Enjoy

Also by DM Paule...

The Monarch of Key West

Highlands-A-Go-Go

Finding Virginia-Highland

DM Paule

iUniverse, Inc.
New York Bloomington

Highlands-A-Go-Go
Finding Virginia-Highland

iUniverse books may be ordered through booksellers or by contacting:

iUniverse
1663 Liberty Drive
Bloomington, IN 47403
www.iuniverse.com
1-800-Authors (1-800-288-4677)

ISBN: 978-1-4401-8056-9 (pbk)
ISBN: 978-1-4401-8057-6 (cloth)
ISBN: 978-1-4401-8058-3 (ebook)

Printed in the United States of America

iUniverse rev. date: 11/5/2009

For Gary

Acknowledgements

Around here, writing is less of a solitary activity and more of a community affair. A lot of people endeavor to keep me out of trouble when I sit down at the keyboard. My special thanks go out to Gary Mann, Sean Dolan, Carol Wyatt, Dennis Maloney, Libby Williams, Beth Davis & Deadra Moore, Rick & Ellen Paule, Cheryl Higgins, Cathi Sciantarelli, Patti DonMoyer, Jon Kupersmith, and Lisa Blackburn.

I also want to acknowledge my attorney, Mike Grider, who diligently protects me from myself, and my editor, Dana Dolan who attempts to tame my use of italics. I'm not sure who has a scarier job.

Finally, I reserve special gratitude for my parents, Marvin & Dora Paule, who never doubted there would be a second book.

Even though a number of people have tried, no one has yet found a way to drink for a living.

- Jean Kerr

Foreword

I ventured south at the lowest point of my life, expecting nothing.

My job was writing entertainment reviews and essays on popular culture for *Manhattan Gothic* magazine. My column was called "A week in the life...of Donovan Ford." I spent the entire month doing things that were new. I went to restaurants the night they opened, well before the critics arrived. I saw shows while they were still working out the kinks in Philly. I attended private parties at clubs that were awaiting their liquor licenses to open to the public. Each month, I told the tale of what would be hip, cool, and popular *next.* I had gone on movie shoots, taken adventure vacations, and traveled with rock bands.

At thirty-five, I was jaded. Worse than jaded, I was a cynic who was passionately in love with his own cynicism. I thought it made me hip. I thought I had seen it all.

But, as it turns out, I had never seen a dogwood. I had never smelled a gardenia. I had never even heard of a Bradford pear.

In case you haven't either, the Bradford pear is an ornamental tree that blooms in March in Atlanta. They put out thousands of tiny white flowers at the first sign of warm weather. They are one of the early signs that winter in North Georgia is coming to an end.

One of the first things I learned about Atlanta is that something is always happening there, just like it was in Manhattan. And for a brief time, I was charmed by the similarities between the two cities. When I took a few minutes to slow down and actually *observe* Atlanta, however, I was enthralled by the differences.

The second thing I learned was that some plant or tree is always blooming in Atlanta, no matter what time of year. Much of the city's character can be correlated to what is in flower at that particular time.

Before I came south, I never would have written about trees or flowers. Frankly, I never would have even noticed them at all.

The Bradford Pear

We walked out of the courtroom silently, side by side, with our lawyers. Olivia was wearing taupe. Olivia always wore some variant of taupe. Tan, beige, ecru: until I had married her, I had never known there were so many variants of neutral. As we exited the courtroom, each of us thanked our lawyers and shook their hands. They departed, and suddenly we were there alone. We looked at each other, no longer man and wife.

"Well," Liv said, "I guess I better get back to the agency."

"Yeah," I said. "I've got to file a story this afternoon anyhow." I was lying.

Neither of us budged. "You know," she said, "it seems like there should be something more, I dunno, *final* that should occur here."

I smiled. "How final could it be? The New York literary community isn't that big. We're going to spend the rest of our lives experiencing awkward occasions where we run into each other."

Liv laughed. God, how I loved it when she laughed. I just wish she had done more of it when we were together. "You're right. We might wind up spending more time together now than we did when we were married."

I chuckled what I can only assume was a sardonic little chuckle. Then, I leaned forward and kissed her cheek. "Take care of yourself, babe." She smiled sadly, and said not a word but turned and walked towards the parking lot at the back of the courthouse. I watched her go, then turned as well and walked towards the one at the front. I knew she would return to our tan-and-taupe-and-ecru apartment in Manhattan. Clutching my folder of legal documents settling the affairs of *Robideau v. Ford,* I headed for the house I was renting in Larchmont.

I hated the house in Larchmont. I think the main advantage of it, apart from a spectacular view of Long Island Sound, was that the famous theater critic Walter Kerr and his playwright wife Jean had once come to dinner there. I had rented it in the hopes that their spirit somehow imbued the place with literary pedigree and that I would be instantly inspired to complete the book that was, ostensibly, the reason that the magazine I worked for had given me a leave of absence. Judging by my lack of progress so far, wherever the spirits of the Kerrs might be, it sure as hell was not in that house.

And, truth be told, I hated the house for another reason. Living here represented the failure of my marriage, and there was nothing I hated or feared more than failure. That fear, more of a terror, really, had characterized every aspect of my life. I made careful decisions, took calculated risks, all intended to carefully avoid the chance of failure. The thought of potential failure created a deep, hollow sensation inside of me. I can only describe it as a type of inner-vertigo. It felt as though there was a bottomless pit starting just below my ribcage and extending downward into eternity. For reasons that are too complex to explain, my father had instilled this fear in me, and it had stayed alive and well long after I was estranged from him.

Even my marriage had been calculated on the facts that we complemented each other so well, that it should have surely succeeded. So, the house in Larchmont sat as a physical manifestation of failure, and every time I saw it, I felt a brief sense of inner-vertigo. Now that the divorce was final, finding someplace new would have to be a higher priority.

I unlocked the door and entered the foyer to a ringing phone. Amidst the jumble of boxes that I had found no reason to unpack for the last several months, I located the phone and answered.

"Donovan?!" resounded from the earpiece and bounced around in my head for a few minutes. It was not so much a greeting as a simultaneous identity inquiry and command for attention, all delivered in the precise, slightly-rising intonations of a Charleston Battery accent.

"Hello, Aunt Laine." DeLaine Wagner Fairchild was nothing if not a force in my life. She was probably the most unique individual I had ever encountered. She wasn't really my aunt, but my mother's half cousin and best friend. They had been opposite sides of the same coin. While both were strong willed and indomitable, my mother was reticent while DeLaine was outspoken. Mother was northern; DeLaine southern. Mother was diplomatic; DeLaine was brash. Mother was proper while DeLaine was carefree. They brought out the best in each other. I was sure Aunt Laine still missed Mom. God knows I did.

"So, Donovan," she intoned in that voice that sounded like Bette Davis reading for the part of Melanie Wilkes, "is today the day? Is it final?"

"It is," I replied wearily. I knew my aunt was quite glad to be able to remove Olivia from her address book. They had not taken to each other in the beginning, and over the years that initial coldness had grown in fullness and bouquet into out-and-out dislike. "I just walked in from the courthouse."

"Well, congratulations." She paused and I could hear the clink of some form of beverage vessel in the background. I thought for a faint moment it might be tea. Realizing it was after two, I knew that it was probably a manhattan instead. "And condolences. I'm sure this is a hard day for you."

"It is," I replied again, not wanting to talk about it. "I don't really feel like talking about it."

"Which is good because I did not call you to talk about it." That was Aunt Laine, always in touch with the feelings of others. "I actually have a business proposition to discuss with you."

"Yes ma'am?"

"It would seem that I have broken my leg."

"What? When? How?"

"And 'where' and 'why,' dear. We're all very impressed with your command of the English interrogatives. I fell down in the parking lot a week ago last Wednesday."

"Last Wednesday? I've talked to you something like three times since then. Why are you just telling me about this now?"

"I knew you had a lot on your mind with the divorce, so I didn't want to bother you. Besides, I was sure it was just a slight break."

"A *slightly* broken leg? How many eighty-year-olds do you know who only slightly break a leg?"

I could hear her sip her cocktail while patiently indulging my sarcasm. She continued as if I had said nothing. "So anyway, they were quite insistent that I couldn't leave the hospital unless I had someone at home to care for me, what with all these steps and all. Brit is here, but I was wondering if you might not like to consider relocating down here for a few months to help me look after this place."

"A few months?"

"Well, yes. With Brit planning the wedding it's not exactly convenient for her right now. And with you not working, I thought it might kill two birds with one bush." My aunt has no remorse when it comes to murdering metaphors.

I paused to light a cigarette and considered the situation. No one in the family had any concept that I had been given a leave to somehow turn a collection of my columns from the magazine into a book and so was not, technically, out of work. In the south, if you stayed at home all day pounding on a keyboard, you were out of work.

My aunt owned and resided in an apartment building somewhere in Atlanta that I had never seen. All I knew about it was that it was old and probably, therefore, a lot of work, which would distract me from the task at hand of converting said columns into said book. I really couldn't afford the time to go to Georgia.

On the other hand, she was being cared for by my sister, Britany. I have to be honest and admit that, although I love her, she has all the sense of duty and responsibility of a pack of breath mints. Years ago, when we were children and lamenting some form of abuse we had taken at school, Laine had taken us aside and given us what I'm sure she considered a sage bit of advice.

"Van, Brit, just tell people you're retarded, and then they'll never expect anything from you. They'll leave you alone." Although I didn't really pay attention, Brit embraced that advice and adopted it as a lifelong mantra.

Moreover, the month before Brit had, against all odds, succeeded in securing a proposal of marriage, and for the next several months I expected wedding preparations to occupy all of what few mental faculties she elected to devote to external matters. My aunt would fare a distant second.

I was probably silent a little too long, as Laine asked, tentatively, "What do you think?"

I took another drag on the cigarette and flicked ashes into an ashtray that really needed to be emptied. "I'm trying to think if I can make that work. I'm a little concerned about finishing the book..."

My aunt will draw encouragement from anywhere she thinks she can find it. "Oh *come*, Donovan. It'll be like a long family weekend. It's a fracture. I should be up and around in no time and you'll have plenty of time to finish your book.

"Besides," she added as an afterthought, "You've got nothing keeping you in New York right now."

Well, that was the crux of the matter, wasn't it? There really wasn't. My job could be done anywhere, and because my mother had left me an inheritance that gave me a small amount of financial security, it wasn't really that important that I be here to do it. My family was all elsewhere. Most of my friends were really *our* friends, as in Olivia's and mine. And, although I was fairly certain I would be able to secure custody of them with a small amount of effort, I was not certain whether I wanted to keep them. They were mostly the kind of mediocre friendships that married couples tend to relegate themselves to, and I was silently dreading the day when those same couples started inviting me over to dinner with whatever single cousin/coworker/close friend was "absolutely perfect for me."

I rotated the cigarette around my fingers and glanced about. I was surrounded by cardboard boxes holding the detritus of my married life. The house was cold and damp. Outside the window, a cold gray fog was descending on the sound. Although I was raised with a typical Yankee disregard for all things southern, I also knew spring came much, much earlier in Atlanta than Larchmont. I wanted to feel warm.

And, when all is said and done, we *do* for family.

"Okay, Laine. I'm in."

She greeted the news with a long, genteel, "*Mah*-velous!" and a swig of her manhattan.

A week later, I was in my Jeep speeding down the interstate towards Atlanta. Most of said marital-life detritus had been relegated to a friend's garage or disposed of. The house in Larchmont had been released back to its landlords. I had with me nothing but my clothes, a box of books, my cameras and my trustworthy laptop. There is something awfully freeing about shedding personal property.

Once I was below the Mason-Dixon line, a bright, glorious sunshine broke through the clouds that had haunted me since leaving the city. I took the doors off the Jeep, despite the fact that the weather wasn't really warm enough to justify it. I had my bomber, an old Aran Island sweater and a scarf to keep the cold at bay.

As I crossed the border, Georgia was not much warmer, but its clear skies and early March sunshine could make you believe that it was summertime. As early evening approached, Interstate 85 flowed ahead of me into the Atlanta city skyline in much the same way that the yellow brick road had led into the Emerald City. Brit had repeatedly forgotten to email me directions despite many reminders, but had left them in a message on my cell phone. I had transcribed these during a gas stop in South Carolina onto a scrap of paper, which I now held in my fingers as the city rose to greet me.

How can I describe my first impressions of Atlanta? Traffic, mostly. I have come to learn that complaining about traffic is one of the main pastimes of Atlantans. Sitting in it is apparently the other. I-85 crosses Atlanta's beltway, which they call the Perimeter, at Spaghetti Junction, a mesmerizing tangle of flyovers, off-ramps and bypasses which resembles less of a cloverleaf and more of an Escher painting. From there, the recurrent high-rise clusters of Atlanta's many urban areas cascade along the ridge of Peachtree Street, one after another all the way to downtown.

Atlanta rush hour, which is comprised of alternatively hurtling along thirty miles above the speed limit and careening to sudden immediate stops, is not unlike coming off of a heroin trip. (Or so I'm told.)

I somehow managed to navigate the darting circus of cars changing lanes (without signaling) like the Keystone Kops in an old Mack Sennett comedy, and pulled off the interstate onto Tenth Street. The traffic carried me along across Midtown past The Dump, where Margaret Mitchell wrote *Gone with the Wind*, and over Peachtree Street. A moment later, Piedmont Park glided past on my left for a good six city blocks. The street ended at Monroe Drive and I took a right and then an immediate left on Virginia Avenue. I now know that, with that left turn, I came home to Virginia Highland for the very first time.

Virginia Highland. Depending on who you talk to, it's an intersection, a neighborhood, or a state of mind. Originally defined by the intersection of Virginia and North Highland Avenues, it began life in the early 1900s as one of Atlanta's first "streetcar suburbs." It grew and developed and was a typical middle-class neighborhood until after World War II, when its narrow lots and small Craftsman, Spanish Revival, and New English bungalows could not compete with the sleek, long, low ranches and wide, rolling front yards in the outer suburbs. It declined into near-slum status in the sixties and seventies, but became one of the first neighborhoods to be gentrified in the early eighties as young intellectuals, artists, musicians, and multiple counterculture "others" began to acquire and restore the housing stock and small retail spaces. Now, it is an area encompassing maybe five square miles, bordered by Piedmont Park (the emotional heart of the city) on the west; Amsterdam Avenue on the north (although it really isn't much of a border since neighboring Morningside looks much the same); stately Briarcliff Road on the East and a road that simply defies description, Ponce de Leon Avenue, on the south.

I followed Virginia to the very center of this roughly square area—nothing can ever be square in Atlanta—where I found a small business district at the intersection with North Highland. And just adjacent to the intersection, as the directions promised, I found an English-Tudor apartment building, all of red brick, built in the early 1920s. And, somewhere in that building lurked its contemporary, Aunt Laine.

I got out of the Jeep and stretched. I had driven the last three hours of the trip straight through, and my muscles were tight. I took a minute to put the doors back on the Jeep before going inside to find my aunt. As I was reattaching the passenger side door, I looked around the neighborhood.

My aunt's building, the Highlandhurst, straddled a steep, narrow lot on Virginia near the corner of Highland. It was the next-to-last building before the business district. On the other side of the next apartment building was a long, low strip mall that looked like it had a couple of bars and restaurants and maybe a shop or two. Across the street were some more businesses wrapping around a wide, curving corner. One was named Murphy's; another was something called Taco Mac. In a little park in the middle of the street, a saxophonist played quietly.

It was an early Friday evening and twilight was giving way to the flickering dawn of sodium-vapor streetlights. Even though it was only March, the patios and porches of the restaurants were packed with patrons. More waited on sidewalks, or browsed in the shops. There was an interesting aura to the place; something I could only describe as a relaxed energy.

Once I had the doors on the Jeep, I locked them. I pulled my duffel bag out of the back and hiked up the front steps to the building. I had only seen the Highlandhurst in pictures. It was a narrow building, probably only one apartment wide, but it was a grand, gothic pile of red brick. The apartment portion itself was three stories tall, with elegant Ionic columned porches rising from a tall granite foundation. One entered the building on the right side through tall, leaded-glass doors in the base of something that I guess the architect intended to be some sort of bell tower. It rose majestically to a height of five stories, and looked over the street in a dark, foreboding manner.

I climbed the steps to the terracotta tiled entrance, and let myself through the glass doors into the outer lobby. I located my aunt's name on the door intercom and pushed the buzzer. A moment later, over the fuzzy intercom speaker I heard my sister's high-pitched voice answer, "Van? Is that you?"

"It's me, Brit. Buzz me in."

"Oh hurray! I'm so happy you're here. Apartment 1A." The door buzzed and I pulled it open. It gave way to a lobby that hadn't changed appreciably in the better part of a century. Tan walls were trimmed with dark wood molding, and enclosed a floor of small black-and-white hexagonal tiles. Across from the front door, a small silver elevator door was surrounded with elaborate art-deco trim work. A hallway led back into the building next to it, with a mahogany staircase winding steeply upwards on the left side. All around was bathed in a sickly yellow light from a white porcelain pendant hanging in the center of the ceiling.

On the left wall of the lobby, at the base of the stairs, was the door labeled 1A. I took a deep breath and started to knock, but the door flew open and Brit had me in a bear hug that knocked the wind out of me.

My sister is a little hard to describe. She is possessed with a life and spirit and vitality that don't translate easily into the written word. Physically, you wouldn't ordinarily peg us as brother and sister. We're about the same height, which makes her somewhat tallish for a woman, while I am somewhat average-to-shortish for a man. I haven't seen her natural hair color in years. When we were kids it was a dirty blond, but since she was nineteen it has been a shade of strawberry-yellow that is not generally found in nature. (Mine is true blond, thankyouverymuch.) She is rather squarish in build, while I've always been absurdly thin. It would appear that I was the child who inherited all of the lip genes since mine are kind of thick and hers are almost non-existent. On the other hand, she got the eyes; big, huge, full moon eyes of sapphire blue, while mine are kind of a dull, steel gray. It was in Britany's eyes that you could see a gleam for life that would have inspired artists everywhere.

"Brit," I gasped. "I can't breathe."

She stood back and took a long, appraising look at me. "Jesus, you're even skinnier. Have you eaten *anything* since you split with Olivia?"

"Soft pretzels and Bacardi. Are you going to let me in?"

"Smart ass." She stood back and revealed my aunt's apartment. It took me a moment to convince myself to go in. I had always heard that my aunt collected knick-knacks. I just didn't expect quite the *volume* of knick-knacks. Every conceivable surface was covered with miniature ceramic cattle, or commemorative plates, or decorative planters or salt-and-pepper shakers shaped like tiny cowboy boots. And sitting in a wheelchair in the center of it all was Aunt Laine in all her glory.

Laine is easy to describe. She is that most magnificent example of fauna found in this part of the country: the southern *grande dame.* She was five-foot-six when she was standing (which she wouldn't be doing much of in the near future.) She had a round face with deep green eyes and a halo of vivid red hair, the color of which had not been allowed to change even one shade in the last seventy years. Despite her age, she still sported a rather ample bosom that shot out so straight and pointy I wondered if she was still wearing those cast-iron Maidenforms she'd acquired in the forties. Her eyes lit up when she saw me, and she put her manhattan down on the coffee table, threw her arms wide and cried enthusiastically, "Donovan!"

I went forward and delivered the required hug and kiss to the left cheek. The familiar scent of Worth filled my nostrils. "You certainly are looking fine for such an ordeal," I told her as I stood back up.

"I wish I could say the same for you," she replied while eying me appraisingly. "Brit's right. You weigh nothing."

"I've always weighed nothing," I said churlishly. My lack of physical presence has always embarrassed me, somewhat.

"You've always been thin," Laine corrected. "Not emaciated. Go into the kitchen. Eat something."

Before I could respond to her command, Brit began ringing. Well, her cell phone began ringing, but since the Brit I knew eschewed things like cell phones as bourgeois, I would have been less surprised if it actually *was* her ringing. She rolled her eyes and looked at me as she retrieved the diminutive cell from the back pocket of her jeans. "I know what you are about to say and I don't want to hear it. Charles gave it to me as a gift. He prefers that I keep it with me since I'm all over the place during the day. He's a bit protective." She glanced at the caller I.D. as she opened it. "This is him now. Hey, babe." She wandered away to the kitchen to talk.

I asked Laine where the bathroom was, and was directed to a narrow hall. When I returned to the living room, Brit was just hanging up. "Charles will be here in about ten minutes," she announced. "Van, I hope you like Thai. He's bringing it for dinner."

I was not all that wild about Thai but told her anything was fine. "I can't believe you of all people have a cell phone."

Brit rolled her eyes again as she slumped down on a couch awash with ornamental pillows. "It's a concession to the conventional, establishment lifestyle staring me in the face right now. Charles is a professor in the business school at Emory. He's a bit on the conservative side."

I had a sudden suspicion. "Please tell me my free-spirit, artistic sister isn't marrying a Republican."

"Tory," Laine volunteered. "He's British."

"Isn't that cool, Van? I'll be Brit, the wife of Charles the Brit."

Sadly, she thought that was uproariously funny. "Go on with your story."

"Yeah, so anyway, he's a professor in the business school. Tenured. Does a lot of consulting gigs. I'm staring down the barrel of being Missus Corporate America."

"That doesn't sound like you."

Laine was losing patience with Brit, making me think she had had sat through this conversation before. She cut off whatever reply my sister was about to make abruptly. "It's not, and she's making it sound worse than it is. He loves Brit. He wants her to continue to work and paint and show her art. He has said he is more than willing to accommodate her bohemian lifestyle."

"You can't accommodate a bohemian lifestyle from a townhome in Druid Hills," Brit observed.

"Better than a trailer in Macon," Laine retorted. "There are worse things than marrying money."

"Money can't buy happiness," Brit replied, more to bait my aunt than out of any real combativeness.

"I never said it could. But with it you can certainly shop for happiness in a lot more stores."

The conversation ended abruptly as Brit asked, "So, who wants cocktails?" She departed to the kitchen to make them before anyone could answer. Laine turned her attention to me.

"So, Donovan," she observed grandly, "You're here and I very much appreciate it. This place is a lot of work for an old lady."

"I'm happy to help, Aunt Laine. Tomorrow morning, you tell me where you want me to start. I just need to try and get on a couple of hours of writing each day."

"That should be no problem," Laine observed. "And, since Brit's moved in with Charles, why don't you move into her old apartment upstairs?"

That surprised me. I had assumed I would be staying in Laine's apartment, although the preponderance of stuff made me think there was hardly room for me. "Don't you need the rent?"

Laine cast a sidelong look towards the kitchen, which immediately conveyed the message that regular rent payments had not been characteristic of Brit's tenancy in the building. "Oh, that place is so small and hard to rent, I doubt it will significantly impact cash flow around here."

"Just be careful, Van," Brit observed as she returned and handed me a rum-and-diet. "It's haunted."

"Haunted?" I asked, glancing at Laine.

"It's not haunted," she replied, accepting a fresh manhattan. "It's just old."

"It's haunted."

"It's not haunted, you just have an overactive imagination."

Brit sat down on the couch and repeated flatly, "It's haunted."

Laine looked at me, "Okay, it's a *little* haunted."

I laughed incredulously. "What's a *little* haunted?"

"Well, we have ghosts but they're extraordinarily benign. Years will go by without a peep."

I stared at them, amazed that they actually believed in ghosts. Before I could say anything else though, the door buzzer announced the arrival of my future brother-in-law, Charles Williams.

Charles was—well, he's not dead; he still is—very, very, very British. Although he doesn't actually wear a bowler or carry an umbrella, it's not hard to picture him with one. He's tall and skinny and usually wears dark Brooks Brothers suits that are impeccably pressed, with striped ties whose stripes never vary in width. What he and my sister see in each other is beyond me. It's like imagining Neville Chamberlain married to a Gabor sister.

Charles was admitted to the apartment carrying three white plastic bags with large Styrofoam carryout containers. The room was immediately awash with the smells of lemongrass and curry and cayenne. He kissed Brit and handed her the bags, and then held out his hand and favored me with a tight-lipped, very self-conscious smile. "You must be Donovan."

I shook his hand. "Charles, it's a pleasure. You must be a madman for marrying my sister."

He looked momentarily shaken, and then laughed nervously. "Right, right. Yes, yes, I must be."

My aunt cleared her throat loudly, indicating that attention was not being paid to her. Charles immediately realized his mistake and doted on her with such grace and aplomb one would think she was a member of the peerage. The British really have refined fawning to an art form. Meanwhile, Brit had transferred all of the food to plates and summoned us into the very small dining room. Charles took responsibility for navigating my aunt's wheelchair through the tight maze of her apartment to the table. We had a very nice dinner and, despite my past aversion to Thai food, it was delicious. I was informed that it came from a little restaurant about three blocks away called Mai Li.

"It really is the best Thai in the neighborhood, I think," Laine offered. I was not used to neighborhoods having multiple Thai restaurants and said so, to which Laine replied, "There are five of them in about a three-block radius. God help you if you want Chinese food; there's none to be found. But there's enough pad prik in the neighborhood to feed all of Bangkok."

As I said, dinner was a pleasant enough affair. Despite his reserve, I found Charles to be funny and quite good company. I was more than willing to have him in the family. As we finished, he asked if I needed any help getting my things inside.

Before I could answer, Laine suggested I go upstairs and look at Brit's old apartment to see if it would suit my needs. I had to admit that, even though I loved my aunt, the idea of having my own space to escape to appealed to me. My aunt told me where I could find the keys, and I made my way out into the building to check it out while Charles and Brit did dishes.

The building had two apartments per floor. I would later learn that the "front" apartment on each floor was the larger, with two bedrooms, while the rear was smaller, with one. Brit's old apartment had never really been an apartment at all. When Brit moved to Atlanta to go to college, Laine's late husband Maurice had been smitten with the girl, and in many ways viewed her as the daughter he had never had. So he had enclosed the old "bell tower" on the roof and made it into a studio. It was located above the third floor hallway, adjacent to the elevator machinery flat. To reach it, one had to take the elevator to the third floor, and then cross the hall and climb a set of stairs to the roof access door. That opened on to a narrow covered breezeway overlooking the rest of the roof that led to the front of the building. At the end of the veranda was a narrow glass door with a single bulb glowing dimly above it. Even though I adamantly did not believe the apartment was haunted, I could see how someone might think it was. The whole approach to it seemed slightly sinister.

I lit a cigarette as I walked down the narrow veranda. The night air was cooling fast. Off to my right, across the roof, was a great view of the high-rises on the other side of Piedmont Park, in Midtown. I unlocked the door and fumbled around the frame until I found a light switch. Switching it on, I discovered what is possibly the best-kept apartment secret in Atlanta.

The original belfry, although never home to bells, was almost two stories tall. Uncle Maurice had enclosed the Romanesque opening with huge windows. A pair of French doors in the center opened and led out onto a narrow balcony overlooking Virginia Avenue. The walls were all exposed brick, and the ceiling was the original wood, although heavily stained. The floor was made of wide, heart-pine planks, unstained, but with enough marine-grade varnish that you could have put out to sea on it.

I had often heard from both Brit and Laine that Maurice had doted on this apartment, making it as much his hobby as her home. Since the bell tower was not large, maybe just fifteen feet on each side, he had struggled to fit every possible amenity into the small space. In the corner next to the front door was a small kitchen. It was fully equipped, however. In order to minimize space, the counters were only eighteen inches deep instead of the usual twenty-four. He had compensated by using a wild variety of appliances. The stove was the small kind you would usually see in a camper. The sink appeared to be a bar sink mounted sideways. Inset into the wall next to it was the tiniest dishwasher I have ever seen, just a single rack with room for a couple of plates and glasses. Behind it was an alcove with one of those European washing machines that also kind of dries the clothes as well. On a shelf above the washer sat a small, dorm-room sized refrigerator.

Behind the kitchen was a small bathroom with a stall shower, pedestal sink, and toilet. Next to the bathroom door, a black metal spiral staircase wound up to a small bed area that sat over the top of the bathroom and kitchen. It was just big enough for the bed and a small armoire that served as the closet.

Since Brit had moved into Charles's house, and since Charles apparently had impeccable taste, none of Brit's furniture had been taken along. She had bought all of it from a junk store and it was a single collection of Danish-modern stuff that must have been the height of contemporary fashion in about 1962. There was a long, low sage green sofa that was covered in some indestructible mid-century material. Next to it was a black leather Eames chair. On the wall facing the couch was a "mod" wall unit in dark teak with a built-in desk, fold-down bar, and several bookshelves. Two bar stools at the kitchen counter rounded out the room's furnishings.

I have to admit, it was not the kind of place I had expected to be living at this point in my career. However, it had a certain romantic cachet that appealed to me; sort of the perfect modern garret for a writer to work from. I inspected it for maybe another ten minutes, and then returned downstairs to get Charles. We were able to empty my Jeep and haul everything upstairs to my new abode in a single load.

We stayed up very late talking, laughing, and consuming cocktails in Aunt Laine's apartment. It was well after midnight when I stumbled upstairs, having first seen to Laine's needs. I let myself into the apartment, brushed my teeth, and tentatively negotiated my way up the narrow spiral staircase. I think I was asleep before my head even hit the pillow.

I awoke the next morning to the sound of the toilet flushing. I sat bolt upright in bed. "Who's down there?" I demanded in my best menacing New York voice. No one answered. I jumped out of the bed and descended the steps part way, again demanding to know who was in the bathroom. I peered around the corner of the open door. The room was empty and the apartment silent, save for the sound of the tank refilling. I looked around, and then stepped into the bathroom. I lifted the tank lid and saw that the seal on the flapper valve was dislodged. Relieved, I made a mental note to go to the hardware store and buy a new flapper valve.

My adrenaline was pumping hard so I decided to put it to good use and go for a run. Five minutes later, after checking to see that Aunt Laine was still asleep, I started to run down Virginia back the way I had come the previous night. I decided to start out by just running around the block. That morning I discovered the South's revenge on Northerners for burning Atlanta: the street layout. There's no such thing as a block.

I ran down Virginia and, at a split in the road, turned right on Monroe. From there, I turned right on a street called Park, which immediately carried me back to Virginia. A little confused, I ran down to Monroe again, and turned on Park. This time, when Park began to curve, I took a left on a street called Crestridge. Crestridge looped back and took me back to Monroe. I turned right on Monroe and went a little farther, this time turning on Amsterdam. Amsterdam immediately ended at a split. I went left on Courtenay, but somehow circled back around to Amsterdam, but at a totally different spot from the split. Confused, I turned left and then, thinking I was still heading in the right direction, turned left on San Antonio, which took me back to Courtenay right where it met Amsterdam.

I decided to run back the way I came, although I was sufficiently confused by now that I wound up going up Amsterdam the wrong way. Eventually, it deposited me on North Highland, but by now I was so turned around that I had no idea which direction led back to the building.

At the corner of Amsterdam and North Highland I saw Mai Li, the restaurant Charles had secured dinner from, so I knew I had to be close to home. I rounded the corner and stopped to catch my breath. Looking around me, I noticed a small coffee house a few doors up from where I stood. I walked up to it just as a very attractive African-American woman was emerging with what must have been one of the largest lattes I have ever seen. She turned and began to walk down the street, and I called to her. "Excuse me? Ma'am?"

She turned around and cocked one eyebrow at me, looking expectantly. "I'm sorry to bother you, but I'm lost."

"Lost?" she asked in a full, rich alto.

"Yeah. I was out running and I kind of got turned around. I'm staying in Virginia Highland."

"Okay, well you're still in the Highlands."

"I'm looking for the corner of Virginia and Highland." I received much the same look would have expected if I had been standing on Miami Beach and asked where they kept the ocean, so I kept going. "I'm trying to find an apartment building called the Highlandhurst."

She looked at me quizzically. "You stayin' at the 'Hurst?"

"Yeah, I'm here to look after a family member."

A smile broke across her face and she held out her hand. "You must be Donovan. I'm Rachel Abernathy. Apartment 3B. Welcome to Atlanta."

I shook her hand. "You knew I was coming?"

"Dear, everyone in the building knows you were coming, except maybe Mister Kersey. Follow me; I'm on my way back past there." We began walking down North Highland towards Virginia.

"So, why not Mister...was it Kersey?"

"Your aunt hasn't told you about the tenants yet?" she asked with a grin.

"Um, no."

"Ah. Well. I probably should let her, but I'll fill you in a little. Mister Kersey is apartment 1B, just behind your aunt's. At least, we assume he is. No one has seen him come in or go out for the last nine years."

"Really? Are we sure he's still alive?"

"Quite sure. Laine says she still gets rent checks from him, usually shoved under the door in the middle of the night. He gets all kinds of deliveries from UPS. If you go into the backyard you can see lights on in his apartment. Someone is in there. You just don't see him."

I pondered that for a moment. "Who else is in the building?"

Rachel took a long sip of her latte. "Well, apartment 1A is your aunt, obviously. Apartment 2A is Mac and Clare O'Toole. He works for a dot-com in some technical capacity. She's a flautist with the ASO."

"ASO?"

"Atlanta Symphony Orchestra. They are the prototypical Highlands couple. Relatively well off, very well educated. Slightly left politically. Way left socially. Make enough money to live in the suburbs, but want more from life than minivans and soccer moms. You'll think he's weird as hell and she's way too fun and charming to be so intense musically. But, they're great people.

"Apartment 2B is Jennifer Mathis. She's a bartender at Fontaine's up here on the right. Sort of your generic rocker-girl type. Total party waiting to happen."

"Then I'm in apartment 3B. 3A is Christopher Diaz. He's a flight attendant for Delta. Very cute. Very gay. Total waste as far as I'm concerned."

"And then 4A is me," I observed, as we crossed over Los Angeles.

"So, you're moving in upstairs? Well, good. Laine hoped you might take that space over from Brit."

"Well for the time being. What about you, Rachel? You've given me insights into everyone else. What do I need to know about you?"

She raised her eyebrows and took another sip of her latte. "Me? Nothing really. I live in my apartment. I run a little bookstore down on Ponce de Leon called Ponce Pages. I'm just a typical girl living intown. Sort of a black *That Girl*, only I don't get overdressed to go fly kites."

We passed a small Episcopal church on North Highland and I began to recognize my surroundings. We were only a block from the building. "Certainly sounds like an eclectic crowd of residents," I observed.

Rachel shrugged. '"It's an eclectic neighborhood. The Highlands is like this great cosmic nexus. It's all about balance. Not too hip, not too conventional. Not too rich, not too poor. Not too liberal, not too right-wing. It's a little bit of every one." She took another sip of her latte as we reached the corner of Virginia and Highland. "*Except* those people who are too afraid of people not like themselves. To live in the Highlands, you have to tolerate difference. If you can't, you have to move out to Cobb County." We stopped and she turned around and looked at me. "Know where you are now?"

"I do. Rachel, I can't tell you how much I appreciate you getting me back here."

"My pleasure. Atlanta doesn't work like other cities. You have to learn it all on its own. Welcome to the 'Hurst , Donovan. I'll see you soon." With that, she turned and continued onward down North Highland.

I walked the hundred feet or so to the building and let myself back in. As I was opening the inner door to the lobby, I heard the outer door behind me open and someone say, "Don't let that shut."

I turned around and saw a very good-looking guy, probably about my age, with dark skin and features and wearing evening club clothes.

"Hey," he greeted me with, and favored me with a very wide smile. "Thanks. I don't have my key."

"You have a key?" I asked suspiciously.

"Well, only 'cause I live here."

I looked at him as I held the door open (something I would never do in New York, but this place *felt* different). He didn't strike me as the bizarre recluse type, so I ruled out Mister Kersey. He seemed too hip to be a computer programmer. "So you must be Chris Diaz?"

He turned as he passed. The smile broadened, but his eyes looked unsure. "Um, hi."

I held out my hand. "I'm Donovan Ford, Laine's nephew."

Recognition spread into his eyes. "Oh yeah. She told me you were coming to help out for a while. Nice to meet you."

"You as well." I let the door swing shut behind me.

He started to mount the steps and unbutton his green silk camp shirt simultaneously. "Oh, hey. A favor? My kitchen sink won't shut off. Can you come look at it?"

"Sure."

"But later," he added. "Sometime this afternoon? I've got to get some sleep." My agreement must have been presumed because he turned and continued up the stairs without waiting for me to answer.

I let myself into Aunt Laine's apartment. I asked softly, "You up?"

"Yes, dear," came the cheery reply from her bedroom. "Up and ready for you."

I walked back to the bedroom. My aunt was propped up in the bed, wearing a black silk bed jacket. I took the handles of the wheelchair and rolled it alongside the bed. "Good morning."

"Good morning to you," she replied as she tossed aside the covers and draped an arm over my shoulder. I gently lowered her from the bed to the wheelchair and rolled her towards the bathroom. As we passed her bureau, she pointed at it and requested, "Do me a favor? Open the second drawer and get me out a fresh pair of pajamas."

I did as I was told, and pulled out whatever pair was on top.

"Oh God, not those." She complained. "Not flannel for daytime. Something with a little more sex appeal." I rummaged through the drawer some more and came up with a pale blue pair of Chinese pajamas with dragons embroidered over each breast and feather boa-type collar. "Perfect," she commented approvingly.

I rolled her to the bathroom entrance and placed a bar stool directly in front of the sink. Then, per her instructions, I helped her up from the chair and perched her on the stool. "Are you hungry? Would you like breakfast?"

"Famished," she replied. I closed the bathroom door and beat a path back down the hall to the kitchen.

I very much doubt Laine's kitchen had changed at all since the 1950s. It was like stepping onto the set of *I Love Lucy*. I expected Ethel Mertz to come around the corner any second. I opened her refrigerator and found it awash in carryout cartons, but not much else. After digging for a few minutes, I located some bread, butter, and eggs. I was also able to secure miscellaneous other breakfast necessities such as plates, skillets, and toaster. By the time my aunt called me to liberate her from the bathroom fifteen minutes later, I was setting fried eggs and toast on the table in the dining room.

Laine had not only changed clothes, but also teased out her hair and applied makeup, all from that stool. (I also heard the toilet flush, but decided not to delve into details. If all she needed was me to get her in there, all the better.) I helped lower her to the chair and then rolled her into the dining room. "You cooked!" she exclaimed with glee. "I didn't know you could cook. What a marvelous treat."

"Of course I can cook," I replied as I sat across from her. "I had to learn mostly out of a need for survival. Olivia didn't spend much time in the kitchen."

"I imagine not," Laine observed as she began spooning sugar into her coffee. "Unless neighborhood children were breaking gingerbread off your house, that is."

"Laine..."

She waved away my warning tone. "I joke. Where were you off to this morning?"

I recounted my run, getting lost and my meeting with Rachel.

"Ah, lovely girl," Laine observed as she spooned the last of the jam onto a piece of toast. "Pity she's so hung up on Chris in 3A. If she enjoys a man who plays hard to get, she's in for a wonderful time there."

I laughed. "Met him this morning as well. He has a leaky faucet I'm supposed to fix sometime this afternoon."

She nodded sagely. "No doubt. Was he alone when he was coming in?"

I cocked my head and looked at her curiously. "Alone. How'd you know he was coming in?"

"Because you met him before ten o'clock in the morning. When you own a building like this, you get to learn people's idiosyncrasies.

If he comes in alone, you can go work on his apartment anytime after three. If he comes in with someone, wait until the next day."

I nodded. "Speaking of idiosyncrasies, what's the story on Mister Kersey?"

She shrugged. "What's to tell? He's the perfect tenant. Always pays his rent on time and no one ever sees him. I wish I had a whole building like that."

"Doesn't it you strike you as a little weird?"

She chuckled as she popped the last bite of toast into her mouth. "Everyone is weird, Van. There's no escaping it. When someone like Kersey prefers to keep his weirdness to himself, I call that courtesy." I stood to clear the plates. "That was the best breakfast I have had in weeks, young man. The most your sister ever cooks is cereal, or, occasionally Pop Tarts."

"I'm not surprised," I said over my shoulder as I carried the dishes into the kitchen. "Pop Tarts constitute one of Brit's four major food groups. The others are cheese puffs, Ramen noodles, and sauvignon blanc."

Laine rolled herself (with great exertion) around the dining room table, past the hutch that was crammed full of commemorative plates, circumnavigated a fern stand, and into the doorway of the kitchen as I began to wash the dishes. "Your sister is changing. She might surprise you. One might even say she is growing up."

"I'll believe it when I see it," I replied as I began to load dishes in to the ancient dishwasher that was an integrated part of the aluminum sink cabinet. "Other than fixing Chris's faucet, what's on my 'to do' list?"

She pointed towards the phone. "It's all on a list over there. Not too much for today. I need you to haul the garbage cans out to the street, and leave a message for the elevator inspector. It just had its annual and he hasn't sent me the certificate yet. I've put together the list of things that have to be done every day, and then the list of things that I'd like to get done if you have time."

"Okay, that's easy enough. Since I can't get into Chris's apartment until three, that will give me some time to get settled in upstairs and go to the market."

"Budget some time to spend in Chris's. He'll come up with five other things for you to do while you're there."

"Really?" I closed the dishwasher and dried my hands on a tea towel.

"Oh yes," she said replied nonchalantly as she backed out of the kitchen. "You'll find Chris is extremely low maintenance…in much the same way a Fiat is low maintenance."

Once I had Laine settled in for the morning, I took the list from beside the phone and went upstairs to clean up. As soon as I finished my shower, I wrapped a towel around myself and called the elevator inspector's voicemail. While I spoke to it, I casually walked over to the front door and peered through the glass at the roof of the building.

The building was sort of U-shaped to accommodate a light well between each floor's "A" and "B" apartments. The roof of the building over the "A" portion had been decked over at some point in the past. I had not noticed it the night before, but I had a wooden deck that looked straight into the skyline. *A perfect place to have a party,* I thought to myself, *if I had any friends here to invite.*

While I talked to the inspector I walked outside. Although I wouldn't say it was warm by Atlanta standards, the temperature had climbed to the low fifties, which felt wonderful to my slush-bound New York metabolism. I walked to the edge of the light well. The deck had no rail on the sides and back, so I peered gingerly over the edge. A wrought-iron fire escape worked its way down from each of the apartments, ending on the ground level of the well, which was fenced from the side driveway. There was not much down there: just a few sickly looking shrubs and a couple of decrepit lawn chairs.

I finished the phone call. Even at fifty degrees, being outside in a towel and with wet hair can be a little chilling, so I beat a hasty retreat back into the apartment. It didn't take me long to get dressed and store away my meager possessions. By eleven-thirty, I guess it was officially "home." I sat down at my desk and made out a joint shopping list of provisions for both Laine's kitchen and my own. Then I slipped on some docksiders and my bomber jacket and headed downstairs to check on my aunt and find a grocery.

I came bounding down the steps two at a time, rounding each landing rather jauntily. I should probably point out to you that, although I am hardly morose, *jaunty* is not one of those adjectives that is typically applied to anything I do. So, I was rather surprised. I felt strangely upbeat, but had no reason to be. Knowing myself, that should have bothered me. I tried to force myself to be bothered about not being bothered. It didn't work.

I bounded down the last flight of steps and noticed that Laine's door was ajar. I stuck my head in and saw that she had a visitor. A very attractive woman sat across from her sipping hot tea. Since I knew for a fact that there was nothing even remotely resembling tea in that kitchen I assume she had brought it herself. "Um, hi."

"Hello," she said in a warm, throaty flat accent that suggested Pennsylvania or Ohio or, maybe, Michigan.

"Donovan, come in here," Laine instructed and I complied. "I want you to meet one of our tenants. Clare O'Toole, my nephew Donovan." I shook Clare's hand and we exchanged pleasantries. "Clare is principal flautist for the symphony."

Clare smiled. "Your aunt is always trying to promote me. I'm actually just an associate flautist."

"I understand. She's always trying to promote me as well. I'm not actually her nephew." Clare gave me a courtesy laugh. I turned my attention to Laine. "I was going to head off to the store. If I was a grocery, where would I be?"

Laine chuckled. "There are several. You might want to go to Whole Foods. It's straight down Highland and then right on Ponce de Leon." I noticed something odd about how she pronounced the street name. It came out as *Ponce duh LEE-on.* I corrected her pronunciation. "Not down here. I wouldn't recommend correcting anyone else's pronunciation, either. If you can't say it right, just say Ponce."

I excused myself and made my way out to the Jeep. I passed at least two other grocery stores, a Publix and a Kroger, to get to Whole Foods. I wondered why she had sent me there. I would later learn that she thought its merchandise would be more in keeping with my Manhattan tastes. Admittedly, I did shop at Balducci's and Dean & DeLuca when I lived there, so she was not far off. Laine herself was a Kroger gal.

I meandered through the store, selecting staples, vegetables, and some meat, supplementing them with the occasional cheese or zabaglione. In short order, I had enough to restock both kitchens in a respectable manner, and I made my way through the checkout.

I came out of the market, loaded the groceries into the back of the Jeep, and started back up Ponce. At the intersection with North Highland, I noticed a squadron of people, mostly elderly, tooling around the parking lot to my right in motorized wheelchairs. Not one or two, but a lot of people, which struck me as odd. They seemed to be practicing some sort of synchronized routine. As I waited for the light, I saw Ponce Pages, Rachel's bookstore. I made a mental note of the location so I could come back and see her. The light turned green and I made the left, being on careful watch for more wheelchairs.

The Highlands has five separate "villages" of small shops, bars, and restaurants, each separated by about a mile. I was living in the center village, with two to the north and two to the south. Each was separated by a long lazy strip of houses and apartments and a substantial number of trees, many of which were budding with small white flowers. I was impressed to see signs of spring starting so early.

I turned on Virginia and made the immediate veer into the narrow driveway next to the building that plummeted to the parking lot in the back. As I careened downwards, I noticed that there was a gate in the fence that screened off the small light well. I emerged in the parking lot at the back of the building, and parked in the space with a faded *4A* painted in it.

Five minutes later Aunt Laine, who was sitting at her dining room table playing a rather elaborate form of solitaire, was taken aback by the substantial load of grocery bags that I hauled into her apartment. "Good God. Are we entertaining?"

"You only get half," I told her as I schlepped the bags past her and into the kitchen. "I bought two of everything. One for your kitchen and one for mine." She continued playing as I unpacked cans and boxes and bags.

"Well, I hope it is your intention to cook everything that is in there. I certainly have no intention of it."

"I would never dream of asking you to forgo your life's animosity towards the culinary arts. I will cook every scrap of it. There is more to life than carryout, y'know."

"Yes, I know," she said wistfully as she pulled a red six and a black four from the table. "Your Uncle Maurice certainly proved that. God, could that man cook. He was a maestro at anything involving his hands." I chose this unfortunate moment to emerge from the kitchen, and she gave me a wink while simultaneously grabbing both breasts and inhaling deeply. "And I mean *anything.*"

I fought off the look of distaste that threatened to creep across my face. Not that I begrudge my aunt her sensuality. Far from it. I just actively avoid the risk of conjuring up a mental image of it. I decided to change the subject. "Laine, what are the trees with the tiny white buds on them?"

The full flower of Charleston aristocracy crept into her voice as she replied, "Why, those are Bradford pears." Pronounced, *brahdfohd peyahs*. "Are they blooming already?"

"Looks like they are just getting started."

She clapped her hands together excitedly. "How *mahvelous*. Spring is just around the corner."

Since I wasn't sure of what significance the Bradford pears had that would put her into such a good frame of mind, I held up the shopping bags and told her, "I'm going to run these upstairs, and then go look at Chris Diaz's sink."

"All of the tools are downstairs in the garage."

I unpacked my groceries in my apartment, and judged it close enough to three that Chris Diaz should have his ass out of bed, so I bounded down the stairs to the basement. It was a dark, dungeon-like affair, built from stacked granite. I walked towards the back to a door that I could only presume was the building's small garage. Laine had given me a key chain with all of the building passkeys on it, and after five minutes of fumbling, I found the key that opened it. It was, indeed, the garage.

There was no light switch by the door, just a string that ran through a large number of eyebolts in the ceiling to a single bulb in the center. I didn't need to light it though, since sunlight somehow muscled its way in through the murky, cobweb-covered windows to illuminate the room. There were workbenches on each wall, covered with a wide variety of tools and machinery. None of them caught my attention though, because it was transfixed on the car. There in the very center of the garage sat a vintage 1971 Rolls-Royce Corniche convertible. It was bright red, and I mean *bright*. There must have been a half-inch of dust on it.

When my mother died, I remember going through her photo albums, and seeing a picture of Laine and Maurice with this car. But all those pictures looked to have been taken in the seventies, and so I never would have thought she would still have it. Then again, judging by her apartment, Laine didn't part with things willingly.

I must have spent fifteen minutes with that car. Apart from the dust, she was immaculate. I opened the driver's side door and slid behind the wheel. Even in the dim light from outside, the dashboard gleamed under probably fifty coats of Armor All. I felt sensations of lust that years of marriage had told me I should be ashamed of.

After a few more minutes inspecting the car, I reluctantly found some plumbing tools and a toolbox, and made my way upstairs to 3A. I knocked on the door and waited. No answer. I knocked again. Still no answer. Finally I pounded.

The door swung open violently and Chris Diaz stood there clutching a sheet loosely around his waist. His hair was askew and his eyes had the dazed, confused look of someone just aroused from slumber.

"Hey," I said. "Sorry to disturb you. You wanted me to come look at your kitchen faucet."

"Faucet?" he mumbled, uncomprehendingly. "Faucet?"

"Um, yeah. Thing in the kitchen above the sink. Water comes outta it?"

He closed his eyes tightly and shook his head. "Yeah. Faucet. You're Laine's nephew, what's-his-name."

"Yeah. What's-his-name Ford. Bad time? I can come back."

He shook his head and stood aside. "Nah. Now's fine. What time is it, anyway?"

"Three," I told him as I walked past into the apartment. For the most part, it was the mirror to my aunt's, two floors below, in layout. In decoration, however, it could not have been more different. The living room was painted stark white, with halogen track lights suspended from steel cables around the entire periphery. They highlighted walls that were totally blank, save for one violently colorful canvas hanging over the fireplace. There were two low, boxy, black leather chairs on one side of the fireplace facing a matching boxy black leather love seat across a square glass coffee table with nickel-plated legs. In the center of the coffee table was a large arrangement of silk lilies and dried yucca of such a size and presence that it would completely obscure the view of the persons sitting in the couch from anyone sitting in the chairs and vice versa. Otherwise, the room was empty. I had attended many cocktail parties in similarly decorated lofts in Chelsea and the Village over the last couple of years.

"Nice, um, place," I told him, hating it.

"Thanks," he replied, closing the door and leading me through the blood-red dining room into the kitchen. He showed me the faucet. It was, indeed, running. "See?" he said by way of explanation.

"Yeah, I've got it," I told him, and felt the water. It was warm so the leak must be coming from the hot line. I knelt down, opened the cabinet below and shut off the hot line. The water stopped. As I began to remove the hot water handle, he meandered back into the rear of the apartment.

While I worked, I heard the sound of drawers opening and closing, followed by the sound of closet doors opening and closing, followed by the sound of more drawers, so I assumed he was getting dressed. It took me about fifteen minutes to finish replacing the washer and to reassemble the faucet. I turned the hot line back on, and the leak had stopped. I turned it off and on a couple of times to make sure it still worked. Olivia, had she seen me, would have been amazed that I could do something so handy. She wouldn't have admitted it, but she would have been, nonetheless.

"Faucet's fixed," I called as I repacked my tool case. Diaz emerged from the back wearing only a pair of green plaid boxers. I stared at him for a moment, surprised. I had heard enough activity in the back to make me think he had dressed every extra in *42nd Street.* "Anything else?"

"Yeah, actually. My closet door doesn't seem to want to latch. Would you mind taking a look at it while you are up here?"

Over the course of the next few months, I would learn to never ask him *anything else?* "Sure I replied," and I followed him back to his bedroom.

The bedroom was only slightly less austere than the other rooms in the apartment. I examined the closet and realized that the doorplate was blocking the latch from closing. It would just need a few minutes of filing and it would be good as new. I knelt down and began to file it. He settled in on the bed, took out an ashtray and lit a cigarette.

"So, your aunt tells me you're a writer for some magazine."

"Uh huh," I replied, continuing to file. *"Manhattan Gothic."*

"Ah," he said, taking a long, considered drag on the cigarette. "Hate that magazine."

I stopped filing for a second and turned to look at him. I was not unaccustomed to hearing that people hated the magazine. I was unaccustomed to hearing it to my face, however. As I resumed filing I asked him, "Any particular reason?"

"Yeah," another drag on the cigarette. "One time I picked it up and some asshole had written an article with the title that *flight attendants were only good for a cheap buzz."*

I stopped filing again. "Did you read the article?"

"No. Why would I read something that I knew was going to insult me?"

"Because, if you had read it, you would have discovered that it was a review of a new bar in Hell's Kitchen called Flight Attendant. And, in the review, you would have learned that the airline memorabilia theme, although kitschy, didn't work, although the drinks were amazingly cheap for New York, so there was still a reason to go there."

He blanched. "Oh God. You wrote it, didn't you?"

I began filing again. "And the title of the article, by the way, was 'Flight Attendant: Get Buzzed on the Cheap.'"

He rolled his eyes. "Oops. Sorry. Guess maybe I should have read it."

I smiled. "No apologies needed. It wasn't exactly Pulitzer quality work. Still, you might have checked out the rest of the issue. It's really not a bad magazine."

"God, now I feel terrible. Is there any way I can make it up to you?"

"Yeah," I said. "Give me a cigarette."

He slid off the bed and brought me the cigarettes, an ashtray, and his lighter. I lit the cigarette, thanked him, and resumed filing.

"Be careful not to let the cigarette get inside the closet," he advised me as he returned to the bed. "It's full of uniforms. Even though they tell us they're supposed to be fire retardant, I still bet you could ignite one and it'd take out the entire building."

I spent the next three hours in his apartment. As I finished his closet, I learned that he was indeed a flight attendant, flying mostly Caribbean and Latin American markets because he spoke Spanish. I also learned that he was first-generation American, his parents having fled to Miami during the Cuban revolution.

I next had to un-stick the window in the other bedroom, which he used as a combination office and den. While I worked on it, I learned that the previous night he had been dancing at a club called Amethyst, which was not exactly a gay club and not exactly a straight club, but mostly just a place to get totally wasted and dance without a shirt on. I also learned that he had been dating someone named Rich for the last two years, but they were over now.

Following the unsticking of the window, we moved on to the hallway where I had to check the wires in the phone plug. While there, I learned that Rich worked for Georgia-Pacific and was based in Boston, so Chris only saw him on the occasional weekend, but not anymore because they were through.

The problem was with the phone, not the jack, so we moved on to the bathroom, so I could open the fan/light fixture and change the light bulb. He was afraid to try to open it because he didn't know how. While I was doing this I learned that he and Rich were planning a vacation in Jamaica next month, but were now going just as friends because, as mentioned before, they were done. Finished. Over.

By the end of the three hours, I had given the apartment a thorough once-over and learned *way* more about Chris Diaz than I had ever desired. I now knew that he was irresponsible, self-centered, narcissistic, and something of a flake.

I also discovered that it was nearly impossible not to like him, I enjoyed the entire three hours I spent listening to him babble. As I was letting myself out of his apartment a little after six, he told me, "Thanks for knocking out all those projects. I really appreciate it. Maybe we can get together sometime for a drink."

"I'd like that," I replied. "I'll see you soon."

I didn't know exactly how soon. As I was returning to my apartment at nine, (after feeding Laine dinner and getting her settled in for the night with a couple of magazines and a pitcher of manhattans), he and Rachel Abernathy were standing outside my door, pounding on it absently while arguing with each other. They seemed totally oblivious to my presence, so I leaned against the door to the elevator machinery flat and watched them.

"I told you he wouldn't be up here. He's probably down at Laine's."

"He's not down at Laine's. He's in his late thirties and in a new town. He's probably already gone out."

I was indignant. "*Late* thirties?" They both spun around, looking both shocked and embarrassed. Oddly enough, Diaz continued to knock.

"Um, yeah. How old are you?" he asked, knocking.

"Chris," Rachel interjected. "He's not in there."

"Oh yeah." He stopped knocking.

"I'm thirty-five."

"Really?" he asked, incredulously. "That's how old I am. You seem older."

Rachel punched him, and then turned to me, smiling. "Hey. We thought since you were new to town, we'd offer to take you out and buy you a drink."

I walked forward to unlock my door. "Well, that's awfully nice of you, but you don't have to do that." I opened the door and welcomed them inside.

"Okay," Chris said as they filed in past me. "Then you buy us a drink."

"Either way," Rachel added, "You must come out with us."

"Why must I?"

"Because it's Saturday night in the Highlands. Staying at home is simply *not done*."

I laughed. They both planted themselves on my couch with expectant looks on their faces. Chris declared, "So, that's settled. Now go change."

Despite having spent the bulk of my adult life in New York City, I found their directness a little disconcerting. I looked down at my outfit. I had on grubby jeans and a t-shirt. I frequently went out to bars dressed like this, although something about their emphasis on changing made me doubt myself a bit. I started to protest feebly. Chris held up a hand and would hear none of it. "At thirty-five, you are too old to try and pull off the jeans-and-tee-shirt look anymore. It may have worked in New York, but this is Atlanta. Standards are higher."

I surrendered. "Okay, then what?"

He indicated what he was wearing, which was a reproduction of a bowling shirt, over a black Lycra sleeveless shirt with a pair of black pants and Pradas. "Something like this."

"I own nothing like that."

He rolled his eyes elaborately and swung off the couch. "Dear God, how do you straight people ever get anyone to even look at you, much less sleep with you?" He swung up the steps to my loft, with me trailing behind.

He pulled open the armoire and began to rummage through the clothing that I had crammed in there. "Lord, look at this. It looks like Goodwill vomited in here. Please tell me you inherited all these clothes. No one would buy them."

I became indignant again. "Well, my *wife* found them attractive…"

"Yeah. Apparently. And is she still your wife?" That stung. He pulled out a blue-and-green striped oxford button-down and handed it to me over his shoulder. "Here. This is possibly the only thing you own that even approximates hip. We're going shopping next week." He pulled out a pair of tan jeans. "With these, and these brown loafers."

"You gonna pick out my underwear and socks as well?" I asked, churlishly.

"If you need me to."

"Go downstairs," I instructed him.

"I want to make sure you wear it right."

"I don't typically get undressed in front of gay guys."

He rolled his eyes. "Oh yeah. Right. We might attack you, 'cause God knows straight women are beating down your door." He returned to the first floor.

I changed clothes and then followed him down. He was leaning against the counter.

"That looks nice," Rachel offered.

"Does not," he replied and descended upon me. He pulled my shirttail back out and unbuttoned my cuffs so they hung open. "There, *now* it looks nice. Go do your hair and put on some cologne."

I glanced into the mirror in the bathroom. My hair was combed. "My hair's fine."

He walked in behind me and messed my hair up. "*Now* it's fine. God, how did you write a column about New York social life without ever learning how to dress?"

I opened the medicine chest and splashed some cologne on. "I didn't have to dress. The column wasn't about me, it was about the locale. It didn't matter what I looked like. They had to impress me."

He spun on me. "It *always* matters what you look like."

Rachel stood up and asked, "Are the two of you done with your cat fight yet?" We turned and looked at her blankly. She had been so quiet, it was almost like she wasn't in the room. "If so, then let's go."

"Where are we going?" I asked.

"Little place right around the corner. Fontaine's."

How do I describe Fontaine's? Sort of an early-twentieth-century-neighborhood-pub-turned-oyster-bar-with-salvaged-fifties-lighting-and-nineteenth-century-fixtures. The atmosphere kind of worked, in an unexpected way. The crowd was equally eclectic. Lots of college and young professional types, with a rather healthy representation of bikers. It was ten o'clock and the place was packed, but we somehow managed to squeeze in at the bar. One of the bartenders started to come wait on us, but another down the bar belted out in a brash, nasal Cleveland accent, "Back off, Leon. They're mine." A moment later she was in front of us.

"Hi Jen," Rachel offered.

"Hey," Chris said, a little sullenly. I suspect he would have preferred Leon.

"Hey," she replied to them while surveying me up and down. "New talent, eh? Okay, you datin' him or her?"

I laughed nervously. "Um, neither. Just a neighbor."

"Jen," Rachel interceded. "This is Laine's nephew, Donovan. Donovan, this is Jennifer Mathis."

"Oh right," I said, holding out my hand to her. "2B."

"Oh right," she replied, taking my hand and shaking it. "Just divorced. Welcome to Atlanta. What'll ya have?"

I ordered a draft beer of some type. Rachel ordered a chardonnay. Chris ordered a very dry Grey Goose martini, straight up, with a twist. "He's buying," he told Jennifer, pointing to me.

While Jennifer was off making drinks, I ventured, "Well, obviously my aunt has ensured that *everyone* knows I'm just divorced. What else has she told everyone about me?"

"Usual stuff," Chris replied offhandedly. "Work. College. Grades. Medical history. Moles. First girl you ever slept with. Stuff like that."

Rachel saw my discomfort and interceded. "Relax, Donovan. He's being an asshole. She didn't really tell us that much, at least not me. I know you grew up in Baltimore. Your parents were divorced and your mother passed away a few years ago. You went to Dartmouth, worked for a couple of papers before landing the job at *Manhattan Gothic.* You just got divorced. That's about it.

"Well, that's about all there is." Jennifer delivered the drinks and then hustled off to take orders at the other end of the bar, once again cutting off Leon's access to patrons.

The three of us toasted each other and sipped our drinks. I hadn't really had much to drink since well before the divorce. Most of the time in Larchmont I was too busy feeling sorry for myself to ever make it to the liquor store. The beer tasted good.

Chris turned on me with a smile and an evil gleam in his eye. "So, tell us about your divorce. Especially *all* the dirty details."

I laughed. It was easy to see that he would never give me a break. "I dunno. I guess I should have expected something was wrong when she asked her ex-boyfriend to give her away at our wedding."

"No!" they both cried, in unison, and on key. It was my first indication that they spent way too much time together.

In truth, the statement about the ex was unfair on my part, and more than a little unkind. Olivia grew up in Key West, and hated every moment of it. She got away to New York as fast as was humanly possible, and went back as little as humanly possible. When her father was dying, however, she had to spend a fair amount of time down there and got to know a guy whose house backed up to her father's house. Although Olivia says they never really had a romantic relationship, and I guess I believe her, they shared a bizarre closeness that always disturbed me.

I recounted all of this to Chris and Rachel. "So, even though I guess they weren't romantic, seeing him walk her down the aisle to give her away sat hard on me."

"Did his presence hang over you guys and linger in your relationship like the stench of a dead body?" Chris asked gleefully.

"Not really." Yes, actually. "But because he's a writer and I'm a writer, I always had a sense that Olivia was comparing me to him. And because he's published something like seven books and I'm still working on my first one, I'm not sure that I fared all that well in the comparison."

"What's his name?" Rachel asked.

"Aidan McInnis."

"Oh yeah. Writes under A.F. McInnis. So-so writer, but his books just fly off the shelves at the store."

I stared at her for a long moment. "Thanks. That makes me feel *so* much better."

They both laughed. Then, Chris put a hand on my shoulder. "Donovan, my sense is you are too talented and interesting a guy to worry about comparing yourself to someone else." The statement struck me as being so genuine and sincere, I was caught off guard. I was half expecting the insult that would follow, but none came.

"Absolutely," Rachel added. "And let's not forget something. He may have published more books, but you actually got the girl."

That was true. Aidan and Olivia were each too attached to their respective lives, which were too anchored in their respective cities, to ever get together. I found an odd satisfaction in that thought.

We finished our drinks and ordered another round. I took out my cigarettes and Chris bummed one off of me. I lost track of how long we were there. At least two more drinks and a full pack of cigarettes. I found myself laughing, a lot. And, when I bid them good-bye a little before midnight, as I returned to the building and they left to go to a club in Midtown, I experienced an odd sensation that I hadn't felt in a while. I relaxed.

And so March went. Each day, I would go running, and I slowly learned the streets in the neighborhood. I would settle my aunt in, handle the jobs around the building, and try to work a little on the book. In the evening, more often than not, I found myself in one of the neighborhood pubs with Rachel and Chris if he was in town. Those first few weeks, I thought I would miss the speed and bustle of New York, but I didn't. This place wasn't necessarily slower. It just had a different rhythm. I couldn't exactly pick out that rhythm, but it was there.

And then it was April, and the dogwoods were in bloom.

The Dogwood

As March turned to April, the blossoms fell from the Bradford Pears, while small brown and green buds on the dogwoods began to split into four segments. I had settled into my apartment and into a routine. Despite my relatively unenthusiastic efforts, I had made some progress on the book. After a slightly menacing discussion with my publisher, I was motivated enough to knock out a detailed outline and synopsis.

The weather was beginning to turn warm, and I couldn't spend enough time outside. I trimmed the bushes and cleaned out the weed-choked courtyard at the bottom of the light well. In my spare time, I had managed to get Laine's Rolls cleaned up. It hadn't been driven in ages. Although I know almost nothing about car engines, I tried to get her in good, running condition. Grand old gal that she is, she suffered my ministrations good-naturedly, but I think she was relieved when I finally drove her into a local garage for a thorough servicing.

Much of my writing took place in the early afternoons on the rooftop deck outside my apartment, which now enjoyed a smattering of patio furniture. I had originally intended to just buy some cheap PVC furniture from the local hardware store. Chris instead convinced me that only solid wood, white, Adirondack chairs were acceptable. I had purchased four of these along with a matching cocktail table, and they now sat in a semi-circle facing west towards the midtown skyline. I began to notice, however, that whenever I went out there, there was thick, yellowish powder covering all of them, even if I had just wiped them down a few minutes earlier. I also noticed it on my car and, occasionally in the apartment. I asked Aunt Laine about it one Thursday evening as I was preparing a brisket for her, Charles, and Brit.

"That, darlin', is the cruelest irony of life in Atlanta. Pollen!"

"Pollen?" I asked in disbelief, coming into the dining room. Beyond the arch, Brit was in the living room watching *Entertainment Tonight* on the television.

"It's true," Charles offered as he set the table. "Spring is so long and pleasant that it seems like the perfect season to have your windows open. Unfortunately, the air quality is absolutely abysmal at this time of year. I think air quality is considered unhealthful at something like two hundred parts-per-million. This time of year, our air quality will max out at something like almost *three thousand*."

I shook my head. "Pollen is microscopic."

"Not here. You will typically find that pine, oak, and birch are the worst offenders."

He finished setting the table. Brit's contribution to the conversation was, "Is there anything as traumatizing as looking at Paul Simon and realizing he's starting to look a lot like Mel Brooks?"

Charles came into the kitchen. "What can I do to help?"

I was chopping mushrooms for my gravy and pointed to the potatoes in the sink. "Peel those?"

"Right." He tied on an apron and began chopping. I should mention that I was *not* wearing an apron. I was wearing running shorts, a golf shirt, and flip flops. It was only about fifty outside, but considering that the news reported snow in New York, I was feeling like I was on vacation. Charles however was dressed immaculately—and what else would you expect from the British?—so the apron complemented the look rather nicely. I was sure Chris would approve.

While we cooked, we chatted about an odd variety of subjects, from pollen to papacy. He had an extremely dry sense of humor, and we enjoyed trading puns and double entendres immensely. While I was busy trying to get my garlic-teriyaki-mushroom-and-ginger gravy to thicken perfectly, I told him the story of how Brit, at seven, had finished all of the leftover cocktails from a party my parents had thrown, and had become so ill we had not only been forced to throw away her pajamas but all of her bedding, and had given serious consideration to the mattress as well. He laughed and, while completing the mashed potatoes, countered with a story of a colleague who had come to a meeting drunk and proceeded to pick a fight with the dean.

"The sad thing is," he told me as he followed me into the dining room with the platters and bowls, "is that because of all the tension, they kept focusing all their attention on me, and I was the least important person in the room."

"Oh, you're being modest..." I began to protest.

"No I'm not. I didn't know shit about the subject. I had nothing valuable to contribute to the conversation. I was simply there to add some color and flavor to the meeting. I was like, like..." he struggled for the word as I rolled Laine up to the table. "I was like oregano! Don't get me wrong, everyone enjoys it in small quantities when you add it to something of substance, but no one wants to sit down to a big bowl of oregano."

Brit joined us while I was laughing and all of us took our seats. We were appropriately somber for the few minutes it took Aunt Laine to rattle off grace, and then we began to pass and serve.

"Well," Brit announced grandly as she ladled gravy onto her potatoes, brisket, green beans and, probably, her Jell-O, "Although none of you have bothered to ask me, I had a simply marvelous day."

"I beg your pardon," I protested. "I asked you when you came in how your day was, but you had to watch that damned..."

"My day," she interrupted, "was just grand because I am going to have a booth at the Dogwood Festival."

"That's marvelous, darling," Charles told her as he grasped her arm.

"How exciting!" Laine observed.

"What's the Dogwood Festival?" I asked.

As they explained it to me, the Dogwood was *the* festival of the springtime. I have since come to learn that it is not *the* festival in the strictest sense that italics would imply. In fact, there are festivals nearly every weekend in the springtime, including the Candler Park Festival, the Decatur Arts Festival, the Yellow Daisy Festival, the Atlanta Jazz Festival, and so forth. The Dogwood is the one that really gets the season going, however.

"During the Dogwood, all the pathways in Piedmont Park are lined with artist booths. You can really buy anything there," Laine explained as she held out her glass so Brit could refill it from the pitcher of manhattans perched on the sideboard. "Paintings, pottery, jewelry. And of course the park is just awash in dogwoods, which makes it that much more festive."

"So what are you going to exhibit, darling?" Charles asked.

"I'm thinking just my paintings. I thought about some of the tilework, but I don't think I have enough of it to last three whole days."

I should probably explain that my sister's art is… well, I guess *abstract* is the appropriate term. Frankly, argyle seems more appropriate. All of her paintings (*and* her pottery *and* her tiles *and* her painted furniture) are all dominated with random stripes of color, punctuated with diamonds. Lots of diamonds, in very strictly regimented rows marching across random flowing fields of color. Argyle.

The topic of Brit's art came up again later that evening. Once Laine had been tucked away for the night, Brit had decided to pop around the corner for cigarettes. (Actually, her decision was just as much at my direction as she had finished my last pack without asking.) Charles and I took the bottle of cabernet that we had been drinking and carried it up to the roof to finish it. The night was clear and cool, so I added a sweatshirt to my meager attire, and we sat in the Adirondack chairs and watched the lights of the city.

"So," I asked as I sipped my wine. "Will Brit actually sell anything at this show? Or is exhibiting her art just a wild part of her hobby?"

He shrugged. "You are too cynical where your sister is concerned, Donovan. She'll sell something, I'm sure. Her art can be very powerful."

"I'm not cynical about her, per se," I protested. "But I guess I've never really seen her work to develop her art. She's been painting diamonds for fifteen years now."

He shrugged again. "Some people like diamonds. Donovan, when you look at her paintings, you see diamonds. When I look at her paintings, I see her and me."

That one caught me totally off guard. "How?"

"Argyles painted over rainbows. Two totally unrelated concepts in what should be imperfect juxtaposition, but which rather combine in harmony to form something totally unexpected."

Not the answer I was expecting. I had to think about that for a long moment. Before I could counter, however, the door from the stairs burst open and Rachel and Jennifer emerged. Rachel was carrying several large torches and a jug of some kind, while Jennifer was carrying a cocktail shaker and some glasses. Jennifer had not been up to the deck before and looked around. Her eyes met mine and she said, "Hey. This is nice up here. I approve."

"We brought you a gift," Rachel announced. "Citronella torches. You will need them soon enough up here."

I examined the torches. They were designed to be stuck directly into the ground. "Hey, thanks. That's great. Although I don't think Chris would approve of me poking these through his ceiling. Tomorrow, I'll figure out a way to secure them, somehow."

Jennifer and Rachel settled into two of the chairs. Jennifer began rattling the shaker and asked, "Can I interest you gentlemen in a martini?"

We both declined. She shrugged and began to pour one for Rachel and one for herself.

"Donovan," Rachel said, "Jennifer and I were talking at dinner. Since she's off tomorrow night, and Chris is off, all of us need to go out. You have to go with us. Charles, you and Brit should come too." Rachel and Chris had, to a certain degree, adopted me as their pet project. Chris had, on several occasions, made me go shopping for new clothes with him, while Rachel had insisted I discover all forms of Atlanta nightlife. In the beginning, I believed it was because they felt I was the emotional cripple that my aunt had portrayed me to be, and they were doing it as a favor to her. It took me some time to realize that neither of them was all that magnanimous, and that they seemed to genuinely like me for myself.

"Alas, we cannot," Charles replied. "Dinner with the dean tomorrow evening. Dreadful affair, but sadly unavoidable."

"Nor, I," I replied. "We've been going out quite a lot lately and I'm feeling the financial strain of it."

"But it's Friday," Rachel protested.

"Ah, God bless ya," Jennifer replied. "I know exactly how you feel. It can get expensive. Tell ya what. We don't need to go out. Let's meet up here tomorrow night. I'll make it an easy, inexpensive evening."

I shrugged. "Okay, as long as it's inexpensive."

There were relatively few projects to do the next day, so I spent some time securing the torches to the corners of the deck. Since there was no railing, I ran a rope between them. It wasn't strong enough to stop someone from falling over, but hopefully it was visible enough to keep them from at least straying too close. As I was finishing off the last one, I heard the phone ring in my apartment. It was the mechanic, calling to let me know that the Rolls was finally ready and I could pick it up any time before five.

Excitedly, I told my aunt the car was ready, and set off to walk the mile to Ansley Mall, where it was waiting. The day had been cloudy and gloomy, with occasional lackluster showers, but I managed to stay dry and made it there around four-thirty. The car sat in front, gleaming, the rainwater beading up on its highly waxed hood and fenders.

I paid the small ransom that the mechanics demanded, and set out for home. At just that moment, it began to pour. Remembering that Rachel typically walked to work, I decided to swing by Ponce Pages and pick her up so that she didn't have to walk home in the mess.

The car started with a rumble that was pure testosterone. I slipped her into gear and slowly guided her out onto Monroe Drive. As we cruised south, I could feel not only the power of the car, but also the weight of it. I had been in office buildings that didn't feel as solid as that car.

I stayed on Monroe until I reached Ponce de Leon, rather than meandering though the quiet neighborhood streets as I might ordinarily do. As I turned left, I could see drivers in other cars turning to admire. While waiting at a stoplight at the corner of Ponce and Freedom Parkway, I looked to my left. An elderly African-American man smiled widely at me and gave me a thumbs-up from within a bus stop. I smiled back and gave him a little salute of gratitude.

I pulled up in front of the bookstore just as Rachel was coming out and fumbling with her umbrella. I glided up in front and opened the passenger side door. She recognized me and came forward, smiling.

"Hey lady," I said. "Need a cab?"

"Wow. She cleaned up beautifully."

"Get in. I'll give you a lift home."

"Gladly." She got in, shaking her small umbrella out the door before closing it. We slid away from the curb.

"Wow, this is pure sex," she said as we circled the block and emerged onto North Highland.

"Tell me about it. Of course, I imagine we burn a gallon of gas with every block we cover."

"Don't bother me with political correctness. I'm willing to bet I'm the first black passenger this car ever had."

I laughed. "I don't know about that. Laine and Maurice were liberal far before it was fashionable." I did have to agree with her comment about the car. Driving that sleek piece of engineering artwork with a beautiful woman next to me through this trendy neighborhood was pure sex.

As we approached the turn onto Virginia, she glanced sideways at me. "I'm not in any hurry to get home if you are looking to put her through her paces."

I considered the offer briefly. "I really want to, but rush-hour in the rain isn't exactly the best opportunity. What about Sunday? You're off this weekend, right?"

"I am. Perhaps we can drive up to the lake."

I pulled down the narrow driveway and executed the tight three-point turn required to berth the car in the garage. As I did so, Rachel rattled off who was in residence by noting whose cars were present. Chris was home, as was Jennifer. Mac and Clare's cars were both absent. Mister Kersey, not having a car, was assumed to be present.

We parted company on the stairs and I went in to make Laine dinner and get her settled for the evening. I didn't make it upstairs until about seven forty-five, which gave me fifteen minutes to get cleaned up before meeting everyone on the deck at eight.

As I came off the steps, I came onto a totally different deck than I had left. The rain had let up, and all of the torches burned brightly in the moist air. Jennifer had strung dozens of strings of Christmas lights over the deck, which gave it a bright, festive air. In the center, she had set up a card table and four folding chairs. She was nowhere to be seen.

I ducked into my apartment and changed clothes. Since the evening was cool and since we were apparently going to be doing something outside, I put on fresh jeans and a sweater that Chris had recently insisted I buy. As I was lacing on my shoes, I heard the faint sounds of jazz float in through the open door.

When I returned to the deck, David Sanborne was revving up "Bang Bang" on a boom box next to the elevator machinery flat. Somehow, Jennifer had succeeded in getting a rolling bar cart up to the deck and had quite an elaborate setup on it. As I emerged, she was busy applying salt to the rim of a margarita glass. "You like salt with your margaritas?" she asked.

"No, thanks. Jennifer, this looks fantastic out here."

She smiled and blushed, which I would never have expected from her. "Just a few things I pulled up from my apartment. I never knew this deck was up here. It's got a lot of potential."

"It does," I admitted. "You've already made it look like a different place."

She came from behind the drink cart and handed me a margarita, sans salt. I accepted and held it out for a silent toast. She clinked her glass to mine and said, "Here's to ya," and drank. Then she looked around the deck. "Yeah, that's what's great about these old buildings. If they survive, they can be reinvented into anything. It's almost like they're people, you know?" I didn't know, but I nodded enthusiastically to be polite.

At that moment Rachel and Chris joined us on the deck. Unlike Jennifer, Rachel, and me, who were all dressed casually, Chris was entirely overdressed. Jennifer got excited when she saw them. "Hey! Welcome to Jennifer's rooftop casino. Can I get you a margarita?"

Rachel smiled and agreed. Chris also agreed, although looked around a bit more dubiously. "What are we doing tonight?" he asked.

Jennifer mixed the drinks enthusiastically. "We are playing UNO!" she announced.

"Uno?" Chris asked, somewhat dispiritedly. "Is that some kind of ethnic slam on the one Hispanic present?"

"UNO," Rachel responded authoritatively, "is a game responsible for more verbal abuse than the U.G.A. – Georgia Tech rivalry."

The drinks were served and we took our places around the table. From someplace Jennifer produced a deck of cards and a green eyeshade, and the game was afoot. If you are not familiar with UNO, you may not understand the sheer emotional toll it can take on the player. The ability of other players to screw you just when you are about to win is actually a good metaphor for corporate America. We spent two abusive hours playing cards on the roof, talking and, of course, drinking margaritas.

Sometime after the third or fourth hand it had become apparent that Chris was going to come out the big loser, and his original skepticism towards the game had turned into sarcastic bitchiness. Once he realized that he couldn't win, he had changed his strategy to a strict "screw your neighbor" approach. The game grew progressively more raucous, with the laughter and joking and abuse climbing in fever and pitch until Chris fell over backwards in his chair, spilling margarita all over himself.

As I noted earlier, he was extremely overdressed for playing cards on the roof. He had also been shivering for a while due to the light weight of his camp shirt. Since he had been cold to begin with, we took a break from the game so he could go downstairs and change. The rest of us stepped into my apartment, allowing Rachel the opportunity to use the bathroom and Jennifer to replenish the ice bucket. While we were in there, we talked of idle things. Jennifer, who had not been in the apartment before, meandered over to the French doors, opened them and stepped out onto the small balcony that overlooks the street. I stepped out and joined her.

"Quite a view you got up here," she observed.

"Yeah," I said. "'Course, it has its downside. I can hear every loud-mouthed drunk on the street after the bars close."

She shrugged. "Ah, God love ya. I didn't realize that you could see the top of the old theater up here."

"Old theater?" I asked.

She pointed across the street. The theater wasn't terribly obvious from the street itself. Its lobby had long ago been converted to a coffee house and a flower shop, obliterating most of its street presence, save some boarded-up doors. However, from up here you could make out the mass of the building behind those small storefronts. And, above their signs were grand old Victorian windows which may have once demarked offices or dressing rooms. I could even make out the poles that had probably held up the marquee, hanging listlessly against the building.

Before I could ask more questions, Chris returned, drier, more warmly dressed and apparently in a much better mood. We resumed the game and I thought no more about the theater until the next day when I was returning from my run.

I had taken a southerly route through the neighborhood, which was bringing me home directly past the theater. It was a pleasant and unusually quiet morning. The streets were littered with the fallen petals from the Bradford pears, and the dogwoods were transitioning from bud to bloom. I slowed to a walk for the last two hundred feet to walk off my run. As I reached the theater, I stopped and stretched against the streetlight. As I did, I studied the building itself.

The lobby had been partitioned so that the flower shop had one third and the coffee house had the opposite third. Although I had never noticed before, what I thought was a posting board for various band posters was actually a boarded-up ticket window. Despite the fact that I hate chain coffee houses, I crossed the street on a whim to buy a latte and check out the building, a little more closely.

There had originally been double doors on each side of the ticket window, but drawing up close I noticed that each double door had been divided with a wall. On either side, one half opened into their respective shop. But the doors on either side of the ticket window opened into a dark portion of the remaining lobby behind the box office. I tried to peer in, but the glass doors had been soaped and I couldn't see much in the gloom.

Inside the coffee house, any trace of the original lobby had been covered over long ago with standard-issue "Seattle uber-hip" accessories that chain coffee houses use to decorate. I paid for my absurdly overpriced latte and returned to the 'Hurst to get Aunt Laine up and moving.

After weeks of physical therapy, Laine was now somewhat able to get around her apartment with a walker, but still required the wheelchair for anything more than a few feet. As I came into the apartment, she was easing herself out of the bathroom, festively arrayed in a pair of burgundy silk lounging pajamas.

"I wish you wouldn't try to get around with the walker without me being here," I informed her.

"If I don't try to get better, I'm not going to," she replied cheerily. She eased herself into the wheelchair and rolled herself into the dining room. As her strength was starting to return, she was in high spirits and found it very easy to dismiss me. I considered that I might be returning to New York in another three or four weeks.

I set about making breakfast while she opened the paper. "How was your run?" she asked as she spread out the front page.

"Nice," I said, bringing her a cup of coffee. "The dogwoods are beginning to open."

"Hmm."

I returned to the kitchen and began to beat the eggs. "Jennifer pointed out something last night I had never noticed before."

"What's that?"

"The coffee house and flower shop across the street are actually in the lobby of an old theater."

"Old being the operative word," she said absently. "It hasn't been a theater for almost thirty years. And even then, it spent the last couple of years of its life showing porn."

"Really?" I asked, laughing slightly at the thought of a porno theater in this neighborhood.

"Yep. The problem with it is that the space just doesn't lend itself to much of anything. That's the reason the lobby was subdivided. So we could at least get some income out of it."

I walked back to the dining room door and leaned against the frame. "We?"

She looked up from her paper as she took a sip of her coffee, leaving a bright red lipstick mark on the cup. "Mo and I."

"Wait a minute, you own that building?"

She nodded again. "That one. This one. The gas station down the street, and that little free-standing dress shop up the block." The shock on my face must have been readily apparent, since she added, "Didn't you know that?"

"How would I?" I asked, returning to the eggs.

"I don't know. I guess I just thought your mother would have probably told you." It was a reasonable assumption, and for all I know Mother may have told me, but it didn't register. Mother certainly never told me that Laine was sitting on several million dollars worth of real estate.

As I set breakfast down in front of her I asked, "So why doesn't the space lend itself to anything?"

She shrugged. "It's a theater. The space is huge. The only people who ever want to rent it are nightclubs. Unfortunately, it has almost no parking, and we have minimum parking requirements in this area to get a liquor license for a nightclub. Besides, even if we didn't, I wouldn't rent it to a nightclub. I don't want all that mess right across the street."

"No one else could use that space?"

"I'm sure somebody could, but it's a theater. It would cost a lot to rework it into anything besides a theater. I've never found another application for it. Maybe you can think of something. The keys are in the desk in the living room."

I had a lot of work to do that day, so exploring abandoned theaters was not high on my list. Nonetheless, it stayed on my mind. Theaters have always held a special place in my heart. In college, even though I had majored in journalism, I had taken every possible theater class I could. I was only one class shy of being able to declare it as a minor. Indeed, as I was busy replacing the light fixture on Mac and Clare's porch, I found my attention repeatedly drawn across the street to where that ticket window was hidden behind thirty years worth of concert flyers.

Once I had finished work, I went over to Brit and Charles's house to help her pack up artwork for the Dogwood Festival. It was late when I returned and found Rachel and Chris on the roof sharing a bottle of wine and watching the lights of the city. I had began to sense that the deck was becoming less *my* space and more of the building's space. I wasn't sure I was happy about that. I did notice that a pink plastic flamingo had now joined us on the roof.

I sat down to join them, slipping off my shoes and lighting a cigarette simultaneously. Mostly Rachel and Chris were maintaining their mindless banter about the things that were exceedingly important to them, so I found my mind drifting off. I didn't actually emerge from my reverie until Rachel said "Van?" and I realized she must have asked me a question.

"Sorry, Rache. My mind was elsewhere. What did you say?"

"I asked how the book was going."

"Oh." I grimaced. The book was going, but I couldn't say it was going well. *A week in the life* was a witty, urbane set of observations, hints, and gossip in the front part of the magazine. It all dealt with what was new in New York and why the reader should do it before anyone else. At least it had been when I was writing it. The guy who was currently ghostwriting the column under my name was more bitchy than urbane, judging by that month's column. My publisher had envisioned the book to be sort of a hip tourist guide for New York. Unfortunately, as I went back through the columns, not much that had been hip still was, so I was struggling with the conversion to book form.

I explained all this to Rachel, who listened attentively and Chris who looked slightly bored. "Sadly, not much about my work could be characterized as timeless journalism."

"Is there such a thing?" Chris asked.

"No, I suppose there isn't. Journalism is not the same as literature."

Rachel looked at me quizzically. "Is this the kind of journalism you always wanted to do?" she asked. "This...I dunno. Does it even have a name?"

I shrugged. "It's called gonzo journalism. I'm not sure I ever knew what I wanted to do. I was always impressed by the hard-hitting, timely writing of the great gonzos like Hunter S. Thompson. I kind of thought the column might be my gateway to similar writings. But, I found that maybe I just can't sustain that level of rebellion. It's hard to keep a sardonic nature alive past thirty without just sounding bitter."

"Did you ever want to write something else?"

I shrugged. "Sure. Novels, plays. What writer doesn't? Unfortunately making a living stood in the way."

"Others manage to do both," Rachel observed. Of course I knew she was right. But I didn't feel like sharing with her that I had always been afraid to take the risk of creating fiction. You put a lot of your personal ego on the line when you try to tell a story. Sarcasm is much more defensible, even if it isn't terribly fulfilling. I decided to change the subject. I told them instead that Laine owned the theater. They feigned polite interest.

I didn't sleep well that night. Around two I got up and tried to work on the book, but nothing about it appealed to me. By two-thirty, I was seated on the balcony in a pair of boxers, smoking a cigarette, the brick of the building cool against my back. Saturday night in the Highlands was winding down below me. The bars had closed, and their patrons and employees wandered home, singularly or in small groups. The night above was clear and a full moon sailed high over Virginia Avenue. I stared at the theater.

Something about the boarded-up ticket window and the dark vacant arched windows above spoke to me. The whole place seemed sad and lonely. No, it was more than sad and lonely. Somehow, I sensed from it the melancholy of unrealized—and worse, unappreciated—potential.

I sat there and studied it for a long time, well over two hours. For some reason, it was drawing me. It was more than intrigue. I almost felt like it was calling me.

Behind me in the apartment, the toilet flushed itself. Despite replacing the seals twice, the toilet continued to flush itself. I had resolved myself to the fact that this was the work of our resident dull ghosts. I did, however, decide that this was their way of telling me to go to bed.

Sundays were relatively easy workdays around the building. Everyone was off work and none of them were particularly anxious to have me poking around their apartments, so I usually had a lot of free time. As such, I intended to go check out the theater as soon as I had Laine settled and got myself cleaned up.

It was a little after ten when I had finished my shower. I had just slipped on a pair of shorts when I heard voices outside. I peeked through the door and saw Jennifer, Rachel, and Chris all seated around the table apparently enjoying brunch. A silver champagne bucket and stand had joined the accoutrements. I made a mental note that, with all the drinking that was taking place out there, I needed to install sturdier rails. I grabbed my shirt and shoes and walked outside to join them.

Rachel greeted me with a "Hail and well met, good fellow."

"Howyadoin?" Jennifer asked as she sipped a mimosa.

"Hi doll," Chris contributed.

"Brunching?" I asked as I dropped into the fourth chair and began to put on my shoes.

"Absolutely!" Rachel replied. "Would you care for a mimosa?"

I shook my head no.

"What are you up to today?" Chris asked. Then without waiting for me to answer said, "If you aren't doing anything you should take me shopping."

I smiled at him. "I had actually promised Miz Abernathy that I would take her out for a spin in Laine's Rolls."

Rachel smiled, happy that I remembered.

"I wanna go," Chris whined.

"So do I," Jennifer announced.

Rachel and I exchanged glances. She shrugged. "I suppose so." Then, glancing at me asked, "When do you want to go?"

I answered as I pulled my shirt on. "After you all finish here, I guess. While you eat, I'm going to go across the street and check out the theater."

"Are you going to break in?" Jennifer asked excitedly. "Can I come watch?"

"Not break in," I told her. "Laine actually owns it. But you can come with me if you want."

"I'm coming, too," Rachel announced.

"I'll stay up here and get some sun," Chris replied.

"You're coming with us," Rachel informed him.

I stood and all of them joined me. I retrieved a flashlight since Laine had informed me that the power wasn't on. We then trooped downstairs - me with the key and the three of them with fresh mimosas – and crossed the street to the theater.

The doors were tarnished silver art deco. I had to unlock a deadbolt on the door on the one to the right of the ticket window plus a padlock. It swung open grudgingly, probably for the first time in years.

The air inside was thick and musty, and dust shimmered in the sunlight that streamed in past us. I took a step forward. The three of them simultaneously took sips of their cocktails, and then followed me in. The door swung shut behind us.

"This is exciting," Jennifer mused. "I feel like I'm Daphne in *Scooby-Doo.*"

"Does that make me Fred or Shaggy?" Chris asked.

"It makes you Velma," the three of us replied simultaneously.

I imagine the lobby must have once been a grand affair. Below the rubbish on the floor you could see mosaic tile spreading out to the left and right, and then ending abruptly at the exposed stud walls for the shops that now occupied either end. Above our heads, a fantastic deco silver sunburst light fixture hung, dirt encrusted but still grand. The door of the box office stood open, and I could see that the ugly plywood posting board outside was doing an admirable job of protecting the elaborate bronze grill over the window.

We turned out attention forward and I switched on the fluorescent torch on my flashlight. To our left, a broad terrazzo staircase with silver railings ascended upwards just past the back wall of the flower shop. To our right were doors to the restrooms. Ahead of us, the doors to the theater were propped open: red and gold gates to a yawning dark abyss beyond. We walked towards them.

There was the unmistakable sound of a rat squealing and scurrying away, followed by a shriek. Three of us turned and stared at Chris. He shrugged apologetically and said, "Sorry to yell. I hate rats."

"You didn't just yell," Jennifer announced. "You sounded just like Janet Leigh in *Psycho*."

We proceeded forward. At the door, I shined my light into the auditorium. In front of us, dark seat backs marched forward in orderly rows towards the giant, silent silver screen glowing faintly in the distance. I shined my light upwards to see if there were bats. Mercifully there were none hanging above us. Instead, stained glass reflected the light back dully from some form of panel fixture mounted in a low ceiling. I followed the ceiling forward to its end and realized that it was the balcony. We walked inside, Chris clinging tightly to me lest there be more rats.

As our eyes adjusted to the gloom, we could make out more details. Stained and dry-rotted curtains covered the walls. But in many places, where they had fallen or disintegrated, they revealed the walls behind, which were covered with deco plasterwork. We reached the front and walked up onto the small stage that jutted out in front of the screen.

Above us, the proscenium of three concentric squares with rounded corners gleamed a pale silver, and I could see chains hanging down on either side ending in bare, exposed light bulbs.

"Wow," Jennifer said in hushed reverence. "This place must have been fantastic in its heyday."

"Absolutely grand," Rachel concurred.

Chris leaned back against the screen to look upwards at the ceiling, which had a larger silver deco fixture similar to the one in the lobby. Much to our surprise, the screen was not mounted against a wall, but rather fitted to the proscenium. It swung back and Chris was swallowed up behind it. He was too embarrassed to shriek a second time. We pushed around the edge of the screen and found ourselves in a small backstage space. Just past the arch at stage right, a wrought-iron spiral staircase wound upwards to a catwalk. Rubbish was everywhere.

We climbed up the steps and followed the catwalk. It led to the door of a narrow hallway which, in turn, led back towards the front of the theater, but behind the auditorium's left wall. Much to our surprise, it opened to a theater box that was concealed from the auditorium by the curtain wall. (We would later discover that it had a twin on the other side of the proscenium.)

"You can almost picture Stadler and Waldorf sitting up here ridiculing Fozzie Bear," Rachel said, laughing.

We followed the hallway all the way back to the front of the building. It ended at the top of the grand staircase from the lobby. Here we found a smaller second floor lobby for the left two-thirds of the balcony. The seats had been removed long ago, but a narrow barrier ran down the balcony. It would have divided the seats on the right side from the left. There was no access to that side except from a fire exit.

"That's weird," Chris observed. "Why would you divide up the balcony?"

"Easy," Rachel said darkly. "Remember when this theater was built. See that door over there?" She pointed to what I assumed was a fire door in the far wall. "I'm sure once upon a time that door had a sign over it readin' *colored entrance*."

The reality of that legacy hit the three of us simultaneously. "Hell," she added, "the fact that this place even allowed us in the same auditorium is pretty amazing. Most southern theaters were totally segregated in those days. This place was *way* progressive."

At the front of the building we found three old rooms that must have been used as offices. Up a short flight of steps on the other side of the lobby, we found the old projection room, dominated by a massive, ancient projector. Everything was full of rubbish and dust covered.

We must have spent an hour exploring that place, except for the creepy old basement that none of us had the nerve to go down into. I could have spent the entire day there, but Chris felt dirty, their cocktails were empty and I had promised Rachel a ride. So, I reluctantly locked the front doors, pocketed the key, and we made our way back across the street.

Chris, having been exposed to dust, had to change clothes; Rachel and Jennifer decided we needed to have a picnic, so they all disappeared into the building. I checked on Laine and then went downstairs to retrieve the car. As I sat in front of the 'Hurst waiting for the gang to rejoin me, I stared at the theater and pondered it. For some reason, going inside had not quelled my curiosity about it. It had, instead, increased it.

The three of them returned. Rachel carried a backpack stuffed with cheeses, crackers and a summer sausage. Jennifer had two thermoses of martinis. Chris brought a bottle of suntan lotion and a new club mix CD, and was horrified to discover that the car had nothing more than an AM radio. They all piled inside and off we went.

The noon-time sun rode high and hot over the city and the temperature was in the low eighties, but the legendary Georgia humidity had not set in yet, so it was a perfect day for a convertible. Rachel sat in the front next to me, donned oversized Jackie-O sunglasses and tied a scarf around her hair. "What do you think?" she asked. "Do I look like Doris Day?"

"Maybe Doris Day as played by Lena Horne," I replied as I pulled away from the curb. She punched me in the arm.

"I do not look like Lena Horne," she replied. "I'm too dark to pass."

"Angela Bassett?" I asked as I merged into traffic.

"Better," she replied.

Driving a fifty-year-old car can spoil you for the cars of today. Sure they are lighter and more fuel efficient, but the Rolls had a solid feeling of substance. Driving her was like driving a ocean liner. Solid, sleek, and elegant all simultaneously.

We cruised down Tenth Street, past appreciative onlookers who pointed and smiled, and crossed Peachtree. I was following Rachel's instructions as we headed towards *the lake*, wherever that was. The sun was too good to resist and Chris and I both had our shirts off before we even hit the interstate.

A memory flickered through my head. Long ago and far away during my married life, Olivia and I had once taken a vacation in Miami. We had rented a convertible and on a whim, she decided she wanted to drive to Key West so we could visit Aidan. I had taken my shirt off on that trip as well. The sun had been magnificent all the way down Highway 1, and it wasn't until I reached Key West that I realized I had a perfect tan on my chest everywhere *except* where the shoulder harness had been. My normal feelings of inadequacy around Aidan were now heightened by the fact that I looked like I was wearing a bright white bandolier.

Fortunately, the Rolls doesn't have shoulder harnesses.

We cruised north onto the I-75 onramp. I punched the accelerator and the car engine roared to life like a fighter jet. We hurdled onto the interstate.

In between Atlanta's political talk radio channels, sports talk radio channels, religious talk radio channels and country stations, we found one that played classic rock. As we hit the Perimeter, the three of them were sipping their martinis and all of us were singing "Video Killed the Radio Star" at the top of our lungs.

An hour later we were seated on a small beach on Lake Allatoona just below Red Top Mountain, talking about life. Well, Jennifer and Rachel were talking about life. Chris and I were mostly smoking cigarettes and listening.

Well, Chris was listening. I was mostly thinking about the theater.

"So here's a question for you," Rachel began as she cut a piece of summer sausage and meticulously placed it on a cracker. "When you think about the person you were at twenty, how much of that person is still alive now?"

No one answered. A deep, contemplative silence ensued.

Who had I been at twenty? I turned twenty during the summer between my sophomore and junior years at Dartmouth. My parents had divorced during the previous year and things were just too weird and tense in Baltimore. So, instead of going home, I had taken a job as a tour guide with a company that led bicycle tours through France. (I hadn't started smoking back then.) It had been a great job. Twenty miles on a bike each day through the French countryside, good red wine in the evenings, Paris on the weekends.

Of course, that had nothing to do with who I had *been*, per se. I was pretty enthusiastic about everything back in those days. Life had seemed like one great adventure. I had dreams of myself as a renaissance man. I was going to be a great writer or journalist. I was going to move to Manhattan and write cutting-edge works about modern society. My life in those days was rooted in the creative.

At twenty, I was someone who had laughed often. At twenty, I was someone who was up for any idea, any creative venture. At twenty, I was someone who took risks.

And at thirty-five? I was writing a column that I was truly too old to write about a social scene I was rapidly aging out of. I had not written one damn word I had been proud of in years. Truth be told, I was more proud of the fact that I could rewire a light fixture or repair a toilet than I was of my work. I was also a refugee from a failed marriage, living off a small trust fund, who couldn't remember the last time he took a chance.

Oh, let's be honest. I was a man who had deliberately chosen *not* to take chances since college.

Worse, I was not a man who laughed often anymore. Laughing was banal. My job had been to be a hip and sarcastic observer.

Holy Christ! I thought to myself. *When did I become this person?* It was as if I began a midlife crisis at that moment. I realized Rachel was watching me intensely, waiting for me to answer.

"I'm not sure," I admitted.

"Really?" Rachel asked. "Why not?"

"I'm not sure I remember who I was at twenty. I know I don't know who I am right now."

She stared at me intensely. I smiled sheepishly and shrugged.

"Well," Chris interjected. "I still have the same boyish good looks and charm I had at twenty."

Rachel turned her attention towards him. "So, you were prematurely graying even back then?"

He threw a small block of Colby at her. It bounced off her forehead and landed in the sand.

We spent several hours at the lake. Occasionally we would wade in, but the water wasn't really warm enough for us to stay long. Mostly, we just talked and joked and told stories. Since I was the designated driver, I got the added pleasure of watching the three of them get sloshed. They mostly slept on the long drive back home.

The days were getting longer, and the sun was still high and bright when we arrived home at six. The three of them all disappeared upstairs into their apartments. I checked on Laine, who had spent the day with Brit, and then left her apartment with every intention of going upstairs to get cleaned up. Instead, I found myself crossing the street, heading right back towards the theater.

I let myself in and stood in the door of the auditorium for a long time. I felt the same sense of melancholy that I had experienced the previous evening. Now, however, I wondered if it was for the unrealized potential of this place, or if I was instead just acutely aware of the unrealized potential of my own life.

The next week was a busy one. Since so many of the neighbors had taken to visiting the deck on the roof – actually, Aunt Laine and Mister Kersey were the only exceptions – I went ahead and built a sturdier railing around the periphery. After all, more than a fair amount of vodka and tequila had been consumed up here recently. There was no sense inviting disaster.

Meanwhile, that weekend was the Dogwood Festival, and much of the building was preparing for it. Jennifer would be working extra shifts at the bar since a large number of people from the suburbs would be coming into town for it. The symphony would be playing in the park during the festival, so Clare was coming and going all hours with her flute from one rehearsal or another. Rachel and Chris were planning which of the related events we would and would not attend. Brit was busily producing last-minute works of argyle to display in her booth.

Laine continued to mend. We would be taking her to the park on Saturday, her first outing in about twelve weeks.

I didn't visit the theater that week, but I found myself staring at it often from my balcony in the evening when I should have been writing.

Thursday evening found Charles and me in Piedmont Park setting up Brit's booth. Piedmont Park is a masterpiece of city parks; over a hundred acres of lawns, woodlands, and pathways interspersed with athletic fields, tennis courts, and botanical gardens. A large city pool sits on the shore of a pond in the center called Lake Clara Meer. (Interestingly, it appears there never was a Clara Meer, since no one knows why it's called that.) It reminded me of Central Park, albeit cleaner, brighter, safer, and without traffic.

The evening was warm, clear, and slightly humid. The park was doing its part for the festival, as the dogwoods were a riot of blooms all up and down the hillsides. The festival would be much larger than I had anticipated. Artist booths lined the paths around the athletic fields and the pond, probably two miles in circumference. There were stages and food courts set up in three different areas of the park. Everywhere you looked, someone was establishing some form of commercial enterprise.

Brit had rented one of the plastic nylon booths and delegated the setup to Charles and me. She was still back at their house busily repacking the art she would be bringing. I must admit that, although I love my sister, I had always missed having a brother. I was finding that Charles would be quite an acceptable substitute, even though I questioned his sanity for marrying into our family.

He had, however, surprised me when he showed up at the 'Hurst to pick me up. Charles always looked like he had been mugged by Brooks Brothers. Suits, button-downs, tassel loafers. I suspected he even owned a cravat. I was therefore totally unprepared when he pulled up in my Jeep (which he had borrowed the previous evening) wearing a tank top, denim shorts and flip flops. (Conversely, I'm sure the fact that I was attired in much the same manner came as no surprise to him, as that is what he usually saw me wearing.)

Charles was a year older than me, but because he was British, he seemed much older. Or, more worldly at least. For those reasons, I projected higher expectations on him than maybe was appropriate, because I was shocked to discover that, mechanically, he was totally inept.

"You should worry about my contribution in this venture," he shrugged as he handed me two support poles he couldn't latch together. "Why do you think people get Ph.D.s? It's because, unlike you, they have no useful skills."

I chuckled a sardonic little chuckle and showed him how the poles fit together. "I don't know that I would say I have many useful skills. Being a writer is only useful if you are successful."

Perhaps there was something in the tone of my voice, because he gave a concerned look. "Well, I was referring more to the fact that you know how to *do* things, like build a porch or fix a leak. That said, is there some reason you don't feel successful as a writer?"

I shrugged, and thought I would give a purely noncommittal answer. Instead, all of the angst I had felt the previous weekend came pouring out of me. The failure of my marriage, my inadequacy as a writer, my paralysis when faced with taking a chance and the theater as metaphor for my own unrealized potential all burbled forth miserably. Good bean that he is, Charles listened intently the entire time, but never ventured false sympathy or protest.

My litany of woe ended with me explaining that "I would have thought, by thirty-five, I would be able to point to some accomplishment I felt proud of." We were pulling the fabric over the frame by that point, so I couldn't see him. As I was tying down the tarp to footers, I realized he was standing above me instead of doing the same thing on the other side. "You need to tie down your side," I told him.

"Got it. Van, after we're through here? Would you show me this theater you mentioned?"

"Sure," I told him. "Why?"

"Well, I'm just wondering something. I'll explain when we get there."

We finished shortly after, and the sun was starting to set when we drove back to the 'Hurst. We parked and walked directly across to the theater. (I had put its key on my keychain.) Inside, I took on him on the tour, pointing out features and discussing how I thought it must have looked or worked. He followed me around obediently, listening to everything I said. About an hour later, we had completed our tour and were sitting on the stage, illuminated only by the ambient glow of the flashlight.

I had been discussing something when I noticed Charles was staring at me intently. "What?" I asked him.

"Van, have you been listening to yourself?"

"Yeah. I was explaining how someone should pull down the curtains and restore the walls."

"Yeah, you were. But you've been full of ideas and opinions about this place the entire time we've been walking through here. This place has you totally animated."

"So?"

"So? I've not seen you animated about anything since you got here."

I shrugged, again indicating, *so*?

"So, this place represents something to you. You said it yourself; you might be projecting your own feelings of unrealized potential on it. So do something about it."

"Like what?"

It was his turn to shrug. "I don't know. But if this place represents your own feelings of failure or inadequacy, quit staring at it. Toy with it. Look, no one is going to rent this place. It is going to just sit here and rot. It's paid for. There's no reason you can't make something out of it."

"But what could I do with it short of turning it back into a theater?"

"Why not turn it back into a theater?"

"And do what with it?"

"Who knows? Maybe nothing. Maybe rent it out. Maybe start your own theater troupe. Quit overanalyzing. You do not realize unrealized potential unless you start *doing something.*"

I started to protest. "I dunno, Charles. I'm only going to be down here a couple of months and I'm supposed to be working on the book…"

I stared at him for a long moment. He was smiling broadly.

"Quit looking for reasons not to try. You know you want to tackle this place."

"Sure I want to tackle it, but for what? I don't even know what it needs."

He stood up, walked towards me and laid a hand on my shoulder. "You now the nice thing about unrealized potential, Van?" I shook my head no. "If it's unrealized, then it can *still be* realized."

I could only stare at him.

He shrugged again. "Why not?" he said.

Why not, indeed?

We didn't discuss it any more that evening. We had to go retrieve Brit and move her artwork to the park, and then spend many, many hours arranging and rearranging and rearranging so it fit her thoughts about what had the best feng shui for a good sale. It was well past midnight before I got home. Sweaty and exhausted, I collapsed into bed and thought nothing more about the theater.

The next morning, I went for my usual run and then went about my morning routine quickly, trying hard not to think about the theater. There was absolutely no reason for me to think about it because doing something with it made absolutely no sense. I kept repeating that to myself right up until early afternoon when I was loading Laine into the Rolls to take her to the park. Although I could have probably pushed her wheelchair down to the park and back, I didn't think it was absolutely necessary. Plus, it was an opportunity to drive the car, something I never tired of.

"So," Laine asked as she tied a scarf around her head, "What did you think of the theater?"

I closed the trunk over the wheelchair and came around to the driver's side. "It looks like it was a masterpiece, once upon a time," I replied, noting that there was too much enthusiasm in my voice.

"It was," she said as the car started with a rumble that was the aural equivalent of an erection. "I wish we could get some use out of it."

I didn't take the bait and we drove on to the park.

It was a gorgeous day out and we chatted about nothing in particular until we reached the park. I helped her from the car into the wheelchair and then wrapped a wool blanket around her legs. She primly tucked her thermos of manhattans under the blanket and I pushed her into the festival.

We spent a pleasant afternoon moving from artist booth to artist booth, with Laine acquiring art at about one out of every three. I had attached a cup holder to her chair, which held my beer, and Laine sipped her manhattan as we rolled along.

By five, we had made one complete loop of the park, and I had deposited about thirty-five hundred dollars of art in the trunk of the car when Laine announced that she needed to make a second circuit.

Even though I had no idea where she was going to put the art we had already acquired, apparently there were two or three items that she still wanted to consider.

When we had rolled past Brit's booth the first time, she had been busy with customers. This time as we rolled by, she recruited us to come in and monitor the booth while she went to the restroom. Say what you will about Atlanta's arts community; they find it hard to say no to an eighty-year-old woman sitting in a wheelchair sipping a cocktail. By the time Brit had returned, Laine had sold three pieces for about five hundred each and was busily negotiating with a fifty-something matron from Dunwoody over a fourth. They settled somewhere in the seven-fifty range.

Once the deal was sealed and my sister's largest painting was on its way to a Dunwoody dining room, Brit announced, "So, Charles tells me you're going to fix up the theater."

"You are?" Laine asked, eyebrows raised over her cocktail.

I shrugged. "Charles seems to think it is important for my soul to try to rescue the theater."

"I see. And is it?"

I tried to vocalize half a dozen different denials, but could not. All I could say was, "I dunno."

She stared at me appraisingly for a long moment. "It might well be."

"There's nothing about it that makes sense, and truthfully, I don't have time to do it. I don't even really know what I would do with it. Besides," I added, "I'm going home soon."

"Well, yes," she acceded, " but if nothing else, just getting the place cleaned up might help it rent."

We could take the conversation no further, as one of Brit's argyles-over-a-still-life paintings had attracted the attention of another customer, and Laine was pressed into service to negotiate.

I returned Laine to the 'Hurst late that afternoon, and then went upstairs to knock out a little bit of writing. I unexpectedly found Chris on the deck, soaking in the sun and chatting with Clare O'Toole.

Even though I didn't know her very well, Clare intrigued me. She was probably in her mid-forties, with dark, dark hair that she wore in a simple pageboy. She had hazel eyes that just sort of lit up when she spoke, and a deep chesty-alto voice that was both rich and serene at the same time.

Almost everything I knew about her, I had learned while fixing one thing or another in her apartment. I knew, from seeing the diploma that hung in her dining room while replacing a lightswitch that she had graduated from a college in Ohio with degrees in music and math. I knew, from an overheard phone conversation while I replaced her ceiling fan, that she disliked most of the soprano section in the symphony chorus. I knew, from repairing her refrigerator, that she had a near-fanatical obsession with bread. I knew, from meeting her husband, that she was attracted to intellectual but slightly goofy guys.

"Donovan," Chris greeted me. "Come sit with us. Or, better yet, make us drinks and then come sit with us."

Clare looked at Chris, clearly shocked, "My God. You're awfully demanding for a flight attendant."

"It's because he's a flight attendant that he's like that, Clare," I explained. "By the time he gets back to us, he's used up whatever stock of charm he has on the plane."

"I'm glad you understand me," Chris said, opening his bottle of sunblock. "I'll have a greyhound."

I rolled my eyes. "Clare, can I offer you a drink?"

She smiled brightly and my heart fluttered. It would be easy to have a crush on her. "Sure. Glass of wine?"

I nodded and ducked into my apartment. I glanced at my laptop, sitting expectantly on my desk, and ignored the pang of guilt. Instead, I poured her a glass of wine. I had no idea why Chris thought I could make him a greyhound since I hate grapefruit juice and never buy it. I just poured him a glass of vodka over ice, poured one for myself, and carried them back out onto the deck.

He took a sip of his drink and nodded approvingly. "Good. Hate to give over glass space to too much grapefruit."

I sat down across the table from Clare, who thanked me for her wine. "So, Chris was just telling me you all went and explored the old theater."

"We did."

"What's it like on the inside?"

"Filthy," Chris replied, flatly.

I rolled my eyes again. Clare caught the look, and gave me a conspiratorial smile.

"It's hard to tell," I told her. "I mean, you can tell it was once a show place but the power was off so you only can get a sense of the place."

"It's really too bad no one's ever found a use for it."

I repeated Laine's story about how it only really lent itself to a nightclub, which she agreed no one wanted in the neighborhood.

"Why couldn't it be a theater again?"

I shrugged. "Is there a need for a theater here? There are three cinemas within a two miles."

She shook her head. "Not a cinema. A theater." She explained that Atlanta was a big theater town. There were dozens of ensemble troupes, improv comedy groups and professional companies in town, many of whom shared performance spaces.

"This is a big theater town," Chris agreed, his only contribution to the conversation. He held his empty glass out to me and smiled imploringly.

Clare finished her wine. "I better get going. I'm meeting Mac at the festival. Are you coming to the concert tomorrow?"

I nodded. "All of us."

She placed her glass on the table, expressed her hope that I would show her the theater one day, and made her way back downstairs. Chris jingled the ice in his glass, still smiling. I sighed, took the glass and made my way back inside to refresh his drink.

Chris was beginning to occupy an odd niche in my life. He was extraordinarily high maintenance and flakey, but I found I truly enjoyed his company. There was nothing sexual between us, but he filled some empty companionship role that I had once thought Olivia would occupy. She never did. Jennifer had begun to refer to him as my non-sexual lover.

I ignored my laptop again and returned to the deck. I kicked off my shoes, pulled my shirt off and joined him soaking up the sun.

We were silent for a time, during which I studied the deck. I was somewhat proud of my handiwork. The rail was a combination of wood supports and railings with wrought-iron stiles. While living in Manhattan, I had always thought I would be good with my hands, but had little opportunity to try it. I was pleased to know I had been right.

I stood up, lit a cigarette, and walked to the edge. Standing at the rail, I looked down into the light well that separated the front and back apartments. The area at the bottom was weed choked. I had removed the old, broken lawn chairs that resided down there. It cried out for something else. If I connected the deck to the fire escape, then all the apartments would have access upward to the roof as well as downward to the yard.

"What are you thinking about?" Chris asked. I turned around. He had lit a cigarette and had been watching me appraisingly.

"Oh I don't know," I said, leaning back against the rail. "Building stuff mostly."

He smiled at me. "You're digging this manual labor gig, aren't you?"

I shrugged. "I guess. It's nice to discover that I'm good at something."

The stair door burst open right then and Rachel emerged, home from work. "Ugh!" she said in exasperation, regarding us. "I hate it when you two start cocktail hour without me."

Chris gave her a slightly mincing look. "Cocktail hour waits for no man…or woman."

Rachel came over and handed the newest copy of *Manhattan Gothic* that I had asked her to pick up for me. As I wandered off to make her a drink, I flipped it open to my column. My name was still on the byline even though I hadn't written it. I hadn't written any of the columns in months, and I had heard they had replaced the guy who was previously ghosting for me with a new, young staff writer. Michael somebody. This was his first column.

I was reading it as I returned to the deck. I handed Rachel her drink and she thanked me. I replied absently, continuing to read. Michael somebody's style was somewhat different from mine. It was edgier, and peppered with more of the hip *lingua franca* of the Lower East Side. My style was geared more towards the Village.

He had reviewed two nightclubs that had just opened in Chelsea, a gallery opening in the Flatiron District, and attended a show that was still in tryouts in Scranton, but on its final approach to Broadway. He gave good, balanced reviews but as I read through it a third time, I could sense the unabashed enthusiasm he was bringing to his job. He loved everything, even the show in Scranton that I had planned on avoiding because I thought it sounded like a dog.

There was a passion and joy to his writing that I knew had been missing from mine all through the last year of my marriage.

And that's when I knew that the magazine would be giving my column to Michael somebody.

I can't say the realization surprised me. In fact, it confirmed something I had been thinking for a while. Namely, that reviewing clubs and nightspots and *happenings* was a young man's game. I had reached the point in my career where I should be creating something of substance.

I knew how it would happen; I had seen it happen to other writers before me. My editor would call me into a meeting. They would offer me a different assignment. It would not have the visibility of my column, but would be an acceptable place to camp out while I decided what the next focus of my career needed to be. Some writers were able to use that role to transition into a different genre. Some camped out there for the rest of their lives. Some never recovered from the shock.

I was roused from my reverie by Rachel. She had asked me a question that I had not heard. What she had asked was if I was ready to head back to the park.

This time we walked to the park. It was a beautiful spring evening, and we sipped our cocktails from plastic tumblers as we walked up Virginia. Even at this distance you could hear the sounds of music floating over the neighborhood from the festival's different stages.

We wandered aimlessly from booth to booth. Even though I had already scrutinized them with Laine earlier, seeing it with the two of them was like seeing it all new. Since we were all a bit buzzed from the cocktails, we were also not above quietly making fun of the things we thought were hideous.

When we had finished our first circuit of the park, we stopped at one of the food courts and bought dinner. Chris opted for Chinese and Rachel bought a plate of cooked vegetables from some southern cooking booth. I stopped at a German booth called Edelweiss and bought an excellent Polish sausage that I devoured ravenously.

The three of us sat on the lawn in front of one of the stages and listened to some mellow jazz while the sun set and the lights in the high-rises surrounding the park flickered to life. I reflected on what a charming, easy lifestyle this was. It may have been the drinks or the music, but I felt a surprising wave of affection for these two people I had only known for a month or so.

The next morning, I tried to run but my splitting hangover made me think better of it. I returned to the apartment after just a mile, and got cleaned up before going in to make breakfast for Laine, who remarked approvingly on my appearance.

As we sat over breakfast, Laine informed me that she had called Georgia Power the previous afternoon and instructed them to turn the power on in the theater. "They said they should have it switched back on today."

"On a Sunday?" I asked.

She shrugged.

"What did you have it turned back on for?" I asked, smearing cream cheese onto my bagel.

"Why not? It's only a few bucks a month, and if this place seems to talk to you, then at least you should be able to walk around there safely."

I began to protest. "It doesn't talk to me…" But she held up a hand to silence me.

"Donovan, maybe it does, maybe it doesn't. I wouldn't mind if you cleaned it up while you were trying to decide if so. But, the fact of the matter is, this is the first thing you've shown even a remote interest in since you've been here. In fact, I suspect it's the first thing you've shown an interest in in a very long time. If you have an interest in it, at least go explore it."

I wanted to argue with her, but I was more shocked and appalled that she had stumbled on the truth. I had just been putting in time since, well since I don't know when. Certainly since my divorce. Possibly since Olivia and I had been married, and maybe even since my mother had died. I could only stare at her for a long time, until at last I could muster, "Laine, what am I going to do with a theater?"

"I don't know, Donovan. The larger question is, what are you going to do with your life? I don't mean to be critical, but you're thirty-five. Isn't it about time you decided how you are going to make a difference? I don't know if the theater is your answer. But it's as good a place as any to start looking."

I confided all of this in Chris later that day as we were wandering through the grocery. He and I had been assigned to put together a picnic dinner for that evening for the four of us to have while listening to the symphony in the park.

Chris was uncharacteristically silent as I prattled on about the fact that I would soon be losing my column, I didn't know what to do with the rest of my life, and a wide variety of other angst that would have been more characteristic of someone having a midlife crisis.

I had finally reached a stopping point as he was placing an absurdly expensive log of chevre into our basket. He asked quietly, "Van, why is this bugging you so much? Certainly you know you are not the only person in the world in his thirties to still be wondering what he wants to be when he grows up."

"No, I know I'm not. But I guess I always wanted to make a difference and I don't think I do. I always wanted to feel like I was someone important," I replied as I added a box of fried chicken. "Are you living the life you wanted to live?"

He wouldn't make eye contact with me, but replied quietly, "No, of course not. Very few flight attendants do."

"Well, you see that's the same thing. Why do you continue to do it if it's not what you want?"

He spun on me very suddenly, and I could see something blazing in his eyes I couldn't recognize, but had definitely never seen there before. "Look, Donovan. Here's the truth of my world. No one becomes a flight attendant with the idea that they are going to do it forever. They get in with the idea that they will do it for a year or two, see the world, and then go start their real life. The problem is, pretty quickly, you're trapped. You're making more money than you can if you go into an entry-level job, and you don't have the skills or the job experience to jump into another job and before you know it, you're thirty-five and being a flight attendant has *become* your real life."

The passion in his voice was not something I ever would have expected.

"The difference between us," he almost spat, "is that there is nothing standing in your way. You have no obligations, and you have the desire to do something. So start doing it."

He was trembling. Then, as abruptly as the mood came, it went. His normal, semi-bemused look dropped into his eyes like a curtain coming down, and he asked me brightly, "Instead of fried chicken, what would you think of getting a sushi platter?"

Later, as we pulled into the building's parking lot, I noticed a Georgia Power truck pulling away from the theater. I said something mundane to Chris, and we parted company on the stairs. I hurriedly climbed the stairs to my place, deposited the groceries in the kitchen, and bolted back downstairs two at a time only to find him waiting for me in the lobby.

"What?" he asked. "You think I didn't see that Georgia Power truck? I knew you wouldn't wait to go over there."

I was surprised he would be interested and said so. "Hey, if this is where you are kicking off your search for your new life, I want to be there."

We crossed the street and I let us back into the lobby. Although I didn't see her at the time, I later learned that Laine was watching us from her apartment balcony, basking in the glow of the gift I had no idea she was giving me.

The lobby was as it was before, except that the exit signs now glowed a dusty green over the doors. I found a lightswitch by the door to the ticket booth and switched it on. A few bulbs in the deco sunburst on the ceiling flickered to life.

"Where do you think the switches are for the house lights?" Chris asked as he crossed the floor to the auditorium doors.

"Probably up in the projection room," I replied and walked past him to the staircase. Another switch illuminated a series of silver deco swags hanging in the gloom above that I had not noticed the first time through the theater. I climbed the steps and entered the projection room.

I hadn't really looked in here on my other sojourns through the theater. All I could tell was that it was ankle deep in garbage. As I switched the light on, though, I discovered that the garbage was mostly old movie posters. Even though the ones on top were for pornos, I stepped over them gingerly to the projection window.

The projector had been shoved aside, and the light controls were on a table next to it. I studied them briefly, trying to decipher the labels caked in dust.

From below I heard Chris call, "Did you find them?"

I leaned out of the projection window but couldn't see him below me because of the balcony. "I did," I replied. "Ready?"

"Ready." I placed my hands on the three rheostats and turned them all the way to the right quickly. Nothing happened.

I glanced back down and realized I had missed the switch labeled "Master Power." I punched it and the lights in the auditorium blazed to life.

I had to blink as my eyes adjusted, but it slowly came into focus. I was transfixed for a moment.

"Well?" Chris asked. I glanced downward and saw that he was standing in the lower aisle, smiling up at me broadly. "You coming down or what?"

I bounded back down the steps and burst into the auditorium. The stained-glass panel over my head glowed merrily, if somewhat dimly, and as I emerged from below the balcony, I could see a larger matching one in the ceiling over the main auditorium was also lit. I stopped below the balcony edge and surveyed the room. Despite the leakage stains in the ceiling, despite the torn and dry-rotted curtains on the wall, and even despite the seats, threadbare and stained with God-knows-what, it was impossible to miss the compact grandeur of the place.

It had not been a large theater in its day, although it was sizeable compared to the long, narrow strip-mall cinemas they build now. Ten seats spread out to each side of the center aisle, and progressed downward for fifteen rows. Narrow side aisles wound back against either wall.

I took a step forward. Chris had already mounted the stage and stood staring out at the seats, smiling absently. I walked towards him.

On a whim, I crossed over to where the curtains angled inwards towards the stage.

"What are you doing?" he asked.

I grabbed hold of the curtain, bundled them together, and then pulled downward hard. The dry-rotted fabric tore away from where it had been nailed up and collapsed on top of me. I dug myself out, sputtering and coughing from the cloud of dust they released, while Chris laughed from the stage. When I emerged I was greeted by the sight I hoped to see. The box at stage left, now revealed, had all of its deco grandeur intact.

"I need to tell you right now," Chris warned, "that if you are planning to make a dress out of those drapes, the gag's been done to death down here. Plus, it's not your color."

I yanked down the curtains at stage right and revealed the other box. Some of the plaster ornamentation at the front was cracked, but all still there.

We wandered back stage. With every light switch, we discovered things that we had not noticed the first time. The stage had actually been designed as a working stage. It was small, but still useable. There were a couple of rooms off each side of the stage that may have been intended as shops or dressing rooms. It was hard to tell with the amount of crap stacked in them.

We also discovered the way down to the basement. There was a hallway running from the stage back to the front of the building, running just below the one we had found on the second floor. We had missed it the first time around because the door was partially blocked. We found that it led to a staircase leading downwards under the main one.

"We're not going down there, are we?" Chris asked, nervously.

"Why not?" I asked, switching on another light switch. A bulb hanging from a wire at the bottom of the steps flickered and then stayed lit.

"I dunno. Rats. Dead bodies. Rats."

"You can stay here."

I descended the stairs with him following reluctantly.

We discovered the furnace room, the water heater, and a huge room underneath the stage. The walls were stacked granite; you couldn't see the floor. Again, it was filled with rubbish. Interestingly, some of it was recent rubbish. Most of the stuff lying around the building was obviously very old. But we found chip bags and fast food wrappers that could have been from the last few years.

"Well, someone's obviously been down here." I observed, picking up a fairly recent Doritos bag.

"Let's hope they aren't still down here," Chris said, glancing around nervously.

I walked over and tried to switch on the air conditioner. High above us, we heard a high pitch shriek of metal grinding against metal. I quickly turned it back off.

"Well, no a.c. for us," I observed. Although the basement was cool, I knew the upstairs would quickly become sweltering in the Georgia springtime heat.

We made our way back to the stage and were preparing to start upstairs when I noticed a glint of metal in the corner. I walked to where I saw the glint, pulled back some boxes and found the first major treasure we would discover in that building.

"What is it?" Chris asked, coming up behind me.

"I am willing to bet this is the old marquee." I was staring at four white glass panels, outlined in gleaming brass styled to match the ticket booth. I dug beneath and found a panel of light bulb sockets. It would have not been a big marquee, but it was still a find nonetheless.

Upstairs, we walked into each of the small boxes beside the stage. They had long ago been stripped of their seats, and one of them creaked alarmingly when I stepped onto it.

"How in the name of God are you ever going to afford to fix this place up?" Chris asked incredulously.

"I dunno," I replied as we started towards the front of the theater. "Mostly, I imagine I'll do the work myself."

He stopped cold behind me. I turned to look and see what was wrong. "Yourself?" he asked, his voice dripping with horror.

"Sure. Why not?"

"Van, this is more than putting a railing up around a deck or fixing a light switch."

"How would you know how much work it is?" I asked, laughing. "You call me for everything in your apartment short of drawing your bath."

In the front offices, there were these seemingly indestructible Steelcase desks and chairs that may have been original to the building. Film reels moldered on one of the desks. On another was a stack of unpaid invoices next to an ashtray holding a petrified cigar stub.

Chris glanced at his watch. "We need to go. Rachel will be looking for us."

Reluctantly, I agreed and followed him out. We retraced our steps everywhere except the basement, switching off lights as went.

Jennifer and Rachel were waiting for us on the deck. We hastily changed clothes, threw the picnic into a rolling cooler that Jennifer had, and walked the ten blocks back to the park. As we walked, Chris and I told them about the theater. We kept it up nonstop for six blocks, despite the fact that Rachel made it very clear she was quite put out with us for not waiting to take her as we explored it.

Once we were inside the park, we visited Brit's booth on the way to Oak Hill, where the symphony would be performing. At Brit's direction, Charles had brought Laine to the park to work the booth with her. Brit was having a great time, and had moved a lot of inventory. Laine was having a marvelous (if slightly lubricated) time herself, selling paintings, sipping manhattans and generally engaging in charming conversations with anyone foolhardy enough to step into the booth. Charles looked bored, but in that politely engaged manner the British use to mask their boredom in courtesy.

"How have sales been?" I asked Brit.

"Marvelous, darling. Marvelous. I might well sell out before the end of the festival. Auntie Laine is a natural at selling art." She came closer and said in a softer, more conspiratorial tone, "To be honest, she has talked up my pedigree *way* beyond what is even plausible, but hey, it's moving canvas."

I smirked. "I'm sure that's just the manhattans talking."

"No doubt. Who cares? I'm up almost twelve thousand dollars."

"Wow."

She glanced over her shoulder. "Do me a favor, darlin'? Take Charles with you to go hear the symphony. He's a love to sit here and be supportive, but he's also bored out of his mind."

"Sure thing," I told her and we separated.

Laine rolled herself over to me. "So, how was the theater?"

"How'd you know we went over there?" I asked.

"I watched you two walk over almost as soon as the utility company left. So, was it better or worse than you thought?"

I said "better" as Chris said "worse" simultaneously. We exchanged glances and laughed.

I briefly told her what we had found, and then asked her, "Laine, we found the old marquee, but there was no name on it. Do you remember what its name was?"

She rolled her eyes upwards, trying to remember. "It had a couple of names. I think the last one was something like Adult Arts Paradise."

"Not the porno days. The original name."

I saw a glimmer in her eye that was quickly extinguished. "No, I don't." She looked around and noticed a potential customer and quickly rolled off to sell him argyles across lavender and ochre.

"Hey Charles," I said, "We're heading over to hear the symphony. Want to come join us?"

A flicker of hope passed through his eyes, but then he glanced at Brit. "Oh, I should stay here and help out."

Brit spun around, "Oh Charles, you're sweet. But we're fine. Go. I know you would you enjoy it."

"No, no, I'll stay here."

"No really, I'm fine. Go enjoy yourself."

"God, young love is nauseating," Jennifer announced and walked towards the next booth.

After another volley, it was decided Charles would join us. The five of us set out towards Oak Hill.

I had been appalled by the amount of stuff that Rachel and Chris had had us bring. We had a blanket, candles, five bottles of wine and more food than I typically ate in a week. Sadly, when I saw how others were picnicking, I realized we looked like poor relations. There were small tables, low chairs, citronella torches, silver candelabras and ice buckets. "Atlantans never lose that ol' southern grandeur." Rachel explained as we spread out the blanket. "I once had a sociology professor tell me that it was a characteristic of a conquered people to hold on to whatever elements of pride or glory they could."

"But that's over a hundred years ago," Charles observed as he kicked off his sandals and dropped down onto the blanket. "No one here is a *conquered people.*"

"Ah," she replied as she dropped down next to him and kicked her shoes off as well. "Doesn't matter. They created the culture. By and large everyone who comes to the city afterwards is indoctrinated to it."

The five of us spread out our picnic and poured wine into small wine glasses Chris had managed to sneak off an airplane. We toasted each other.

As the symphony filed onto the stage, the crowd began to politely applaud as best they could with their hands full of wine glasses and canapés. We were able to make out Clare as she and the other flautists took up their positions. Down in front we could see Mac.

The symphony played a wide variety of tunes, from Mahler to Mercury to Lloyd-Webber. We listened, gossiped among ourselves, and drank wine. During the intermission, Charles pumped me for every detail about the theater. I was more than happy to oblige.

Right before the concert resumed, Mac came by. We called him over and he sat down and joined us. We exchanged the usual pleasantries about the concert, and then Mac reported that Clare had told him about the theater. I happily repeated everything that I had just finished telling Charles.

Towards the end of the concert, Charles excused himself and walked back across the park to rejoin Brit and Laine. It was time to shut down the booth and Laine would be getting tired. The four of us finished the last bottle of wine. It was dark as we folded up our stuff and wandered back towards the 'Hurst.

The next day, I finished up all my usual chores and routines as quickly as possible. Laine had a nice little stack of rent checks piled up with a deposit slip. I gathered them all up and walked across the street to the bank to deposit them for her. I slipped each into the deposit envelope, counting to make sure I hadn't dropped one as I walked. They were all there, but I paused on the one signed *I. Kersey.* It was written in elaborate, old-fashioned script on a plain blue check. I momentarily wondered about him. Was he an international man of intrigue, or just a crazy old coot locked up in his apartment? I began to construct a story in my head about him being both.

When I returned to the building, I gathered a couple of boxes of big garbage bags from the basement and went back across the street. I thought, if nothing else, I could at least start throwing rubbish out. I started in the lobby picking up everything on the floor. Mostly it was newspaper, broken sheet rock, cups, and really, really old porn magazines.

It took about an hour to fill up three trash bags and carry them out to the dumpster behind the theater. (After filling it up, I would later discover that it was not the theater's dumpster. The coffee house made it pretty clear that I was not to use it again.) I found a broom in a janitor's closet by the men's room and was able to sweep up. By the time I was done, I had the lobby and box office, if not clean, at least clear.

They would also be the easiest part of the building to clean up.

Before I could do any more, Clare and Mac knocked on the front door. I went and let them in. Clare was carrying a bottle in a bag. She handed it to me as she walked in, exclaiming, "Happy theater warming!"

I blinked, surprised. "Um well, wow. Thanks. You do realize I'm just cleaning it."

She patted me on the shoulder. "That's what you think, sweetie. Per Laine, you are turning the building into something." She took a step inward, followed by Mac, and gazed around the lobby appreciatively.

"Wow," she said looking down at the terrazzo floor. "This must have been beautiful."

"It still is," Mac replied. "They left it intact in the coffee house. Maybe under the carpet in the flower shop as well."

I had not realized it, but the floor *was* indeed still intact in the coffeehouse. I suddenly felt like I had accomplished something. I have no idea why.

I found myself showing Clare and Mac through the theater. I gave them the abbreviated tour – happily discovering I *had* an abbreviated tour – focusing on the auditorium, backstage, and the balcony. When we had finished, we returned to the stage and stood in front of the silver screen. Clare was talking about the possibilities for the theater, and again reiterated the potential for renting such a place out to local theater companies. At that moment, Rachel and Chris entered the theater noisily, and I realized I had forgotten to lock the door when I came in.

"What are you guys doing here?" I asked. "I thought you would be at the festival."

"We came to help you clean up," Rachel announced.

"Really?" I asked, looking at Chris with disbelief.

"Hey, I clean," he protested. "I just don't like manual labor."

As I sat pondering that, Clare suggested we open the champagne they had brought and toast the theater. (Conveniently, they had also brought cups.)

The five of us sat on the stage, sipping the champagne and discussing possibilities of what the theater could be. I hadn't expected to be entertaining. I was glad I had cleaned the lobby.

Once we had toasted the theater, the Dogwood Festival, spring and each other, Clare and Mac made their way back to their apartment. Rachel and Chris looked at me expectantly. "Okay," she asked. "Where do we start?"

"Well, I just finished the lobby. My intent was to do the building from front to back, then clean out the basement."

"So which is next? The auditorium or upstairs?"

I looked around. "The auditorium I guess. It's mostly just clutter."

We got up off the stage. "Hey," Chris asked, "is the water on?"

"Yeah," I said. "Why?"

"Need to use the restroom." He started towards the edge of the stage, but I stopped him by laying my hand on his arm.

"Go across the street," I advised.

"Why? You just said the water's on."

"Have you ever been in a porn theater restroom?" I asked.

It took a moment, but the look of recognition slowly spread across his face, quickly followed by a look of disgust. "Ew. Even the ladies' room?"

I nodded.

"I'll go across the street. Be right back."

Once he was gone, I turned my attention to the curtains. As soon as I pulled each one down, Rachel pulled it into the center aisle and folded it up. Beneath each we revealed blue walls with silver panels and wall sconces that were still in great shape. The whole place needed a paint job. By the time Chris returned, we had managed to get them all down.

The next day, I rented a dumpster.

The three of us met at the theater again after work. We carried all of the rubbish and garbage out of the auditorium and the balcony. I had retrieved a few tools from the basement of the 'Hurst. As we were standing on the balcony, on a whim, I handed Rachel a crowbar. She looked at me blankly. "What do you want me to do with this?"

I looked past her at the wall dividing the "whites only" portion of the balcony from the rest. She followed my gaze as I said, "Anything you want."

A grin crossed her face and she walked over to the wall. Most of the seats had long ago been removed from the balcony, so she had largely unobstructed access to it. She tentatively tapped the wall with the crowbar. All of a sudden, the smile disappeared from her face, she swung the crowbar back and then, with a force I never would have expected she was capable of, she let out a primal yell and swung the bar into the face of the wall. Plaster exploded outwards and lath cracked beneath.

She took a step backwards and stared at it for a second. Then she said under her breath, "That one's for you, Momma." She swung the crowbar again and more plaster shattered. "And you, Daddy." Then, like a woman possessed she began to dismantle the wall, each hit being personally dedicated to one relative or ancestor who had suffered under the injustice of Jim Crow. Chris and I could only watch her as she took swing after swing. She paused once, out of breath, and I offered to take over for her. Her eyes blazed at me. "This wall is mine!" she declared flatly.

She continued to smash away at it, often using her bare hands to break down the lath and the two-by-four supports. Chris and I were forbidden from even picking up the pieces, so we left her to her personal mission and began working in the front offices. Here there were more pieces of memorabilia. Nothing really valuable, mind you, but things that merited looking at and saving. I began cleaning out one of the desks while Chris emptied a closet. The smell of mildew was overpowering.

We worked mostly in silence until I hear Chris mutter "Well, holy shit."

"What?" I asked as I gingerly relocated a mummified mouse from the desk drawer into the wastebasket using a pair of pencils like chopsticks.

He emerged from the closet holding a chrome-framed, lighted sign, similar to the exit signs in the theater. On the milk-glass panel, stylized art deco letters spelled out *Colored Entrance*.

I could only stare at it. It was hard for me to reconcile the elegant craftsmanship of the fixture with the ignorance of its message. "What do you want to do with it?" Chris asked.

I took it from him and found a way to open it. I gently slid the lettered glass panel out and laid the fixture itself on the desk. With him in tow, I carried the sign out to the balcony.

The wall had been broken down to its sill plate. Rachel, covered in grime and plaster dust, knelt on the floor, carefully selecting large pieces of the broken plaster and placing them in a plastic garbage bag.

As we came in, she glanced at me over her shoulder and said, "I hope you don't mind, but I'm taking souvenirs. It's kind of like my own personal Berlin wall."

"Nope," I told her. "I don't mind, but if you want souvenirs, you may want to take this." I held out the glass sign to her. She stared at it with an expression that conveyed both sadness and distaste. Reluctantly, she took it from my hands and stared at it for a long time.

"Chris, do you have your phone?" she asked, without looking up.

"Yeah," he replied, taking it from his back pocket.

"Take my picture." She turned and held up the sign. He obliged, snapping the shot twice. As he started to put the camera away, she informed him, "Keep shooting. I'll tell you when you're done."

Chris continued to snap shots as she picked up her crow bar. She gently tossed the sign into the air like a softball, and then expertly swung the crowbar around like a bat. She hit the sign squarely, shattering it with a spray of white glass. Chris caught the shot at the moment of impact.

As the shrapnel settled she looked at him triumphantly and said, "*Now* you are done." It was close to ten at that point, and we decided to call it an evening. We returned to the 'Hurst , helping her lug the heavy bag of plaster remains to her apartment. Years later I would discover that, every evening after we left the theater, she sat down with that bag and wrote a long letter to a different member of her family who had grown up in or lived under the segregated South. Although she herself was too young to remember the world before the civil rights movement, she was old enough to have experienced its aftermath. Everyone she wrote to received a chunk of the plaster and two pictures of her, one with the sign and one shattering it to pieces.

On various visits I have made with her to different relatives' homes over the years, those pictures are uniformly framed and displayed, sometimes with the plaster chunks, as if they were Pulitzers.

For the next two weeks, we cleaned out the front half of the theater building, leaving the backstage and basement areas for later. Among the other treasures that it surrendered were vintage movie posters, including a very valuable one for *Roman Holiday;* a photo album with pictures from the early sixties just before it went porno; and some sheet music that apparently went with a silent movie to be played on the long-gone organ.

After the single most unpleasant Saturday of my life, I managed to get the bathrooms clean and functioning. Brit and Charles had thrown in to help us as well. Brit painted the entire lobby and Charles attempted to steam clean the carpet in the auditorium, which promptly disintegrated. Chris and Rachel discovered an attic catwalk that accessed the ceiling light fixture. Working above, they cleaned all the glass and replaced all of the light bulbs. Now, when we entered each evening, instead of the dingy glow the theater was now bathed in a bright shower of blues, reds, and yellows. Even Laine had made the trip across the street in her wheelchair and, after thorough inspection, approved of our handiwork.

By the last week in April, although still threadbare and peeling, the theater was at least clean and no long disreputable. I found myself now having to consider my next great challenge: what should I do with it?

It had been a rainy April, and so spending the time inside cleaning and stripping had been no great hardship. However, as the last weekend of the month approached my comrades had informed me we would not be missing the Inman Park Festival. Work on the theater was suspended for the weekend.

Inman Park was the first "streetcar suburb" of Atlanta and was the next neighborhood south on Highland Avenue. It had gentrified in the seventies, but had never lost its funky, counterculture persona. Indeed, a walk through the neighborhood's main business area, Little Five Points, could make you think you were in Haight-Ashbury during its heyday. Their festival, which began as the Inman Park Funky Tour of Homes, snaked through the streets, outlining two full blocks with arts booths, antiques booths, beer booths, and food vendors. Stages were strategically placed around the neighborhood and an unusual blend of blues and zydeco floated down the streets.

So, on the last Saturday in April, we took an outing to Inman Park. The rains that had plagued us for the last two weeks had abated, and just about everyone in the building, apart from Mister Kersey, repaired southward. Hell, for all I know, he was there as well.

We had, all of us, staked out seats for ourselves along Elizabeth Avenue, which Clare had identified as the best possible place to watch the parade. The weather was beautiful and, actually, so was the crowd. The pleasant spring weather was beginning to give way to the first warning shots of summer humidity. Clare and Mac were sharing bloody marys with Laine, all served from a large silver samovar that she had forced me to lug all the way down from the Highlands. Jennifer, Rachel, and Chris were all drinking mimosas from a Coleman pitcher. I was sitting in the middle, fidgeting and nervously smoking cigarettes. Even though it was a beautiful day and even though I was very happy to be amongst family and friends, I really wanted to be in the theater. I was moody and largely removed from most of the conversations, and didn't even notice the start of the parade until it was upon us.

A guy in his early twenties with less than one percent body fat came roller-blading up the street. His bare chest was shaved, and he wore a very short, tight pair of black leather shorts. Some form of leather harness crossed his chest and supported two large diaphanous butterfly wings so that they appeared to be sprouting from his back. I made some comment about the quality of drag and was informed that the butterfly was the official mascot of Inman Park. I was unaware that butterflies and club kids were synonymous. Chris later reprimanded me for not making that connection.

The parade was a grand celebration of non-conformity. Following *butterfly-boi* was the Seed & Feed Marching Abominable band playing a medley of John Phillip Sousa and Bob Marley. Next came a group of women in home-decorated flower hats pushing flower-covered toy lawnmowers who identified themselves as the Digging Dykes of Decatur. They carried a sign announcing, "It's a garden club, silly." Next came several cars of various city and state officials, and then a group of men and women dressed in business attire executing precision marching drills with their briefcases, the Marching Attaches. Then the parade began to get a little weird.

One of the interesting little interpersonal dynamics in our building was between Jennifer and Clare. They didn't particularly like each other. Not that they disliked each other, mind you. They were just so dramatically different in personality and interests that they had absolutely no common ground from which to base any kind of relationship. However, by virtue of the fact that Jennifer was an amateur actor and Clare was with the symphony, they were forever finding themselves thrown together in situations where they had to make polite conversation. This situation presented itself yet once again as a float of pagan gods and goddesses from a wide variety of mythologies made its way up the street. It was the float for Bachannalanta, an improvisational comedy troupe. A solidly built woman with long, curly brown hair dressed as Sigrid from some Wagnerian opera yelled out to Jennifer in a resonate, projecting alto voice with just a hint of a Texas twang.

"Miranda!" Jennifer yelled back, waving. She began walking towards the float.

"Miranda?" Clare said from next to me, turning. "Miranda!"

"Clare!" Miranda shrieked, hopping down from the float with a clatter of iron mail.

As it turns out, Miranda, who had been in several shows in Atlanta with Jennifer in her early years in Atlanta, had also studied with Clare at the Cincinnati College Conservatory of Music. Reunions like this happen all the time in Atlanta, especially to Clare and Jennifer.

Fortuitously, the parade stalled for a minute. One of the city council cars had accidentally nudged one of the Digging Dykes of Decatur and there was a lot of drama over the need to retrieve a Birkenstock from under a tire. Clare, Jennifer, and Miranda took advantage of the opportunity to stand in the street and catch up by all three talking simultaneously. They agreed that all of them would meet that evening at George's, a small restaurant around the corner from the 'Hurst. The parade began moving again and Miranda clambered back on the float. She stood up and waved her mace over her head, and the float sailed majestically up the street.

Clare and Jennifer smiled at each other awkwardly, and turned and walked back to their respective positions on either side of me. Each was oblivious to the expression of horror on the other's face that they were going to be stuck together in such an intimate social setting that evening.

After the parade, most of the building went off to listen to the Swimming Pool Cues, a local band, play on one of the stages. Neither Clare nor Laine had any desire to hear the band, and I was too antsy to sit, so the three of us set off to explore the marketplace. In the middle of three different pottery vendors, there was a booth of antiques and collectibles. Laine was in heaven and began some heavy dickering with the proprietor over a group of tiny Hummel figurines representing the characters in *Sweeney Todd.* Clare and I found nothing that we were interested in, so we hung along the side of the booth making small talk and sipping our drinks. After a particularly compatible pause, Clare turned to face me and ask, "Can I ask you something personal?"

I glanced sideways at her. "Well…I guess that depends on the question."

She blurted out, "Are you dating Rachel?"

I was rather taken aback by the question. But, I also had to admit that I did spend rather a lot of time with her. "No, not really. We're just friends, I think."

She continued, "Well then, are you dating Chris?"

And I thought her previous question had taken me aback.

"Um…no…not…um, really." I stammered, trying to figure out where the question even came from. "*Why?*"

She smiled and shrugged. "Surely it hasn't escaped your attention that they both have a crush on you."

I choked on the beer I was drinking. "*What?!?!?*"

She smiled indulgently. "Oh, Donovan, come on. The two of them have been working nonstop on the theater with you for a week. I admit Rachel may be doing for altruistic reasons. But when have you *ever* seen Chris do anything that even remotely resembled altruism?"

I had to admit that was unlikely. "Well…" I could not think of anything to say. The concept of one of them having a crush on me was a little intimidating, much less both of them. I shrugged helplessly. "I got nothing."

She turned to look back at the crowd. "I could be wrong. You may just want to watch for it. Just be careful. One should *never* trifle with the affections of a southern woman. God only knows what happens if you trifle with the affections of a Cuban queen."

As I laughed, she abruptly changed the subject. "So, now that you've cleaned up the theater, what are you going to do with it?"

I was happy to have a different topic, if not a happy topic. I sighed as I pulled out my cigarettes. "I have no idea, Clare. It's a real struggle for me. Some mornings after my run I'll just go sit in the auditorium and try to think about what it could be. It's got a lot of potential for some things, but it's not *perfect* for anything."

"So what's wrong with not perfect? What potential does it have?"

"Well…it could be a movie theater, obviously. I could turn it into an art house theater, y'know showing classics and foreign films. *But,* there are three other old theaters in the area doing the same thing, plus the theater at Georgia State."

She gave me a little nod that conceded the point. "What else?"

"I could turn it into a comedy club, except there are already three comedy clubs in town. Even in Manhattan we only had three major clubs, and that pretty much saturated the market."

"Sure…plus you would never get a liquor license for that kind of club from the neighborhood association. So, Option Three?"

I lit my cigarette and took a deep drag. Clare tried hard to disguise her distaste. "Well, I could convert it into a theater, of course, like you suggested. But I can't help but compare it to the theaters in New York."

Clare punched me in the arm. "Donovan! If you are going to compare this place to Broadway, it's never going to be good enough for anything.

"Forget Broadway. Even the off-off-off-Broadway theaters were bigger and better. This place is awfully…" I struggled for the word. "*Intimate*…for a theater, so it's kinda limited. And no surprise. It was built as a movie theater. The stage was almost an afterthought. So it's not going to support many shows."

I took another drag on the cigarette. "And, let's face it, if I take in one of the theater troupes in town, I tie myself to the non-profit world forever. If I'm going to put all of this work into the place, I'd like to see *profit* associated with it."

"Standard platitude reply: money can't buy happiness."

"And to quote my dear Auntie Laine, I never said it could. But with money, you can look for it in a hell of a lot more places."

Clare gave me a little toast with her drink and winked. Laine came rolling up triumphantly with her tiny ceramic musical-comedy neatly bagged and resting in her lap. "Success?" I asked.

"Success!" she confirmed. "Now roll me away. We *must* dish."

"Oh goody!" Clare said as I tossed my cigarette away. I obediently took rein of the wheelchair and steered her out into the road.

"I've done business with that woman before. Did you get a look at her? Bless her soul, I swear every time I buy something from her she goes and uses the money to get another facelift."

Clare glanced over her shoulder. "Are you sure that's not just Botox?"

"Dear girl! Did you see those cheekbones? Twenty years ago, they were her tits."

Later that evening, I begged off going out with Rachel and Chris. I didn't know if one or both of them had a crush on me, and truthfully I didn't have the mental bandwidth to deal with that at the moment. I had a quiet dinner with Laine during which I repeatedly answered concerned queries about why I *wasn't* out with them. In a vain effort to distract her, I tried to get her to tell me more about the theater's history, but she didn't seem to be interested in answering questions about the past. I could also tell she was tired from our outing earlier. Her physical therapy had been much more strenuous this week, and I attributed her vagaries to exhaustion. I put her to bed and went out to walk. I started towards the theater out of habit, but forced myself to walk past it into the heart of the village.

Few restaurants or bars can survive in Atlanta's temperate climate without some form of patio or deck, and with warm weather after two weeks of rain all of the city seemed to be dining al fresco. As I walked past George's patio a crouton bounced off my head. I turned to see Clare, Jennifer, and Miranda all smiling at me innocently with barely concealed laughter. I bent down and retrieved the crouton from the ground, sauntered over to the rail running around the patio, and leaned across it, holding it out to the three of them.

"Ladies...by any chance might one of you be able to explain this projectile to me?"

Behind the wide-eyed mock innocence, I could tell that at least two bottles of very mediocre merlot had been consumed. I leaned down, placed my elbows on the rail and folded my hands beneath my chin, waiting expectantly. The three of them exchanged glances and suppressed laughter, each expecting the other to come up with some witty bon mot. None was forthcoming. Perhaps it was three bottles of merlot.

After a long moment, I ventured. "Let me tell you what I think. I think one of the two of you," I pointed at Jennifer and Clare simultaneously, "pointed me out to Miranda. But, either you couldn't get my attention or didn't try, so Miranda lobbed the crouton at me, thinking that maybe it would stimulate some action on the part of the other two."

The three of them stared at me wide eyed and dumbfounded. Finally Miranda broke the silence. "Wow! How did you know that?"

I shrugged. "Secret superhero powers."

"That was amazing," she said. "You could be like a detective or something."

I held out my hand, and she shook it with a painfully firm handshake. "Hi Miranda. I'm Van."

"Hi. I'm Miranda. Well, you already know that." She took a sip of her wine.

"Seriously, Van. How did you know that?"

I shrugged again. "What can I say? I know the two of them."

"Not for that long," Clare ventured.

I gave her what I hoped was a dazzling smile. "Some things don't take that long."

"You know," Miranda observed. "I suppose we could invite you to actually join us rather than just make you stay on the sidewalk and watch us drink wine."

I accepted the invitation and hopped the fence. Generally, fence-hopping is frowned upon at most dining establishments, but not George's. It's just that kind of place. Within moments a wineglass was procured and I was toasting them.

"So," Miranda said flashing a dazzling smile and pale blue-green eyes at me. "It has become readily apparent to me that the only thing these two have in common to talk about is you. I hear you are restoring a theater."

I smiled and gave a sidelong glance at Clare. I was getting an inkling that Clare found all writers romantic, and anything we did became heavily romanticized.

"I'm not sure I'd say restoring it quite yet. Cleaning it might be a better description."

We began discussing the Atlanta theater community, and I quickly learned that Miranda was a rather widely sought-after director among Atlanta's non-profit theaters. I knew several directors in New York who were professionals, but I had never met a professional director who made a living by working in community theater. I was mesmerized.

So, let's cut to the chase, shall we? An hour later, the merlot drained, I was unlocking the theater to show it off to Miranda with Jennifer and Clare in tow. As we toured, I recapped the same conversation I had had with Clare earlier about the theater's relative merits and faults. Miranda listened, but also refuted several of them.

"I don't know, Donovan. I can see your concerns, but I know several theater troupes that would love to have this as a home. The stage might be small, but most community theater troupes aren't staging *42nd Street.* Most of the shows in town right now could be adapted to this stage."

"Ah, well there's the rub," I replied sitting on the stage, rather proud of myself for inserting a Shakespearian reference. I pulled my cigarettes out of my pocket. "The property is worth an awful lot to turn over to a community theater. With what rents are in this town, I kind of owe it to my aunt to ensure that the property is profitable."

Miranda came over and took the cigarettes and lighter away from me before I could light one. "Never smoke in the theater itself. The smell lingers forever and actors and actresses will sabotage every show unconsciously because they hate the smell."

She sat next to me and continued. "The problem, Van, is that you are confusing the profitability of the venue with the profitability of the troupe. If you give control of the stage to a theater troupe then, yeah, you are never going to make a dime off of it. However, if you keep control of the stage, then you can run a for-profit theater."

"How can I do that if I don't have a troupe?"

She sat and pondered for a second. "It's not unheard of. I know of a for-profit troupe in San Francisco that has moved from space to space. They've been running one show for over thirty years."

"Thirty *years?*"

She nodded. "Yeah. It's called *Beach Blanket Babylon.* It's an ongoing musical revue that celebrates and parodies San Francisco. I've only seen it once. It involves hundreds of giant hats and a Mister Peanut costume. Anyway, they are performing on a stage not much larger than this one. The only problem is, do you want to run the same show for a hundred years?"

"Well…"

"What you might want to do is let a theater troupe rent it temporarily, but not make it anyone's permanent home. That lets you get shows running in here, but still gives you the flexibility to decide what you want to do with it."

I was silent for a long time. Miranda looked at her watch. "Well gang, I've got to get home. Look, Donovan, think it over. If you decide you want to do it, let me know and I'll get you hooked up with a couple of options."

I promised I would think it over.

And then it was May.

The Azalea

May began the following week with me spending less time in the theater. Laine's physical therapy increased in intensity, which was a good thing. She was no longer using her wheelchair in the apartment, although her confidence with the walker suffered when she was outside on the sidewalks. The increase in therapy, however, had me hauling her back and forth to the physical therapist in Buckhead daily. I didn't mind overmuch because it let me drive the Rolls.

At the same time, the amount of work to do around the 'Hurst increased. The pollen had abated somewhat just as the azalea blooms burst open, and the warm weather began to pick up speed towards the hot summer sun. As such, all of nature responded, and the shrubs around the building needed to be trimmed. Additionally, the porches, window frames and doorways all required painting. The rooftop deck needed to be resealed, as did the parking lot.

With all this going on, I had no time to work on the theater. I only visited once. On Wednesday, Britany and I rolled Laine across the street so she could see the work we had done since her first visit. She told us she was impressed, but her manner was more wistful than enthusiastic.

During April, Thursday evening had emerged as Family Night. Laine and I ate dinner together most weeknights, but on Thursday Charles and Brit joined us. Usually Charles and I made dinner while Laine and Brit discussed plans for the wedding, now scheduled for September. That particular Thursday, I was making scallop enchiladas and Charles was wrestling with how much spice to add to his black beans. He and I frequently debated spice. Having spent his entire life eating English food, he wrestled with any culinary preparation other than boiling. As a result, he approached spices with the same caution others might reserve for plutonium.

I had just slid the enchiladas into the oven, and was busy adding ancho to Charles's beans behind his back when there was a knock at the door. Laine pulled herself up and gently crept her way across the room with her walker. I was momentarily distracted and Charles caught me adding the chile. I received an arch-indignant look followed by a smart rap on the knuckles with a wooden spoon. I escaped to the dining room, and nearly collided with Clare and Miranda coming in from the living room. Without much of a greeting, Miranda informed me that the purpose of her visit was a business proposition. All of us sat around the dinner table.

"Here's the deal, Van," Miranda began after politely refusing one of Laine's high octane manhattans. "I'm directing a show at Second Ponce church…at least I was until last night." The church in question, Second Ponce Existentialist Evangelist was a sort of new age, neo-Unitarian Congregationalist church with strong Wiccan-lesbian overtones located halfway between downtown Atlanta and Decatur. Its sanctuary was often leased out to different theater troupes to help fund the congregation. It had been damaged a few days earlier when, during a celebration of the Celtic festival Beltane, the historic reenactment of the Beltane Fires had accidentally spread to the building itself. It had been doused before doing too much damage, but the sanctuary itself would be unusable for the next several months.

"It's a stage adaptation of *Duck Soup*," Miranda continued.

"The Marx Brothers' *Duck Soup*?" Laine asked. "That was a classic. Oh, how fun."

Miranda nodded. "Anyway, we'd still like to stage it. Can we rent the theater?"

Laine and I exchanged glances. "I don't know, Miranda," I replied. "You saw it. It's hardly ready to stage a show. Hell, it's barely clean."

"It doesn't have to be perfect, and we aren't staging the show until July. What would you have to do to get it up and running?"

My mind began to reel as I ticked off the possibilities. "Well, to start with, paint it, clean it, repair the seats. The air conditioning doesn't work. I have no idea about the sprinkler system...which is important because we would have to pass a fire inspection."

"You also have to replace the carpet," Charles added, somewhat apologetically.

I nodded. "And that's just to get it able to be occupied. There are no lights, no sound system..."

"We can handle that," Miranda said. "We've got the lights and the sound system from the church. It can be borrowed temporarily and moved here for the show."

I didn't hear her. "We'd need a curtain...we'd need a concession stand...hell, we'd need a *name.* Miranda, I don't know how we could be open in July. I don't think we can..."

Before I could finish my refusal, I was cut off. "We'll do it," Laine announced.

All heads spun on her. "Laine?"

She gave me a look that reminded me I was just cleaning the theater. It was still hers. "You already know what needs to be done, so therefore it can be done."

"But what about the work I need to do here? I can't take care of this place *plus* do everything over there."

"Donovan! Who says you have to? There are contractors that can be hired."

That hit me like a bucket of ice water. I had been hoping to do most of the restoration work myself. That must have shown on my face, because she continued more gently.

"Van, it doesn't have to be perfect, it just has to be livable."

My mind was reeling, and in the ensuing silence, Brit offered, "You know, I've already painted the lobby. Maybe we could set up some of my paintings for sale there...kind of like a site gallery."

"Marvelous idea!" Laine enthused.

Clare then ventured that she could probably help with a new curtain. Charles thought he could probably help with the work around the theater since he was wrapping up the spring semester and would not be teaching during the summer term.

As their excitement grew, my mind reeled. I felt like Andy Hardy, albeit an unwilling one, consigned to build a stage in the barn. I was about to excuse myself to go get the enchiladas out of the oven when Miranda brought silence to the room, "I will need to know what cut you will want so I can take it back to the troupe."

All of us blinked at her, blankly. Of course there would need to be a business deal. And, sadly, there was only one person I knew who would know what I needed to put together. I sighed at the thought of calling her.

"Before we can answer," I told Miranda, "I need to ask the advice of my ex-wife."

That evening I returned to my apartment to mix a drink and prepare myself to call Olivia. As I approached the door, I noticed a manila envelope leaning against the frame. At first, I assumed that Rachel had left the latest copy of *Manhattan Gothic* for me. However, when I picked it up, I saw that the envelope was old and dusty, and much too full for a magazine. I looked and there were a lot of different things inside, including pictures. I set it on the counter to look at it later, picked up the phone, and dialed the apartment in New York.

Liv worked as an agent for a wide variety of artists, mostly actors and visual artists, along with a couple of writers. One of the things I had learned early on was that she wrote a damn good contract. She would know exactly what I needed to ask for.

I really didn't expect Liv to answer. Liv typically screened calls at home. Since she also spoke to clients all day long – many, many high maintenance clients – the phone at home typically went unanswered unless I felt like answering it. As expected, the machine picked up.

"Thanks for calling," her outgoing message intoned severely. "Please leave a message." Beep.

"Hi Liv. It's Donovan. Hope you are well. I need to ask…"

The phone was yanked off its receiver. That meant she was spread out on the couch in the living room, probably reading contracts. "Donovan! Hi. *Where the hell are you?"*

I laughed. "Wow. What a greeting. Almost phone sex."

"I'm serious," she said, unamused. "I've been calling your cell phone for weeks. No one knows where you are."

I was glad she couldn't see me blush. She probably *had* been calling my cell phone. I wouldn't know because it had been dead in the glove compartment of my Jeep for the last five weeks or so. I hated my cell phone. It had been the source of a fair amount of stress during the last years of our marriage.

"I'm in Atlanta. Aunt Laine broke her leg, so I came down to help take care of her while she recovered."

"You've been staying with Laine all this time? God, how is that?"

"Eh. It's not bad. I occasionally feel like we've got this Waylon-and-Madame act going, but other wise it's fine." I decided to get down to business. "Hey, I need some business advice."

I explained the whole situation. We spent about an hour on the phone together, during which she guided me through putting together a pretty elaborate agreement. She even reminded me that I had once toyed with the idea of writing a play myself.

Once we were finished, a long silence fell over the line.

"Listen, Liv, I appreciate the help."

"My pleasure, Van. I'm glad you were willing to ask me for it."

Another long silence. Before I hung up, it occurred to me to ask, "Hey, why were you trying to get in touch with me?"

"Oh, no reason. I just wanted to know you were all right."

Poignant. "Yeah. I'm fine."

After she extracted a promise from me to go recharge my cell phone and begin carrying it again, we said our goodbyes. I sat and thought long and hard about her. My chest felt strangely hollow.

I made another drink and turned my attention back to the envelope. I dumped out the contents. Old movie programs, newspaper clippings and black-and-white photographs came tumbling out. There was no note, and nothing on the envelope, apart from dust.

Confused, I began to sort the material. The common thread suddenly became apparent with a photograph of the front of the theater. Judging from the cars and the fact that the theater was screening *City Lights,* I assumed the picture had been taken during the late twenties. The theater's name was spelled out in shiny metal letters atop the marquee. It had been called The Briarcliff.

I sat the picture aside and continued to sort. I had several different programs for movies, and another photograph that showed the theater, probably also in the twenties. Then, I found another photograph from the late forties or early fifties. The theater's name had changed to the Orion, and it now advertised air conditioning. I started to lay the picture on top of the earlier one, when something caught my eye. Picking it up and examining it, I noticed a woman standing in front of the ticket window, smiling. It was almost certainly Aunt Laine.

There was a bundle of clippings describing different showings, premieres and parties that had taken place during the war, which I decided to read later. Another photo, this time from the late sixties showed that the theater was now sandwiched between a head shop and a record store. Its name had become the Highland Art Cinema. The marquee was still there, but just barely hanging. The theater was screening *Barbarella.*

Whoever had assembled this envelope for me must have been building a history of the place. My thought went first to Aunt Laine, but I dismissed it immediately. There was no way she could navigate the steep stairs that led up to the roof.

Near the bottom of the stack was a large, folded document. The paper was brittle and brown with age, and I worried that it might crumble to dust as I opened it. Gingerly, I spread it out on my counter. It was the jackpot of the envelope.

There, staring up at me from early in the previous century, was the floor plan of the theater's main floor. I couldn't tell if it was the original construction design or some latter rendering because much of the handwriting in the drawing data block had faded to illegible. Nonetheless, it answered many questions that had perplexed me. The rooms backstage had been intended as stage shops, as I had suspected, and the staircases had once led to "dressing roomes."

The theater organ, which I had assumed must have existed, had in fact been in the center of the stage in a little semi-circular pit that I guessed had been floored over. I imagined some poor organist having to crane their head way back to watch the action on the screen.

The flower shop occupied the space that had been the original concession stand, and the coffeehouse had been the lounge area of the lobby. Someone had written notes all over the side. An arrow indicated where the pulley system for different curtains and scenery flats would have been installed. I didn't know if they were still there or not since we had not cleaned out the stage at all yet.

I looked at the remainder of the papers, hoping to find a similar plan for the upper and lower floors, but there was none there. Looking back at the design, I wondered who would have had all these treasures and left them for me without so much as a note.

The next morning I showed the papers and pictures to Laine. She said she did not know who would have had them or who would have left them for me, but something about her demeanor didn't convince me. She did confirm that it was indeed she pictured in front of the theater in the one photo.

Laine had been up most of the night thinking about what she had committed us to the previous evening. She gave me a budget to handle the major issues like carpet, paint, and repairing or upgrading the systems. While I was not empowered to spend lavishly, I could at least get it habitable pretty quickly.

Once my daily chores around the building had been completed, I ran across the street and purchased a large double-shot latte, and then went to rouse Chris. I knew he was flying a pretty easy schedule that month that gave him weekends free and so I planned to recruit him into the project. Even though he was not particularly handy, he could still cart and carry and clean and paint.

I pounded on his door several times before I heard him yell, "Who is it?"

"Me," I called.

"Go away."

At that point, I figured I could push the envelope of super-tenant relationship a little, so I unlocked his door. "Wake up," I called in. "I need you."

I heard a heavy sigh from the back bedroom. I let myself in and went to his bedroom door. He was splayed across the bed, nude, with a sheet barely covering his butt. "Seriously," I said. "Get up."

He rolled on his side. Flight attendants, as a rule, are not big on modesty. "What?" he asked in a mixture of irritation and resignation.

"We're going into the theater business."

He stared at me for a long minute, trying to decide what his reaction was. Curiosity won out over agitation. He pulled his cigarettes off his nightstand and got up to go pee. "Give me a minute."

He emerged from the bathroom a moment later, now with a towel wrapped around his waist, and accepted the latté. "Okay, I'm listening."

I explained the entire situation I found myself in. Although I couldn't describe him as a willing volunteer, he grudgingly agreed to help. His participation secured, I left him to get dressed and went immediately across the street to the theater. Charles and Brit met me there and together we began to lay out a plan of attack for getting the theater up-to-snuff.

The troupe needed rehearsal space, so our highest priority was to get the stage and auditorium cleaned up and presentable. While we were working on that, we could clean out the basement and they could hold rehearsals there until the stage was ready to be occupied. Once Chris arrived, we divided forces. Brit would get to work painting the restrooms. Chris and Charles would begin cleaning out the basement. I would find contractors to get the air conditioning fixed, and then arrange to have the sprinkler systems checked.

I laid claim to one of the offices upstairs and sat down to work with my newly recharged cell phone. By four o'clock, I had not only lined up the contractors I needed to come out and provide estimates, but I had also made appointments to get a bid on re-carpeting the auditorium. I was beginning to turn my attention to trying to figure out how I would get a couple hundred seats reupholstered, when Chris and Charles appeared at my door.

The theater had grown stuffy in the hot midday and both of them were bare-chested, sweaty and grime covered. Much to my surprise, Chris was not complaining about the physical labor. They waited patiently until I got off the phone. As soon as I pushed the End Call button, Charles said, "You probably need to come downstairs and see something."

Perhaps it was his British accent that made it sound sinister so I asked, "It's not a dead body, is it?"

He chuckled. "No, not a dead one. A live one perhaps."

I crushed out my cigarette and followed both of them back downstairs. As we entered the basement, I was impressed by how much rubbish they had removed. They had also uncovered many things that they had elected to leave, including an old, battered leather chesterfield sofa and some sturdy metal cabinets that might be good to hold costumes.

Charles led me to a small alcove that they had discovered while moving the metal cabinets. It was directly under the ticket booth. Inside were perhaps ten milk crates, all stacked neatly three high. In a couple were clothes, neatly folded. In others were a few six-packs of sodas, some crackers, a few cans of spray-cheese, a box of Pop-Tarts and a box of cereal.

There were also a few bowls and some plastic silverware. On top of the rack were some textbooks, notebooks, a couple of candles, and a lighter. A sleeping bag was neatly rolled up and leaning next to the shelves.

I turned and exchanged glances with Chris and Charles. "It would appear we have a boarder."

"Do you think they've been here recently?" Chris asked, a little uncomfortably.

I checked the expiration date on the Pop-Tarts. It was several months in the future. "Yep. Possibly very recently."

"How do you suppose they got in here?" Charles asked.

We all looked around. There was nothing readily apparent. There was a bulkhead entrance that opened to the parking lot behind the building, but I knew it was padlocked. I even walked over and pulled on the lock and it was still secured. In fact, it was so rusty I imagined I would have to cut it off.

I turned back to the guys. "No idea. Maybe through the roof?"

After a long pause, Charles ventured, "Should we, um, throw this person's stuff away?"

That would, of course, be the logical course of action. However, something about the meager collection of personal belongings spoke to me.

"Not yet," I said. "Let's figure out who he is first."

"How do you know it's a he?" Chris asked.

I pointed to a pair of jockey shorts half folded over in one of the crates.

Chris ventured, "You don't, er, suppose he's still here, do you?"

We all glanced around. In the long, ensuing silence, no one moved. All of us listened intensely. There was no sound save our own breathing. If our guest was in there, he would have been a fool to have moved. He wasn't in there.

"Well," I said. "Let's leave our phantom's stuff alone right now. Let's get everything else cleaned out. Maybe, when he sees we're on to his lair, he'll relocate someplace else."

The level of energy was pretty intense that afternoon. As soon as Rachel got off of work, she was included in the story and pressed into service as well. Brit, much to my amazement, took my Jeep and returned with several sheets of sheetrock, which she then proceeded to hang, finishing the walls that divided the coffee house and the ice-cream shop.

"When did you learn to do that?" I asked her incredulously.

"That summer I spent with Dad after the divorce," she said more lightly than the comment deserved. Our parents' divorce had been particularly contentious. It had surprised everyone as my otherwise mild-mannered and polite mother had sweetly leveraged her role as the woman scorned to litigate one hell of a divorce settlement. (Years later, she would give Laine credit for her transformation during that period by teaching her the "southern art of passive-aggressive womanhood.")

Anyway, Dad's affair had rallied Brit and me around our mother. However, while I tried to emotionally separate myself from the whole scene, Brit could not help but feel sorry for my father. She saw a once-successful lawyer lose his home, his family, and much of his wealth. I would hardly have described him as a tragic figure; he still had his law practice and his girlfriend, Ansley, who had graduated two years ahead of me from the same high school. But, Brit saw him as broken. So, when he bought a rundown row house in downtown Baltimore, Brit had spent a lot of time with him, helping him renovate it. At least, until she was so fed up with the non-stop inane drivel coming from Ansley that she had gone back to Mom, never to return. It was nice to see that she had at least gained a skill for all the heartache.

Meanwhile, in the auditorium itself, Rachel had managed to get most of the tattered upholstery off the chairs. She had worn enormous rubber gloves while working on them to avoid the "genetic remnants of porn audiences."

The interesting thing was, although the work was hard, hot, and dirty, we all had a ball. All of us came out of the theater at ten that evening, sweaty, filthy, and babbling happily about what we were going to do the next day. Both Rachel and Chris separately asked me to go get dinner. Instead, I invited both up to my apartment and made them Chinese. They were both polite, but I sensed maybe just a hint of tension between them. I decided I was flattering myself, and that Clare was full of shit.

Around eleven, after I sent them on their way, I took a glass of wine and went and sat out on my balcony. I watched the theater for a few minutes, trying to identify where and how someone was getting inside. No one stealthily climbed up the drainpipe and let himself in through the vent stack.

About thirty minutes later, there was a knock at the door. I leaned back inside, but before I could call out to whoever it was, the door opened and Rachel let herself in. She was carrying a bottle of wine and a rolled up magazine. She was barefoot, wearing only a pair of pajama bottoms and a camisole.

"Hey," she said, as she crossed the room. "I forgot to give this to you earlier." She handed me the magazine. I was the latest copy of *Manhattan Gothic.*

"Thanks," I said, Then, indicating the wine added "And, that?"

She smiled shyly. "I was having a hard time sleeping so I thought I'd see if I couldn't entice you to have one more glass of wine."

I held up my nearly full glass. "I've got one, but feel free to pour yourself one and come join me."

She went to the kitchen, retrieved a wine glass, filled it with the modest malbec that she had brought, and came over to join me. Since the balcony is only a French balcony, barely more than a rail running in front of French doors, she sat on the floor in front. We talked of minor things, while I kept an occasional eye on the theater, watching for the phantom.

I asked her if she had read my column…well, Michael somebody's column under my name. She had not. I flipped the magazine open and, after ensuring my name was still on the masthead, flipped back to my traditional spot, just aft of the full-page Bacardi ad. My name was still on the column, but my face had been dropped.

"And so it begins…"

"And so what begins?" she asked. Her hair was coming due for its regular relaxing, and she worried a curling lock that was brushing her neck intensely.

I explained how I expected to lose the column this month. In fact, I was sure it had already been promised to Michael somebody, and the publisher and editor were trying hard to figure out what to do with me. "I suspect, sometime late next week, I'll get the call telling me they've 'decided to go in a different direction' and offering me an occasional feature spot."

Mercifully, Rachel knew enough about the world of publishing that she did not try to soothe me with empty protests that surely they wouldn't let a brilliant writer like me go. Brilliant writers, alas, are not that hot a commodity, much less uninspired ones. Instead, she took her index finger, the one that had teased the wayward curl into an angry kink, and began to stroke it down the top of my bare foot.

The gesture, I'm sure, was meant to be soothing. It was anything but. I don't mean to imply there had never been any physical contact between us. We had begun to hug chummily, and she more than occasionally punched me. (Actually, "frequently punched me" is probably a more accurate description.) But this gesture was just ambiguous enough to draw my attention more to questioning the intent than being soothed.

It actually triggered quite a rush of emotions in my brain. Liv and I had not slept in the same bed since we separated over a year earlier. Although I dated occasionally during the separation, I had been chastely faithful until we both agreed that it was probably better to divorce. Then followed a period of about four months that could only be described as revenge sex. Although I had never tried the trick before, I experimented with what all columnists knew. A promised mention in the column was frequently good for meaningless sex. I had abated a bit during the holidays since they were leading up to the divorce, and I had been largely celibate since, what with an aging aunt to care for and an insane idea of restoring a theater.

There had not, however, been a relationship since Liv. There had not even been sex with a person I cared about. I was very much aware that I had not rebounded. Now I was receiving a totally ambiguous signal from Rachel, someone who I had begun to think of as a very close friend in a very short time. And, while I had to admit she was incredibly sexy, I also had to ask myself if I needed a friend more than I needed a lover at that moment.

I was fortunately saved from having to decide what to do at that moment by the sound of metal clanging from across the street. It had not been particularly loud, but in the suddenly intense silence of my apartment, it sounded like a gunshot. I jumped up and leaned out of the doors, scrutinizing everything about the theater. Rachel got up and looked with me.

"What was that?" she asked.

I continued to study the theater. There were a couple of people walking on the street, but nothing really moving. I could see no one on the roof, nor anyone moving about the doors.

"I dunno," I replied. "I thought maybe it was our houseguest, but I don't see anything. Do you?"

She studied for a long minute and said "No."

"Maybe I should go over and see if they are there," I ventured.

She put her hand on top of mine where it rested on the rail. "Don't do that. If you think they are there, call the police. Don't go inside yourself. It could be a crack den for all we know. They'll shoot you."

I smiled. "A crack den with textbooks?"

She did not smile back. "I'm serious. Promise me you won't go over there tonight."

I smirked.

"I mean it, Donovan. Promise me."

"Okay. Not tonight."

She sighed, satisfied. She reached down, picked up her wine and drained what was left in the glass. Whatever moment that may have almost happened was not going to happen now. "Hate to tell you," she said walking back inside, "but there is worse news than losing your column."

"What's that?" I asked, following her.

"Aidan McInnis is coming to town."

I stopped and stared at her. "So?" I said, hopefully nonchalantly.

"So, he's doing a book signing at the store at the end of the month. He just published another book and is out promoting it."

An old, clammy jealous feeling washed over me. I wasn't proud of it. I shrugged. "Aidan is part of Liv's life, not part of mine. Who cares if he comes to town?"

"Well you better be nice to me," Rachel replied as she crossed the room and put her glass in my sink, "Or I'll bring him to find you."

I followed her to the door. She opened it, then turned and gave me a small, chaste kiss. Her lips tasted a little of the wine and I could smell the warm, nutty fragrance of her.

"Sleep well," she said, and was out the door.

I didn't have the energy to contemplate what might or might not have happened that night. I closed and locked the door behind her.

The next morning, I was over at the theater early to see if I could catch the phantom. I knew Rachel would kill me if she found out, but I was obeying the letter of my promise if not the spirit. It wasn't night.

I slipped in the front door and silently crept down the aisle to the stage. Then, letting myself through the door to the side hallway, I crept along the wall in the dark until I reached the stairs that descended to the basement. Taking a deep breath, I crept down, feeling my way with my hand until I found the door. I reached inside and flipped on the light, hoping to gain the advantage by surprising him.

There was no one in the nook, although things had been moved and the sleeping bag was missing. I looked around the basement again, but was unable to find whoever was living down there. I occurred to me that they may be elsewhere in the theater and I had now, effectively trapped myself. If I found myself killed, Rachel would have the right to be pissed at me. How stupid.

I walked authoritatively to disguise my sudden nervousness and returned to the front of the building as quickly as possible. I went running and then returned to the 'Hurst to make Laine breakfast.

Although Laine was becoming able to take care of herself, she had made it clear that she liked being cooked for and so I kept it up.

Typically, each morning she was waiting for me when I came in, and while I made her breakfast, she sat at the dining room table and read the *Atlanta Journal-Constitution*. This particular morning, an article in the Metro section held her attention tightly. I had tried several conversation starters, but none of them really took. It wasn't until I sat the eggs benedict down in front of her that she looked up at me, smiled brightly and said, "The Rolls runs on diesel, right?"

"It does," I replied as I sat down across from her.

"Good." She took a bite of her eggs.

"Why?" I asked as I began to cut an English muffin.

She swallowed her eggs and took a sip of coffee. "I want you to take it in and have it converted to run off of vegetable oil."

I paused with a bite hovering right in front of my mouth and stared at her. "I beg your pardon?"

"There's a place in East Atlanta that coverts diesel cars to run off of recycled vegetable oil. I want to convert the Rolls."

Despite having held my breakfast in stasis while waiting for clarity to arrive, clarity failed to do so. Therefore, I allowed the muffin to resume its course. Around my mouthful of food, I informed her, "Okay, that's an interesting opening gambit. Explain, please."

She informed me, "Well, apparently this place converts diesel cars so that they run off of a mixture of vegetable oil and eth..eth..."

"Ethanol," I replied, cutting another bite.

"This says the vegetable oil is recycled from deep fryers at fast food restaurants. It's totally natural, and a completely replenishable resource. Plus, you get to drive in the HOV lane because it's an alternative fuel."

I took a sip of my coffee. "So if it runs off of old fryer oil, I suspect we'll crave French fries every time we get a whiff of exhaust."

"Nonsense," she said dismissively. "How often do you actually smell your exhaust?"

"Ironic comment considering that we live in the city with the worst air quality in the Southeast."

She ignored me again. "I want you to call them and have them give us an estimate of how much it will cost to have the car converted."

Obviously Madame was serious. "Well, the issue is that there aren't ethanol-and-veggie-oil stations everywhere in the country. You'll limit the Rolls to driving in Atlanta."

She folded down the paper and stared at me sardonically. "Van, the Rolls is made out of stainless steel. It gets about seven miles to the gallon. I don't plan to drive it to the West Coast anytime soon." She laid the paper on the table and took another bite of her breakfast. "Besides, it's reversible. So if you're worried about the condition it'll be when you inherit it..."

My fork clattered loudly where I dropped it on my plate. "Jesus, DeLaine. How could you say something like that?"

She looked up, startled. "What?"

"I've never thought about an inheritance. Christ, is that why you think I'm here?"

"No darling, of course not. But surely you realize that you and Brit are really the only family I have. All of this will be yours one day," she gestured broadly. "Such as it is."

It had never occurred to me that I might inherit all of Laine's empire, and I briefly considered what in the world I was going to do with thousands of ceramic salt-and-pepper shakers. Laine, sensing that she had stepped on a nerve, handed the paper across to me.

"Don't be mad. Here, read the article. I think it is actually a very responsible thing to do."

I accepted the paper sullenly and read the article. Reluctantly, I had to concede, it did have a certain allure. I promised her I would call them later that day.

Since it was Saturday, I had the full benefit of everyone in the building waiting at the theater to help out. Well, apart from Laine and Mister Kersey, of course. All of them, even Christopher, were milling around in front of the theater at ten o'clock waiting for me to let them in.

They went immediately to their tasks. Clare and Mac had joined the cadre. Mac had signed up for tracing and labeling the wiring in the building so we could get a sound system working. Clare, in the meantime, had shown up with her sewing machine and thirty or forty swatches of material. Clare was, in addition to a professional flautist, a frustrated decorator. She was forever offering to "do my colors" for the theater. She planned on making new stage curtains herself, which was no small undertaking. I spent much of the morning looking at swatches with her, along with a large number of paint chits. We decided to paint the theater in the same gray with silver metallic trim that it currently sported, so we opted for deep royal blue curtains with silver piping and a maroon pongee dust ruffle on the bottom. To be truthful, I had no idea *what* pongee was – or a dust ruffle for that matter - but she seemed psyched by the concept so I went along with it.

When I finally sent Clare off to get the fabric, I found a minute to disappear downstairs. The basement was empty, although the sleeping bag had returned to its spot next to the rack. I looked around, but my guest did not seem to be in residence.

On a whim, I took one of the notebooks off the shelf and opened it. I briefly considered reading it, but that seemed like a violation of privacy of someone I'd never met…even though he was living in my basement. Instead, I flipped though the notebook until I found a blank sheet. I ripped it out, pulled a pencil out of my back pocket and wrote a note out to the Phantom.

> Dear Sir:
>
> As you may have noticed, we are in the process of restoring the theater. This space that you are living in is about to become a rehearsal hall. As such, it would probably be in your best interest to find other accommodations.
>
> Rehearsals are due to start next week. Thanks for understanding.
>
> All the best…Donovan Ford

I sat the note on top of the sleeping bag in a way I was sure he couldn't possibly miss it, and went about my business for the day.

Late that afternoon, my friends excused themselves one by one to go about their evening. I could only marvel that these people, who had not known me from Adam three months earlier, were giving their time and energy to this project. It wasn't until years later that I discovered that the denizens of VaHi are a great underleveraged resource. They have more spare time and money than most, are more community minded than most, and are more desperate for a creative outlet than all. I had unwittingly plugged into that dynamic.

Eventually, it was just Chris, Rachel, and me. Each of us was filthy, but it was possible to see some of the impact we had made that day. The theater was at least clean and ready to begin remodeling. We had mostly emptied the new rehearsal hall, and I had moved some bookcases to partially conceal the Phantom's alcove. The next day we could begin painting. There was still much to do to make the stage useable, but I was confident we could get there.

"Let me make you two dinner," I suggested as we stepped outside the front doors. "I owe you both. I really appreciate all you two are helping me to do."

Chris and Rachel exchanged glances. "Sure," they both replied in stereo. They had been friends sufficiently long enough that they often said the same thing at the same time, something they described as *hag-and-fag-surround-sound.*

"Great," I told them. "Let me check in on Laine and go get a shower. Meet at my place in, say, an hour?"

They both agreed as we crossed the street, and I sent them on their way while I checked on Laine.

She was sufficiently ambulatory to leave the building and had been dying to go out to dinner, so Charles and Brit had retrieved her and were taking her out. While she got ready, she had me make us each a cocktail and then sit and regale her with the details of everything we had accomplished that day. It took almost forty-five minutes before the rest of the family arrived and were off on their way to the latest hip restaurant in midtown.

I climbed the stairs to my place. As I turned the corner on the deck, Chris was sitting at the other end of the breezeway, his back against my front door, sipping a martini and flipping through a stack of paper.

"What are you doing here?" I asked as he stood up.

"I was invited," he protested.

"I know, but you are early. You're never early. I suspect your mother carried you for eleven months."

He ignored me. "When I got up here, there was the envelope full of stuff in front of your door, so I'm reading it."

"Another one?" I asked. There was no point protesting the violation of my privacy or even the legal sanctity of mail. In Chris's world, boundaries were strictly one way.

I unlocked the door, and took the stack of paper from him as we went inside. I sat it on the counter and flipped through it. More of the same theater memorabilia.

Chris had showered and had put on a pair of cabana pants and a white gauze Henley that laced up from the sternum to the throat. He smelled of Versace. As he stood next to me, I was acutely aware that I smelled like sweat and industrial solvents, a fact that he confirmed by asking, "You want me to make you a drink while you take a long shower?"

"Sure," I replied and left my newest stash of memorabilia to head towards the bathroom.

"What do you want?" he asked as I was pulling off my shirt.

"Bacardi and diet," I replied as I closed the door behind me.

The shower felt incredible. For an old building, there was no shortage of hot water. I sighed happily, and the lights flickered briefly, which I took to be a sign of acknowledgement from our resident ghosts. Although I didn't really believe in ghosts, the apartment had a habit of doing odd little things that I decided was easier to attribute to them than try to explain myself. I had begun referring to them as the Feldmans.

As I was rinsing the shampoo out of my hair, I heard the bathroom door open and Chris pulled the shower curtain aside slightly to hand me my drink.

I thanked him, but something about my face must have conveyed my discomfort because he rolled his eyes. "Jesus, Van. You've got nothing I haven't seen before. Hell, you've got nothing I probably haven't had in my mouth before." He pulled the shower curtain closed and stepped back out of the bathroom.

It is probably worth digressing a moment to discuss whether I was comfortable with Chris's sexuality. I will freely admit I was not a "man's man" growing up. At the prep school I had attended in Andover, sports were the dominant interest, and business or law were the dominant career aspirations for boys. Although I enjoyed being outside, and wasn't a bad shortstop, I had little of the kind of interest in sports that other boys had. I rowed and sailed in college, but being more interested in writing, music and theater, I had not been one of the "in" crowd. Granted, I had been popular enough and wasn't branded "fag" like other outsiders had been, but I certainly felt some camaraderie with them even if I wasn't. I didn't exactly fit in either.

My best friend in college had been gay, and although he had hit on me once at a party, I had never been in the least attracted to him. I had occasionally wondered what it would be like to be with a man, but had never been tempted to find out. Then, when Liv and I had married, I had lost all interest in sex with other people. Candidly, on her worst days, Liv could make you lose all interest in sex, period.

All in all, being gay never bothered me. It just never interested me, either.

I took a sip of my drink. It was unbelievably strong. One of the interesting things about flight attendants I have learned is that most of them are terrible bartenders. If the liquor doesn't come prepackaged in mini bottles, they have no idea how to measure it out.

I finished my shower, dried off, and wrapped a towel around my waist. As I came out of the bathroom, he was sitting on the couch, sipping a fresh martini and flipping through the papers from the previous night. "Looks like quite a lot of memorabilia," he commented as I padded up the stairs to the loft to change.

"Yeah." I felt a little foolish being self-conscious in front of him, but was self-conscious nonetheless. I quickly dropped the towel and pulled on a pair of flannel pajama bottoms and a baseball jersey.

As I descended the stairs, he smiled mischievously at me and said, "You're cute when you're bashful."

I was saved from answering by a knock on the door. He went to let Rachel in.

For dinner, I made chicken lo mein and vegetable pot-stickers using my brand new Peking pan. We talked and gossiped during dinner, all the while I drank Bacardis, Rachel drank wine, and Chris drank martinis.

After dinner, the three of us sat on the floor sorting through the contents of the two envelopes. Like the one the previous evening, tonight's held a wide variety of pictures, programs, and sheet music. It also contained the warranty on the air-conditioning, which I decided to investigate to see if I could get any financial benefit from it.

The pictures were far and away the most interesting. There were several of Laine, all taken seemingly from above. All of us noticed it, and at one point Rachel stood up and carried one to the French doors. Looking out, she said, "I am willing to bet this one was taken from up here. The angles are very similar."

I stood, looked over her shoulder and had to agree. It was taken either from the bell tower or from Chris's balcony one floor below.

Chris had stood as well and went to the kitchen to make us fresh drinks. The booze was getting to all three of us, but it didn't really stop any of us from drinking. "So," he began. "What are you going to name the theater?"

I dropped back to the floor and lay on my back. "I have no friggin' idea," I replied.

Rachel dropped down on the floor as well and lay with her head on top of my stomach. "You could always resurrect one of the earlier names," she ventured. "I like the Orion."

"There's some merit to that," Chris added as he returned with the drinks. I caught a flicker of something in his eye as he handed my drink down to me, but I couldn't tell what it was. He dropped to the floor as well, stuck a hand under my head and lifted it, sliding his stomach beneath as he rested his head on Rachel's. I smiled inwardly as I remembered doing this with friends in junior high and the sensation of feeling someone laugh in the stomach beneath you.

"Lots of the theaters in town have retained their historic names. The Fox, the Rialto, the Roxy…"

"The problem is," I replied, "is that I don't like the names *Orion* or *the Briarcliff*."

"Okay," he ventured. "Let's just play lightning round. We'll take turns saying the first theater name that comes to us. Rache, you start."

Rachel was holding up one of the pictures that showed Laine, taken during the porno days. "Highland Art Cinema," she replied.

Chris tapped my head, "You," he replied. His hand remained lightly on my hair.

"Uh, the Helen Hayes," I replied.

"The Loews," he said referring to the long-gone landmark where *Gone with the Wind* had premiered.

"Radio City," Rachel added.

"The Minskoff." I was stuck with New York theaters.

"The Gaiety."

"Graumann's Chinese."

"It's Mann's now," I corrected. "The Schubert."

"The Schubert Alley."

"That's not a theater," Rachel objected.

"Shh," Chris countered. "Just name a theater."

A long pause. "I can't think of one," she replied.

"Then just say anything. You've got to keep lightning round going fast."

She struggled for a minute while still studying the picture and then blurted out "DeLaine."

"DeLaine?"

I sat upright and looked at the pictures. The DeLaine? After all, it was her theater. She was underwriting this whole project. Why not the DeLaine?

"We could call it the DeLaine," I mused.

"She'll hate that," Chris said as he propped himself up on one arm to take a deep draught of his martini.

"Maybe you're right." I immediately forgot all about it.

We chatted for a long time. Neither of them seemed particularly anxious to leave, but I was getting quite tired. The conversation drifted into Hollywood gossip, and without intending to, I drifted off to sleep.

I awoke suddenly to Chris's finger gently playing with the hair on my sternum. He was next to me on the floor. My shirt was open and he was propped up on one arm, staring at me intently. It took a moment for me to figure out what was going on, and as the meaning slowly crept into my sleep-addled mind, I was aware enough that I must not overreact.

"Where's Rachel?" I asked.

"She went home about a half hour ago."

"Ah. You didn't?"

He grinned at me. "I did. I came back."

I pulled my hands up over my eyes. The action of bringing my arm up gently moved his out of the way. He pulled it back slowly.

I kept my hands over my eyes and said, "Wow, the rum hit me hard. I think I better head up to bed."

There was silent hesitation in the room, and I could tell he was calculating whether that had been an invitation or not, so I added, "You heading back downstairs?"

I felt the sexual tension break. "Yeah," he replied cheerily. "I just didn't want to leave you on the floor."

I stood up slowly and offered him a hand, which he accepted. He walked towards the door, and I followed to lock it behind him. He turned as he opened the door, and his bare foot came to rest lightly on mine. "Van…" he began.

I faked a yawn, and then said sleepily, "Yeah?"

He smiled. "Nothing. Thanks for dinner." The he leaned in, gently kissed me on the lips in much the same manner Rachel had the night before. "Night." He turned and walked out.

I locked the door behind him, ran my hands through my hair and said to myself, "Y'know, Donovan old boy. You always hoped you would have an interesting life. You ought to be writing this down."

I pulled my shirt the rest of the way off and walked to the French doors. I pulled them open and a rush of cool air flowed into the room. I leaned out over the rail, letting the night breeze blow over me. There, below me, the theater gleamed in the bright light of a full moon that was ascending over Druid Hills. It was just after two, and the bars had all closed, so the streets were pretty much empty. On the street a couple of people strolled by, and I noticed one, a kid of maybe twenty wearing a heavy backpack, disappear around the corner of the theater into the alley. A moment later, I heard the same heavy-metal clang I had heard the night before. I watched for several minutes, but he never came back around the building.

On Sunday, we began painting. Charles, Chris, and I succeeded in erecting a rolling scaffolding that we had rented and started with the ceiling. Our intent was to work our way from the top down. Because the air-conditioning still wasn't working, we opened all of the windows on the second floor and the doors at the back of the stage to try to get some air moving through the theater. Nonetheless the air was still stifling, probably not helped by the number of cigarettes Chris and I were smoking between us (despite Miranda's admonitions to the contrary), and all of us had stripped down to shorts before noon. Meanwhile, Clare sewed away diligently on the stage in a tank top and running shorts, and Rachel, wearing cutoffs and a sports bra, hauled garbage from the prop rooms and dressing rooms to the dumpster. To help make things more bearable for my all-volunteer workforce, I had some reggae playing from a boom-box in the balcony and Laine, who was beginning to feel left out, had a steady stream of food and beverages delivered from the neighboring restaurants.

The old curtains had been removed and the movie screen retracted upwards on its roller, so that one could see all the way through the theater. It was early afternoon and the scaffolding had been placed in front of the proscenium. Charles clung to the top, painting the ceiling, and Chris and I hung from each side painting the arch. Subconsciously, I suppose, I heard metal clang and I looked towards the open door at the back of the stage. The kid with the backpack that I had seen the previous evening was outside the door. He was passing slowly, subtly looking inside the theater. After watching him for a moment, our eyes met, and a spark of recognition passed through his. He hurried on his way, but something on a gut level told me he was the Phantom.

I finished the section I was painting and leapt down from the scaffolding. Without explanation, I slipped down to the basement. The note had been moved from the sleeping bag, and there appeared to be fewer things down there. I took comfort in the knowledge that the Phantom would be moving out, and thought no more about it.

On Monday morning, the serious work of converting the theater into a business got underway. I first met with the building inspector and came away with a long list of items that would have to be installed, repaired, or replaced. Next came the upholsterer, who left me with a heavy estimate of what new seat covers would cost, and a stack of fabric swatches from which Laine and Clare would pick.

The heating and cooling engineer came and broke the news to me that the air conditioning would have to be replaced entirely, and the warranty had expired sometime during the Eisenhower administration. And I received a visit from the health inspector with a long list of things I would need in order to be permitted to sell refreshments.

At lunch, I carried the sheaf of estimates over to Laine's and we sat and reviewed them together while we ate lunch. I was taken aback by the amount of money we were looking at spending, almost fifty-thousand. My aunt shrugged it off. Yes, it would hurt, she admitted. But no more so than paying taxes on a property that was moldering into ruins. She told me to go ahead with everything.

I returned to the theater after lunch. As I was unlocking the door, a gold Mercedes pulled up and parked directly in front of the fire hydrant that was outside. I stopped and watched as a tall, leggy blonde in a surprisingly short white leather miniskirt got out of the car, looked at me, smiled, and said, "I'll be right back. Don't call the cops."

With that, she was off, walking up the street at a brisk pace. I chuckled a little, and let myself into the theater, thinking no more about her. The day was hot, so I left the door open a crack. I was working alone, painting the left wall of the auditorium.

I had been up on the scaffolding for perhaps ten minutes when I heard a throaty "Hello?" called from the lobby.

Now I, like most northerners, had never known that there was more than one southern accent. But, after living in the south for a while, I have discovered that a Charleston Battery accent differs from Louisiana Cajun as much as French differs from Mandarin Chinese. This *hello* was delivered in the Buckhead accent, an accent that was limited to the natives of that wealthy Atlanta neighborhood. The accent itself is hard to explain. Almost every word originates in the middle of the throat, and is said with a smile and a slightly clenched jaw. It sounds very much like Thurston Howell on the old *Gilligan's Island*.

"In here," I called.

I heard the sound of heels striking the floor, and a moment later the blonde appeared in the lobby door. She looked around, gave me a broad smile with a gleam in her eye, and said, "Oh. Hello." She proceeded down the aisle, the sound of her Manolo Blahniks echoing off the walls like gunshots. "You wouldn't happen to know where I could find the proprietor of this establishment, would you?"

I put down my brush and leaned against the scaffolding. "I would be him. How can I help you?"

She cocked her head, still smiling, and winked. "I think the question may be, how can I help you?"

I flipped a leg over the scaffolding and slid down the sides. I turned to shake her hand and introduce myself, and as fast as lightning she slipped a card into it.

"I'm Talbot Van Hessel. I'm an account rep for Midtown Wine Wholesalers." She looked around. "Are you, by any chance, turning this place into a restaurant?"

I slid the card into the pocket of my badly paint-smeared shorts. "Why do you ask?"

"Well, this is Virginia Highland. Is anything else financially viable here?"

I laughed. "Well, I'm hoping a theater will be."

Her face lit up. "A theater? Perfect! Just exactly what the neighborhood is going to need. Something to do before or after dining out. And you, of course, are going to need wine."

I smiled, crossed my arms, and leaned against the scaffolding. "I am?" I asked coyly.

"Come now," she replied, making my coyness look shallow and amateurish. "Of course you are. What good theater doesn't have a concession stand? And what great concession stand in this part of town doesn't have beer and wine? It's a must."

I hadn't really considered that, and said so. I wasn't even sure we were going to *be* a theater after the run of *Duck Soup* finished. "I don't know. I haven't even considered applying for a liquor license."

"You'll get a special event license to start. Once you've been running a show for a couple of weeks, we can apply for a license to serve. We'll have to go in front of the neighborhood planning commission, and it'll be a battle, but ultimately we will win."

"We?"

She smiled and shrugged. "I'm connected, Donovan. I can help you to navigate Atlanta's arcane liquor licensing process."

"And why, pray tell, would you want to do that?" I have no idea where the *pray tell* came from. I never talk like that.

She took a step forward. "I would do that in exchange for being your exclusive wine distributor. You buy from me exclusively for three years."

There was something cunning in her sales approach. She was not a southern belle, not by a long shot. She was a different breed of southern woman: one who could dispense with the feminine wiles when she needed to hold her own with the boys. She had the forthright demeanor of New York women, but without the hard edges. I couldn't help but like her.

We talked for perhaps fifteen minutes, and she gave me her wine catalog so I could think about it, and then left just as she was about to get ticketed. I returned to painting.

By five o'clock that evening, I had a fresh coat of paint on all the walls, and everything trimmed out except the balcony and the boxes. I was sore, tired, sweaty, and very, very dirty. I also had an appointment, so as soon as I had cleaned the rollers and brushes, I ran across the street to shower and dress.

At six o'clock the actors were coming.

Miranda had planned to bring the entire troupe to the theater that evening to see where they would be playing. She wanted them to get comfortable with me and with the theater. She had never once mentioned that it was an entirely lesbian cast.

I had donned a pair of white cotton pants, a camp shirt, and a pair of flip flops for the first cast meeting, which was a bold move in a theater covered in wet paint. For all the notice I received from the cast, I could have been wearing nothing but pants made out of toast. As I came across the street, there were twelve women milling around in front of the theater, several of whom were arguing with Miranda.

Jean Kerr once wrote that a "young person who wants to be an actor has an addiction only slightly less dangerous than heroin." Having lived in Manhattan, written for a lifestyle magazine, and been married to an agent, I was accustomed to actors. Indeed, they formed a major part of the backdrop of my life. Professional actors, especially on Broadway, I have learned, are a different lot from actors who have decided to "make it" in community theater. In New York, they are "very serious" about their craft. You know they are "very serious" because they tell you it frequently in tones that manage to convey the quotation marks.

Community theater actors, especially in a town with a thriving arts scene like Atlanta, are no less serious. In fact, I have witnessed many performers that would have had bright careers if Liv had managed to get her hands on them. But they are less uptight about it. Their interests and personalities are broader because they aren't trying to market themselves as a type. They get parts or not based on the type they already are. There is some argument that they are what theater should truly be.

As I came across the street, a smile lit up Miranda's face and she immediately lost interest in the woman who had been arguing with her. She held out her hands wide and announced in a loud, dramatic voice, "Ladies, our savior approaches."

All of the women turned and looked at me. Even the ones who had been angry the moment before beamed at me, and a spontaneous round of applause broke out. I paused in the middle of the street, took a dramatic bow, and then hurried across to avoid being run over by an approaching MARTA bus.

I was introduced to the whole gaggle of them. (I'm not sure if gaggle is the right collective noun. I know *flock* and *bevy* aren't right. Chris has always made it very clear the queens travel in a *cadre*, and a large number of fag hags travel in a *hagella*, but he's never filled me in on lesbians. I must remember to ask him. But, I digress.)

Anyway, I was introduced to the cast. Cara would be playing Groucho's part, Rufus T. Firefly. Sara would be playing Chico's part, Chicolini. Tara would assume the role of Pinky, originally played by Harpo. And, of course, Lara would be playing Zeppo as Lieutenant Bob Roland.

"You're kidding," I said, laughing. "Groucho, Harpo, Chico and Zeppo are being played by Cara, Sara, Tara, and Lara?"

C/S/T/Lara failed to see the humor in that.

I was also introduced to the other seven leads, whose names were not nearly as interesting. They all greeted me in various degrees of warmth, or lack thereof. The chilliest probably came from Kelly, who would be playing Mrs. Gloria Teasdale, the part originated in the movie by Margaret Dumont.

I opened the doors and led them into the theater, explaining as we went what changes would be made before the show. In no time at all,

Miranda had the cast marshaled on the stage, and they lost whatever interest they may have had in me. They disappeared through the side door down into the basement, and I was left alone.

I wasn't exactly sure what I should be doing at this point. I couldn't very well paint in the clothes I was wearing currently, and besides, everything needed to dry. I wouldn't be seeing Chris or Rachel this evening. He was off flying until Wednesday night, and she had to close the store that evening. I glanced at the stage. Certainly there was more work to do up there. Although we had removed most of the garbage, we still needed to get the marquee moved out of the way so that the troupe could begin building the sets.

At something of a loss, I returned to the lobby, climbed the stairs, and went to the front office. Cleaning these rooms had been my lowest priority. So apart from throwing away petrified food products and wildlife, there was still a lot of crap about. I sat at the desk I had claimed as mine, lit a cigarette, and looked around. I knew, soon enough, that I would no longer be allowed to smoke in the building in order to comply with fire codes and Georgia workplace laws, so I savored the drag on the cigarette. Idly, I pulled open the lower left file drawer.

The file folders inside predated manila. They were a dark brown, almost like a glossy kraft paper. I pulled out a couple to determine if there was anything worth keeping.

Each folder was a file on a different film. Pretty quickly, I was able to determine that the folder in the front of the drawer was the last film shown in the theater, an artsy little porno titled *Whores of Babylon*. In each folder was the receipt logging the film in from the distributor, a copy of the shipping receipt for its return, and tally sheets documenting the audience and revenue for each showing during the film's run. The meager take of *Whores* made it pretty clear why the theater had closed.

I pulled the file at the very back of the drawer. It was still a porno, so I put it back. I stood up, my cigarette dangling from my lips, walked over to the file cabinet, and pulled open the top drawer. The foremost file was for a showing of *Pillow Talk* in 1959. I pulled it out. The file told a tale of a happier time. Higher box office takes, longer runs. As I flipped through the folder, a photo fell out. It was a picture of the marquee, advertising Rock Hudson and Doris Day's film. There, beneath, Laine stood talking to Uncle Maurice.

I carried the file back to the desk and crushed out my cigarette in an old green glass ashtray. As I studied the receipts in the file, something about the handwriting stuck me as familiar. At the very bottom of one I realized why. There, acknowledging the receipt of the film from the distributor, was the stylish signature of the theater's manager, Isadore Kersey.

"So that's who's leaving me pictures," I said aloud. Laine must have known that. I quickly dug through the other files, finding many other pictures of Laine beneath that marquee.

At that moment, I heard Miranda call me from the auditorium. I stuck the picture into the *Pillow Talk* folder, and resolved to discuss it with my aunt the next morning.

The cast wasn't really rehearsing. They were more negotiating how they were going to rehearse. I was invited into the negotiations, which were often extremely intense, to work out logistics. We didn't finish the discussions until after ten, at which time I escorted all of them upstairs and sent them on their way. Once they were outside, I ran back up to the office, grabbed the file folder and switched out the light. Glancing out the window, I saw the kid who I suspected was the Phantom. He was across the street, sitting on a park bench in front of the Italian restaurant next to the apartment building, reading.

I decided to test my theory. I nonchalantly descended the stairs, extinguishing lights as I went, and emerged from the front doors. Once I had made a great show of locking the door, I crossed the street, flipping through the contents of the folder, making sure not to look directly at the kid. I let myself in the front door, laid the folder on the table next to the mailboxes and then made a mad dash downstairs to the garage. I let myself out the back door, and then snuck up through the unlit side yard, glancing around the corner of the building.

The kid had put his book back into his backpack and was zipping it shut. He glanced around. There were not many people on the street, and the ones that were, were not paying attention to the theater. He nonchalantly crossed the street, and then purposefully strode around the corner into the alley.

I kicked off my flip flops so they wouldn't make any noise and then dashed across the street after him. I actually crossed to the other side of the alley and squatted down in front of a mailbox. He had not heard me, and was walking past the stage door to the bulkhead doors that led into the basement. I watched, perplexed, since I knew the doors were padlocked from the inside.

He reached the doors and glanced around. Seeing no one, he bent down to one side of the door and lifted. The door on the left was off its hinges, and he folded it back over the other. I could see the padlock I had trusted dangling beneath.

I shook my head, disgusted. I was so confident in the padlock, it had never occurred to me to check the hinges. The kid walked down the steps and lowered the door back into place. It came down on its rusted frame with the same muffled clang I had heard each of the previous evenings.

I stood up and considered what I should do. I could follow him, but the fact that he was young didn't mean he wasn't dangerous; quite possibly the opposite. I considered calling the police, but then thought better of it. If he was homeless and about to lose his home, he had more than enough problems, and calling the police would only make it worse.

Ultimately, I shrugged, and went back to the building. I decided that patience was probably the most appropriate course of action. I walked back across the street, retrieved my shoes, and then let myself back in the front door. I came to the table in the lobby and stopped short.

The folder was gone.

The next morning at breakfast, I pressed Aunt Laine on this. She admitted, grudgingly, that yes, she had suspected Mr. Kersey was who had left me the two envelopes.

"Do you know him?" I asked.

She grimaced impatiently. "Of course I *know* him, Donovan. He lives in my building, after all. I just haven't seen much of him in the last several years."

"But you do see him," I pressed.

"I do," she replied flatly. "He comes and goes. He's getting old but he's not dead."

"So why the Boo Radley act?" I asked.

She rolled her eyes upward a little, and nodded knowingly at my comparison.

"Well, I guess, like Boo Radley, Isadore Kersey is a troubled and melancholy man. He was a man who lived his life largely though movies. He was more content to watch than participate. When the theater closed, he really didn't have much else. No family. No other interests. Just a tiny pension and a tiny apartment here, across the street."

She took a sip of her coffee. "Life, unfortunately, just kind of closed in around him."

I contemplated Mister Kersey's lot. Deep in my mind I suspected a truth, but didn't know if I should voice it. *What the hell*, I decided.

She was spreading cream cheese on her bagel. I rested my chin on one hand and asked, "He was in love with you, wasn't he?"

She paused for a moment, but did not look up. Although she maintained careful control over her expression, I could tell she was contemplating her answer. Finally, still without looking up, she resumed her knife-work and replied, "Yes, I suspect so."

I contemplated whether to ask the next question, but she saved me the decision. "I was *not* in love with him. Oh, he's a kind man, a good man. And in his own way might have been attractive, even. But he couldn't compare to Maurice. No one could, really."

That morning, after doing the dishes and getting cleaned up, I took Laine on an excursion. We motored off in the Rolls for the automotive shop in East Atlanta where the car would be converted to run off of vegetable-based fuel.

I had previously spoken with the shop's owner a good bit about the cost, the availability of the fuel, and other such practical matters. Laine had called him separately and discussed the environmental ramifications, the socially conscious decisions one made every day in the products they used, and the relative impact of corn futures on fuel prices. The decision was made to convert the Corniche.

When you drive a Rolls, you become aware of—and ultimately somewhat revel in—the pointing and stares from other cars. That was on a normal occasion. On this particular occasion, Laine had decided to put on her fur coat, despite the temperature in the high seventies, and a large pair of sunglasses that even Yoko Ono would have passed on as oversized. She rounded out the ensemble with a Dior scarf wrapped into a turban and fastened with a rhinestone pin. To complete the effect, she elected to ride in the back seat with a martini as we drove south at a majestic fifteen miles per hour. We created a sensation all the way down North Highland.

If we thought the stares and gawking we received on the road was impressive, it was nothing compared to the reaction as we pulled into the garage. East Atlanta, although largely the same vintage as Virginia Highland, was about fifteen years behind in terms of gentrification. The action in the garage came to complete halt. While they might have been accustomed to working on luxury cars, they weren't accustomed to a Rolls-Royce with Norma Desmond in the back seat.

We met up with Phil, the owner. I signed the work order and handed over the keys while Laine enthused over the how environmentally responsible she felt.

"Environmental activists seldom wear mink," I observed, dialing Checker Cab from my cell phone.

I heard a chuckle behind me. A large African American mechanic whose shirt identified him as George smirked and laughed as he leaned under the hood of a Jetta. Laine, recognizing she had an audience, immediately turned on the charm and somehow seemed to increase in volume.

"Minks are weasels," she observed. "They are a totally replenishable resource. It's not like I'm wearing California condor."

George laughed again and said something I missed because the cab dispatcher answered. I gave her the address and was assured that a cab would be there in five minutes.

Forty minutes and two calls back, there was still no cab. Laine, meanwhile had George in near hysterics over her views on environmental extremism, Republican sexual peccadilloes, Atlanta's archaic sewer system, and how racial politics influences watershed management policies.

I shut off my phone in disgust. "You don't happen to know another cab company's phone number, do you?"

George shook his head. "Sorry, no. Where are you folks headed?"

"The Highlands."

"Tell you what. I'm about to go on break. I can give y'all a lift home in the truck."

I snickered at the image of my mink-attired aunt riding home in a tow truck. Before I could say anything, however, she told him, "Why, thank you, George. That's very generous of you. We accept."

George excused himself and disappeared into the building to get the keys to the truck. I glanced at my aunt, incredulously. "We do?" I whispered.

"It was a gracious offer. In the South you're never too good to refuse someone's hospitality. It invites bad karma. Besides, my drink is empty and the sooner we get home the sooner I can have another."

George pulled the truck around, and Laine stepped up into the cab with all the aplomb of Queen Victoria.

I had a fair amount of work to do around the building that day before I could go work on the theater. I actually was feeling a little stressed about that. Both buildings required a lot of maintenance. There were things at the 'Hurst that I needed to knock out, including painting all of the hallways and sealing the parking lot. I had mentioned the stress to Laine, and she suggested that maybe we should hire a handyman. I was not certain I was willing to share my turf, however, especially knowing that I was facing an impending job loss at the magazine.

I finished up my 'Hurst "to do" list around five, with just enough time to trot across the street and let the troupe in. I didn't bother getting cleaned up since Charles and I had to remove each seat from the theater floor so the carpet installers could come the next day. When I arrived, most of them were there, along with Charles, who stood on the outskirts, largely ignored by the troupe, looking both bemused and horrified at the same time. For the record, "bemused horror" is a facial expression I have only seen the British master.

I made all the polite introductions, and then led the ladies downstairs to begin rehearsals. Once down there, I glanced into the alcove the Phantom had been occupying. It was empty. I sighed, satisfied, and silently wished the kid well, wherever he had landed in the world. I made a mental note to fix the hinges on the bulkhead.

Charles and I began removing seats, identifying where they needed to be reinstalled, and then stacking them on the stage. Clare arrived shortly after, carrying a floor lamp that was missing its shade.

"What's that for?" I asked as she lugged it past me, up the aisle to the stage.

"Old theater superstition. If a theater is ever left completely dark, a ghost will take up residence. The fact that you don't have a light on the stage has been bugging me, so I brought one." She plugged it in to a socket next to the stage. The bare bulb cast a harsh glare over the stage. "It's called a ghost light."

I glanced at the light. "What other superstitions should I be aware of?"

She sat down at her sewing machine and began sewing. "Well, let's see. It's unlucky to open an umbrella in a theater. It's unlucky to whistle in the theater, or wear squeaky shoes, or use a Bible on stage."

Even though we had the doors open, and the windows upstairs, the theater was still stifling. As Charles pulled off his shirt and used it to wipe the sweat running down his face, he added, "Don't forget the Scottish Play."

She pointed at Charles and winked. "Ah yes, the Scottish Play. Never say its real name."

I turned that one over in my mind. "You mean Mac…" I was unable to finish the sentence as I was struck in the face by Charles's sweat-soaked tee-shirt.

"We just told you not to say it," he exclaimed.

Discretion being the better part of valor, I elected not to say it. "Well, we'll see if your light works. I sent a phantom packing today. Perhaps the light will keep him away."

As if on cue, a tightly clipped Battery accent said aloud, "And what Phantom would that be, dear?"

I turned to see Aunt Laine come through the double doors, pushing her walker ahead of her and accompanied by Mac. "What are you doing here?"

"I wanted to see how the paint job looked." She smiled mischievously. "And, I own the theater, dear. Besides, my physical therapist has been telling me I needed to exercise more."

"Well," I said, waving my hand broadly. "What do you think?"

She turned slowly, taking in the auditorium. I stared at the back of her turbaned head as she rotated. As she came back around, she was smiling broadly. "Honestly, Van, you are on the right track. It hasn't looked this good in fifty years."

"Well, thanks. It has sort of become a community effort."

She nodded at Charles, Mac, and Clare. "So it has."

She clapped her hands together. "Now! Enough small talk. Take me to meet our lesbian thespians."

Needless to say, a rich, opinionated octogenarian who travels with a flask of manhattans was a hit with the troupe. It was well after midnight before I got her home.

I climbed the stairs to my apartment, and got into the shower. While I was in there, the lights in the bathroom, flickered incessantly. Thinking it was the fixture, I made a mental note to check it in the morning.

It was not, however, the fixture. It was, apparently, the Feldmans. Something had them worked up that night. No sooner had I climbed into bed than the toilet flushed. It did so every ten minutes, reawakening me just as I was about to drift off. After about an hour of that, the ceiling fan began to creak, and then one of the French doors blew open.

Having had enough, I got out of bed, stomped down the steps, slammed the door and said aloud, "Hey! Feldmans! Knock it off!"

The fan creaked once, and stopped. An odd silence fell over the apartment. I considered whether or not to apologize but thought better of it. They didn't sleep, what with being dead and all, but I did. I snarled slightly and went back to bed.

Just as I started to drift off to sleep again, the toilet flushed.

The next day, we received carpet, and work began on replacing the air-conditioning. I had hoped that they would just be able to repair it, but a menagerie of wildlife had nested in it over the last fifteen years, and it was unsalvageable.

I was amazed at what a difference the carpet made in making the place *feel* complete, even though it was far from ready. That evening, Charles, Clare, and Mac all rejoined me. We were also joined by a the troupe's technical director, a jovial if rather butch woman whose name I didn't catch, who spent much of the evening climbing around the catwalks above the stage trying to figure out how she was going to light it.

Mac had identified and labeled about half of the wiring that ran through the theater. Much of the rest of it seemed to disappear someplace under the stage, and he was having a hell of a time figuring out where it went.

Clare had one panel of the stage curtains nearly finished and sewed like a mad-woman. Charles and I began reinstalling the seats.

Charles seemed to have something on his mind, and was a little absent. It was taking much longer to reinstall the seat banks than it had to remove them and we only finished about a third of the auditorium that evening. Around ten, we had bid farewell to Clare. I was tightening down the bolts when he sat in the row behind, put his hands on his knees and a stared at me pensively. A little unsettled, I asked him, "Um, something on your mind?"

"You could say that," he said a little morosely. "I need to ask you a favor."

I glanced up, eyebrow raised, indicating that he should continue.

He cleared his throat with a proper little *ahem*, and then continued. "Well, right. Here's the thing, what with Brit's and my wedding coming up, it would appear....the thing is...well..."

I stopped tightening the bolt, leaned my arm on the nearest seat and stared at him. He returned the stare with a bit of a pained expression and then blurted out, "Donovan, would you be my best man?"

That surprised me, and my face must have shown it, because he began to quickly explain. "The thing is, I don't really know that I have anyone I would describe as a *best friend*, per se, and my brother lives in Thailand and we're not even sure he's going to be able to even come to the wedding, so..."

I held up a hand. "Charles. I'd be honored. Thank you very much for asking."

Charles smiled broadly. "Right. Well, yes. Thank you as well."

Before leaving, I went downstairs to check on the alcove. The Phantom's stuff was still missing. I nodded approvingly and went home.

I was tired and a little cranky the next morning as I was making breakfast. Mostly, it was due to stress over how much I had to do that day, exacerbated by the fact that the Feldmans had made the building creak all night. They had also rolled a chair across the living room. Although I was still sure there was a rational explanation for everything happening – like the fact the building was nearly a hundred years old – I had to admit that it was becoming easier to blame the Feldmans than to try to explain all of it away.

Laine eased herself into the room with her walker, now almost totally free of her wheelchair. "Good morning darling," she told me brightly, delivering a dry little peck to my cheek as she crept through the kitchen. "Today's an exciting day!"

"Morning," I replied quietly. The tone wasn't lost on her.

"Rough night?" she asked as she made for the table in the dining room.

"Feldmans," I replied.

"Ah," she replied. "I know a lesbian shaman. We should probably have her come release their spirits one day." Since she couldn't see my face, I felt free to roll my eyes. "Regardless, perk up. We get the Rolls back today! Won't it be exciting to be so socially conscious, yet still stylish."

I smiled, despite myself. *Socially conscious, yet still stylish* could be the brand statement for the Highlands. I sat the coffee down in front of her and said, "I'll get Chris to take me over there after lunch to get it."

She took a sip of her coffee, and opened the paper. I returned to the kitchen, collected the oatmeal and bagels and carried them into the dining room. She looked up brightly, "Returning to the Feldmans, I meant to ask you a question. The other evening when I visited the theater, you made reference to a phantom. What were you talking about?"

"Oh, yeah," I said as I sat down. "It appears we had a young, homeless kid living in the basement."

She paused with a spoon of oatmeal halfway to her mouth and stared at me intensely. "Are you sure?"

"Quite sure." I recounted for her how we had found the Phantom's stuff in the basement, how I had seen him climb through the basement bulkhead, and how he appeared to now be relocating elsewhere.

"So that's what you meant by 'sent him packing?'" she asked, coldly. Her tone caught me off guard.

"Well, yes…"

She threw her spoon down into her bowl and stood up. Her eyes blazed at me. "Without so much as a thought of how we might help him?"

I started to stammer something, but didn't really have an answer. She wouldn't have let me get one out anyhow.

"Honestly, Donovan. How could you? The homeless situation in this city is bad enough without you adding to it. And especially a kid."

"What was I supposed to do, Laine? Move him in here?"

She rolled her eyes, exasperated and pulled her walker towards her. "There are any number of things you could have done, Van. Maybe get him info on a shelter. Maybe get him into a rehab program. Maybe help him find a job. At very least you should have talked to him, instead of just leaving a note telling him to be on his way." She started towards the door.

"Where are you going?"

"*We* are going to see if it isn't too late. Let's go."

Obediently, I put down my spoon and followed her out the door. As we crossed the street, she continued her diatribe about what a thoughtless, uncaring, unchristian cad I had been. As I started towards the front door, she hissed at me, "Not that way. You always come and go by the front door. He can probably hear you coming and be gone well ahead of you."

I followed her around the back to the bulkhead. "We won't have any light," I protested.

"I'll wait here at the top of the steps. You go find a light. If he comes up, I'll talk to him. If you get him first, for God's sake, be nice to him. He won't let us help him if you treat him like street trash."

Against my better judgment, I opened up the bulkhead doors and let myself down the steps. I crossed quickly to the other side of the rehearsal hall and switched on the light. No one was there. I looked into the small alcove where the Phantom's stuff had been. It was empty.

I slowly came back towards the bulkhead. My aunt stared down at me expectantly. I shook my head and said. "He's gone."

Her face fell. "Is any of his stuff still here?"

"No ma'am."

She closed her eyes, and turned away from the door. I followed her as she went back across the street. I still didn't exactly understand, but I tried to mumble an apology. Once she had reached the far side of Virginia, she turned and said to me sadly, "Van, you don't understand. This is not New York. I realize in New York you step over and around homeless all day long. But they aren't objects. The homeless are people with stories. They got there *somehow*. The circumstances of their life got ahead of them in some way.

"Look, I'm not saying that you have to move all of them into your guestroom. I am saying, however, that down here we at least ask if we can help. This kid, whoever he is, has some natural sense of dignity that needs to be respected. Instead, you became just another part of his life that doesn't work." She turned sadly and walked back into the building.

I stood there for a moment, lost in the difference. Laine was right in one respect. The homeless were objects to me. I had never thought to ask if I could help. There were services out there for them. I always assumed that people were homeless because they chose to be, or because they couldn't function within the guidelines of those services. I gave money to charities. I had always thought that I had been doing my part. It never occurred to me to ask if I could help *directly*.

I spent the morning fixing the stairway banister between the second and third floors. (Chris had brought home a rather drunken date one evening who had fallen against it with some force and loosened it.) As the morning progressed, I proceeded to feel more and more like shit.

Around noon, I checked on Laine, who didn't particularly want to see me. She accepted lunch grudgingly, so I returned upstairs to wake Chris. He answered the door wearing a white fleece robe that was *way* too gay while trying to light a cigarette.

"You look weird," he observed as he let me in.

"I am weird," I replied. "Are you ready to drive me down to get the car?"

He yawned. "I just need to get cleaned up first. Did you bring me coffee?"

"I'm not your valet," I snarled, and immediately regretted it. His wide-eyed sardonic look told me he hadn't missed it. "I'm sorry. I don't mean to be rude. I'm feeling like an asshole."

"And acting like it," he said curtly as he went into the bathroom. I went into his kitchen and made him a cup of coffee. This being Chris, it couldn't be as easy as dumping Folgers into a coffee maker. By the time I had measured and ground the fresh, lightly-roasted Peruvian beans, brought the water to boil and poured them into his Belgian coffee press, almost fifteen minutes had passed. I poured a cup, added some half-and-half and two tablespoons of raw sugar and carried it to the bathroom door.

I heard the shower inside, so I knocked, cracked the door and asked, "Want coffee?"

"Please," he said. I walked into the bathroom. It was thick with steam and the aroma of five or six different, expensive botanicals. His hand extended out from behind the Pierre Cardin shower curtain. I placed the coffee in it and the hand disappeared back into the shower. As I was turning to go, he asked from within, "So what's eating you, anyhow?"

I leaned against the bathroom door. "Remember that homeless kid that's been living in the basement? Well, I caught hell from Aunt Laine for sending him on his way."

There was a long silence on the other side of the curtain, before he asked, "So is the fact that she gave you hell what's eating you?"

"No, not so much. I'm used to her giving me hell. She just made me *feel* like hell, because I didn't do anything to help the kid first."

"Why does that make you feel like hell?"

"I don't know. I guess it's because that would never have occurred to me. In New York, the homeless aren't real people. By that, I mean, they aren't real to you. Sure, something happened in their life to get them there, but that's not my responsibility."

He switched the shower off and his hand stuck out from behind the curtain. "Towel?"

I pulled one of his Kate Spade bath towels off its bar and handed it to him. "I guess why I feel like shit is that it never occurred to me to *want* to know this kid's story, and now I feel like less of a person."

The curtain pulled back as he wrapped a towel around his absurdly narrow waist. "You don't think you are maybe being a little hard on yourself?"

I shrugged.

He stepped out of the shower and began to apply multiple American Crew products to his hair. "Look, here's the most likely scenario. The homeless kid is probably gay."

"How do you know that? You think everyone is gay."

"I only think attractive people are gay," he corrected. "Statistically, however, over half of homeless kids identify as gay or lesbian. There's a homeless shelter in town for gay and lesbian youth run by CHRIS Kids that is pretty good about making those kind of stats public.

"So anyway, here's the deal. He's probably gay. He was probably thrown out by parents when they found out he was gay. With no money and no opportunities, he's been turning tricks on Ponce during the evenings, and sleeping it off in your basement during the day." He finished hand sculpting his hair and applied a roll-on. "Meanwhile, he keeps himself going with a dream of being an actor or a singer or a model, all of which are continually reinforced by the bastards who cruise hustlers and will tell them anything because they are slime." He returned the deodorant to the medicine chest and shut the door. "In truth, while I respect your aunt immensely, he is probably trapped by his own circumstances and you offering help would have not done a lot to spring him from the trap."

He slipped past me, heading towards the bedroom. "Let me get dressed and we'll go."

Thirty minutes later, Chris had deposited me at the garage, and I had secured the Rolls, freshly fueled on an ethanol-vegetable oil mixture, and was cruising back home. The car didn't run appreciably differently; in fact, it might have run slightly better. And, despite the best efforts of my imagination, I couldn't actually smell french fries.

I picked up Laine and took her for a ride. She seemed in much better humor and my indiscretion with the homeless community hopefully forgotten. She approved of the car, and announced her plan to begin driving it again as soon as she could walk. I deposited her back on the front steps and returned the car, now dubbed by Laine as the VeggieRoll, to its garage.

I somewhat forgot my depression, although I couldn't say my good mood had recovered in any way. After I had fed Laine dinner, I made my way across the street to the theater. One of the local street musicians who periodically sets up shop in the Highlands was playing saxophone on the median. As I crossed the street, I recognized the melody, but couldn't think of the song. It didn't hit me until I was unlocking the front door.

It was "Anatevka," the song the suddenly homeless Jews sing near the end of *Fiddler on the Roof.* I immediately felt like shit again.

The evening proceeded pretty much as usual. Charles and I finished installing the seats while Chris and Clare straddled ladders hanging the new curtains. In the basement, the troupe rehearsed *Duck Soup.* Their technical director, whose name was something like Lois Common-Denominator had joined our little troupe, and she joined Mac to scour the building trying to find where cables disappeared and reappeared.

Late that evening, Mac came upstairs and motioned for me to join him. I followed to the front of the stage as he explained, "Y'know how we've been trying to find where all those cables run?"

"Yeah."

"Well, there is an old well or pit right here," he stomped his foot on the floor in front of the stage and I heard the hollow echo below. I immediately remembered seeing the plans that Mister Kersey had left me.

"There is!" I said excitedly. "It's the old organ pit."

Mac nodded. "That makes sense. Anyway, there is a metal panel where you can access it down in the basement. It was hard to find because we thought it was one of the electrical panels. Anyway, when we looked inside we found where all those cables originate."

"Great. So you can get the sound system hooked up?"

He nodded. "We can. However, it looks like your Phantom just relocated his stuff into there."

My heart flipped, and I had an odd sense of apprehension in my stomach. "Show me."

He led me downstairs and showed me the panel that I had also assumed was one of the fuse boxes. Inside, however, was a shallow, semi-circular room, perhaps only four feet tall. The milk crates, books and clothes had all been moved in here, and the sleeping bag lay spread out in the center. A single lamp and a clock radio were plugged into a scary-looking electrical outlet at the side of the door. Dozens of cables were bundled up to one side.

"We're going to have to move all this stuff so we can get those cables reconnected," Mac said. "What do you want us to do with it?"

"Do me a favor," I asked. "Let it alone for tonight. I'll have a better idea in the morning."

Mac nodded and went off to make plans for the next day with Lois. I climbed inside the organ pit and looked around. Idly, I pulled out one of the notebooks. It was a school notebook. After a few minutes of study, I recognized the subject as Psychology 101. Opening to the front cover, there was a name inside: *Zachary Wells Covington.* There was also a phone number. I tore a blank sheet out of the back, wrote both down, and then gently returned the notebook to its milk crate shelf.

As I emerged from the panel, the cast was busy arguing loudly over the appropriate key for the lead to sing the Freedonia Hymn. None of them noticed me as a I slipped past and went back up the stairs. In the comparative silence of the stairs, I thought back to what Chris had said that morning. It was hard to reconcile a Psych 101 notebook with a teenage prostitute. Maybe I had an opportunity to redeem myself with Laine after all.

That night, I loudly said my goodbyes to the troupe, and escorted all of my friends back across the street. Then, I immediately ran upstairs and took my perch on the balcony of my apartment to watch. Around one, the Phantom (who I was beginning to think of as Zachary) came strolling up the street. He was wearing a black golf shirt and jeans, with a backpack slung over his shoulder. He had a black apron folded over his arm. On any given evening at around that time, you could see hundreds of waiters, bartenders, cooks, and barbacks walking home from the dozens of restaurants in the neighborhood in exactly the same way. They made up the flip-side of the Virginia Highland citizenry. Seventy-five percent of the neighborhood was made up of artists and intellectuals who lived there because you could walk to everything. The other twenty-five percent were the people who provided everything.

Zachary walked purposefully across the street and leaned against the boarded-up ticket office. He glanced at his watch like he was waiting for someone, but I could tell he was actually studying the inside of the theater for light. He subtly pulled on the door to see if it was locked, and then sauntered away. Once he was past the coffee house, he looked around again to see if anyone was watching. Seeing no one, he disappeared around the corner. A moment later, I heard the telling, metallic clang.

Okay, so I knew he was home. I also knew I had one more chance to do right by him.

I had no idea how to do it, and more than a fair amount of uncertainty whether I should even risk it.

I quietly descended back to the street. I didn't want to make too much noise since I didn't want either Rachel or Chris to hear me. As I was coming out the door, I collided with Jennifer, who was coming home from her bartending shift.

"Hey doll," she greeted me as she came in the front door.

"Hey. How was your evening?"

"Oh, we had a busload of Japanese tourists in that just wouldn't leave. They came in at six and by ten I was tempted to put on a Godzilla mask and stomp through the restaurant to get them out. Where are you off to at this hour?"

"Just back across the street for a minute."

"Don't you spend enough time in that theater?"

I had to think fast. "I left something unlocked." Technically, not a lie.

"Ah, well, God love ya. Don't get distracted. I know you, you'll go over to lock up, and start digging an orchestra pit."

I laughed and bid her good night. She started up the stairs and I slipped out the front door.

I made my way across the street. I wasn't sure the best way to approach him, or what I was going to say, or even what I was going to do. I also was more than a little scared. He was surviving on the streets, something I knew I couldn't do. He was a lot tougher than me. Hell, he might have a gun. This was probably the dumbest thing I could do.

I figured I would walk downstairs, knock on his metal panel, and invite him out to talk. I would position myself on the steps that ran out the bulkhead to prevent him from escaping. Of course, there was nothing that would prevent him from running up the stairs into the theater.

I reached the front door. As I stuck my hand into my pocket for my keys, movement caught my eye. It was a triangle of light, receding across the carpet. I recognized it as light being thrown from the men's room as the door closed. I silently opened the door and eased inside, closing and locking it behind me. I could hear water running.

I switched on the lights in the lobby and sat down on the staircase to wait. He spent perhaps fifteen minutes, during which I could hear him go through a nightly ritual that sounded very much like my own. When the door opened, he walked out, wearing only a pair of boxers, zipping closed a shaving kit.

He was only a half step out of the restroom when it dawned on him that the lights were on. He looked up at me, wide-eyed with fright. I tried to give him an open, non-threatening look. I knew I couldn't look happy to see him. I didn't want him to think I was a lunatic. But, I didn't want him to run, either.

The look of fright gave way to one of recognition. He closed his eyes and tossed his head upward over his left shoulder in disgust. After a moment, he opened his eyes, looked at me, and said, "Crap."

I laughed despite myself. "Hi Zachary. I'm Donovan."

He took a deep breath. He was clearly expecting something from me other than a laugh and a warm greeting. Since that was all being proffered, he didn't appear to know what to do.

"You probably shouldn't walk around the theater barefoot. There's a lot of loose nails and sharp stuff that I haven't had the opportunity to clean up."

He still looked terribly unsure of himself. The door had swung shut behind him, and the noise of it settling into its frame seemed to make him look around. He really didn't have many options. Out the front door would put him on the street in his underwear. He couldn't get back to the basement without passing directly in front of me. His only other option for flight was to retreat back into the bathroom and hope I would go away.

Seeing no option for flight, he leaned against the door frame, looking uncomfortable and said, "Okay, you caught me."

I shrugged, indicating, I hoped, that I wasn't really trying to. Even though I was.

He wasn't a bad-looking kid. He had long, dark brown hair that fell forward across his forehead and low over his right eye. His eyes were blue, and a little sleepy looking. He had a long straight nose, and small, triangular mouth with full lips. Despite being homeless, he wasn't emaciated. Rather, his chest showed a lean muscular frame that suggested he got a fair amount of exercise.

"I'm sorry I didn't move out when you told me to."

I nodded. "I'm sorry I asked you to."

That was clearly not the answer he expected, and shook his head disbelievingly. "When I realized you were living here, I should have probably made sure you had someplace to go. I didn't. I'm sorry I was so thoughtless."

I watched as the apology slowly registered, and hoped he couldn't hear my heart pounding. "Um, don't call the cops. If you let me go get my stuff, I'll get out of here now." He took a tentative step towards the auditorium doors. When I didn't say anything he took another.

And then I heard something come out of my mouth that even I couldn't believe I was saying. "Maybe you don't have to."

He stopped and looked at me. "Look, I'm not sure what you want, but I don't put out."

I laughed. He *was* a tough kid. "Not interested in you putting out." I took a deep breath, still not knowing exactly what I was doing. "Tell me your story."

"My story?" he said, unsure of himself.

I nodded. He looked extremely uncomfortable standing there, nearly naked, holding his shaving kit. I decided to throw him a line. "Look, I really need a cigarette, so I'll tell you what. I'm going up to my office. You can go downstairs, get dressed and run and I'll put all your stuff out on the street. Or, you can come up to my office and tell me your story, and maybe we can find some other solution for you." I stood up. "If you haven't come up by the time I've finished my cigarette, I'll assume you decided to run and tomorrow I'll throw your stuff out."

I walked up the stairs. At the landing, I glanced back, and he was watching me, uncertainty still painted on his face. I ascended the second flight.

In my office, I took more time lighting and smoking that cigarette than at any other time in my life. I was extraordinarily uncertain of myself. Hell, I was playing a game that could very easily make me a victim.

I had nursed the cigarette down to the point that there was no tobacco left, and I was going to have to smoke the filter when he peered around the frame of my door. Although he was still barefoot, he had pulled on a pair of jeans and an oversized knit sweater which had gone out of style about five years earlier.

"Um, hi."

I stubbed out the cigarette in an ashtray I kept outside my office window in the mistaken belief I was hiding the fact that I was smoking in the theater. "Hi." I indicated the battered green leather couch that sat opposite my desk. Reluctantly, he came in and sat down.

"You prefer Zachary or Zach?"

"Zach is fine," he replied quietly.

I nodded. "I generally go by Van, but you can call me that or Donovan. Just no *Don.*"

He nodded.

I stretched back in my chair. "Okay. So, what's your story?"

He scrunched up his face. "What do you mean by that?"

"You weren't born living in my basement," I replied. "You came to be living here somehow."

He grimaced, then stared at his feet, uncomfortably. "What do you want to know?"

I shrugged. "I dunno. Let's start with how long have you been here?"

"Two years. Almost two years."

"How did you find your way in? I mean, I know you've been coming and going from the basement doors, but how did you discover the theater at all."

He looked up, and almost smiled. "Luck, mostly. It was raining. I didn't have anyplace to go and I was standing under the fire stairs waiting for the storm to blow over, but it was taking a long time. A truck drove over the metal doors and I saw one pop up. I figured it was better to get under there and wait it out. I had a flashlight in my backpack, so I had a look around. When I realized the place was abandoned, I figured I'd stay there for a while, until I could find some other place. It just kept working out for me."

"How old are you?"

"Twenty...one."

The long pause made me suspicious, so I asked, "Really?"

"Yeah," he replied, looking away. Then looking back he said, "Well, almost. But that's how old they think I am at the restaurant where I work. Can't work in a restaurant with a liquor license unless you're twenty-one."

There was a long, uncomfortable silence, so I decided to opt for the money question. "How'd you find yourself homeless in the first place?"

He stared at me for a long moment. His face was a mixture of emotions. He had no reason to trust me, and all of his experience obviously told him not to. However, there was also an almost childlike need to communicate. He opened his mouth a couple of times, but no sound came out. He took a long deep breath. I wasn't sure what to do.

"My friend Christopher was telling me some stats today. He said that over fifty percent of all homeless youth are gay." He watched me, wide-eyed, wary. "Are you gay?"

He nodded once.

"His theory was that you probably were thrown out when your parents found out. That true?"

He nodded again. There was a little glimmer in the corner of his eye, but no tears emerged. I suspect none would have dared.

"Okay," I said. "I'm not going to throw you out for being gay. Now, his theory is also that most homeless gay kids wind up hustling to survive. Are you using this place to turn tricks?" He shook his head, vehemently. "Good answer. Are you turning tricks at all?"

The silence broke. "No!" he snapped. "I'm a waiter at Village Pizza up the street. The rest of the time I'm a student at Georgia State."

I smiled at him. "Okay. So first things first. I'm not going to throw you out tonight. Second, we are going to have to find other living accommodations for you. I'm not being mean. I've got a theatrical troupe moving in here to put on a show, and they need to hook up wires in the alcove where you've put all your stuff. So, we're going to have to move it temporarily."

He sighed deeply and relief spread across his face. He nodded.

"Third, you aren't going to get off the hook. You still have to tell me your story."

He took a deep breath and began.

That night Zach gave me a glimpse of a world that had never been real to me before. My privileged, protected childhood in the heart of Anne Arundel County, Maryland, didn't overlap with Zach's much.

He had been raised in a north Georgia town called Rome. It was an old-money town, but there was also a pretty large blue-collar working community. Zach had been raised in the heart of it. Although his parents had been working class, he had not been raised as a redneck. He had been a Boy Scout, made it all the way to Eagle Scout in fact. And had been a good student in school, qualifying for Georgia's Hope scholarship, which guaranteed him free tuition at any Georgia state college or university. He had chosen, and been accepted, to the University of Georgia in Athens. At eighteen, he had been a kid pretty much on top of the world.

Then, his father had caught him making out with another boy on the night of their high school graduation.

They had taken a bottle of gin that they had sneaked out of the other boy's house and were drinking it in on the bank of the Etowah River. The liquor and hormones were taking effect when his father, recognizing his car parked on the side of the road, had stopped to investigate. Finding the boys, and having consumed a fair amount of Jack Daniels himself, he flew into a rage, dragged Zach home, and promptly beat the crap out of him.

The beatings had continued for the better part of a week, and Zach had overheard a discussion between his parents over whether it was safe to send him to college, or whether he should be forced to get a job or maybe join the military; something that would *teach him to be a man.*

It would not be the first time his parents had held money over his head, but it was the first time it had the potential to impact his entire future. He had a dream of graduating from college and going into television, and college was the only way to get there.

Something hardened in him that day, and he laid out his plans very carefully. He had to do things quickly, and in a very tight sequence, or he knew he would be just another "homeless, penniless fag" on the streets of Atlanta or some other nameless city.

That night, after his parents had gone to bed, he slipped out to the garage and quietly moved his tent, backpack, sleeping bag and other backpacking supplies to his room. He packed just enough clothing to survive at college—jeans, shorts, t-shirts and rugbies. It came down that, if it didn't fit in his backpack, he didn't take it. That night, he hid the backpack under his bed.

The next morning, he was kicked out of his bed by his father. The days had developed a Dachau-like cadence. His father would dress him down each morning, and then deliver a list of tasks that must be completed by the time he got home from work. He was out of the house by seven, his mother shortly after.

Zach moved quickly, taking nothing that wasn't his, save papers he knew he would need: his birth certificate, his social security card, and his transcripts. He also took his acceptance letters to UGA, Armstrong State in Savannah, and Georgia State, which had been his fallback school. He specifically tore a sheet of paper and wrote Savannah on it, and left it crumpled in his wastebasket. He snuck out and hiked across town to a different branch of his bank than the one he normally used, and withdrew his entire life's savings. It wasn't much, but enough to take care of himself for a few weeks.

Not wanting to involve or implicate any of his friends, he made contact with no one. Instead, he hiked out of town towards Atlanta.

He would hike almost twenty miles over the next four days, relying mostly on his Boy Scout skills to hide and survive in the shadow of Interstate 75. When he reached the outskirts of Atlanta, he hitchhiked to the first MARTA station he could reach, and took the subway into town, personally delivering his acceptance letter to Georgia State.

Once he had been admitted and met with the Financial Aid office, he spent the night under an overpass, scared to death. It took him almost a week to come upon the theater, which he took as a sign from God, and it had been home ever since.

I listened half in awe, half in disbelief at his hesitant yet calm delivery. I marveled at his ingenuity, both in escaping Rome, Georgia, and in surviving homelessness. He would get up at six every morning, hike to the Tenth Street MARTA station, and ride to school, where he would shower and get cleaned up at the student athletic center. Then, he would go to classes, alternating with studying in the library. Once classes were complete, he would work waiting tables, which did not pay much, and then come home to his basement. His lifelines to the world were a PO box and a cell phone.

"To tell you the truth," he said, staring at his toes, "you coming in here was a mixed blessing. You made it a pain in the ass, because I couldn't come home until I knew you were gone, and I couldn't be here on the weekends." He glanced up under his over-long bangs and smiled slightly, for the first time. "On the other hand, you got the bathroom working. You can't underestimate the value of that when you've been peeing in the alley for the last two years."

I was sitting forward in my chair, my elbows resting on my knees. "Why did you stay? I mean, two years is a long time to live like this. Didn't you ever make friends at school? Find some roommates?"

He shrugged. "The Hope grant doesn't cover living expenses, just tuition. Money is awfully tight for me to actually take on additional expenses like a lease. Besides, I didn't want too many written records that led to me."

"What about your parents? Didn't they ever try to find you?"

He looked out the window. "I dunno. If they did, not hard. I'm less than fifty miles away, attending a major university. There are kids from my home town who see me at school." He turned and looked me straight in the eye. "I guess, by leaving, I made it easy. They didn't need to *explain* me if I was a runaway."

I felt a physical sensation in my chest, much like something tearing. I had no idea what the feeling I was experiencing was. Months later, Rachel explained to me it was called *empathy.*

I glanced at my watch. It was almost two. "Listen Zach, here's the deal. You don't need to move out right now. We probably need to talk about what your long-term plans are at some point, because I don't know that living in the theater is possible. But right now, the only important thing is that we get your stuff out of the organ pit so we can rewire it tomorrow."

He nodded. "Sure. Here's my deal. The pizza place where I work is going out of business. I need to find another job, and then I can try to find a place to go. But if you can just let me stay until then…"

Jesus, I thought, *I was about to evict him just as he lost his job.*

"Sure," I said. "In the meantime, can we move your stuff up here? You can sleep on the couch until we figure out where you are going." I heard that word, *we* come out of my mouth and wondered why I was taking any responsibility for his life. Nevertheless, we spent the next hour hauling his stuff from the basement up to my office. We chatted while we moved. I learned about his classes, about how the pizza place where he worked was about to be put out of business by the bakery next door, and about the myriad of Boy Scout skills that had come into play to help him survive. By a quarter to five, he was settled into his new home in my office.

The organ pit was not a particularly clean environment and we were both pretty grubby. Plus the air conditioning was off, and sweat left trails of clean in the grime on our faces. I looked at him and said, "Look, you're filthy. Do you want to come to my place and get cleaned up?"

He looked at me, warily. "Um…"

I held up a hand. "You don't have to worry. I have no interest in you apart from concern as another human being." *Who the hell was operating my mouth?*

He paused for a beat, considering, but the dirt and discomfort won out. He shrugged, and grabbed his shaving kit from off the top of the filing cabinet and said, "Sure. Why not?"

He slipped on a pair of sneakers which had seen better days, and followed me out of the building and across the street. The neighborhood was silent and so was he. As we walked, the silence intimidated me, and so I began to tell him about Aunt Laine. As we climbed the stairs, I explained how she owned the apartment building and the theater. He listened, perhaps out of courtesy, perhaps exhaustion. He followed me up the stairs, silently, obediently.

We crossed the rooftop, and I opened the door to the apartment. I held the door open for him, and he stepped inside, tentatively. I closed it behind him, flipped on the lights and stepped past him. I opened the bathroom door, switched on the light and said, "Towels and washcloths are in the cabinet over the toilet."

He stepped into the bathroom and closed and locked the door. I climbed up the steps to my loft and pulled off my grime-encrusted t-shirt. I took off the rest of my clothes and pulled on a pair of sweat pants, then descended the stairs to wait my turn in the bathroom.

I started a pot of coffee and heard the shower come on. I sat down on the couch to wait, but quickly dozed off. I wasn't sure how long I was out, but I awoke with a start when I heard him say, "Donovan?"

I opened my eyes. He was leaning out of the bathroom door. "Yeah?"

"Can I borrow a t-shirt? This sweater is pretty filthy."

"Sure," I said. "Do you want some sweats as well?"

He nodded. "Yeah, if you don't mind."

I pulled myself off the couch and climbed the stairs. I retrieved a t-shirt and sweats from the armoire and came back down and handed them to him. He thanked me, pulled them inside, and emerged a moment later, repacking his small shaving kit. "Bathroom's all yours."

"Thanks," I said. "If you want, throw your stuff in the washing machine."

"Thanks, Van. I appreciate it."

I closed myself in the bathroom, brushed my teeth and jumped into the shower. As I was showering, the water pressure suddenly dropped and turned quite cold. I realized I should have probably suggested he could use the washer *after* I got out of the shower.

I rinsed off as best I could in the cold trickle, got out and toweled off. I ran a brush through my hair, considered shaving and thought better of it, and then pulled my sweats back on. I opened the door and looked across at the couch. Zach sat in the spot I had vacated, holding a cup of coffee, sound asleep.

I switched off the light and ascended the steps to the loft. Running could wait this morning. I lay down on the bed and was almost immediately asleep.

I was awakened at nine by the phone ringing. I sat bolt upright and dropped down the steps to the phone. I glanced over at Zach, who was blinking hard, trying to make sense of where he was. I answered the phone; it was Laine.

"Donovan?" she asked in that rising intonation. "Are you all right?"

"Yes ma'am. Sorry I'm late with breakfast. I had a late night."

"Ah. Out with Rachel and Christopher?"

"No ma'am." I glanced at the couch. "The Phantom."

"The Phantom?" she asked, her voice not comprehending. "You mean you found him?"

"I do. Want to meet him?"

"Absolutely."

"Be down in a minute." I hung up the phone and turned to see him looking at me warily.

"Phantom?" he asked, a slight look of bemusement on his face.

"That was our name for you."

"As in opera?"

"Of course. What else would you call someone who lives under a theater?"

He smiled openly this time. "Who were you talking to?"

"My Aunt Laine. Want some breakfast? Meeting her is the price."

He glanced at his watch. "Sure. I only have one class today and it's too late to make it."

I grabbed a shirt, poured myself a cup of coffee and replaced his cold one with a warm one. Then, I led the way downstairs.

I knocked on the door, and Laine bid me enter almost immediately. She was standing with her walker in the doorway to the dining room, dressed in a royal blue caftan and her pearls, of all things.

"Laine, this would be Zachary, our erstwhile phantom. Zach, this my Aunt Laine, your benefactor for the last two years."

He padded barefoot across the thick Persian rug, extended his hand and said in a very professional manner, "Please to meet you, ma'am. I'm sorry I've been living in your basement."

Laine's face burst into a glowing smile as she took his hand. She was clearly smitten. But then again, Laine has always had a soft spot for cute young boys, even after they had grown into cranky, divorced, practically unemployed thirty-five-year-olds. God bless her for that.

"Nonsense, darling. Everyone has got to live somewhere."

"I've invited Zach to join us for breakfast," I reported.

"Marvelous!" she said with same animation of Gloria Swanson discovering she was going to be given the Cecil B. DeMille Lifetime

Achievement award. "You go make it, and Zachary and I will get to know each other a little better."

Laine led him into the dining room. As I went into the kitchen, I heard her ask in her sweetest, grandmotherly voice, "So dear, you aren't a hustler, are you?"

Over the course of breakfast, Laine covered much of the same ground with Zach I had covered the previous evening. However, she covered it in a much more goal-oriented, solution-focused way. There was a small room in the basement with a toilet in it. Laine offered to have me (!) install a shower and sink, and we could convert it into a small studio apartment for him to occupy until he could get himself on his feet. When she heard that he would be losing his job, she immediately offered him a position working part time as my assistant handyman, paying him roughly what he made at the pizza place. (This, despite the fact she did not, in fact, pay me anything.) She also suggested that I might pick him up at the train station each afternoon so he could have more time to work at the building.

Although it may sound like I'm grousing, truth be told I took an active, willing role in volunteering my aid and assistance. I have no idea why. It felt weird, out of character and yet oddly exhilarating to be doing something for a total stranger.

For his part, Zach was also acting out of character. He would later tell me that he had absolutely no idea why he was willing to trust me, or by corollary, Laine. It may have been that, after years of seeing and believing the worst about people, he was subconsciously desperate for someone he could trust and rely on. Or, it may have been that he simply had no other options open to him. Regardless of the reasons, we offered assistance and he accepted willingly, albeit warily.

By ten o'clock, we had laid out Zach's new future. I gave him a pair of old sneakers to replace his and took him down to the room in the basement. It wasn't much. It originally had been the home for the massive boiler that heated the building, long since replaced by HVAC units in each apartment. A *maid's toilet* sat in one corner, a relic from the days when white residents would never tolerate black help using the same facilities. Off to one side, I could see some stub pipes off of the lines to the laundry room where I knew I could hook him up a sink and a shower. *There might even be enough room for a small kitchen of some kind*, I thought.

The room itself was dusty, but dry and cool and relatively empty. Zach studied it for a long time, and then turned and smiled at me. His smile began as a glow from behind his long-lashes and spread downward, culminating in an almost triangular smile. "This could have some real possibilities," he said. "Do you think you can build me a real bathroom?"

I nodded, trying not to think about my miserably long "to do" list. "I probably won't be able to get to it until this weekend, but yes. If I'm going to, though, I'm going to need a lot of help from you."

He nodded solemnly. "Hey, I'm your assistant handyman. You're the boss."

"Okay, first things first. Let's get to Home Depot."

Zach got quite a workout that Friday afternoon. I had him cut the yard, trim the hedges, and edge all the walks, something I had been remiss at while working on the theater. In the meantime, knowing that he was working over there, I was able to go get some critical changes made to the theater. The lack of sleep wore heavily on both of us, but he obviously felt he needed to prove his earnestness, and I was too embarrassed not to match his energy.

At five, I admitted the troupe, plus Mac; Lois; Mort, the sound technician (who, despite the name was also a woman); Keisha, the set designer; and a host of others, all of whom began the mechanical transformation from cinema to theater.

Around six, Rachel and Chris came across the street with a shaker of martinis to see what mischief they could recruit me into for their weekend amusement. They found me sitting on the stage, trying to figure out how I was going to hang the marquee. Rachel called my name as she climbed the steps to the stage, but came up short as I turned and smiled at her.

"Ye gods! You look like hell."

"Thanks," I said sarcastically even though I was sure she was probably right. Lack of sleep does not make me pretty.

"What happened to you?" Chris asked, coming up from behind Rachel.

I briefly explained how, in the last twenty-four hours I had gone from trying to evict Zach to being his benefactor. If either of them thought to remonstrate me for failing to heed their warnings, my patently exhausted demeanor convinced them otherwise.

After listening to the tale, Rachel said, "You're exhausted. Why don't you go home and go to bed?"

"I've got to be here to lock up after the troupe leaves."

"Leave me the key," Chris said. "I'll stay and do it." Since Chris is not known for ever volunteering for selfless acts, or even for anything that might be inconvenient, Rachel and I just stared at him.

"What?" he said, self-consciously. "I can be responsible."

"No one doubts you *can*, per se," Rachel explained. "It's just no one has ever seen you do it."

I briefly considered protesting, but the exhaustion won out. I handed him the key and gave him a brief rundown of what I needed him to do, and walked slowly back up the aisle towards the front door.

In the lobby, I met Zach who was carrying his backpack, his sleeping bag, and his shaving kit.

"Where you off to?" I asked.

"Thought I might spend my first night in my new place," he replied brightly and I cursed his twenty-year-old metabolism.

I held open the door for him and he led the way across the street. As we reached the front door, he asked permission to use my shower to get cleaned up since he had endured a pretty hot, sweaty day. I told him he could, and that he was welcome to use it as necessary until we had his hooked up. We agreed to meet at my place in twenty minutes, and while he carried his stuff downstairs, I checked in on Aunt Laine.

He was waiting outside my door when I arrived, obviously tired but still in a bright mood. He chatted a little bit about a couple of things he was planning to do with *his place,* and asked me if I could help him change the lock on the door tomorrow so he could lock it. I agreed, although I don't really remember saying much of anything, and sent him into the bathroom. I dropped onto the couch and was asleep immediately. I never heard him leave.

The next day and the following weekend are still a blur to me. A little sleep deprivation combined with a lot of work left me largely out of touch with reality.

First of all, there was Laine to look after. As she became more ambulatory, she actually seemed to require more attention rather than less. It wasn't just the need to haul her to doctors and physical therapy; weeks in her apartment had made her a bit stir crazy and desperate for intellectual stimulation.

Then, there was the theater troupe. The technical staff succeeded in getting the sound system up and running, and several lighting tracks were improvised on the stage, with controls run down to the side of the proscenium. But, every time I turned around there was someone with a toolbelt and a roll of wire demanding attention from me.

Separate from the theater, I had my new assistant to keep busy. While I was getting more accomplished with his help, it also required more mental exertion on my part to explain to him, and occasionally show him, exactly what I needed him to do.

There was also the matter of Zach's apartment, which I found odd moments to work on. I replaced the toilet right off since it looked like it hadn't been cleaned since the late sixties. I was also able to install a pedestal sink fairly easily, so he had some semblance of a bathroom. We brought home a prefab shower stall, but for the moment it sat in pieces in the corner. I knew where it would go and how to install it; I just didn't have time to do it.

Also competing for my time were my friends. Chris and Rachel had been very supportive of my new theater obsession, but they had also made it clear that they missed our periodic sojourns to neighborhood bars. After all, what was the point of living in a bar district if you didn't go out to them.

And then, of course there was the troupe itself. They were quite anxious to move to the stage to start rehearsing, which meant that I needed to get the marquee out and hung. And, to get the marquee hung, I needed to figure out what to name the theater.

That particular problem was solved over cocktails on Saturday evening. The troupe had knocked off and gone home around five. Charles and Brit had taken Laine out for dinner. Jennifer, Chris, and Rachel sat cross-legged on the stage with a pitcher of martinis, staring at me as I rearranged parts and letters of the marquee, trying to make sense of it.

"You know, it's like a big brass Scrabble game," Chris observed, holding aloft a big C with one hand and examining it, while sipping his martini with the other.

"The highest point word ever made in Scrabble was *quixotry* for eight hundred and eighty points," Rachel observed, playing with her skewer of olives. "By a carpenter."

"Who knows that?" I asked, looking up from the letters that I had just arranged into *Roxy*.

"Who knows what quixotry is?" Jennifer asked. "Someone used *temerity* today at work and I had to go in the back room and Google it."

"I work in a bookstore. A good vocabulary is a side effect." Rachel observed, sucking the pimento out of one of her olives. "There's already a Roxy in town."

I removed the letters and started over.

"How long do we have to watch you spell?" Chris whined.

"Until I have a name."

"Your name is Donovan," Jennifer observed. "Done."

"A name for the theater."

"We could call it Jennifer," Jennifer said.

"We could call it Christopher," Chris replied. "That has a much nicer ring to it."

"We could also call it Lincoln Center," I retorted. "But we're not."

The door of the auditorium opened, and Zach stepped inside tentatively. I smiled. "Hey, Phantom. No need to be shy. C'mon down."

He came down the aisle tentatively and I introduced him to everyone sitting there.

"Hey doll," Jennifer said, smiling up at him as he mounted the stage. "Welcome to the daylight side of life. Want a martini?"

"Um, I'm not twenty-one," he said shyly.

She took the plastic cup she had brought for me and poured him a drink. "Neither am I, doll. Neither am I."

He took the drink, sipped it hesitantly, and winced. "What are you doing?"

"I," I announced, before anyone else could interject, "am trying to come up with a name for the theater. And, if I can figure out a name that uses these letters, all the better."

He took another sip of the martini, sat his drink on the floor and began rearranging letters with me. "My English composition teacher in high school used to say, if you can't find inspiration, think of someone or something that used to inspire you. Who or what used to inspire you?"

I had an odd sense of déjà vu and remembered *my* English composition teacher saying the same thing to me about twenty years earlier. It was a technique I often used when I was struggling to find something good to say in an article.

I closed my eyes and tried to think of someone who inspired me. The drone of my friends' voices kind of blended together, and for just a moment, it was the drone of the crowd in the subway. The interesting thing about subways is that there is always an intense, subliminal pressure not to speak, much like standing in an elevator. Or, at a urinal.

I think, because of that pressure, no one stands out. However, here I was with four people whom I had not known three months ago, who were rapidly becoming the most important people in my life. They all stood out. That inspired me.

That led me to think about Brit. I had to admit, I had never taken Brit seriously. Yet, I also had to admit she had made a life for herself. And with no one's help. Well, no one except Aunt Laine's. And Uncle Mo's. And Charles's.

That, in turn, focused my attention on Aunt Laine. Talk about someone who inspired me.

Laine had grown up in Charleston, in a house on the Battery that had been in her family since shortly after the Civil War. Her branch of the Wagners (a family never exactly known for their timing), had relocated from Cincinnati to Charleston with the mistaken belief that it was a city in need of a brewery, immediately before the seizing of Fort Sumter. Because most of the family's wealth was still in the North, they were spared the privations of the war's aftermath. Since the war started in Charleston's harbor, the city was not treated well by the occupying

Union troops after the war. But they treated the Wagners quite well as the only local source of beer in the city.

The city itself, however, did not treat the wealthy German immigrants particularly well. Charleston is an aristocracy without being a plutocracy; social power comes from history, not from wealth. Johan Wagner was marginalized until he did the smartest thing of his life: convince Lydia Beaumont's father to give him her hand in marriage in 1866 in exchange for a familial "loan" that enabled his new father-in-law to keep his dry goods business. While Johan was never welcomed, he graduated from marginalized to silently tolerated in deference to his wife's family.

Their son, Gustavus Beaumont "Beau" Wagner followed his father's lead, marrying himself another impoverished pedigree and gaining polite entrance, if not welcome, to Charleston society. By the time his granddaughter, DeLaine, had her "coming out" in the late thirties, the family was a fixture in Battery circles. They *belonged* there.

That said, the Battery may not have been fully prepared for DeLaine Russell Wagner to belong there. Born shortly after Prohibition inflicted radically different economics on the family, she was a woman of the twentieth century. Very early in her life, she became aware of Eleanor Roosevelt when the First Lady, driving herself through on the way to visit Franklin in Warm Springs, Georgia, stopped for the night at the Francis Marion hotel and had dinner next to the Wagner family in the dining room.

Laine, much to the shock and horror of her parents and brothers, struck up a conversation with Mrs. Roosevelt, and in the course of the next three hours found endorsement for every radical, liberal, and socially progressive thought that had ever entered her head, but which she had previously been afraid to share. She would transform herself almost overnight into a high-spirited champion of liberal causes, without ever losing her polished southern veneer. Long before the word *integration* was ever uttered in Charleston, she held the city's first integrated coming out. Of course, it was sparsely attended by the scandalized city elite, leaving the family eating leftover hors d'oeuvres for months, but Laine had made her mark.

While studying business at the College of Charleston she met Maurice Fairchild, a poor but ambitious student at the Citadel. He thought she was too worried about niceties; she thought he was needlessly argumentative. They fell in love almost immediately, and when it became clear he was going to be drafted, they had a quiet wedding at Saint John's Lutheran followed by a weekend honeymoon in Savannah. Then Mo was off to training, and Laine back to school.

After the war, she and Mo lived with her parents while he finished up college. But Laine's increasing maturity and liberal politics put her at odds with her mother's southern gentility. As soon as Mo graduated, they moved to Atlanta, where they would ultimately build a small real-estate empire by buying up properties that were a little unusual or off the beaten path. She had a good instinct for when a property had something special about it; he could make one heck of a business deal.

Laine had always had a knack for finding people and properties with hidden potential, and convincing them to realize it. I glanced around at the theater and thought, *She's doing it again.*

On the stage, Zach was idly rearranging the letters. I silently reached past him and took the letters from him. I discarded an S and made quick work of the rest.

The others stood and came and stood behind me to look. I felt a hand on my shoulder and turned to see Zach smiling at me shyly, but approvingly.

The theater would be called THEATER DELAINE.

The Hydrangea

Laine typically started almost all conversations in the middle, assuming I was fully grounded on what the hell she was talking about. It did not matter what the subject was. If it was a discussion of Bitsy Hollander's operation, the story was based on the assumptions that (a) I knew who Bitsy Hollander was (good friend of Laine's. Known her for years. Used to live two doors down from the theater); (b) I knew what surgery Bitsy was having ("Hysterectomy, which is just amazing because, bless her soul, with that little mustache you would have thought she had all the plumbing ripped out years ago"); and (c) I understood that Bitsy's recovery would be greatly complicated because that up-north, new-money snot of a daughter-in-law of hers was simply *not* going to reschedule her golf game and haul her madras-covered butt out of Peachtree City to drive the forty minutes to Piedmont Hospital to check on her more than twice a week.

In the beginning I had given her blank stares when she did this, assuming she would notice and fill in the blanks for me. It didn't work. I later realized she did not associate the blank stares with a lack of information but rather thought I was just slow. So when, over breakfast on the morning of June first, she began reciting a long litany of things I was going to have to get done before the festival, I held up a hand and asked, "Festival?"

"The Virginia Highland Festival, dear, so anyway…"

I kept my hand up. "Before you go on, give me the details on the festival so I can understand what you are telling me to do."

She took a deep breath and gave me the remedial explanation. The Virginia Highland Festival was a two-day arts and music celebration very much like all of the other festivals I had attended that spring. For this one, Virginia Avenue would be closed for a half mile, from Highland down past the park. The street would be lined with booths much like the other festivals, and all of the neighbors who would be largely trapped in their homes and apartments would plan to have house parties that weekend. Many of Laine's subsequent directions to me involved the provisions I would be expected to lay in and the things I needed to do to ensure that the place "looked presentable." It was also suggested that I find a parking space on one of the side streets now for the Jeep in case a last minute dash to the grocery or liquor store was in order.

Duly charged, and with the breakfast dishes done, I descended the stairs to the basement. As I cleared the last step and turned towards the garage, Zach emerged from his apartment and bid me good morning. His world had changed a great deal since the middle of May. For starters, the building had adopted him, and everyone had taken on turning his tiny basement apartment into a "real" home as an additional mission to reopening the theater. We had installed the shower and managed to enclose the bathroom with some prefab wall panels. I had also found a small all-in-one kitchen unit with a sink, refrigerator, and two-burner stove at a yard sale. Charles had given him an old futon that sat in his basement, and Rachel had given him an armoire from her bedroom so she could have an excuse to buy herself a new one. Clare had contributed sheets, towels, blankets, and pillows. I accused her of also looking for a reason to buy new, and was summarily informed that Clare did not need a reason to go pillage Ikea.

He had received a gift of lamps and a chair from Laine, some mismatched dishes and glassware from Jennifer, and an old television from Mac. Brit was latch-hooking a rug to cover the bare concrete floor. Mister Kersey didn't contribute anything directly to Zach, per se, but I continued to receive occasional, anonymous gifts of movie memorabilia, which found their way onto his walls.

And then there was Chris.

Now, I admit I had always suspected that under Chris's shallow, superficial exterior was an equally shallow, superficial soul. And, of course, Chris gave Zach nothing from his own apartment. But, one evening, he descended to the basement (after calling my cell phone for detailed instructions on exactly how to find it) with three enormous bags of new clothes, shoes, belts, ties, jackets, and an absurd amount of toiletries. Since Chris only bought expensive brand names, the clothes represented a kind of windfall a young gay man like Zach could only dream of.

At the time I had been in there installing the shower, and listened to them for the next two hours. While Zach excitedly tried on the clothes, he and Chris had a talk that was almost paternal. Chris began the gentle explanation of the ins and outs of being an openly gay man. I'm not sure about Zach, but I certainly learned a few things.

Zach was initially self-conscious from all the attention. However, as the weeks went by and we folded him into our little society, he began to lose the strangeness. He seemed to smile a little more openly now. Classes had wrapped up for the summer so he worked for me full time, which meant many more things were getting accomplished at the theater and around the building. It also meant I had a near-constant companion, fifteen years my junior.

"Morning, sport," I said as he pulled his apartment door shut behind him. He fell in step beside me as we made our way to the garage. We typically began our mornings together there, where we would lay out the day's projects.

"Mon Capitan," he said brightly. "How do you plan to make me earn my meager wages today?"

"Meager wages! You mean the money I pay you on top of the free lodging you are enjoying?"

"You don't pay me. Auntie Laine does." I had no idea when he had started calling her Auntie Laine. But he had, and she didn't seem to mind at all. "And I wouldn't be so sarcastic about free lodging. I don't see you writing rent checks."

"Yeah, but I don't even get meager wages." I unlocked the garage and led him inside. "We have a couple of missions today. Laine has a ton of supplies that she needs us to lay in. Apparently there is a street festival coming up this weekend and we'll be trapped in here. Also, she wants us to plant impatiens along the front walk and trim the hedges around her porch. We've got to clean the front-door windows and mop the lobby. Plus cut and fertilize the lawn. And, on top of that, I want to see how much more of the marquee we can get hung."

He nodded sagely. "Good. Lots of outdoor stuff. Where do you want to start?"

"I guess we should go to Home Depot first and get the stuff for the yard."

He grabbed my spare keys off of the hook by the back door. "I'll drive."

I let him drive my Jeep occasionally when I needed him to run an errand. After living nearly three years without wheels, it was one of those things that you could tell gave him immense pleasure. "You will, huh?"

He stopped and cast his eyes downward in mock humility. "May I please drive, sir?"

I shrugged. "What the hell." We exited out the back of the garage and jumped into the Jeep. I had taken off the doors for the summer, so the seats were a little damp with the morning dew. But, the air was already warm and thick. I was learning that Georgia and humidity were synonymous.

He pulled out of the driveway and sped down Virginia. As we worked our way through the side streets to the Home Depot on Ponce, he chattered brightly about all manner of things. We talked about the show he had watched the night before and how, when he finally graduated and started making real money, he was going to buy the Jeep from me. He also talked about the Highlands Festival, since he had lived in the middle of it for the last two summers, explaining in elaborate detail to me exactly what he enjoyed about it, and also what he thought was overrated. He also informed me that he would be buying me dinner Friday evening at the festival.

"Why are you buying?" I asked as he made the turn into Home Depot's alarmingly inconvenient parking lot.

He glanced sideways at me. "To thank you. You've done a lot for me."

One of the things I had come to realize about Zach is that the last two years living in the basement had been extraordinarily lonely for him. Between the hours he had to work to survive and the embarrassment of being homeless, he had not really made any close friends at school. With all the intense interaction he had with the rest of us, he was lonely no more, and benefiting from it.

We did a power tour of the Depot. Flat of impatiens from the garden center. Concrete anchors from hardware. Outdoor wiring and light sockets from electrical. Back out the door in under fifteen minutes. I considered the trip a victory.

We returned to the building and got to work. Georgia summer days typically are pleasant until eleven, hot until two, and ungodly until six. So if you can, you are smart to get as much outdoor work done as early as possible. Since we had mostly outdoor work that day, I wanted to try to have everything done around the building by one. That meant we would be working on the marquee in the midday heat, but I would rather do that than be pushing a lawn mower.

While Zach cut the grass, I began trimming the hedges that nestled along the base of Laine's porch. While I was trimming, she opened the door and hobbled out on the porch carrying two tumblers of ice water. She handed one to me and held the other up for Zach to see. He waved, acknowledging it, and she set it on the porch rail.

"You should have your walker," I told her before drinking. "At very least your cane."

"Bah," she said, leaning on the rail for support. "I can walk from the kitchen to the porch." She gazed down the street. "I see that monstrosity has sold."

The monstrosity in question stood on the former site of Bitsy Hollander's bungalow. At that time, there was a lot of real estate speculation going on in midtown Atlanta and the Highlands. Builders were snapping old two-bedroom bungalows that had been built in the thirties and forties, bulldozing them, and then building four-thousand-square-foot houses in their place. The new houses, which the locals referred to as McMansions (usually with a disapproving sniff), almost always overpowered the houses and streetscape surrounding them.

Everyone freely admitted there was no particular architectural significance to the old Hollander place. It had been nothing more than a little white clapboard cottage that was seriously overpowered by a mammoth tulip tree in the front yard. And, the developer had paid Bitsy quite well for the house that he summarily bulldozed. But the new house, which literally spanned from lot-line to lot-line, looked like *Architectural Digest* had vomited on Virginia Avenue. Palladian windows and craftsman brackets formed a painful juxtaposition with the Corinthian columns and Tuscan stucco, all under a chaotic jumble of rooflines. When neighbors walked by, they generally dismissed it with disparaging statements like "Brand spanking new money."

I looked down the street to where she pointed. There was indeed a Sold sign in front. I shrugged. I thought the house was tacky as well, but having never seen what was there before, it didn't mean a whole lot to me.

We finished the yard work and, after lunch, crossed the street to start work on the marquee. One o'clock was also the time that I now typically took up residence in the theater each day so I could let in the plethora of people who came and went as work on the production ramped up. I was continually signing for set pieces and production equipment that arrived at all hours of the day and night. In the evenings, the stagehands would convert these into the presidential palace of Freedonia that was taking shape on the stage. The set designer, in an attempt to help visualize the stark, Texas two-step mentality of a world where you "are either with us or ag'in' us," was rendering the elaborate art deco set where most of the action took place almost entirely in black and white.

We saw none of that this afternoon, however, as we clung to the front of the building in the hot midday sun, assembling brass marquee panels. We had been working on them for the better part of a week and had resecured the base (which formed a lighted rain canopy over the ticket window and doors) to the building using a series of brass rods and steel cables to suspend it from the anchors in the wall. Today, working from the inside, we were attaching the frames of the frosted milk-glass side panels. The sun was hot, and sweat ran down our bare chests and backs, leaving marks where it dripped onto the brass panels.

The reassembly process required one of us to gingerly lift each piece out of the window, and then Zach would hold them in place while I would fasten bolts or tighten screws. Because of the heat, the awkward nature of the work, and the overriding fear that we would drop and ruin one of the antique pieces, we didn't speak much except as was necessary to install the pieces.

Around two-thirty, we had both of the sides installed, and I was leaning far out the window securing the last milk-glass panel in place on the very front. The position was awkward, requiring me to lean way out over the marquee. There was no way to support myself, so Zach was straddling me from behind, holding me by my belt so I couldn't fall out of the building. It was at this time, in this precarious position, that my cell phone chose to ring.

"Crap," I said, continuing to tighten one of the glass braces. "As if this position wasn't compromising enough…"

"Do you want me to reach in your pants and answer it? At this point, I couldn't be getting much more personal anyhow."

I laughed despite myself. "Yeah, go ahead." I felt him reach into my pocket and pull out the cell phone.

I heard the beep as he punched the answer button, and his voice say, "Hello? Donovan Ford's pants." I rolled my eyes. After a moment he said, "It's Rachel. She's laughing."

"I'm sure she is," I replied as I began work on the last brace. "What does she want?"

"Van can't come to the phone. I'm holding his ass out the window. No seriously. He wants to know what you want." There was a long pause that ensued, during which I dropped the wrench and had to retrieve it. I felt ridiculous. "Well, we've almost got the sides of the marquee done, and then Laine wants us to go buy a bunch of stuff so we don't have to leave the neighborhood this weekend. What time? I don't see why not. Hold on, I'll ask him."

He pulled the phone away and said, "Rachel's short-staffed and can't leave the store. She wants you to go up to Peachtree-DeKalb Airport at five and pick up some author that's doing a book signing and bring him to the store."

Ordinarily, I have pretty good instincts for what's going to piss me off, but apparently they don't work when hanging upside down by my belt. "I suppose I can," I sighed. "Find out where and how we'll know him."

He turned his attention back to the phone. "Van says okay. How do we find him?" Long pause. "Van knows him?"

I knew him? The light bulb finally snapped on over my head. (Apparently it's fluorescent: slower but more efficient.) "Pull me in," I barked.

"Hold on, Rachel." He pulled backwards and I regained my footing. I hit my head on the upper sash of the window.

"Son of a…" I growled, and snatched the cell phone from his hand. "Tell me this is a joke," I said.

"Donovan, *please,*" she said plaintively. "I know you don't like him, but I have no one else to ask."

"Can't he take a friggin' cab?"

"There's no cab stand at PDK. You won't have to take him back. But I have no way to get him here in time." I sighed heavily. No, angrily. In truth, more angrily than she deserved. "*Please* Van. Don't make me beg."

I sighed again. "All right. You have no idea how much you owe me."

"I promise I will make it up to you."

"Yes. Yes, you will." I replied sourly and snapped the phone off. I glanced at Zach, who was watching me wide-eyed with a mixture of surprise and concern on his face.

"You okay?" he asked tentatively.

"We're knocking off early," I told him, shutting the window perhaps harder than I should have. "We have to go give a lift to my wife's best friend."

Olivia, God love her, is a complex woman. The reason we fell in love is each of us saw the potential of what the other *could* have been. She didn't see me as a trust-fund child of privilege trying too hard to hold on to my youth past the point it made sense. She saw me as a writer of incredible caliber who, with her guidance, could dominate the literary magazine circles of New York.

I, in turn, saw her as an incredibly smart and sophisticated woman who had the potential for great joy if only she would think a little less about her clients, her job, and her image.

The thing both of us missed is that neither of us *wanted* to be the person the other saw that we could be.

Her father had died about the same time as my mother, and we met about six months later. It was at a small reception for one of the other writers at the magazine who had just published his first book, the bastard. She was his agent. She always represented writers of great potential.

We dated for about a year before I asked her to marry me. Our courtship had taken place almost exclusively in New York, and truth be told the city was probably what made us work at all. There was always something to distract our attention. After a disastrous weekend in the Hamptons we discovered we did not travel together well. However, right after we became engaged, it was decided that I would travel with her back to her hometown, Key West, for the opening of a small retrospective of her father's work. Her father, Louie Robideau, had been something of a famous portrait artist and some of his lesser-known works were going to be displayed.

When we got to Key West, I met her best friend, Aidan McInnis. I found I disliked him almost immediately. Now, in retrospect, I think the reason I disliked him so much was because Aidan and I were very similar. However, he was much more stylish and successful at it than I was.

Over the years, Aidan continued to be successful. He, too, was Olivia's client, and she helped him parlay his writing into financial security, if not out-and-out wealth. I wasn't sure which book tour he was on, but I thought it had to be at least his seventh. He averaged a book about every ten or eleven months so it made sense.

All of this was running through my head as I piloted the VeggieRoll up Buford Highway towards the city's largest general aviation airport, Peachtree-Dekalb. Zach sat next to me. My hope was, at least with company along, I could avoid having to talk to Aidan too much. However, I wasn't getting much peace on the ride since Zach continually pumped me for details about Aidan, Olivia, and my life in New York.

"Why isn't he coming into Hartsfield?" he asked.

"He owns this vintage airplane. He uses it to run a charter business during the tourist season in Key West. If he tours during the summer, he uses it to fly himself around the country."

"Really?" he said, his voice reflecting the awe over how adventurous Aidan's life sounded. I hated that tone of voice.

We pulled up at the Mercury Air terminal at the airport and walked to the waiting area where we were supposed to meet him. Parked out on the tarmac were a multitude of private jets, probably almost a hundred. "You forget how wealthy the city is until you come to some place like this," I mused. "There's probably twenty billion dollars' worth of aircraft out here."

We sat and talked for about five minutes before I heard the plane. At an airport that is overwhelmingly trafficked by small jets, the sound of the old rotary-powered propellers was unique. I turned towards the noise and saw the sun glint off the silver-and-blue fuselage of an early airliner as it banked out of a turn and into the final approach to the runway. "And here's Aidan," I said sarcastically.

We watched in silence as the plane touched down and slowly taxied to the terminal. Once it arrived, the propellers switched off and spun down for about five minutes before the hatch at the rear of the plane opened and he jumped out.

Even despite my dislike for him, I had to admit he was aging well. He was still thin and well tanned and his hair, which he wore rather long, still looked thick and wavy, despite the gray that heralded the fact we were both closer to forty than I perhaps wanted to admit.

He was wearing jeans, flip flops, a starched white oxford button-down and a blue-and-yellow awning striped sports coat. He pulled a backpack and duffle bag out of the aircraft, closed and locked the door, and then secured the plane's tail to some kind of lock in the ground. He then walked to the terminal office, I presumed to pay for the plane's lodging for the night.

Once he came out of the terminal, he glanced around, looking, I'm sure, for Rachel. I took a step forward, forced a smile on my face and said, "Aidan."

The expression crossed his face that indicated he was trying to reconcile an unexpected face in the context, before a smile lit up his face. "Donovan? Hey! What are you doing here?" He crossed the distance between us in three wide strides, knocked my extended hand away and hugged me.

I should probably mention that, although I disliked him, Aidan never gave me any indication he disliked me. Quite the contrary. It may have been just because I was Olivia's husband, or it may have been because Aidan couldn't conceive of anyone not liking anyone, but he always treated me with a warmth and genuineness that lumped guilt on top of all the other complex feelings I had for him.

"I'm your ride," I told him as we emerged from the hug. "Rachel Abernathy had a last-minute emergency at the store and asked me to come get you." I indicated Zach. "This is Zach Covington. We work together."

Aidan turned and greeted Zach graciously, then turned his attention back to me. "Olivia told me you were staying in Atlanta, but she never told me what you were up to." The word Olivia seemed to trigger a thought and he added on a more serious note, "Sorry 'bout the divorce, by the way."

I smiled, I'm sure without warmth, and said, "Me too. We need to get you to the book signing."

I turned and led him to the parking lot. I had expected Zach to get in the front seat with me, but when Aidan whistled and said, "Wow! What a beauty!" he immediately offered it to our guest. I made a mental note to punish him for that. Without a word, I slid the VeggieRoll into gear, and glided out of the parking lot.

Aidan gave me a playful little punch in my right arm. (I detest playful little punches.) "So, man, tell me. What have you been up to? What are you doing down here?"

I shrugged. "Well, a family emergency brought me down here. My aunt took a fall and I had to care for her and look after the apartment building she owns. In the meantime, I've been restoring an abandoned movie theater."

"Cool!" He enthused. "Are you keeping it a movie theater?"

"Well, I'm keeping the capability. In the meantime, we've broadened its use. It'll actually be a working playhouse when we get it done."

"God, that's fantastic. Man, I'm jealous. What a find. I'd love to see it."

I smiled and nodded, thinking it would be a cold day in hell before I took him to see the theater. "What about you? Obviously you're doing well. What is this, your seventh book?"

"Eighth," he said as he pulled his sunglasses out of his breast pocket and settled them on his nose. "Well, if you count *Manheim*, which most people don't."

Manheim's Lament had been his fourth book, and his first out-and-out bomb. At the time I had taken a perverse joy in that, until I actually sat down and read the book. It was disgustingly well written. Its lack of commercial success had been primarily due to its bold challenge of Republican politics at a time when political discussion was viewed as dissension, if not outright sedition. I am sure that, in the future, it will be hailed as his forgotten masterpiece.

"What's the story this time?" I turned onto Buford Highway and began driving south.

"Midlife crisis. It's called *The Biscanya*. It's about a man, facing forty, who can't reconcile his real life with his fantasy about being a pirate."

I smiled despite myself. "Olivia would say that is totally autobiographical."

He chuckled. "Olivia would be wrong. I've always lived my life with the express intent of avoiding a midlife crisis." He looked around at the odd character of Buford Highway as it slipped by. Asian restaurants tucked in with Latino carnicerias and Baptist churches. He asked, absently, "What about you? Still writing for *Gothic*?"

"Well, my name's still on the masthead, although I doubt for long." I was surprised to find myself adding, "I think I've outgrown it."

He nodded. "It happens. A writer of your caliber is bound to grow tired of that scene." I can't recall Aidan ever paying me a compliment before. That said, if he had, I'm sure it would have just pissed me off. "I actually admire you for having been able to stick to the grind of turning something out every week. I'm nowhere near that disciplined."

I exited from the highway and turned onto Cheshire Bridge Road. There's really no way to describe Cheshire Bridge; it's just weird. Fine old restaurants share the road with light industrial businesses, gay bars, strip clubs, and at least one porn-and-fetish boutique, all of them garishly advertised. In a span of three blocks you could procure anything from auto parts to oral sex without too much trouble. He seemed mesmerized by the signs. "So, are you writing anything right now?"

"I was supposed to be working on an anthology of the columns, but the project is going to die. Not enough of them are timeless."

As we passed a long line of cars waiting to pull into a strip club he glanced at his watch. "Strip clubs start early here."

"Happy hour, I presume."

He turned his attention back to me. "So, since the book isn't going to work out, what's next?"

The man had an amazing ability to hone in on raw nerves.

If nothing else, for the last ten years I had been a disciplined writer. Churning out a column every week kept me busy, and my talent well honed. I had hardly sat a word on paper in months, and I felt more than a little guilty about it. Actually, the word *guilty* was not accurate.

I was terrified.

I hadn't written because I couldn't find my voice anymore. I felt like I had lost my muse after the divorce. (And, wouldn't it be just like Olivia to sue for custody of my muse?) I had sat down at my computer numerous times, but nothing seemed to want to come out. In the beginning I had attributed it to stress, but lately I found the theater to be consuming more and more of my creative energy, and less seemed available for the written word. I was worried I was losing it.

Fortunately, I was saved having to answer his question as a car cut me off. All three of us chose a different epithet for the driver simultaneously, and then all shared a laugh at his expense. Cheshire Bridge ended at Piedmont and I turned left. "Where are you staying tonight?"

"Some place called the Virginia Highlands Inn. It's affiliated with the same innkeeper's association that we are, so I want to check it out." I forgot to mention that, in addition to writing books and owning a charter business, Aidan was also part owner in a highly successful bed-and-breakfast in Key West. Damn overachiever.

We chatted about minor things until we reached Ponce Pages. I pulled up in front and he climbed out. Zach handed him his bags and climbed into the front seat. As he closed the passenger door, Aidan leaned over it and said, "Well, as always, thanks for the ride. If we can, let's get together for a drink before I leave town."

"Sure," I replied noncommittally. "Rachel knows how to get hold of me."

He slapped the door, stood back, and gave a dapper, self-confident little wave. I put the car in gear and pulled away.

As I circled the block to get back to the Highlands, Zach said, "Okay, I'm not really much into older men, but he is *hot.*"

I don't know what pissed me off more; that I had to listen to Aidan get complimented, or the fact that Aidan and I were the same age. The term *older men* always hurts.

"So why, exactly, do you dislike Aidan so much?" Zach asked as I pulled the VeggieRoll into the garage.

I grimaced as I shut off the car. "What makes you think I dislike him?"

"Oh, I dunno," he replied as he got out of the car. "Maybe the fact your voice was, like, dripping with hostility."

"I'm sure I did not drip," I replied as I shut the driver's door. "In fact, compared to how I treated him while I was married, I'd say I was downright motherly."

He followed me out of the garage and walked up the stairs beside me. "Well, motherly if your mother was Charles Manson."

I popped him in the back of the head.

"Seriously, why?" We walked out the front door and started across the street.

"It's too complicated to explain," I replied. "Especially when we have a theater full of lesbians waiting for us."

We crossed the street to where the whole gaggle of them were waiting. The troupe had really taken to me, and they had practically adopted Zach once they heard his story.

Zach, unfortunately, had a hard time with names, so he struggled to keep Sara, Cara, Lara, and Tara straight, so to speak. Failing that, he had elected, instead, to give them their "native American tribal names."

"Look," he whispered as we jaywalked. "Angry Vegan Chick got her hair colored."

I snorted back a laugh but said nothing. Some of the other troupe members were "Claims to Know the Indigos," "Alpha Mullet" and "Dances with Corgis."

We were greeted warmly by the cast, and as I prepared to unlock the door I said, "Ladies, I know you have waited long and patiently for this evening. Tonight, we welcome you to move to the stage."

There were a lot of appreciative comments as Zach and I held the doors open for them. The set was far from complete, and the lighting and sound systems only a third done, but there was enough of the Palace of Freedonia built that they could have delivered the show that evening. Miranda strode up the brand new steps to the stage triumphantly, turned dramatically and announced in a tone previously only mastered by Hermione Gingold as she commanded the River City Ladies' Auxiliary to form a Grecian Urn, "Ladies! We have, at last, come home!"

All of the cast politely applauded Miranda, and then immediately set about second-guessing every one of the stage directions she had issued in the rehearsal hall. Miranda found herself busily debating every single decision made over the last few months, while Zachary and I watched from the doors of the auditorium.

"Lesbians," Zach observed, smirking. "They're always just so busy. It's like watching hamsters in a Habitrail."

I smacked him in the back of the head again and sent him off to clean the bathrooms. Although he was, strictly speaking, only employed to take care of the 'Hurst , I usually paid him a little extra to do odd jobs around the theater as well. I remained, leaning in the auditorium door to watch Miranda.

Miranda had been an actress for years. Although she was pretty, she was not a classic beauty. She could never play the ingénue. Instead, she was meant to be a character actress. That fact worked out for her extremely well as she *preferred* the roles given to character actresses. She liked to point out that most of the truly successful women in theater and in Hollywood were the character actresses, not the ingénues.

She had moved more into directing a few years ago and had become something of a quiet force in Atlanta's professional theater community. She freelanced from theater to theater, and was highly sought after. Her shows usually played long and paid well.

I personally admired her. Unlike me, who had never really decided what to be when I grew up, she had made up her mind at thirteen and pursued it with a dogged determination that made her a little intimidating.

As I watched her commandeer and corral her players around the stage, a woman's voice behind me said, "Nothing says 'sounds of summer' like a bunch of butch women arguing about the true definition of *stage right*."

I turned around to see Talbot, my friendly wine merchant come striding across the lobby towards me. She was dressed in a black pinstriped blazer over a low-cut maroon blouse and a high-cut matching leather miniskirt. She had on maroon Manolo Blahnik pumps with impossibly high heels. It was definitely a power ensemble.

"Hey Talbot," I said, smiling as I closed the auditorium doors behind me. Miranda was having enough problems with the cast. They didn't need to add the distraction of Talbot's legs. "What brings you here?"

She rolled her eyes. "Oh, I'm using you as an excuse to get away from my sister. She belongs to one of those churches…oh, what do they call themselves? Southern Pentecostal…Evangelical…Disciples of Tom Cruise or some such thing. It's one of those churches where half the congregation is in the choir and everything is being projected on PowerPoint screens. She dragged me off to a revival tonight, of all places."

"A revival? They really have those?"

She nodded. "Oh yes! Big white tent in the parking lot. People getting healed. Speaking in tongues. All of it. I let her keep me there for an hour and a half before I faked a page and had to get away."

"I'm surprised you lasted that long."

She nodded. "Truthfully, I wouldn't have if it wasn't for a purse full of vodka miniatures." She looked around the lobby. "Things are looking good, but there is no refreshment stand yet."

I nodded. "You're telling me what I already know. It's time to stop focusing on the theater building and start focusing on the theater business."

She nodded a quick little nod. "You know it, sweetie. You've got a lot to get together if you are opening next month. But, let me be honest with you, you need to let me go to bat for you on the liquor license. You don't have much time, and no one downtown knows you."

"The thing is, Talbot, I can't commit to buying from you for three years. Hell, I don't even know if the show will run three days."

She smiled. "Look, you give me your word that, if you decide to make a go of this place I get an exclusive, I'll get you the event license, line you up with an attorney who'll get you the permanent one, and hell, I'll even hire your bartenders for you if you want. But, you've got to get this place going."

I thought about it for a minute and said, "Okay, deal. What do you need to get me started?"

"I need a check for five hundred to get things rolling."

I took a deep breath and suddenly felt a moment of terror rush over me. I was committing to something. I hadn't committed to anything terribly substantial in my life apart from my wife, and I wasn't bragging about how that had worked out. I began to think I would go tell Talbot to forget it, send the actors home, and just lock the door and go hide in Laine's attic. Then Zach came out of the men's room carrying a sponge and a can of bathroom cleaner, and I thought of him, my neighbors, my sister and future brother-in-law, my aunt: all the people who were rallying around this project for no real reason other than that I asked them to.

I took another deep breath. "Okay, sure. Checkbook's upstairs." I led her up.

Forty minutes later, I had sent Talbot on her way and had begun work on a business plan. Over the course of the next hour I made a ten-page list of things that needed to be done. I kept thinking it should depress me, but with each additional action item I recorded, I felt an odd sense of exhilaration. At least I had an idea of what I had to get done. Admittedly, one of them was to check Amazon to see if there was a book called *Starting a Theater for Dummies*.

Around ten, I heard Miranda call me from the auditorium. Assuming the troupe was ready to knock off for the night, I jumped up, folded the sheets and stuck them in by back pocket and dashed down the stairs. As I burst into the auditorium, I instead almost collided with Aidan.

I took a step backwards as he laughed at me. I couldn't believe he was there, and I don't mean that in a good way. I noticed Rachel standing behind his back silently pleading for me to understand. Her facial expression said to me that he wanted to come and she had no choice because he was an important author so please be pleasant. It's a powerful expression.

Aidan looked awed. "Van, this place is *amazing*. I hope you don't mind, *mon ami*, but Rachel was telling me about how much work you've done and I just had to see for myself." He suddenly noticed the bottle of wine he was holding. He quickly recovered and held it out to me. "Hey! Here! Congratulations! Consider this your theater-warming present."

Hesitantly, I took the bottle. It was a wonderfully gracious gesture on his part.

Damn it.

"Aidan! Thank you. You shouldn't have done that."

If I have learned nothing from my association with southern women, it's how to mask resentment with graciousness.

Zach, who had been sitting in the theater watching the rehearsal, said, "I've got some plastic cups tucked away downstairs."

Feeling trapped, I told him, "Well, go get them." A few moments later, I found myself sipping wine and escorting Aidan on a tour of the theater while the cast busily rehearsed "Hail, Hail Freedonia." Rachel and Zach tagged along, and I led him around behind the stage and up to one of the side boxes.

He took a step into the seatless box, looked over the edge below, and said, "I feel like a Muppet."

"Better that than Lincoln," I replied, momentarily fantasizing I was John Wilkes Booth.

Below, the cast sang out, "We're not allowed to tell a dirty joke. Hail, hail, Freedonia!"

"Who's the guy playing Groucho?"

"Her name is Cara."

At that moment Kelly, who was playing Mrs. Teasdale backed into the set, and came away covered in white paint.

"That's a woman?"

"Yep."

The rest of the cast, realizing Mrs. Teasdale's backside was now white, began to snicker. Groucho, née Cara, sang, "If chewing gum is chewed…"

Mrs. Teasdale realized people were laughing at her, and tried to look over her shoulder to see what was wrong with her backside. As she did, she stumbled into Lara, (a.k.a. "Wears English Leather"), who was nominally playing Harpo, and knocked her off balance. Lara stumbled towards the edge of the stage and, just before toppling over the edge, grabbed a large set pillar, knocking it over onto the rest of the cast.

The singing stopped.

Aidan turned and looked at me, "They, um, seem, um…"

I saved him from his struggle for the right word. “This is their first night on the stage. They’re still getting used to it.”

From below I heard Miranda say, “Okay, maybe Tara’s right and Groucho shouldn’t be standing next to Mrs. Teasdale.”

I led Aidan back out of the box, up the small hallway to the front of the theater. As we walked, I explained that the troupe was fairly young and their rendition of D*uck Soup* was being staged as a form of political protest theater against American adventurism in the Middle East. We reached my office and the four of us settled in to drink our wine.

“So, this show opens when?” he asked.

“Next month.”

“And how long is it supposed to run?”

“The month of July.”

“And then what?”

I looked at him blankly, not knowing what he meant. “It closes?”

He rolled his eyes. “I mean, what are you going to book in here after that?”

“I don’t know. Maybe nothing. I’m still not sure exactly what I’m doing. I find myself on the verge of running a theater with no real experience.”

He shrugged off my self-deprecation. “Previous experience is highly overrated. It can be bought. What do you *want* to do with it?”

“I don’t know,” I replied, realizing for the first time I was lying.

“You’re lying,” he told me, grinning. Again, I don’t like him.

“Why do you say that?”

“I can just tell. You’re different than you used to be. You’re doing this because you want something.”

A small alarm I had not heard since college sounded in the back of my head; the alarm that indicates someone was drifting dangerously close to my emotional perimeter. I decided evasion was the best response tactic. Pouring a little more wine into his cup, I replied, grinning, “Save the psychoanalysis for Manheim.”

He accepted the cup, winked at me over the rim, and said, “You know I’m right.”

I tried to ignore that Zach and Rachel were watching the two of us intently. “I know no such thing.”

He put the glass down, glanced at them, and said, "How far is this Virginia Highlands Inn?"

"Back south," I replied. "About a block from the bookstore."

"So I could walk it back?"

"Well, sure," Rachel replied. "But there's no need. I'm happy to..."

Aidan held up his hand. "No need. Actually, Rachel, I appreciate it, but I want to take my old friend here out for a drink."

"But your bags are in..."

I glanced at her, oddly intrigued. Although Aidan's never been hostile to me, he's also never shown any more desire for my company than I have for his. "Zach, pull Aidan's bags out of Rachel's car and throw 'em in the back of the VeggieRoll. I'll get him to the hotel."

Rachel looked slightly disappointed. "Well, okay."

Aidan jumped up. "Okay, it's settled."

He thanked Rachel and Zach, and before I knew it, we were all outside on the sidewalk saying goodbye. Then, he and I were walking towards Fontaine's. He put his arm around me in a collegial kind of way that implied an intimacy *we have never, ever shared!*

"Can I tell you a secret?" he asked.

He wasn't drunk. If there was one thing I was confident of, Aidan could hold his liquor. At my wedding I watched him polish off two full bottles of vodka and he was still able to shag.

I truly hoped he wouldn't tell me the secret. "Sure," I replied, hesitantly.

He held the door open for me. "Did you ever notice anything familiar about Manheim?"

It was one of those rare occasions when there were open seats at the bar. I took a moment to introduce Aidan to Jennifer, and to order drinks. She talked to us while she mixed them, so it was almost ten minutes before we could get back to the conversation. Unfortunately, he didn't forget, although I had hoped he would. We toasted each other, and then after drinking, he asked, "Well, did you?"

I sighed. "Familiar about Manheim?"

"Yeah."

I considered telling him I never read it, but something told me to behave. "Honestly, no. I think it's your best book, but no."

He grinned. "The reason I know you are looking for something else is because Manheim was." I was confused, and my face must have said so. "You still don't get it, do you? I based Manheim on you."

That caught me off guard. "You did what?"

"You're Manheim."

I considered Manheim. In the book, he was an office drone: a working man with brilliant political opinions who really desires to accomplish something, but was too terrified of taking a risk to actually make a difference.

In the book, Manheim has a brilliant legal mind, but he never pursues it. Life's circumstances conspire to force him into the middle of a labor-management dispute where he must take a stand. He conceives of a brilliant plan for resolving the dispute, but it requires him to risk everything: his job, his marriage, and his very concept of who he is as a man. The plan goes horribly wrong. In the end, Manheim is sitting in a bar, nearing his fiftieth birthday, contemplating the disaster his life has become, and yet congratulating himself for finally having taken a chance.

It took a long minute for what he was telling me to sink in, and I ignored the gentle sounds of Roberta Flack in the back of my head singing "Killing Me Softly."

"You son of a bitch."

He grinned. "C'mon. You really didn't know?"

I resisted the urge to punch him in the face. "Did Olivia know?"

He snorted his laughter. "Olivia? Do you really think Olivia ever actually *read* one of by books? Peddled them? Sure. Made money off of them? Of course. But read? Surely you jest."

I was speechless. I knew I should be angry, and perhaps was, a little. But more intrigued. "Why?"

"C'mon, Donovan. You have built your entire persona on being the slacker savant. The man who deliberately chose not to realize his potential. I've always believed that you don't really find any satisfaction in it though, and if you ever really put your mind to something, you would be hell on wheels. That inspired Manheim."

I drained my glass and signaled to Jennifer for two more, even though Aidan was still working on his. "But Manheim fails miserably at the end of the book."

"Yeah, well, if he had been an outrageous success, it wouldn't be a social commentary on Republicans. Hence why it was *so* successful." The emphasis portrayed a bitterness I knew he didn't really feel. He drained his drink. "Look, I never said it was a good book, I just said you inspired it."

After a long moment I said, "Despite your sarcasm, it *was* a good book. I'm not kidding when I say it's your best. It'll be the book you are remembered for."

He slid the empty glass across the bar as Jennifer brought his fresh one. "I never really think about how I will be remembered. All I care about is going to my grave knowing I tried something. Other people dream about trying things but don't. I wanted to try." He took a sip of the fresh drink, smiled approvingly and abruptly spun on me. "So! Because I know Manheim so well, I also suspect I know you better than I really do. And, here you sit, with a theater all your own. You wouldn't be busting your ass to restore it if you didn't secretly want to do something with it."

I rolled my eyes. "I'm not Manheim. I don't have any secret ambitions."

He stared at me a long minute before replying flatly. "Bullshit. In the years I've known you, you have only dedicated yourself heart and soul to two other things: your marriage and *Manhattan Gothic*. Neither would have got off the ground without you shouldering way more than your load. And now you are pouring yourself into this theater. You want it, and deep down, you even know what you want it for."

A sudden wave of emotion swept through me as the man I did not particularly care for paid me compliments I did not expect. Underneath the emotion, I knew he was right. I did want the theater. I wanted it desperately. I also knew I couldn't articulate it to this man who I had resented for so long.

No, let's be fair. I did not resent Aidan. I admired him. He was the writer I wanted to be. Hell, he was the man I wanted to be and I was insanely jealous.

As all of these realizations swept through me like waves crashing against the shore, I smiled weakly at him. "Olivia might have issue with you for saying that I carried more of our marriage."

He laughed and peered deeply into his drink. "Don't I know it."

We spent a very nice evening together during which I never answered his question, which he pointed out as I delivered him to his hotel at one in the morning. He got out of the VeggieRoll, leaned against the windshield and said, "So give. What is it? What's driving you?"

"I want to stage my own show," I admitted helplessly.

He smiled triumphantly. "I *knew* it!"

I shrugged. "I don't know where to start. I don't know the first thing about producing a play."

"Well, it seems to me you have a whole theater full of women who do. In the meantime, you're a writer aren't you? You absolutely do know where to start."

I felt a smile creep across my face, and our eyes met. We both said simultaneously, "At the key board."

I was up early on Friday. The festival vendors would begin setting up that afternoon, so Laine had decreed that there would be no work that weekend. "Since we are going to be trapped, we may as well enjoy ourselves." Her enjoinder extended to rehearsals as well. Every year, she had a tent set up in the front yard, and held court over a weekend-long hospitality booth. It would not be a hospitality booth open to the general public, however. It was *by invitation only.* Of course, everyone in the building had been invited, along with thirty or forty of Laine's neighbors and close friends. And the entire cast and crew of the show. Plus several flight attendants that Chris brought with him each year. And the staff of Ponce Pages. And the symphony.

Just an intimate little gathering.

At noon, Virginia would be closed so the vendors and artists could set up their booths. It was a juried show, which meant you had to be selected by a panel of judges to get in. (In case you are curious, Brit had not been selected. Not one to be discouraged, she was going to display her wares discreetly within Laine's pavilion.) The show would officially begin around six with a cookout in the park for neighborhood residents only, but Laine explained that most of the artists would open anyhow.

So, while trucks and trailers busily came and went on Virginia, depositing crates of pottery and photographs and jewelry and paintings and sculpture and ...well, you get the point...Zach and I helped the gentlemen from the rental place to erect a small circus tent – appropriate for wedding receptions and commitment ceremonies – across the length and breadth of the front lawn. We finished at noon, and the truck pulled away as the police began pulling barricades across the street. We were now officially trapped in the festival for the duration.

After lunch, the real setup began. We followed behind Laine as she descended the driveway to show us where all the party decorations were.

"You really don't need to go to the basement," Zach protested. "Just tell us where things are and we'll figure it out."

"Zachary dear, I'm not an invalid. Besides, I want things set up a specific way."

Under her careful supervision, we set up a portable bar in the corner of the tent with multiple ice chests. Then, elaborate strings of lights were strung back and forth across the tent. She had a couple of silk ficuses that were placed in the corner opposite the bar, and a fairly complicated metal arbor that served as the gated entrance. We ran a silk rope all the way around the perimeter of the tent, draping it from each of the poles at chest height, and she came behind us hanging small signs from it that informed the curious that it was a private party and for invited guests only. I noticed that the signs were white and used the same font as Olivia had chosen for our wedding invitations.

Around three, as Zach and I, huffing and puffing, tried to drag a large faux-stone fountain up the driveway to its designated spot in the center of the pavilion, we heard a large number of expletives being shouted loudly from in front of the building. Whereas that would have hardly merited my attention in Manhattan, it was so far out of context in Atlanta that it jarred me. Not that Atlantans don't curse, mind you. They just usually do it discreetly, usually while smiling through clenched jaws.

We completed hauling the fountain to the pavilion, and dropped it about where I thought it should go. "This right?" I asked Laine, who was busy picking dead leaves off of a boxwood, so no casual observer would *dare* think she was watching the spectacle in the street, which she was.

"Hmm?" she asked absently without turning around. In the street, a man, red faced, was leaning out of an absurdly oversized SUV, yelling at a police officer manning the street barricade. Idling behind him was a Bekins truck.

Zach and I came up on either side of her and I asked, quietly, "What's the scene for?"

While still picking at the hedge she replied quietly, "As near as I can tell, the uncouth fellow is the new owner of the monstrosity. He was apparently unaware that the street would be closed for the weekend, and this is the first of three loads of furniture that need to be delivered to his house."

Zach began fiddling with the shrub as well. Being from New York, I felt no compunction about watching. The police officer patiently tried to engage the guy in the truck, smiling in a friendly manner, only to be repeatedly cut off by another tirade.

At that moment, I learned that southern subtlety also extended to the police...but only so far. The officer in question was a large, friendly guy who regularly patrolled our neighborhood. I had seen with him on a couple of occasions and knew that, despite his friendly demeanor, he could be menacing. It became quite clear that he had had enough of the tirade. The smile left his face, and he pushed his sunglasses up onto his forehead. He stood up, not so subtly unsnapping his holster as he did so, and walked directly to the truck. I couldn't hear what he was saying, but two catcher's-mitt-sized hands grabbed the car door and yanked it open. The man in the SUV was commanded down onto the street.

The guy had suddenly caught on that yelling at a Georgia cop was not the smartest thing he could do. (It's not officially the dumbest, either, by the way. I know of another guy who discovered the very dumbest thing you can do is to kick a Georgia police dog, but I digress.) He stepped nervously out of the truck. He was about five-foot-five, with short blond hair and round steel wire frame glasses, and a softness that suggested a profound need to exercise. The officer, on the other hand, at six-six, two-eighty, loomed over him, glaring down and explaining something in a very controlled, menacing manner. He pointed south down Highland and then jabbed his finger indicating the man needed to be headed in that direction immediately.

I could actually see the guy's Adam's apple bob up and down as he swallowed. He scurried back to the Bekins truck, said something quickly to the driver, and they were off immediately heading south.

As soon as they were gone, Laine called out, "Hey, Raymond. It's awfully hot out here. You want a Coke?"

The smile immediately returned to the cop's face. "Love one, Miss DeLaine. Thank you. Any kind is fine."

I should mention that, in the South, all carbonated beverages are called Cokes, even if they are Schweppes diet tonic water.

Laine instructed Zachary to go inside and retrieve a soda for the officer. He did so as Raymond sauntered across the street.

Laine introduced me immediately since to have not done so would have been rude. While we shook hands, she treated each of us to a brief biography of the other. Once Zach returned, introductions were repeated, although Raymond received a significantly scaled-down version of Zach's biography.

As he accepted the Coke, Raymond asked how Laine's leg was healing. She recounted a brave tale of her recovery from total incapacitation that may actually have been the plot of something by Tennessee Williams. He countered with a story of his Aunt Selma who had endured the same thing, and several family remedies that had helped her recover.

Finally, in the most offhand of manners, Laine asked innocently, "Was there some sort of trouble with that truck before?"

Raymond, being a southern gentleman, would never dare point out that the lady had been standing there eavesdropping on the whole damn thing, and explained that our newest neighbor had been unaware of the festival and things had become a little heated. However, Raymond had directed him to a back route that would take him to a cross street "near his new house where they could park the truck, and it would be just a short walk to carry the furniture up the street to his new home."

The cross street Raymond had directed him to was Ponce de Leon Place, a major connecting street in the neighborhood, and a good six blocks from where the monstrosity sat.

At six o'clock, we were instructed to open the bar. Laine arrived in the front yard wearing black pedal pushers and a long purple, gold, and green paisley silk jacket with a long purple scarf draped across her throat and over each shoulder. Both Zach and I had earlier been dispatched to shower and get cleaned up, with explicit instructions to be back at five forty-five. I was attending as a guest; she had engaged Zach to be the bartender. It occurred to me that Zach's earnings this year might well be on track to exceed my own.

Laine settled herself onto a white wrought-iron chaise lounge near the front of the tent where she could have a grand, unobstructed view of the street below. As she sat, she told me, "I very much approve of the outfit you have chosen. It's the way a true southern gentleman should dress for an afternoon event like this."

I was wearing a pair of linen pants, a blue and yellow striped shirt, and a pair of topsiders. Being a man who is not typically complimented on his attire, I'm sure I blushed as I thanked her. "Can I get you a drink?"

"Of course, dear. The usual."

Zach had never heard of a manhattan, so I had to show him how to make it. Laine had very strict standards. It had to be made with Canadian Club, and she always liked a dash of maraschino juice from the jar tossed in when it was mixed. He sampled it and smiled approvingly. I reminded him that he was underage and not to do anything that would get Laine into trouble. He rolled his eyes, but nodded understandingly.

As I brought the drink back over to Laine, she let me know she had overheard me. "Don't come down too hard on him," she informed me. "Although things have certainly changed around here in the last twenty years, there is still a basic understanding that children should learn how to drink at home. Why, every mother in my circle considers it a point of pride that their daughters know how to serve a drink before they can drive. It's the making of a good host."

"Do you think the cops would agree to that?" I asked, settling into the Adirondack chair next to her.

"If they had a proper upbringing, they would," she replied, sipping the drink.

We shared a few moments of companionable silence, just as my mother and I would occasionally. Emboldened by the comfort of the moment, I ventured, "Laine, I've been thinking about trying to keep the theater open after *Soup* closes."

She seemed to be expecting the conversation, but kept her tone light. She took another sip of her manhattan, and gazed down the block to where moving men were huffing and puffing a pool table up the front steps of the monstrosity. "Really? Well, I would certainly like to see us get some use out of the place if we aren't going to get income. What did you have in mind doing with it?"

"Um, I was considering staging my own show."

She turned to regard me with one arched eyebrow. "Do you have a show written?"

"No..."

"Then, my dear, hadn't you better get to work on it?"

"Get to work on what?" a familiar voice asked, and we turned to see Miranda come walking across the tent, accompanied by her partner, Liz. I had never met Liz before, but had heard from many people that she was charming, soft spoken, and probably the most ruthless litigation attorney practicing on Peachtree.

"Miranda, darling," Laine exclaimed. "I'm so glad you could join us!"

Miranda introduced Liz, and cocktails were immediately secured for them. As they gathered around my aunt, Laine informed them, "Donovan was just telling me that, when *Duck Soup* closes, he would like to keep the theater going to stage a show of his own."

I stared at my aunt, aghast that she would blurt this out. She regarded my shocked expression for a moment, and then waved it away, commenting, "Don't be embarrassed, darling. If you are going to go into theater, you are going to need the pressure to actually produce something."

"I think it is a great idea," Miranda observed. "There are a lot of theater companies like ours that need venues. And, there's a real appetite for original material in this city."

"Well, thanks," I stammered, "but it is still conceptual at this point. I don't even have the faintest idea of a storyline yet."

The conversation ended abruptly as Charles and Brit rounded the corner and came up the steps to join us. We exchanged greetings and then, almost immediately, Clare and Mac emerged from the building. This began a long procession of friends and neighbors arriving to pay their respects as Laine held court over Virginia Avenue.

"Did you ask Mister Kersey to come?" Clare asked Laine.

"Of course dear. Well, I left him a note. He won't come, but I never want him to feel unwelcome."

At that moment, Bitsy Hollander arrived. Laine struggled to her feet as Bitsy was helped up the steps by a man in his late twenties or early thirties who I later learned was named Kenny. I assumed Kenny was a grandson, but later realized by the discreet lack of engagement he was receiving from Laine, the he was actually Bitsy's current boy-toy.

Bitsy herself was probably Laine's contemporary but had not held up nearly as well. Admittedly, the woman was only three weeks out of a hysterectomy, but the short white bob surrounding a plethora of wrinkles were the tell-tale sign of a woman motivated more by golf than emollients. She had on a teal pantsuit with a yellow blouse and spanking white accessories.

"Bitsy! What in the world are you doing here? The doctor said you aren't supposed to be up and around yet."

Bitsy smiled warmly and came forward to kiss Laine on the cheek. "M'dear, the absence of a uterus is not sufficient reason to miss one of your shindigs. Besides, I thought it would be easier to get here tonight then try to navigate the crowd and traffic this weekend."

Laine waved me over and started to introduce her to me. Bitsy, however, mistook me for a waiter and glanced at me, smiled absently, and said, "Scotch. Neat."

Laine and I made eye contact, as a mortified look spread across her face. "No, Bitsy, darling, this is my nephew."

I held up my hand. "Drinks first," I walked behind the bar to pour the drink myself.

"Who's the walnut?" Zach asked quietly.

"Bitsy Hollander," I replied, seeing no reason to correct him. "Old friend of Laine's."

Having figured out my identity, Bitsy accepted the drink from me a little more graciously. Before I had a chance to talk to her, they were joined by Frieda Harrelson, a local magazine publisher in her late forties, and her date, who knew Laine from a stint on the board of directors of Callanwolde Fine Arts Center. Following them were Pamela and Phipps Harrington, who had met Laine years earlier at the Piedmont Driving Club.

I sat on the periphery of this polite gathering of southern gentry and watched something fascinating happen. As soon as everyone had met everyone, and drinks had been passed about, the party almost immediately divided. The women sat in a circle of chairs next to the fountain, politely gossiping about people not present with a heavy peppering of "God bless her soul," while the men gravitated to the edge of the tent and discussed business and politics. What became apparent is that, although these two societies co-existed harmoniously, the South, for all practical purposes, is a matriarchy.

"His name is Archer Bellamy," Bitsy informed the crowd, referring to the identity of the new owner of the monstrosity. "He's moving into town from Alpharetta."

"Good God, why?" Laine asked, horrified. Alpharetta is a town out in the northern suburbs that contains opulent new-money subdivisions. Its residents were all stereotyped as terrified of coming inside the Perimeter.

"Same reason they all come," Bitsy sniffed. "To get away from the traffic out there. He does something at FCOTLIC and the commute was getting to him."

"Well that explains the horrific styling of the place," Frieda observed. "It's sort of a neo-gothic, tudor-brothel look. It would fit in perfectly in Alpharetta."

"I suppose the house could be forgiven," Laine observed, "but his behavior in the street today concerned me. He seemed a little too self-important for his own good."

"That's that Alpharetta mindset, darling," Bitsy concluded. "As I always say when I'm up there: 'an ounce of pretension is worth a pound of manure.'"

Sometime a little before eight, Miranda detached herself from the group to get another drink, and then joined me on the sidelines where I was observing. "Your aunt is quite the character."

"She is, indeed," I replied. "Then again, being 'quite the character' seems somewhat mandatory for southern society women. From what I've seen, the real power lies with the women."

She nodded her agreement and took a sip of her beer. "It is indeed. Funny you should say that. I never thought about it before, but you're right. The real power of the south is its women. I wouldn't just stop at genteel society though. You ever go to a poor black church and watch the dynamics there, it's the same thing. The South may be run by men, but it's *owned* by women."

She turned and winked at me. "That's where you should look for your play."

Most of the guests meandered away around eight, and so Laine told Zach and me to close up the bar. Even though the festival didn't officially begin until the next morning, most of the vendors went ahead and opened up that evening for the benefit of the locals. Once we had locked up the liquor, Zach reiterated his offer to buy us dinner from one of the vendors. So, we loaded Laine up into her wheelchair, and the three of us set off to explore the show.

The art was mostly quite good, some of it certainly on a par with some openings I had been to in Soho. Of course, there was also a plethora of folk art from the Howard Finster school, which I'm not at all fond of. But, since I know what the Whitney paid for a Finster, more power to those artists.

The food vendors were about three blocks down, well over half way to the other end, so it was a nice leisurely stroll. As we passed the monstrosity, we could see the two movers huffing and puffing as they carried yet another widescreen television up the sidewalk. Laine reached into the bosom of her blouse and produced a twenty, which she handed to Zach. "Zach, be a dear and go fetch two bottles of water from that vendor over there."

Zach complied, and we spent a few moments lingering over a tent filled with raku pottery. He returned just as the two movers were emerging from the carved teak front doors. Laine took the bottles and instructed me to roll her over to them.

"Gentlemen," she announced. "I've been watching you from my yard and you must be absolutely dehydrated. Here. Please take these."

The smiles that broke across their faces indicated that she was correct. They both smiled, came forward to meet her and accepted the water with grateful "Thank you, ma'am"s.

Being the South, it would have been rude not to linger for a minute. So, they each opened the water and drank. "Mighty lot of furniture going in there," Laine observed.

The taller of the two men nodded, wiping sweat from his forehead. "Is indeed. We still got one more truckload to go."

"Well, I imagine it takes a lot to fill up a place so grand."

Before either could answer, they were interrupted by the owner of the house, who emerged, fairly shrieking, "Hey! I'm paying you two losers to move furniture, not stand around. Get moving!"

The two beat a hasty retreat back towards the truck and Laine, although a bit startled, took her wheels and rolled herself forward a little. "My apologies, sir. I'm the one who distracted them. I'm your new neighbor, DeLaine Fairchild. Welcome to..."

Archer Bellamy stomped down the front steps, mostly ignoring her. "Yeah, whatever lady." He stopped, put his hands on his hips and stared at the retreating backs of the movers, as if his menacing look could somehow intimidate them from behind.

Laine, a little nonplussed, continued. "Um, well, anyway, I'm sure you're going to enjoy living here in the Highla..."

Bellamy spun around, still irritated, as if he had just noticed she was talking to him. "Huh?" he snapped.

The most indulgent smile I have ever seen her muster crept across the lower half of her face, noticeably absent from her eyes. Her voice fairly dripped southern hospitality. "I can see you're quite the busy man, so let me cut to the point. A bit of advice: no one in this neighborhood will hold buying one of these gawd-awful, white-trash, new-money infills against you. Lack of graciousness, however, will turn the neighbors against you as resolutely as if you were Al Qaeda." The shocking contrast of the biting sarcasm against the syrupy sweet tone began to slowly register across his face as she turned herself slowly and majestically around. "Again, welcome to the neighborhood." With that, she gave herself a jaunty little push forward and rolled on towards a booth of sepia-tinted photographs, Zach and me in tow.

I glanced over my shoulder briefly as a variety of emotions played out across Bellamy's puffy red face, and exchanged smirks with Zach. "That was quite a welcome to the neighborhood," I told her.

She cast her eyes heavenward ever so briefly from the matted five-by-seven she was examining and sighed, "Poor benighted rube, God bless his soul."

The festival kicked off the next morning with a 5K road race. I was oblivious to it, however. I had given myself the morning off from running, and was sitting on the deck wearing a pair of boxers and working on my laptop, trying to capture some of the dialog I had heard from the previous evening. On some level, I was aware of a lot of footsteps, and someone talking over a loudspeaker, but not enough to actually get up and look over the parapet.

The door from the stairs opened and Chris stumbled out, bleary eyed, in a pair of boxers and a tank top. He was carrying an empty coffee mug. Without saying a word, he went into my apartment and filled it from my coffeemaker.

"Morning, Sunshine," I said as he slumped into the chair next to me. He favored me with a look of sarcastic affection, and then stared deeply into his coffee cup. "You're up early."

"I couldn't sleep with all the noise from the street."

It occurred to me that there *had* been a lot of noise from the street and I asked him, "Yeah, what's going on anyhow?"

He took a sip of the coffee. "Virginia Highland's 5K. They run it every year at the start of the festival." He reached over and helped himself to a cigarette from my pack.

"Really? I didn't know."

He nodded as he lit the cigarette with my lighter. "It's one of about ten neighborhood 5Ks leading up to the Peachtree."

"The Peachtree?"

He took a deep drag on the cigarette and leaned back in the chair, his eyes closed against the morning sun. "Peachtree Road Race. The world's biggest 10K."

"The world's biggest?" I scoffed.

"*Es verdad.*" When he wanted to be cute, he occasionally slipped Spanish in with English. "Fifty-five thousand people running down Peachtree Road from Lenox Mall to Piedmont Park."

"Really?" I said again, seeing he was serious. "Fifty-five *thousand*?"

"Uh huh. It's run on Fourth of July morning. Biggest street party you will ever see."

"Have you ever run it?"

He opened his eyes and shot me a sardonic look. In lieu of answering, he held up the cigarette and waved it slightly. As he closed his eyes again, I mused loudly, "We should run it."

At that moment, Zach emerged from the stairway, also with an empty coffee cup. "We should run what?" he asked. Zach had begun to assume he was included in all building goings-on.

"Run the Peachtree."

He snorted as he crossed to my apartment door. "Yeah, right."

I sat there, indignant, waiting for him to return. "What do you mean 'yeah, right'? And by the way, when the hell did my apartment become Starbucks?"

They both ignored my latter question. Before Zach could answer my first one, Chris leaned forward, cleared his throat dramatically, and held up his cigarette in my face again.

"So what?" I said defensively. "I hardly smoke at all. And besides, I run two miles every morning. That should more than make up for the smoking."

"There's a difference between running two miles through the tree-lined streets of the Highlands at six in the morning when it's still cool and running six point two miles down Peachtree at nine when it's like a million degrees."

"Besides," Zach offered in a conciliatory tone, "It's not all that easy a race. The first two miles are downhill, but the next four are all uphill. The grade is so steep in front of Piedmont Hospital, they call it Cardiac Hill."

"Wait a minute," I said to Zach, taking another drag on my cigarette. "You've run it?"

He nodded. "In high school."

"Well, if you can do it, I can do it."

Chris snorted laughter. "*Sure* you can. The fact that he's a healthy, non-smoking twenty-year-old, and you're in the latter half of your thirties and smoke a pack a day should have *no* bearing on your performance."

I gave him a churlish look, and stood up to go refill my coffee cup with *my* coffee. As I returned, Chris tried to sound a little more conciliatory. "Besides, race numbers are incredibly hard to come by. If you haven't registered on the day they come out in March, you're S.O.L. Tell you what. A bunch of us meet that morning at a place on Peachtree call The Mug. Come watch it with us. You can run it next year."

"I may not be here next year. I've got to go back to my real life at some point."

Our eyes met, and something indefinable passed between us. Zach interrupted the moment by saying, "Well, with all her contacts, I'm sure Auntie Laine could score us numbers."

"You want to run it?"

He nodded. "Sure. Someone's got to be there to call the ambulance when you collapse."

I rolled my eyes, but said nothing. He continued, "Seriously Van, it's not an easy course. If you are going to run it, you really ought to give up smoking. Cut back, at least."

I stared at my cigarette for a moment. I had taken up smoking when my mother was dying. It had given me something to put energy into at the hospital. There is no bigger waste of energy than that generated by people sitting in hospital waiting rooms. If we could harness it, we could power a city.

It was also a legacy from my past life. Olivia hated it. Truth be told, I hated it. Even though I couldn't smell it, I had always been embarrassed when people I trust told me how bad it smelled on me. I took a drag and looked at Chris. "Whaddaya say?"

He regarded me warily through narrow eyes. "What do I say to what?"

"Give up smoking with me."

He grabbed his throat and said dramatically, "Clutch the pearls and gasp!"

"Seriously, let's give it up."

He rolled his eyes and took another drag defiantly. "You're the one who wants to run the stupid race. I'm perfectly happy spending my July fourth sitting on the sidelines, drinking mimosas and *smoking my damn cigarettes.*"

I grinned at him. "No you're not. You sit on the sidelines, because you don't believe you can do it. Take a chance."

I saw a momentary flash in his eyes that indicated I had hit a nerve. There was a deeper truth there than I suspected. "It's too late for me to start training. The fourth is only a month away."

"No one says you have to run the whole thing," Zach offered, swept up in the camaraderie. "We can run-walk it."

"Besides," I said, "You know you are starting to get a little pudgy looking. You've got sort of a mid-thirties spread going on."

His eyes narrowed further, clearly unamused. "That's a cheap shot to take at a gay man and you know it. Besides, if I look like I'm gaining weight, the last thing I'm going to do is give up smoking. What will I hold in my hands when I'm drinking if I don't hold a cigarette? A canned ham?"

I stubbed out my cigarette in the ashtray and held it out to him. "C'mon. We'll help each other through it."

He inhaled on the cigarette defiantly. There was a long, long pause, during which he never took his eyes off me. He exhaled the smoke in two sharp, angry streams through each nostril and then reached out and stubbed it out in the ashtray.

"Good job," I congratulated him. "Trust me, you'll be glad you did this."

"Maybe I will," he said dubiously, "but I doubt you will. I reserve the right to be an unholy bitch to you whenever I crave a cigarette."

Chris, Zach, and I spent much of the rest of the festival camped out on the front lawn, working on our tans and having cocktails with whoever came and went. Laine continued to hold court under the awning. When no one was about, she would lament the fact that she couldn't go out and shop. Finally, the three of us succumbed to guilt and wheeled her out through the festival, checkbook in hand. One of us would push her and the other two were delegated to carry her purchases.

We had finished the south side of the street and were turning to amble back up the north when she asked me, in the most offhand manner, "What have you been scribbling in your notebook all morning?"

It may have been that the alcohol and the humidity were magnifying each other's effect, but I think it is more likely that I was extremely self-conscious about my writing, because I became painfully aware of the rivulets of sweat running down my bare back. "Oh, not much. Just some ideas I had for a story," I said.

Much to my surprise, I did not miss cigarettes at all. But I needed to do something with the energy that, in the past, would have been channeled into the activity of smoking. Most people I know in the same situation had channeled that activity into eating, which Chris and I were committed to prevent each other from doing. So instead, I had channeled it into writing, while he was spending the afternoon agitatedly stirring his martinis.

But the truth of the matter was that I had been scribbling furiously about my aunt. Miranda's comment from the previous evening had struck a cord with me. The southern *grande dame* was a fascinating source of material. I realize others had mined it before, but from what I could see the motherlode had not run dry yet. I could milk it for a bit more.

"What kind of ideas?" Zach asked, earnestly.

I pretended not to hear him. "Laine, do you know of any way for us to score three numbers for the Peachtree Road Race?"

"I'm sure I do. Why?"

"The three of us are going to run it."

"Really!?!? How marvelous. Is that why you aren't smoking today?"

Chris and I exchanged glances. Not much escapes my aunt. "It is."

"Well, I can't say I look forward to the two of you going through nicotine withdrawal, but I certainly applaud your efforts. Let me think a minute." We endured a long pause while she admired a collection of wrought-iron sunflowers. "Analise Schuler has a son-in-law who is very big in the Atlanta Track Club. I'll call her tomorrow and ask if she could prevail on him for some numbers. I'm afraid they will be well in the back of the race, however."

"That's okay," Chris replied. "I wouldn't want to embarrass myself in front of the Kenyans."

Laine and Zach both laughed appreciatively. "Kenyans?" I asked.

Chris explained, "The first two time groups are seeded times. Meaning you have to qualify for those groups through times you've achieved in other races. People come from all over the world, and for the last couple of years the winners have all been from Kenya. It's something of a joke. Each year when I'm at The Mug, they announce that the race has begun. Half of us immediately order a new drink. Five minutes later, when you go back out on the patio, all the Kenyans run by. Then the rest of us go get a drink. Ten minutes later, the rest of the runners come by. It's nicely timed."

I put an arm around his bare shoulder, noting he was sweating as much as I. "And just think, this year you'll get to run by, instead."

"Yeah," he replied. "Somehow that doesn't strike me nearly as desirable as the cocktail."

When we returned to the house, Miranda and a couple of the members of the troupe were lounging under the awning. Several of them had bags of art, including Cara, who had an enormous galvanized metal sculpture of Kokopelli. All of them were sipping beers, and greeted us enthusiastically as we rolled Laine up the driveway.

"Ah, my lovely Marx Sisters are here," Laine gushed as she struggled to her feet and up the steps. "How are y'all enjoying the festival?"

They were all enjoying it quite well. Miranda jumped up from a chair, and Laine eased herself down into it. Zach carried the bags of art into the house, and Chris stepped behind the bar to begin mixing us a fresh batch of martinis.

"Miss DeLaine," Miranda began, "We've been talking about you as we wandered the festival and we had an idea we wanted to discuss with you."

"What's that, dear?" she asked as I removed the thermos of manhattans from the back of the wheelchair and replenished the Baccarat rocks glass she had been drinking from while rolling along.

"Well, you may not know this but Gay Pride is the last weekend in June," Miranda began.

Laine smiled at her indulgently over her cocktail. "Dear girl, I lived in midtown for sixty years. I'm intimately aware of when Gay Pride is."

"Of course you are," Miranda beamed. "Anyway, to help drive publicity for *Soup,* we've decided to all march in the parade this year."

"Of course you have, dear. That makes perfect sense. But what does that have to do with me?"

"Well, here's the thing. You are doing a great thing by opening up the theater for us to put this show on, so we'd like to recognize you. We also think there is a story there that we can capitalize on in the gay and lesbian media. So, we'd like to have you join us in the parade."

"But she's not gay," I blurted out.

"So?" Miranda asked, favoring me with a smile that was a bit strained. "The parade is open to everyone."

"How marvelous," Laine exclaimed, clapping one hand against her knee and nearly upsetting her cocktail. "But I'm afraid I'm not up to walking that whole route dear, and I absolutely will not be pushed in a wheelchair."

"There's no need to," Chris added, as he walked up and handed me a fresh martini. "You could ride in the back of the VeggieRoll and Donovan can drive you."

My head snapped about. "Me?"

"Sure. Why not?"

"Why not indeed!" Laine exclaimed. "Miranda, could we have the car in the parade?"

"I don't see why not. We might have to pay something extra, but I doubt it will be much."

"I'll pay it," Laine exclaimed. "Oh what fun. I haven't ridden in a parade since the Charleston Christmas Parade when I was seventeen."

"Um," I began, "Laine, you do realize this is *Gay Pride*? It'll be a lot more like Mardi Gras than anything Charleston ever staged."

She rolled her eyes at me. "Of *course* I do, dear. I've been to it before. Christopher, you must ride with us as well. And Zach. Hell, the car's big enough, we could probably get the whole *building* in it if we tried."

I started to say something else, but Chris took me by the arm and steered me backwards, away from my aunt. As soon as we reached the front steps, he said quietly, "Quit looking for a way out of this. You are going to do it."

"Look," I began, "the issue is…"

He held up his hand, silencing me. "No issue. This is important to your aunt. It's important to the theater. You're going to do it."

I startled to bristle. No one *tells* me what to do. "Look…"

"No, you look. I've helped you restore your theater because you asked me to. I'm giving up smoking because you asked me to. I'm getting up early on July fourth and running the goddamn Peachtree Road Race because you asked me to. I'm asking you to do this."

My anger immediately gave way to shame. I nodded, helplessly, as the front doors open and Zach emerged. He took the two of us in and asked, warily, "What's going on?"

Chris smiled, released my arm and turned to our young protégé with a more open, joyful expression than I've ever seen him muster. "Donovan is going to drive you and Laine and me in the parade at Gay Pride."

I had had relatively little to drink the previous evening, so I was surprised to awake on Sunday morning with what felt like a monstrous hangover. I had a headache, my mouth was dry, and my throat unbelievably sore. I was also craving a cigarette so badly, the thought of having one practically gave me an erection.

I forced myself out of bed and put on my running togs, even though running was the last thing I desired to do. Both Chris and Zach had committed to begin training with me that morning, so I descended the stairs to meet them. Predictably, Zach was waiting, Chris was not.

Impatiently, I pounded on his apartment door. After several minutes of pounding, he answered the door, looking like hell. He was wrapped in the comforter off his bed, and his hair most closely resembled an artichoke. He opened the door and said sourly. "Not going this morning."

"C'mon. You promised."

"I only got about twelve minutes of sleep last night. And I woke up once in the middle of that."

"You're not going to be able to run if you don't start training."

Chris hardly ever displays any mood except bemused sarcasm, so I was unprepared for the nostril-flaring snap I received. "I *said,* I'm not going." The door slammed shut in my face.

I turned and looked at Zach, who was watching wide-eyed. "I guess he's not going."

While nicotine withdrawal may have made Chris an irritable insomniac, it made me loopy. In addition to feeling like hell, I was unable to concentrate on anything. Fortunately it was Sunday, so I didn't have much to do except sit under the awning, watch the festival, and write. But it extended into the next day. At breakfast, I had intended to make soft-boiled eggs, but instead cracked them into the pot of boiling water. Laine suffered through her breakfast of egg drop soup with a minimum of commentary. I also managed to back over a bougainvillea with the VeggieRoll, tried to wax the foyer floor with oil-soap, and called Bitsy Hollander Olivia. (I'm sure, somewhere in Manhattan, Liv got indignant at the moment with no idea why.)

All the action at the theater had not gone unnoticed by the community, and almost every day we had drop-ins from curious neighbors or bar patrons. Eventually, one of them turned out to be a young reporter for a local free paper. He couldn't have been more than twenty-four. On a whim, I bought him a couple of drinks, and in exchange we got a article on the show, with a small insert article about the theater and an interview with Laine. That kicked off a bit more media, and soon we had notices for the show in every free publication in Atlanta.

By the third week in June, I had outlined my entire script. It was about a man—loosely based on me—who finds himself the object of affection of two close friends— loosely based on Chris and Rachel—while caring for his eccentric aunt, Virginia Highland—a blatant rip-off of my aunt. Miranda and I had been spending quite a lot of time together, so I gave her a copy of my work one evening after rehearsal and asked her to take a look at it and give me her thoughts.

She arrived early for rehearsal the next day and wandered upstairs to find me in my office. She gingerly laid the outline down in front of me, carefully placing it in the center of my desk.

I looked up at her nervously and found myself wishing for perhaps the fortieth time that day that I still smoked. "What do you think?"

She took a deep breath and sat down. "Well, I think you are a very good writer. And, I think you have done a very good job of capturing what an aging southern grande dame should be like. But Donovan, there is no way in hell you should *ever* finish that script."

My heart sank. "Why not?"

"Because there is no doubt who those characters are. I don't even know Chris and Rachel all that well and I can tell from the outline you are writing about them. Once you actually assign dialogue to them, there will be no question. And I will tell you I have been in the theater long enough to know that very few people are *ever* happy with how they are portrayed on stage."

I sighed heavily. "Maybe you're right. I just thought it would be a good story."

"I think it *is* a good story. The characters are just too close to reality. Plus, you've already figured out that the real star of the show is the grande dame dialogue. The thirty-something characters don't play well into that."

I had an inspiration. "Hey. Suppose I still made the main character the center of the love triangle, but I made the Chris-type character and the Rachel-type character peers of the aunt."

Her eyes brightened. "Now *that* could really work. A grande dame, an elderly queen, and an elderly, African-American woman would let you capitalize on three southern archetypes."

"And, then *all* the dialogue could reflect that southern sensibility."

"And, if you set the show specifically in Atlanta, you can use those characters to make fun of the people we all know. For example, if you write the Rachel character as having spent her life in Sweet Auburn, every black member of the audience is going to think they know who she is. If the aunt is from Buckhead, then you can make fun of all those stereotypes. Same thing with the old queen. The only other character you might need is an old dyke from Decatur."

We both laughed. "I think I could write this."

"I'm sure you can write it. And, if you let me, I know I can stage it in such a way that it'll be a hit."

We smiled across the desk at each other. "Is this the start of an artistic partnership?"

"I believe it is. We could be the next Gilbert and Sullivan!"

"Didn't they not speak to each other?"

Gilbert and Sullivan's personal differences aside, that began one of my most prolific weeks ever as a writer. I could think of nothing else but the script. In all my years of writing, I had never been in such a zone. Almost everyone noticed that my mind was elsewhere. Chris commented on it while we were out running in the mornings. Zach commented on it while we were doing yard work. Laine and Brit both commented on it over dinner. For the most part, I just explained it away as having a story on my mind. Only Miranda knew what I was really working on.

I delivered the first draft to her the following Saturday. She arrived to my office before rehearsal on Sunday, beaming. She slapped it down on my desk, leaned forward and said, "This is screaming to be a musical."

The Monday of the fourth week in June officially kicked off Atlanta's Gay Pride festival. All of us in the building –apart from Mr. Kersey, of course - began the week by attending the Premiere Party as Laine's guests. Unbeknownst to me, she had signed up *Theater DeLaine* (our new moniker) as one of the sponsors for the event. It was held at a special events venue downtown to benefit CHRISKids Rainbow program, a transitional living program for homeless gay and lesbian youth (a program Zach could have benefited from had he actually ever asked anyone for help).

Although I really did not want to be away from my computer for an entire evening, it was communicated to me that I was more or less expected to be there. Plus, I had been pounding away on a keyboard nonstop for a week, and I probably needed some company.

Laine, Chris, Zach, and I arrived at the event in the VeggieRoll, which commanded no small amount of attention. The event was a mammoth cocktail party surrounded by an incredible silent auction. As soon as we came inside, Laine found someone she knew and they wandered off into the VIP room. Chris and Zach disappeared into the crowd, leaving me alone. I began to examine the items in the silent auction. Idly, I bid fifty dollars on a pair of comedy and drama masks.

Unbidden, a glass of wine appeared over my left shoulder. Turning, I saw Talbot holding it out to me. "Hello dahling."

"Hey babe." I kissed her on the cheek and accepted the wine. "What brings you out to this?"

She glanced around. "How can you ask? So many lovely men."

"Well, yeah...but this is the kickoff for Gay Pride."

She shrugged. "I like a man who plays hard to get."

"Well, in that case you're in for a wonderful evening."

We wandered the tables and tables of items, bidding on various things according to whim and chatting idly. After about maybe fifteen tables, Talbot stopped suddenly, knocked a very petite young woman out of the way, and bid on something.

"What are you bidding on?" I asked.

"A bartender."

"Beg pardon?"

She held up a picture of a very cute young guy with a description of what was being sold. She read it aloud. "Six hours of professional bartender service from Ian Grace, experienced, licensed bartender."

"What a great auction item," I observed. "You buy that and use him for, say, a Christmas party or New Years."

She gave me a perplexed look. "Well, yeah. I suppose you could use him for entertaining as well." Her customary leer returned to her face and she winked at me. "I've got another type of party in mind."

I didn't win my masks. After nine up-bids, she won her bartender.

During the rest of the week, things began to get a little heady at the theater in anticipation of opening night. Rehearsals were running much better. I spent a lot of time in the theater observing the show coming together, and wishing I could play a more active role. Instead, I channeled the energy into writing.

And then, it was Pride Weekend. The whole of Piedmont Park was given over to the event. Much like the other festivals, the paths were again lined with food and art vendors. Several stages were put up around the park, and the sounds of music wafted throughout the neighborhood. It was nearly impossible to drive during the afternoons, as the city was predicting that over four hundred thousand people would come into town over the weekend. That, coupled with the fact that most of the cast were involved with some community pride group, led us to put rehearsals on hold until Monday.

On Sunday morning as we prepared to head out for the parade, we opened the paper and saw the article on the front of the Arts & Books section. There, in all of her turbaned glory, was a four-column picture of Aunt Laine, a smaller picture of me, and the story of the theater. The headline read "Theatrical Resurrection."

We met in the garage. After much ongoing discussion, it had been decided that there would be seven of us in the car. Laine wanted Chris and Zach, as well as Brit and Charles *and* Rachel. ("After all, this is a family affair.") I thought the ride down to the parade start was going to be a little cozy, but all of us fit in just fine.

We pulled into the Civic Center parking lot and checked in with a woman at the gate who directed us to our place in line. I pulled up to a spot just behind the Atlanta Freedom Marching Band and ahead of the big flatbed truck that the cast of the show would be riding on. Once in place, I released the hatches and punched the switch to send the Corniche's top sliding backwards into its boot.

Everyone emerged from the car. We had some magnetic signs to stick to the side of the VeggieRoll that identified who Laine was, as well as advertised the theater and the upcoming show. We also had some balloons to blow up and tie to the windshield and the antenna. And, of course, we had a cooler full of manhattans in the trunk.

All of us set to decorating the car, except Laine, who sat in the car trying to figure out the most comfortable way to sit on top of the boot for the entire parade route. The noonday sun was hot, even for June, and the heat index had already hit ninety and was climbing. Laine had a parasol to shade her. Being recently from New York, I found it hot as hell, and it was worse for poor Charles. Even though he had lived here for years, he had never adapted to the heat. Within minutes of getting out of the car, his shirt was soaked.

"Bloody subtropical climate," he muttered as he tried to tie balloons together. Unfortunately, the perspiration on his hands prevented him from getting a decent grip on the rubber closures.

"How can you complain?" I asked, trying to get the magnetic sign aligned on the door for perhaps the thirtieth time. "I thought the more unpleasant the climate, the more the British loved it. Y'know, that whole 'mad dogs and Englishmen' thing."

He fixed me with a disapproving stare, dropped the balloons and stripped off his t-shirt, saying, "I am sure if Noel Coward had known what a curse that sentence would be on his fellow countryman, he never would have uttered it."

He tossed the drenched shirt on the hood. I cleared my throat loudly, and gave him a disapproving stare, glancing pointedly at the shirt, which was going to smudge my wax job. He rolled his eyes, retrieved the shirt, and draped it over the tire. "My apologies, your grace."

Chris looked up from the streamers he was affixing to the trunk. "Charles, what are you doing?"

Charles looked at him blankly, a balloon in each hand. "Tying balloons together."

"No, I mean taking your shirt off."

He blushed. It is, after all, appallingly easy to make the British self-conscious. "It's hot," he offered meekly.

"Hey, you don't hear me complaining," Brit offered from where she was running streamers down the front of the car. She leered at her betrothed.

"You do realize what you're doing, right?" Chris continued. "If you are shirtless at Pride, no one is going to think you're straight."

"Even with me on his arm?" Brit asked. "Why would they think I would be there if he wasn't straight?"

Rachel, Chris and Zach all answered in unison, "Fag hag." I chuckled under my breath, and proceeded around the car to the other side to attach that sign.

"Fag hag!" Brit repeated, laughing.

"Hey," Rachel observed as she tied a balloon to the radio antenna, "I say it with the utmost respect, being as I am a confirmed grand ole hag."

Charles sighed. "I'll put it back on when we are ready to drive out. I'd rather people think I was gay, than yet another sweat soaked European."

Laine rattled the ice in her glass, so I took the glass from her and went to the trunk to refill it. As I was pouring the drink from her Baccarat shaker, Rachel ventured an opinion. "Actually Charles, you should leave it off. In fact, all four of you should have your shirts off."

I glanced around the trunk lid to see if she was serious. Her bemused expression told me she was. It was a nice counterpoint to Chris's horrified one.

"You can't be serious," he said.

"I am. Don't you think it would be a riot? Laine riding in the parade surrounded by four sexy, shirtless guys?"

I closed the trunk. Chris's discomfort was palpable, and I took a certain amount of pleasure in that. I handed Laine her drink and asked, "What do you think?"

Laine shrugged and stirred the cocktail with her finger, sucking it dry. "At my age, dear, I never say no to looking at sexy men. It's certainly nothing to complain about."

I turned around and looked at Chris. He was more than uncomfortable. He was significantly self-conscious. I grinned at him, pulled my tee-shirt off and said "I'm in."

"I'm not," he announced flatly.

I said nothing, counting on Rachel to do the dirty work. "Why not?" she asked.

"Because one does not go to Pride shirtless. It's *declasse.*"

"Oh please," she said, reaching into the glove compartment to find the suntan lotion I kept in there. "It's Pride. The park is full of men looking to get laid. You can't pretend you aren't one of them."

"While I may *be* one, I am not about to look like I'm one. No man wants someone who looks easy to get."

Charles and I exchanged bemused glances. "Bullshit," he said. "Every man wants easy sex. Gay or straight."

"Chris," Rachel began, "Think of it as marketing, not as cruising."

"I'm not taking my shirt off," he said flatly.

Rachel rolled her eye. "Vain queen." She fixed her eyes on Zach. "Zach?"

Zach blushed, grinned, and pulled his shirt off. "Yet another gay man falls victim to the influence of his fag hag."

"Zach's not afraid," Rachel declared, triumphantly turning back to Chris.

I reached under the dashboard and popped the hood.

"Zach is twenty."

"So?"

I lifted the hood and put the support in place.

"So, a gay man at twenty is not supposed to be worried about his image. Cruising is considered appropriate at his age."

I pulled the dipstick out of its sleeve.

"Dear," Laine asked Chris over her drink, "Are you being, perhaps, a bit overly uptight about how you're perceived?" I walked around the car.

"I'm not," Chris protested. "I'm thirty-five. There are certain things gay men *shouldn't* do at that age. Two that come immediately to mind are buy clothes at The Gap and appear at Pride shirtless."

I tapped him on the shoulder. He turned around and looked at me. "What?"

"Take your shirt off."

"No. Van, you don't understand…"

He didn't have a chance to finish. I took the dipstick and pulled it diagonally across his chest from his right shoulder downward. He didn't move, so I pulled it back upward towards his left shoulder, making a greasy black X on his tee-shirt.

There was a long, uncomfortable pause during which everyone backed away from the car. Even Laine, sitting in the back seat, looked apprehensive.

He stared at me, clearly pissed, for perhaps thirty seconds. Finally he said, "You unspeakable bastard."

Through the three weeks of nicotine withdrawal, we had pretty much confined our irritability to each other, and the most extensive time we had spent together was when we were running in the morning. Most of that irritability manifested itself as snippy comments, and me cajoling him to run harder. During all of this, Zach had kept us company. At first, I think he thought we were just teasing each other, but after a week or so, he had come to realize there was a lot of biting energy behind the biting sarcasm, and he had kept his distance. Now, he cleared his throat hesitantly, and let me know he thought I had gone too far.

"Van," Zach said, warily.

I didn't turn and look at him. Chris and I had our eyes locked on each other.

"Chris," he said, "You can wear my shirt if you want."

Chris said nothing, to Zach. Instead, he said to me, "Obviously this is important to you." His voice was icy. Slowly, he pulled his shirt off and folded it up. I returned to the front of the car and put the dipstick back in its sleeve. Rachel came around to the front of the car and said to me under hushed breath, "What the hell was that about?"

I looked at her innocently. "You wanted all of us to have our shirts off."

"There was no reason to humiliate him," she snapped. "Once the parade started, he would have felt left out and he would have done it anyhow."

I shrugged, and removed the hood support. "Who has time for these kind of silly games?" I let the hood drop.

The tense energy hung over the family for several more minutes. Laine held out her drink to Chris, who gave the vaguest smile of acknowledgment, and accepted it. Although I knew he was pissed at me, I didn't particularly care.

A guy came by with a clipboard and a headset on. He checked Chris out appreciatively and then informed all of us, "Parade is starting. Y'all need to be ready to roll in five minutes."

We finished with the decorations, and returned everything to the trunk. Once we had freshened Laine's drink, we all piled back into the VeggieRoll. I noticed Chris was not making eye contact with me. Laine and Rachel sat on the center of the boot with Chris and Zach flanking them. Brit sat in the front seat between Charles and me. She had taken to collecting hats a few years ago, and so each of us had a specific hat. Chris and I had panamas. Charles had a porkpie and Zach had a bowler. Actually, Brit had intended the bowler for Charles, but he refused to put it on his head, deeming it to be too stereotypically British.

For their part, the ladies were no less lavishly adorned. Brit was wearing a bright blue pillbox with a spray of black netting and a red rose that I remembered had been part of her bridesmaid's dress at our cousin Panda's wedding. Rachel was wearing a black disk from the forties that required a massive hat pin to hold it to her thick, straightened tresses. "You realize everyone is going to think I'm wearing this 'cause I'm nappy," she informed Brit as she secured it in place.

The biggest and most absurd hat was, of course, reserved for Laine. It was a massive, floppy white disk, probably thirty inches in diameter that was lined with black-and-white spotted feathers. On top, a dome of black feathers mushroomed out of it. She had a matching black-and-white boa that she draped loosely about her neck. Brit also had a boa, and had brought one for Rachel. Rachel, however, steadfastly declined to have anything around her neck because of the heat. Undeterred, Brit draped hers across her throat, and let it drop down the back of the front seat.

A biodiesel Rolls festooned with hats and balloons was relatively tame compared to the floats that marshaled ahead of us. We were at the start of the third wave of the parade, just behind the Atlanta Freedom Marching Band. I could not really discern an order to how groups were staged, and guessed aloud that it must be by similar interests; e.g., community groups walked with community groups, etc. Rachel scoffed.

"Oh, please. They are grouped by who is willing to be seen with whom. Watch when they roll by. *Everyone* will want to walk with PFLAG or a float of cute circuit boys, but there will be a sizeable distance between anyone and the leather-bears."

I got a sense of what she was talking about. One of the local bars was using a trailered pontoon boat as their float, and every single guy on it was stripped down to a Speedo, totally shaved and probably under twenty-five. The other floats were crowded so close to it I thought there was going to be an accident. Meanwhile, no one wanted to be within fifty feet of the gay science fiction geek float, an enormous Starship Enterprise rendered in pink tulle.

The last float in the second wave was manned by the camp-band, The Jane Hathaways. Ten guys, all dressed in bad drag impersonations of Nancy Kulp riding atop a flatbed truck struck up a song that I didn't immediately recognize as they rolled passed us and out onto the street. (I later learned it was a zydeco version of the theme song from *The Beverly Hillbillies*.) The parade ops director blew a whistle and waved us into formation.

And then we were moving. The Atlanta Freedom Marching band, who had all been standing at parade rest, immediately struck up "Before the Parade Passes By." As soon as there were a few feet between us and the tuba section, I slipped the car into gear, and the VeggieRoll slid out onto Peachtree. The truck carting the cast turned in behind me.

I'm not sure what I was expecting from the Pride Parade. I had never attended the one in New York because, usually, the gay scene was not my beat. There were not many things I attended if I didn't cover them. But I had always been told it was a very political affair. This was not. I drove the VeggieRoll straight into the middle of a street party fifteen blocks long.

Right after the start of the parade, we drove into a part of midtown called Jesus Junction, where four of the biggest, oldest churches in the city were located. (A similar spot up the road with newer old churches was referred to as Brimstone Corner.) Outside the gothic, terracotta Catholic cathedral, Sacred Heart, a group of men and women stood watching politely. Two blocks later, we reached Redeemer Lutheran, where the crowd was much larger, still. A giant banner fluttered from a terrace above the street announcing "*EVERYONE* is welcome at Redeemer!" Not more than a hundred feet beyond, at Saint Mark's United Methodist, a larger crowd was picnicking under a larger banner that commanded "Celebrate Your Diversity at Saint Mark's!"

On either side of Peachtree, people crowded the streets, some gay, some clearly not. There were families pointing out the parade to their children, beaming members of the clergy, and of course, men and women. And cocktails. Lots and lots of cocktails.

There was a lot of happy banter among everyone in the car, but I could feel an icy silence emanating from Chris towards me. I tried to make eye contact with him in the mirror, but he steadfastly refused. I began to feel bad about what I had done.

On the whole, though, we seemed relatively well received by the crowd. We were following the marching band, which was a great hit and certainly gave us a nice intro. And, some of the ladies of our ensemble ran alongside the car and the truck passing out flyers. But I noticed a number of people pointing out the car, the family, and, of course, Aunt Laine. It wasn't until the end of the parade I understood why.

The parade turned right on Tenth, and then just sort of abruptly ended at Piedmont Park, where we were directed off onto a side street. The going was slow as the crowds from the parade were starting to make towards the park. Several guys surrounded the car and loudly congratulated Laine. "You look ravishing, honey," one of them gushed.

"Why thank you," the belle of the ball replied warmly.

"You do," another added. "The hat, the boa, the whole ensemble is just grand."

She cast her eyes downward, blushing.

"And whatever you use on your face, your complexion is flawless." She looked up at the unexpected comment.

"Truly. You must use a straight razor to get it that close."

"I beg your pardon?" she asked, slightly confused.

The horrible truth of what these three guys were talking about dawned on Chris and me simultaneously and, despite himself, his eyes met mine in the rear-view mirror and we smiled at each other.

"She does," Chris offered them. "Never a sign of five o'clock shadow on her."

"What?" Laine cried.

"Sorry," I said to the guys as they continued to walk along side. "Our dad gets a little hard of hearing when he is in drag."

They all nodded sympathetically, and I saw the terrible realization dawn on Laine's face that they thought she was a man. She popped me hard in the back of the head. "I am NOT a drag queen!" she announced indignantly.

The realization had dawned on most of the rest of the car at the same time. Brit turned halfway around in her seat and said, "Oh, c'mon, Dad. They can *see* your Adam's apple."

The three guys walking with us were saved from Laine's tirade as we were directed to turn again into the park's parking lot. "I can't believe they think I'm a man."

"Laine," Rachel said patiently. "You are wearing a boa and a feathered hat, riding in a forty-year-old convertible in the Gay Pride parade, surrounded by four sexy shirtless guys. *Of course* they think you are a drag queen."

I parked the car, and everyone got out. As we were reassembling, I took Chris aside. "Sorry about earlier," I said, hoping I sounded sincere.

He looked directly into my eyes—something he doesn't do very often—and there was a deep emotion there I couldn't understand. He started to say something, stopped, paused, and then said, "Okay."

I was a little taken aback by the emotion beneath. "Um, am I forgiven?"

"Not yet," he said flatly.

"Chris, I…"

He held up his hand to stop me. "Not here. Not now. Later."

The silence was awkward. "I've got to take Laine back to the building. Can I meet up with you guys later?"

"No." He looked away to make sure we were out of earshot of everyone else, and then turned back to me. "Look, I know you don't think this was a big deal, but it was. I don't really want you around me right now. I'm sure I'll get over it, but right now I'd rather not be with you."

I didn't know what to say, so I just nodded. I reached into the car, retrieved my shirt and held it out to him. He looked indecisive for a minute, then accepted it. "Thanks," he said lightly.

He walked over and joined Rachel and Zach, and they walked off towards the festivities. While Laine and Charles and Brit got back into the car, I watched them walk away, suddenly feeling very much the outsider.

It was the first time I had felt that in Atlanta.

The Gardenia

There is a massive gardenia at the front left corner of the property, truly one of the biggest I have ever seen. It must be twelve feet tall. July of that year began with it detonating into bloom. The rich, heady fragrance of its perfume hung over the yard like a convention of southern matrons, strong enough to smell it all the way up on the roof.

It was a busy time for all of us. Rehearsals were proceeding at a frenzied pace in the theater, because opening night was two weeks away. Britany and Charles were in the throes of wedding planning. We had to finish getting the theater ready to open, and run a 10K on the fourth. You could almost feel the energy humming between the apartment building and the theater.

You could also feel that things were different between Chris and me. We still ran together every morning, but I didn't see him after that. The one or two times I tried to engage him in conversation, or tried to apologize again, he waved me off or changed the subject. But a certain iciness had crept into our friendship and I missed him a little.

I sought advice from Rachel who explained that Chris hated conflict and couldn't deal with it directly. "His only coping mechanism is this passive-aggressive withdrawal," she told me on the evening of the third, as we sat on the rooftop sharing a beer. "He'll either get over it, or repress it away for three years, and then tear your head off when you least expect it."

"That hardly sounds healthy," I mused.

She shrugged. "To each his own demons."

"Fair," I replied and took a sip of my beer.

"What are yours?" she asked, looking at me quizzically.

"My what?"

"Your demons."

I smiled at her and leaned my head back on the Adirondack to think. "Olivia?"

"Nope. Doesn't count. The ruling from the judges is that demons must be internal. Ex-wives are strictly external."

I took another sip of my beer. "Well, your good friend Aidan seems to be of the opinion that my demon is realizing my potential. He thinks that I prefer the image of being a rebel against what people expect me to be, rather than taking a chance at achieving something myself."

"Ah, Manheim syndrome."

I gave her a cold, sidelong glance. "I'm not Manheim."

"Never said you were. Is he right though?"

"I dunno. I've been thinking about it a lot lately. He may be. I've never taken much of a chance on anything."

"Technically not a demon unless you know *why* you've never really taken a chance."

I shrugged. "I guess the demon would be a fear of failure. Never try, never fail."

"Nor succeed."

"True, unless you view never having failed as a success."

"Can't argue with circular logic," she replied. "You have a race tomorrow. Let's go next door to LaTavola so you can carbo-load."

Independence Day morning arrived hot and muggy. The warmth hit me as soon as I opened the door of the apartment and I questioned my sanity. Regardless, I clumped down the stairs, knocked on Chris's door to let him know I was ready, and descended to the lobby.

There was quite a contingent in the lobby waiting for me. Charles and Brit were busy getting Laine out the door and into Charles's car. They would be watching the race from a balcony in Park Place on Peachtree, a trendy condo high-rise where many of Laine's friends had retired to. Separately, Jennifer and Rachel were waiting as well. They would be dropping Zach, Chris, and me at the subway station, and then watching the race from the roof of a bar in Buckhead.

Laine was dressed in a prim white pantsuit with an enormous hat. She looked for all the world like she was dressed for Ascot. I hadn't even showered and I felt a little awkward trying to kiss her without touching her. I had notice she had stepped up the wardrobe a bit in recent weeks. After what happened at Pride, she was making sure no one ever mistook her for a drag queen again.

There was a lot of pre-race banter as we waited for Chris and Zach to join us. Zach came upstairs first, struggling to get his race number pinned to his tank top. While Jennifer helped him, Rachel called up the stairs to Chris. "Diaz! Let's go!"

He rounded the corner and began to descend the stairs. "I'm coming," he said flatly, betraying no emotion. "I'm short MARTA fare. Do you have an extra quarter?"

Rachel nodded and produced one from the pocket of her shorts. We said our goodbyes to Laine, Brit, and Charles, and made our way down to the parking lot.

Fifteen minutes later, we were at Lindbergh MARTA station. Although the race only started a few miles away at Lenox Mall, the streets all around it were closed to traffic, so we could either walk to the start or take the train. We elected to take the train. As we stood on the platform with perhaps three thousand other runners, Zach informed us that there were people "who park above the race, run the six miles to the park, get the t- shirt, and then run all the way back to their cars."

"They're idiots," Chris replied under his breath, as he was jostled by the press of the crowd. A train rumbled into the station, but the inside was packed with runners. Not another person would be able to squeeze on.

"Now what do we do?" Chris asked.

I shrugged. "Wait for the next train?"

"We're in the last time group," Zach reminded us needlessly. "We'll have time."

Two more trains rumbled through before we were actually able to board. Once on, the crush and close proximity to others on the train was worse than anything I had ever experienced in New York, even during a transit strike. Moreover, the racing togs worn by the crowd left little to the imagination for *any* sense. I was grateful that I would not have to endure the ride northward after the race with the same crush of people. I imagined the smell would be horrid.

We were deposited at Lenox station and joined the crush of people riding the escalator upwards to the street. Next to me, Chris began to sing "Another Hundred People" from *Company*. "And another hundred people just got off of the train..."

Once on the street, I was amazed by the throng. Thousands of people walked through the streets, each sporting a different colored race number. As we walked towards Lenox Mall, a sign directed the runners in the 00000–19999 groups to the left. All other numbers were to go to the right. We turned right.

At the next intersection, runners in the 20000–29999 group got to turn left. We continued to walk on.

Chris, Zach, and I were 90965, 90456, and 90337. Ten blocks later, we got to turn left and join the last group. We walked a block up to Peachtree Road and were directed into a large, sort of mobile holding pen, which kept us separate from the other eight time groups. There were roughly five thousand of us standing together.

"Just in case you're curious," Zach said in a tone that was menacingly chipper, "We are about a mile from the starting line at Lenox." Chris curled his lip in response, but said nothing.

We eased our way to the front of the time group, so that we were standing up against the orange mesh barrier that separated us from the back of group eight. We were on a slight incline and, looking downward, there were more people than I had ever seen together in one place in my life. I could see a multitude of heads between me and the sign defining time group eight, and then more ahead of that, dissolving into a hazy, undulating mass of running Atlantans. "Wow," I said appreciatively. Even Chris seemed awed, albeit still irritated.

A loudspeaker announced the playing of the national anthem, and all of us sang along with the gathered crowd. A few moments later, they announced the beginning of the wheelchair race which preceded time group one. Although I couldn't see it, I'm told the wheelchair racers were moving at forty miles an hour when they reached the end of the downhill portion of the run.

We stood and waited, checking our watches, wondering. I tried to make polite small talk with Chris, but didn't receive much in the way of response. Finally, I just stood and watched.

Periodically over the next hour, we would get to walk forward about a quarter mile as each time group was moved to the starting line. I was also aware of the sun moving ever higher in the sky. As time group seven approached the starting line, the announcer told us, "The first runner has just passed the finish line, so just take it easy and enjoy your run."

An hour after the national anthem, time group nine made its way towards the starting line. Interestingly, I expected a certain amount of resignation over being at the back, or the crowd to be subdued from the heat. Quite the opposite was true. These people were here to have fun, and the cheering, shouting and rebel yells that went up from the crowd as we moved forward were infectious. I felt buoyed along by the good will around me.

And in an instant, the orange barrier dropped in front of us and we were running past the starting line. I glanced at the race clock to my left. We were one hour, four minutes into the race.

If I thought the runners were excited, they had nothing on the people lining the streets. The sidewalks were *thronged* with people. Every mile or so, a radio station had set up a mobile booth, and their morning shows were broadcasting live, blaring whatever music they deemed appropriate for the runners. As soon as we passed Lenox Mall, the road began a gradual descent, and I leaned back into my run, thinking it best to pace myself.

The runners began to spread out as each found his or her natural speed. Since the three of us had been running together for a couple of weeks, we had learned to pretty well match each other's pace. Zach tended to run a little faster than Chris, and I learned I tended to power up hills and take it easy down. As we fell into rhythm, we passed some people, and were passed by others. To our left, four guys ran by, each carrying a twelve-pack of beer on their shoulders, chanting something about their fraternity. To our right, we passed a man from time group eight easing his way along with a cane. Chris and I exchanged glances.

The grade became a little more steep as we crossed Piedmont Road. On the corner, a woman in a scarlet blouse and jeans yelled at the crowd, "You look fantastic! You all look fantastic!"

Zach turned as we passed her and shouted back, "So do you!"

Although she couldn't see who had shouted it, she called back, "Thank you, darlin'."

Two blocks later, on our right, was the imposing edifice of Peachtree Presbyterian church. A huge crowd was gathered outside of it. Of course there was a huge crowd everywhere and I probably would not have noticed it if Zach hadn't pointed towards it and said, "Look!"

In the center of the crowd were two old ladies, twin sisters, probably at least in their eighties. They were dressed in matching navy blue skirts, matching red sequined jackets and red-and-white striped top hats. They stood in front of two lawn chairs. Between them was a small folding occasional table with a giant silver ice bucket cooling a bottle of what looked to be very expensive champagne.

"Those two were here when I ran it in high school," Zach said.

A woman who was running alongside of us said, "They're here every year. They were two of the first women attorneys in Georgia. Big Atlanta boosters."

They waved genially, like a pair of Queen Mothers reviewing the troops, and several runners stopped briefly to talk to them or acknowledge them. Out of the corner of my eye, I could see Chris smiling broadly at the sight of them.

We approached a turn in the road marking the entrance of the Buckhead Village, the city's primary nightlife district. I had never been to the bar where Jennifer and Rachel were going to be watching from; I just knew it was coming up on the right. "I wonder if we will be able to find the girls," I said.

"In this crowd?" Zach said.

"We'll find 'em," Chris replied confidently.

I needn't have worried. As we rounded the corner, a huge crowd stood on the roof of a bar identifying itself as "Wood's." At the very front of the roof, Rachel clung to the bar's art deco sign and leaned way out over the sidewalk below scanning the crowd. She held a flute of champagne with the arm that was hooked over the sign's support line, and held her other hand over her eyes against the sun. Jennifer stood behind her, pouring champagne into her own flute, looking a little unsteady. "There they are," Chris announced, pointing.

The three of us all called "Rache! Jen!" They both scanned the crowd, saw us, and shouted excitedly. Rachel jumped up and down, nearly dislodging the sign and herself from the building. Jennifer grabbed her and pulled her backwards. They shouted something that I couldn't exactly decipher, and that's when I realized they were blasted. We all waved and continued past the bar.

Zach observed, "Oh, they're trashed."

"A fine old Independence Day tradition," Chris replied.

"At eight thirty in the morning?"

Then we were in the heart of Buckhead. The scene at Wood's was repeated at every bar and restaurant along the way. As we passed one with a huge patio just below West Paces Ferry Road, a bartender stood in the streets handing out cups of beer from a tray to any runners who wanted one. To my shock, several accepted. (Chris sighed wistfully.) Two blocks later, one of the bakers from the Publix stood in the street handing out fresh glazed donuts to the crowd.

In another few blocks the street became more residential, as shopping and restaurants gave way to condo high-rises and apartment blocks. Ahead, I could see Park Place, where Laine would be watching from. I also began to notice more than a few half-consumed beers and donuts lying in the streets.

We reached Brimstone Corner, and in front of the Cathedral of Saint Philip, one of the priests stood on a riser, blessing the runners by throwing holy water on them from an aspergillum. Instinctively as I passed, I crossed myself. I noticed Chris did the same thing. Suddenly we were passing mile marker two of the race.

"Hey, what happened to mile one?" I asked.

"We passed it right after we saw the girls," Zach responded.

We were coming closer to Park Place. It was a big, octagonal tower of gray concrete with floor after floor of balconies marching skyward. Several Atlanta celebrities lived there, but of course Laine was not visiting any of them. She was visiting one of her "respectable" friends from the Arts Center. It was a forty-story building so none of us expected to see her, but then we noticed the sign. From one of the balconies hung a white bed sheet with the words "Van! Chris! Zach! We're Proud of You!" The letters stood out bright against a pale sea of pastel waves in the back, and I could just make out a couple of argyles. I started to point it out to the guys, but realized they both saw it. Chris beamed, smiling wider than he had at any time since before Pride. Zach was misty eyed and choked up.

On the balcony behind, I could make out Laine's hat. I thought about yelling, but she was ten floors up.

And then the hard part of the race began. We reached the end of the downhill portion. Peachtree suddenly leveled off for about fifty feet and turned abruptly, menacingly upward. We had reached Cardiac Hill.

I had been aware of the rapidly increasing heat and humidity for some time, but now as the course turned more difficult, the run became excruciating. We began to ascend the steep grade, and next to me I noticed that Chris was muttering something to himself.

"Did you say something?" I asked.

"I'm just reciting to myself all the other things I would rather be doing right now."

"Oh, c'mon…"

"I'm alphabetizing the list. Do you want to hear it?"

"Not really."

"First, accessorizing the outfit Laine was wearing this morning. Second, bathing. Third, calling a cab."

Zach suggested that maybe we should walk a bit. Although I had personally vowed that I would run the entire race, I also knew it was important to stay with Chris. Before I could say anything, though, we reached Shepherd Spinal Center.

The Shepherd specializes in the medical treatment, research, and rehabilitation for people with spinal cord injuries, acquired brain injuries, multiple sclerosis, chronic pain, and other neurological conditions. On the sidewalk in front of the hospital were perhaps twenty patients. Some in wheelchairs, some on gurneys that had been rolled outside. They cheered if they could. Some waved. One, obviously totally paralyzed and breathing with the help of a respirator, had a small American flag propped in his hand, giving as much salute as he could muster.

I glanced at Chris to ask him if he wanted to walk a bit and noticed him staring at the patients, wide eyed, somber looking. As soon as we were past the hospital, he glanced at Zach and said "Hell no we're not walking." He put his head down and began to pick up speed.

The grade became steeper again as we passed the Shepherd Center. A radio station booth in front of Piedmont Hospital was playing the Village People's "YMCA," and suddenly Chris and Zach were dancing up the hill. In a matter of minutes, just as we were repeating that you *could get a good meal*, the grade suddenly leveled out and we passed Collier Road. Although the race would still continue resolutely upwards for another three miles, we had conquered the worst part of it.

Below Collier, the streets convert to mostly numbered streets, and we began a countdown starting at Twenty-eighth. In eighteen blocks we would turn left on Tenth, the last leg of the race.

Just below Twenty-fifth, we saw The Mug, the bar Chris usually frequented to watch the Peachtree. Suddenly he veered to the left towards it, grinning madly and we saw he was heading directly for a group of his friends, flight attendants all. They were drinking mimosas and smoking cigarettes on the patio. Zach and I trailed behind and as we got closer, he screamed out, "Hey you bitches!"

They all turned, saw him, and screamed collectively. Several things were shouted, some encouraging, some sarcastic. He called back, "This is what a *healthy* lifestyle looks like." They favored us with a bunch of catcalls as we ran past.

We passed over the interstate, and then the climb became steeper. All along the way there had been water stations to stop and get a drink before running on, but none of us had stopped. Now, in addition to water stations, there were huge sprinklers hooked to the fire hydrants that were blanketing the street in water. Two guys were running beside us and I heard one say, "Oh crap. There's no avoiding getting wet."

"So?" asked the other.

"New shoes, y'know."

The three of us passed under the shower together. It was cold and bracing, and my eyes burned from the sweat that it washed into them. It didn't make sense to me at first why everyone had to be hosed down, but then we entered the shadeless concrete canyon that ran from Seventeenth Street uphill to Fourteenth. The peach trees that had once shaded this stretch had long ago succumbed to blight, and the concrete and brick edifices that lined the street radiated the heat of the sun back to us. I was panting hard by the time we reached Fourteenth.

The crowds seemed to thin a little in this stretch as we passed some closed nightclubs and restaurants, and we continued our steadily uphill climb to Tenth. In my mind, since Peachtree ran along a granite ridge, I assumed that once we turned left at Tenth, it would be straight downhill to the park. Instead, as we rounded the corner, the street rose sharply, and we climbed another two blocks towards Piedmont Road. The crowds thickened up again, although not as thick as they had been when I had driven through this intersection in the parade two weeks prior.

Ahead of us I noticed a metal framework spanning across the street as if it were the finish line, but we had just passed the sixth mile marker and I knew we had another two-tenths of a mile to go. Up on the framework were dozens of photographers, each shooting pictures of the runners. Once we realized what they were doing, I put my arms across each of the guys' shoulders. They did the same, and we ran triumphantly past, hoping someone was getting a picture of us.

The road sloped downward and we could see the finish line. Perhaps forty thousand people milled around in the park, and I glanced over my shoulder at another fifteen thousand coming up Tenth, and more still rounding the corner from Peachtree. As I turned back around, my eyes met Chris's. He was smiling maniacally. Suddenly he broke out singing the theme song from *Bonanza.* "Bumdadabumbum, bumdadabumbum, bum *bum!*"

I laughed and picked up the second verse. "Dadadadum, Dadadadadum, bumdadadadadum!"

Zach, having never heard of *Bonanza,* had no idea what we were doing, but smiled indulgently as we sang at the top of our lungs all the way to the finish line.

As we crossed it, announcers alternatively yelled "Congratulations!" and admonished us to keep walking. Chris threw his arm around my shoulder, as did Zach, and the three of us turned off Tenth Street and into the park. We were quickly paraded past a tent reserved for those requiring medical assistance, and into lines where we were made to take bottles of water. Then, all of us funneled into one of several lines marked "T-Shirts! Men's Medium." We were handed a bag with the coveted shirt, which we all immediately pulled out to admire. It was a deep blue shirt with Atlanta's skyline rising over the horizon of an immense peach-planet, with Peachtree Road running along the peach's crease.

"I never, *ever,* believed I would do this," Chris said proudly, beaming at me.

I decided to take a chance. "Does this mean I'm forgiven?"

He paused, considered for a moment and said, "No. Not at all. But it does mean I love you again." He gave me a sweaty kiss on the cheek, and the three of us joined the procession through the park.

We made it back to the 'Hurst by eleven, and I marveled that we still had the entire day ahead of us. As I slid off my sneakers, I experienced something that members of the Atlanta Track Club call a footgasm. Barefoot and sore, I did something I had never done before. I rode the elevator up to the third floor.

I bid farewell to Chris, agreeing that all of us would meet later to walk around the Highlands in our t-shirts and let other people compliment us on our superior athletic prowess. Then, I ascended the stairs to my apartment. There was a message on the answering machine, and I punched the button to listen as I pulled off my shirt. It was from Rachel, calling from her cell phone on Wood's roof.

"s'HAAAAAAAAAY!" she slurred. "You guysh jush ran by and you look fantastic. I'm so proud of you. We'f had some champagne and now I haff to go to sleep. I'll shee you this affernoon." I could hear Jennifer cackle in the background, and the message ended.

Once out of the shower, I climbed the stairs gingerly to my bed. The muscles in my legs had begun to cramp following the run, and I dropped into the sheets thinking I would never get to sleep with them so sore. I was out immediately.

I don't think I moved until I heard Brit say, "Van? C'mon and wake up, darlin'." I opened my eyes. She was sitting on the bed next to me.

"Hey," I said, stretching languidly beneath the sheet. I glanced at the clock. It was three. "Thanks for the sign. It meant a lot."

She smiled beatifically. "I'm so glad you saw it. We think we saw the three of you, but Bob's condo is so far up, who can be sure. I either got a picture of you, or three guys running close together who look enough like you no one will care."

I took her hand and kissed it. "You have a marvelous heart," I told her. "Were you always this great?"

She winked at me. "I'm one hell of a nice lady. You must get to know me some day. I think you'll like me. Now, I need you to get up."

"Why?"

"Just do. Get up, get dressed, and meet me downstairs."

She stood up and descended the spiral staircase. As she reached the front door, she paused and said, "Feet on the floor?"

I remember our mother asking the same question from the foot of the stairs when trying to get me up for school. I smiled, flipped back the sheets, gingerly swung my legs out and called back, "Feet on floor, ma'am."

"Good. Hurry up." I heard her close the door. I achingly slid on a pair of shorts, pulled my brand new t-shirt on and slipped my feet into a pair of flip flops. It took me a minute or two to navigate the spiral staircase downward, and I noticed that the Feldmans had moved everything to one side of the coffee table. "Y'know," I told no one in particular, "for ghosts, I can't decide if you are benign or simply boring." They of course said nothing. As I crossed the apartment, I could see people on the deck beyond the glass door. As I walked out, Laine, Charles, Brit, Clare, and Mac all began applauding.

"Laine! How did you get up here?"

"I climbed the steps, dear. It was slow going, but I imagine you know how that feels this afternoon."

She came forward and gave me a kiss. There was a large table set up on the deck covered with food, and the banner we had seen while running now hung on the side of the elevator shaft. Charles handed me a mimosa and said, "Congratulations, old man."

The stairway door opened and Rachel led Chris out onto the deck. Everyone cheered and called congratulations again. He blushed for a minute, and then held his hands upward like a gymnast who had just stuck the dismount. Jennifer followed almost immediately leading Zach, and everyone cheered again.

Mimosas were passed around, and the gathered residents of the building toasted us all. There was a fantastic variety of food, none of it healthy, which seemed to totally defeat the purpose of running ten kilometers that morning. Regardless, we dug into it with ravenous enthusiasm. Brit lugged my stereo speakers out onto the deck, and we all sat down to eat while John Fogarty serenaded us from a CD.

There was not a lot of conversation while we ate. It seemed a lack of respect for some of the best fried chicken ever made. There was a pleasant lull before seconds during which we recapped the race, described our adventures and challenges, and the oddly motivational aspect of passing the Shepherd Spinal Center.

Rachel reached down to Zach, who was seated on the deck at her feet, and wiped some breading off his face with her napkin. I teased her about displaced maternal aspect, and she favored me with a smile and gently tussled his long dark hair.

Chris grinned at me and said, "Don't kid yourself, Van. She's always been a collector of young queers. We're like Hummels to her."

She looked at Chris, aghast. "I beg your pardon?"

"It's true. Me, Zach, a third of your store…"

"Clare's the same way," Mac injected. "She hags for half the symphony."

Clare started to object, but then just shrugged, acknowledging the truth of the statement.

"And don't forget Vijay," Laine added, pointing at Rachel.

"Vijay?" I asked.

"Former tenant," my aunt informed me from under her parasol. "Used to rent Jennifer's apartment. Nice Indian boy." She took a sip of her manhattan, and then thought further clarification must have been in order, so she added, "Dot, not feather."

"Laine!" I replied, scandalized at her lack of political correctness. She held her hands up, feigned a look of wide-eyed innocence and mouthed *what?* to me.

"Vijay doesn't count," Rachel protested. "We don't know if he was gay. If he was, he wasn't out."

"Oh please," Chris answered, rolling his eyes and pouring more champagne into his glass. "He was more out than a fat kid in dodge-ball."

The party lasted until about six. Laine was tired, so Mac and Clare escorted her downstairs. We cleaned up the deck and carried the table back down to Rachel's apartment, and then the seven of us went out to walk the Highlands. It was an ego-building walk, as many people stopped Chris or Zach or me to admire the shirt and compliment us on running the race. We might have stopped into one of the bars for a drink, but Zach would not be twenty-one for another month and it would not have been right to leave him behind.

Fortunately, it was a beautiful night to be on a walk, and the Highlands was quiet. The big crowds were at the fireworks displays at Centennial Park or at Lenox Mall. Brit had assured me that the fireworks were visible from the roof, so we stopped into a nearby market, bought a couple more bottles of champagne, and returned home. Charles and Brit said their goodbyes and departed for their house in Druid Hills.

The sun had set by the time we wound back up at the 'Hurst. Everyone else disappeared back into their various apartments to get comfortable, and we all agreed to meet up on the roof in fifteen. I carried the champagne upstairs to my apartment, unlocked the door, and tossed my flip flops inside. Then I turned on the stereo to the radio station that would be broadcasting one of the fireworks shows. I turned back around and, much to my surprise, Chris was right behind me. Since Chris was never on time for anything, much less early, I was surprised. He was leaning against the elevator shaft, arms crossed.

"I would kill for a cigarette right now," he stated flatly.

I smiled. "Me too."

We walked across the deck and sat in two of the Adirondack chairs. We were facing westward. Ahead of us, the skyline was silhouetted against a beautiful sunset. The sky exploded in teal and orange and mauve.

"You know, I have a fantasy," Chris began.

"The one about having martinis with Bea Arthur?" I eased the cork out of the bottle and filled two glasses that may or may not have been the ones we had been drinking out of earlier.

He smiled. "No."

There was a long pause. Handing him his glass, I finally asked, "Were you going to share the fantasy, or was it just a broad announcement for the benefit of the media?"

He chuckled and took a sip of his drink. He leaned his head all the way back against the chair and turned to look at me. "You're not gay, are you?"

I shook my head. "Nope."

"You're sure?"

"I was married."

"Yeah, I know. Means nothing. I know lots of gay guys who were once married. But you aren't one of them, are you?"

I sighed deeply. "I've never been attracted to a guy. I don't rule anything out in life, but statistically I have to say probably not."

He nodded sadly and took a sip of his drink. "That's what I thought."

I sensed a land mine ahead, but decided to proceed anyhow. "What's that got to do with your fantasy?"

He closed his eyes and smiled serenely. "My fantasy is something like this. Having a great guy who loves me and who I could sit with and watch the sunset. A great guy who would make me do things I never would think to do on my own, like give up smoking or run the Peachtree or, hell, appear at Pride without a shirt, and make me feel great about it. And afterwards, who I could sit and have a quiet moment with, and being with him would just be enough." He took another sip and, with his eyes still closed, held the glass out to me to refill. I did so obediently. When I finished, he nodded, pulled the glass back, opened his eyes and looked at me. "But that guy's not you, is it?"

I considered which way to proceed. He had shown me more vulnerability in thirty seconds than Olivia had shown in almost six years of marriage. "I can be a lot of those things for you, but I don't think I can be in…in the way you really want me to be."

He nodded. "I suspect you're right."

I decided to go for broke. "Is that what's been driving radio silence for the last two weeks?"

He nodded and stared far off into the twilight. "I had thought you might be gay when I first met you. I really had *hoped* you might be gay. At least that you might be curious. But I realized at Pride that, when you had no idea how *big* a deal it is for your average guy to take his shirt off in that environment, that you really had no clue about what it is to be gay."

"Explain to me why it's such a big deal."

He shook his head. "Unless you've ever been in the closet, it's not something you could grasp. When you are living in subterfuge, extreme conformity is one of the first tools you learn."

It dawned on me that there was a long, complex path that had led Chris to this moment. I resolved to ask him about it one day, but I also immediately doubted he would ever tell me.

The door of the deck opened, and Jennifer, Zach, and Rachel all joined us. Jennifer had changed into a nightshirt with a giant number five emblazoned on the front; Zach was wearing a pair of flannel pajama bottoms that had been Chris's, and Rachel was decked out in sweat pants and a yellow-and-denim sweatshirt with a lace-up collar. Because it was still nearly eighty on the deck, I asked about the attire as I poured a glass of champagne.

"I'm not really feeling all that well," she replied, declining the proffered glass. "I'm sure it's all the drinks today, and the heat. As soon as the fireworks are over, I'm going to turn in."

I finished passing around glasses, and we chatted idly for about ten minutes, until the radio station announced that the fireworks were about to begin.

"Rache?" Chris asked. "Do you still have my new dance mix CD in your stereo?"

"Huyup," she said, combining a belch with the affirmation. "Excuse, please."

He got up. "Your apartment open?"

"Yeah." He started towards the stairs. "You can't just listen to the music that accompanies the fireworks?"

"It's the same freakin' mix year after year after year after year after..." His voice faded out as the fire door closed behind him.

"He's right, y'know," Jennifer observed. "I can almost guarantee it'll start with 'They're comin' to America,' then go immediately into James Brown singing 'Living in America.'"

"Don't forget Lee Greenwood," Zach added. "No patriotic event can take place in Georgia without 'Proud to be a 'Mercan.' It's the law."

"That accent scares me," I told him.

He shrugged. "You can take the fag out of Rome, Georgia, but..."

"And the whole thing ends with the *1812 Overture,*" Rachel announced.

"But that's patriotic Russian," I replied.

"Ah," Jennifer announced sagely. "Miss Clare downstairs would point out to you that the vast majority of Americans think it's the overture to *our* War of 1812. Besides, it has cannons in it. What's more patriotic than cannons?"

The fire door opened and Chris emerged. "…after year after year after year after year…"

He crossed the deck and entered my apartment as Neil Diamond began the first notes of "America." The music cut off abruptly as the first firework exploded over Centennial Park, three miles to the west. We could just make it out over the tree line. The second firework was greeted with the powerful baseline of some house dance mix.

A firework burst brightly over the trees and I instructed them, "Okay, everybody. Mandatory *ooh.*"

"Oohs are mandatory?" Zach asked.

"The summer after my freshman year in college, my roommate and I worked in an amusement park. They had a fireworks display every night and the crowd never changed it's cadence. First firework is *ooh.* Second firework is *ah.* Third is *appreciative murmur.*"

Another one exploded over the trees. The crowd obediently *ah*ed. As soon as the third burst, they all said, "Appreciative murmur," and laughed.

As the fireworks proceeded, something about the music Chris had put on struck me as horribly, horribly familiar. I turned on him, aghast.

"What?" he asked, irritably.

"This is 'The Wreck of the Edmund Fitzgerald.'"

He grimaced and shook his head. "Is not. There's no Gordon Lightfoot on here. It's the Edmund Fitzgerald Dance Remix."

The fireworks concluded, and Rachel disappeared downstairs almost immediately. Zach followed soon after, and Jennifer lasted perhaps another fifteen minutes. Chris and I were alone. We sat in silence for a long time, a pleasant compatible silence. I finally offered, "Hey, if I were gay, you would be the guy I would fall for."

He laughed, looked sideways at me, and said, "You realize that means nothing at all, right?"

The next day began early with a phone call. It was from Ben, my publisher at *Manhattan Gothic*. He was calling to offer me a different position as my column would now be written by Michael somebody. I was tempted to be bitter, arrogant, sarcastic. Instead, I listened to everything he had to say, and then politely declined. He was not surprised. We said all the pro forma things that you are supposed to say to each other at this point, and then we hung up. I knew his next call would have been to the pressman, telling him to go ahead and run the magazine using a masthead that already had my name removed.

I tried to feel something about losing my job, but I couldn't. My life in Manhattan, after four months, seemed far, far away. I decided not to think about it for now. I had to get to the theater to meet Talbot.

As I crossed the street, she pulled her gold Mercedes up on the sidewalk, hopped out, and placed a very small notice high above the newly uncovered window of the ticket booth. I examined it over her shoulder.

"This," she informed me, " is the public posting of your application for a liquor permit. Don't call it to anyone's attention. With any luck, it'll be illegible in a matter of days."

"Is that legal?" I asked as I unlocked the door.

"You're compliant with the letter of the law. I don't worry overmuch about the spirit."

She accompanied me inside. We had an appointment at city hall for me to fill out all the papers for my special event liquor license. She had handled most of the behind- the-scenes work including, I suspected, one bribe. My instructions were very clear. I was to show up with a checkbook, dressed presentably which, she insisted, meant no flip flops. While she waited in the lobby, I ran upstairs and retrieved a couple of files from my desk and my checkbook. Then we were back in her car and off to City Hall.

The experience at City Hall wasn't hard or intimidating, just long. I had to certify I was aware of Georgia's laws concerning selling liquor to minors, my liability in case I willingly over-served someone, and my understanding that I could only sell liquor on Sundays if it accompanied food. Finally, after three long hours, and one expensive check, we emerged from the building at Trinity Place, permit in hand, and headed for the car.

"That wasn't too bad now, was it?" Talbot asked as she touched up her lipstick while walking.

I shrugged. "It seems to me that we had less difficulty launching war on Iraq than getting a liquor license."

She snapped her lip-liner case shut. "Same sides of the argument, babe. Atlanta may be a liberal city, but it is still the capital of Georgia. This is the heart of Southern Baptist land. In their mind, waging war on alcohol consumption and Muslims both qualify as God's work."

"Sad, but true."

My cell phone rang at that moment. My ringer is of an actual telephone bell. Talbot smirked at me and said, "Quaint. Ironic, but quaint." I pulled it out of my back pocket, hit answer and said hello.

"Donovan!" Brit's plaintive wail was loud enough that I had to pull the phone away, and even Talbot could hear it over the traffic on Martin Luther King Drive.

"What's wrong, Brit?" I asked as we crossed the street towards the parking lot.

"My wedding has been outbid!"

"It's what?"

"Another bride has offered the church more money to bump my wedding."

We entered the parking lot. "They can't do that. Don't you have a contract?"

She sniffled. "They want to walk me."

"Walk you?"

"I can't explain. Can you just meet me?"

"Where?"

"At the church? In half an hour?"

"Meet you at what church?"

"Friendship Church of the Light in Christ."

I glanced at Talbot. "Friendship Church of the, uh, Light in Christ?" She rolled her eyes and nodded. "Yeah. We're on our way."

"Thanks, Van," she sniffed and we hung up.

"Do you know the church?" I asked as we got into the car.

She nodded. "My sister goes there. It's a multimedia megachurch."

"A what?"

She started the car. "Very modern reinterpretation of the gospel, all done with modern music, live-action video, and hymns projected on PowerPoint screens. All on a huge scale; they have something like fifty thousand members."

I will admit I had fallen away from organized religion long ago. I was unaware of the rise of megachurches in the world, much less multimedia ones, and said so. "What's their affiliation?"

"None. They're probably an offshoot of Pentecostal, but strayed pretty far from the language. There are a couple of them in town. They preach a very different gospel."

"How so?"

"Well," she said as she turned out of the parking lot. "It's less of a gospel that says 'help the poor,' or 'do onto others.' Its message is more, 'God wants you to have all the material things you want and the way to get them is to pray and give money.'"

I scratched my head. "Well, giving money to ministries and charities has always been preached as a way to salvation…"

She shook her head and took a left onto Piedmont. "Different message. Not give to God or give to the poor, but give to the church. You've got to see this place to believe it. Private school affiliated with it, and a day care plus a credit union, *plus* a health club. It's got this huge campus up in Buckhead and it's very insular. Their message is your business and God's business are one and the same. Invest in the church, and God will pay you earthly dividends. The poor are on their own."

Talbot can be pretty cynical, so I took everything she said with a grain of salt. Even so, I was unprepared for when, fifteen minutes later, we turned into a Buckhead office park that had been converted into the FCOTLIC campus.

There was a school, and a credit union, as described. The health club was massive, with tennis courts, ball diamonds and a horse stable. There was a pavilion, an outdoor amphitheater where they apparently held concerts, and a "retreat house" that looked a lot like the Elizabeth Arden spa. A sign announced the construction of their new golf course.

And then there was the Jesus.

In the center of the campus was a pond. It might have once been a peaceful pond, but now there was a turbulent effluence of water surrounding an enormous concrete head-of-Christ. Well, more than his head, really; his entire upper torso. It emerged, easily five stories tall, from the end of the pond. It was rendered as if he was bursting forth from the pond, hands up-stretched in worship. He stared upwards towards the sun, and torrents of water churned up and outward around him, I suppose to give some sense that the savior had literally just burst out before we rounded the corner, and not that he was rendered in millions of cubic yards of concrete.

"Oh…my…" I said, horrified.

"Oh yeah," she said as she maneuvered around him and towards the church. "I forgot about the concrete Jesus. It's worse at night. There's actually a chapel inside his head. The irises of his eyes are skylights. At night, if you drive by and they have the lights on inside, it can be pretty disturbing. These enormous blue eyes staring out over Peachtree."

"Wait a minute. They gave a first-century Middle Eastern Jew *blue eyes?"*

"They gave him *glowing* blue eyes."

The church itself was rendered in a kind of Spanish mission revival style on a massive scale. We parked and walked up under the faux stucco arches and into the sanctuary itself.

For all the money, they didn't spend a lot of it on decorating the church. It could have easily been the atrium of a large mall. There were plasma television screens everywhere, and ferns cascaded from the balcony. Another, enormous statue of Christ, arms outstretched, hung over the congregation, easily forty feet long.

I couldn't help myself. I laughed. "Look," I said, pointing. "He's flying."

"Welcome to Our Lady of Ostentatious."

Brit came running down the aisle. "Oh Donovan, this is terrible. Another bride has outbid me for the church."

"Outbid you?" I asked, walking forward to meet her. "I thought you had signed a contract."

"I did," she said handing it to me. "But apparently there's a walk clause."

"What's a walk clause?"

Talbot answered. "It's actually a term from the hotel industry. It means that, if they can sell the space you've reserved for more money, they reserve the right to 'walk' you to another facility."

I took the contract, walked forward and sat down in the front pew—well, front row of comfortable padded seats—to read it. While I did, Brit fiddled nervously with a hymnal and Talbot wandered around, inspecting the church.

Having been married to an agent, I have seen a lot of contracts. This one, in particular, was pretty intense. Up until one month out, if another bride "outbid" the reserving bride (in this case, Brit), the reserving bride could meet the bid to hold the church. Otherwise, the higher bidder would get the church, and the first bride's wedding would be moved to either the ballroom in the spa or the chapel in Jesus' head.

"This is pretty watertight, Brit," I told her, folding up the contract. She wailed again.

"What's the bid up to?" Talbot asked as she climbed the steps to the altar.

"Forty thousand."

"Jesus!" I cried, forgetting for a moment where I was.

When our mother died, Brit and I were each left small trusts. Brit, having no head for or interest in money, had made me trustee over hers. Mom had also left a little extra for me to use to pay for a wedding for Brit, when that day arrived. We had nowhere near enough to cover a forty-thousand-dollar rental. We were already over budget as it was.

Talbot stood at the lectern and looked at us. "Tell me the truth. Does this pulpit make my ass look big?"

"Brit, there's no way we can cover that amount."

She closed her eyes and tried to hold back tears. "I simply *can't* get married in Jesus' head."

"We don't have a lot of guests," I consoled. Maybe the ballroom will be okay."

Talbot came down from the pulpit, flipping through a sheaf of papers she had found. "Do you *really* want to get married here?" she asked. "I mean, if they are willing to walk your wedding, they seem kind of sleazy."

Brit opened her eyes and wiped away the tears. "Of course not. Walking a wedding is *very* sleazy. But the wedding is in six weeks. Where in the *hell* would we find another church on this short of notice?"

"Why not do it someplace else. The park? The theater?"

She shrugged. "I'd love to get married someplace unusual. But Charles's coworkers are going to be there. I don't want them to think he's marrying some flake."

Talbot put an arm around her shoulder. "But honey, you *are* a flake."

Brit burst out laughing. "I guess we *could* get married in the theater…"

"Talk to Charles about it."

Back in the car, Talbot tossed the sheaf of papers into my lap. I glanced at them and saw that it was some form of church bulletin and directory. As we pulled away from the church, I noticed a parking space in front of the building housing the credit union. It said *Reserved for Archer Bellamy.* I opened the bulletin and saw his name in the directory. He was their director of property management.

As Talbot pulled up to the theater to drop me off, I noticed an ambulance pull away from the 'Hurst. Worried that something may have happened to Laine, I said a quick goodbye and ran across the street.

I ran into the lobby to see Laine talking to Clare and Zach. She saw me and a look of relief spread across her face. "Oh, Donovan. There you are."

"What was the ambulance for?" I asked as the lobby door swung shut behind me.

"Rachel," she announced dramatically. "They've taken her to Atlanta Medical."

"For what?"

"We don't know. She was running a terribly high fever and had very strong abdominal pains, so they think maybe her appendix burst.

"Is anyone with her?"

"Chris is. But I told them you would come along behind with a car to bring him home."

I nodded. Of course I would. "Zach, run across the street and open the theater so the cast can get in, and I'll pick you up out front." He nodded and ran out the door.

I ran downstairs, jumped in the Jeep and pulled up the driveway. Zach ran across the street and got in. As I drove off I told him, "You're going to have to navigate me to Atlanta Medical."

He turned and regarded me with a blank expression. I started to say something, but realized there was no more reason for him to know where it was located than I did. Instead I threw the Jeep into reverse, backed up to the building, and he ran in to ask Laine how to find it.

Thirty seconds later we were off again with instructions to turn left on Monroe, follow it to Boulevard and you can't miss it. As we drove, I noticed a tense, concerned look on his face. I shook his knee gently and said, "She'll be okay."

Monroe becomes Boulevard once you cross Ponce, and the entire character of the neighborhood changes. The manicured bungalows of the Highlands and the shabby-chic of Midtown immediately give way to the rougher character of Bedford-Pines and the Old Fourth Ward. I had driven through here occasionally before, but always found it a little intimidating. I subtly accelerated.

The hospital was on the right, just before Boulevard met Freedom Parkway. I pulled into the parking deck and parked, and we ran across the street to the entrance. We found Chris in the emergency room admitting area with Rachel's purse, trying to answer the many questions that the admission rep had for her forms.

I came up behind him as he was rummaging and asked, "Where is she?"

"They took her back for tests. Do you know what her blood type is?"

"No idea."

Once she had been admitted, there was nothing for us to do but sit down and wait. Well, there was nothing for me to do but settle down and wait. Chris and Zach, having the collective attention span of a gypsy moth, set off to explore the hospital.

After about an hour, I was informed that she was upstairs, and I set off to find her room. I opened the door gently, only to see her sitting up in bed, flipping through a magazine.

"Well," I announced as I walked in. "You hardly look like you are at death's door."

She smiled wanly at me. "It appears I either have a bad bladder infection or a kidney stone. They are waiting for the tests to come back."

I sat down on the bed and felt her forehead. She was hot, but not outrageously. "How do you feel?"

She shrugged. "Kinda sucky, but I suspect I'll live. I didn't think so earlier. I was up all night vomiting and I couldn't even get out of bed this afternoon. Chris said I was so pale I looked mocha."

I chuckled. "Are they going to keep you overnight?"

She nodded. "Probably."

"Do you want me to get you anything from home?"

"A pair of sweats. And could you take the ones I came in home? They're in the bag by the sink."

"You don't just want to keep those here?"

She shook her head. "Can't. I learned one of life's valuable little lessons today. Never startle your urologist."

I laughed. The door opened and Chris and Zach both looked around the corner sheepishly. "Can we come in?"

"Sure," she replied. "Might as well have the entire building here."

They came in and Rachel quickly recapped what she had just told me, except the urologist part. I could see relief spread across both their faces.

"Where have you two been, anyhow?" I asked.

They exchanged guilty looks. "Exploring," Chris said, unable to meet my gaze.

"Exploring?" I pressed.

"We, um, took a wrong turn and found ourselves in obstetrics," Zach confided. "It took us a while to find our way back."

Rachel smirked. "See anything that validated a lifestyle choice?"

They both nodded emphatically. Chris leaned in to confide to her, "I now know that gynecologists do not find the concept of Pappcicles amusing."

Visiting hours ended. Rachel rejected offers from each of us to stay the night with her, so the three of us piled into the Jeep and returned to the Highlands. I parked the Jeep and the two of them disappeared into the building while I walked across to lock up the theater. I noticed the lights were on upstairs in my office. The auditorium was dark and the entire cast had gone home, so I ascended the stairs to switch off the lights.

Miranda was lying on the couch in my office, shoes off, humming quietly to herself while making notes on a pad. I was surprised to see her as she usually left as soon as rehearsals were over. "Hey," I said pleasantly, happy that she was there. "What are you still doing here?"

"Liz is out of town working on a case in some god-forsaken place like Missoula, so I decided to hang out. Nothing gets the creative juices flowing like an evening in an empty theater, after all."

I smiled and crossed to a small refrigerator that I had installed behind my desk. "Want a beer?"

"Love one."

I removed two beers, opened them on a Coke bottle opener that was mounted to the side of my desk, and handed her one. "How was rehearsal?"

She rolled her eyes. "If you are ever asked to collaborate with a bunch of lesbians on a piece of political performance art, don't do it. Every bloody sentence uttered on stage has to be diagrammed."

"What do you mean?" I asked as I dropped into my chair and kicked off my shoes. I noticed the floor was a little dusty beneath my feet. I was going to have to get busy cleaning the non-public spaces soon, or else buy carpet.

"Oh, everyone has their own issue. Cara is a power-feminist, so we have to quibble about Groucho's lines to Mrs. Teasdale all the time."

"Even though they're in the original script?"

"Even though. And Tara can't understand that comedic delivery and satire are totally compatible with political rhetoric. Her natural tendency is to bark every joke like she's Stalin delivering a speech at May Day ceremonies. Lara has no issues with delivery or feminism, but she's totally hung up on subject-verb agreement, which is somewhat loose in the original script."

"And Sara?"

She rolled her eyes. "Sara has begun dating Tara's ex, so the entire cast is snubbing her. Where were you tonight?"

I explained about my whole day, covering all the ground between Rachel's bladder and Christ's head. "What are you working on?" I asked, pointing at the pad in her lap.

"I'm trying to write some lyrics for your show. If we can get a couple of poems written that have a good meter, I'm sure Clare or one of her friends could help us score them." I must have been beaming because she looked at me and added, "I know I haven't been much help as a collaborator recently, but I'll have a lot more time when we open."

"I understand." I actually did. We were opening in days and there was still much to work on.

The windows were open, and outside the sounds of our neighborhood saxophonist floated in. He was playing something that was familiar, but I couldn't quite place it. "Blues riff on saxophone."

"Huh?" she asked.

"Outside. The saxophone player is playing the blues."

"Does he have a name?" she asked. "I mean, besides *saxophone player*."

I shrugged. "I'm sure he does. I just don't know what it is. But he's playing the blues on a saxophone."

She smirked. "Who has the blues in Virginia Highland? This is preppy heaven." Miranda lived two neighborhoods over in Candler Park.

I reared up in righteous indignation. "I beg your pardon. We have the blues in the Highlands."

"Oh please. Over what? Your Bass Weejuns?"

"Well, yes, that's as good as any reason." I started singing. "*I've got those Weejun wearin' blues...*"

She joined in immediately. "*I've got those Weejun wearin', ethanol drivin'...*"

"*...Microbrew drinkin'...*"

We joined in chorus. "*I've got those Weejun wearin', ethanol drivin', microbrew drinkin', Virginia Highland left-wing livin' blue-ues.*"

Over the course of that evening, we wrote four songs together. In addition to the "Virginia Highland Blues," we also wrote "The Atkins Park Rag," "The Amsterdam Avenue Altercation," and "The Rhythm of Piedmont Park." We worked late into the night for each of the next three nights. The next night, we would write "The Moon over Saint Charles Bar and Grill" and "The Great Buffalo Wing Boycott of 1989." Then during the third night, we wrote "Requiem for Darryl the Dogwood."

I had never collaborated on writing with anyone before and, candidly, had always dreaded it. I was certain that I would always find my own creativity overruled by another. Instead, I found each of our ideas became great fodder for the other.

The next day, Zach and I retrieved Rachel from the hospital after an interminable wait. At one point Zach wandered off, leaving me alone for quite some time. The next time I saw him, he informed me a nurse had instructed him to write one hundred times *I will not crack walnuts with the mammogram machine.*

Once we had Rachel home, however, we found she made a lousy patient. Since she couldn't be at work *and* couldn't be with us working on the theater, she had nothing to fill her time. She called my cell phone just about every half hour. Finally, in a fit of desperation, I spoke to Laine, who hobbled upstairs to make her some tea and spend the afternoon talking to her.

That afternoon, Zach and I hung the letters on the marquee announcing *Duck Soup* and took delivery of all the costumes. As soon as that truck pulled away, Talbot's gold Mercedes berthed itself on the sidewalk, and she unpacked into the lobby a copious amount of beer and wine, which Zach and I had to schlep up to the office.

"You know, it's just a little show," I informed her. "We don't need this much wine."

"You've never seen an Atlanta theater audience," she replied. "This may not be enough."

No sooner had Talbot left than the portable bar we had rented arrived. We set it up in the lobby beneath the staircase.

And finally, as I was signing for the delivery, the cast arrived. Tonight would be the first dress rehearsal, not just for the cast, but for all of us as well. Shortly behind the cast came the citizens of the 'Hurst. Jennifer was going to man the bar with Rachel, although Laine had commanded her patient to stay at home in bed that evening. Charles and Brit were going to run the ticket booth, and Zach and Chris would be ushering. Clare's contract with the symphony prevented her from actually "working" for us, but she was quietly giving us advice and direction. Laine had no "official" duties, but intended to exercise her right as landlord to supervise all activities not taking place on the stage.

There was a great deal of hubbub. The cast was not having a good rehearsal. Clare's copious amount of advice was not appreciated by Miranda. Charles and Brit were snippy with each other. Zach and Chris were snippy with each other. Laine and I were snippy with each other. All of us were desperately trying to have things together before opening night, and unfortunately, nothing was coming together.

And then, much to my chagrin, Rachel arrived.

She was dressed in an oversized football jersey, a pair of sweat pants, and some fuzzy slippers. She wore no makeup, and her hair was all pulled up and crammed under a baseball hat. She was carrying a big shopping bag.

When she arrived, Chris, Jennifer, Laine, and I were in the process of arguing or how best to set up the bar for two servers. I probably would not have even noticed her, but I heard Brit open the ticket booth door and say aloud, "What the hell are you doing out of bed?"

I turned to see Rachel trying to quietly shut the lobby door. We made eye contact, and she favored me with a sheepish grin. "Opening night's just two nights away."

I came around from behind the bar and said, "You should not be out of bed."

She shrugged. "I'll go back soon. I brought champagne."

Laine came up behind me. "That's nice, dear, but really you need to be in bed."

She proceeded past us, smiling politely, as if we were speaking some foreign language she did not understand. "No , really, I brought champagne. It's important."

"What are you talking about?" Chris asked, snippily.

"What I am talking about is that the marquee needs to be relit, and we can't just throw a switch." She unpacked a bottle of Cuvee and a smaller bottle of Freixenet. "I've been reading a lot about theaters and theater history at work lately. The marquee needs to be lit before the show, and everything in the theater involves creating tradition for good luck and bad luck. So, we need to christen her."

I could tell she was weak and did not feel good. It was also obvious she was on a mission, so I asked, helplessly, "If we comply with this, will you go back to bed?"

"Oh yes." She began to assemble plastic champagne flutes. "Could you go ask the girls if they could take a break and meet us on the front sidewalk?"

I had not really, ever, thought of the cast as *the girls*, but I did as she asked. Miranda was just about ready to pull her hair out, and she actually welcomed the distraction. She marshaled the entire cast and they followed me up the aisle and out the door.

While I had been in the auditorium, Rachel had managed to get everyone else outside, except Zach, who sat in the ticket booth. Once all of us were outside, and several people had protested to Rachel that she should not be out of bed, she held up her hand and said, "Friends, many of you may not understand this, but us *chicks of color* are descended from a line of women who believe there is a lot more in this universe than what meets the eye. I believe that all great adventures start with a great beginning, and it seems to me that it is time to start this adventure. So, since the marquee has not been officially lit yet, I thought it was probably appropriate to christen the theater. So…"

Even though I had switched on the marquee to make sure all the lights worked, it had only been in daylight. The marquee had yet to be lit at night, and certainly not *officially.* She handed Laine the cheaper bottle of champagne. "Laine, I thought it would be most appropriate, since the theater is named in your honor, for you to break the bottle across the ticket booth."

Laine, smiling, took the bottle of champagne, and looked at a loss. After a long moment, Rachel ventured, "My idea was that you would actually hit the building with the bottle."

"And waste this good champagne?" she replied, indignant. "That hardly seems fitting."

"We have a better bottle for us to drink," Rachel replied, a little impatiently.

"We should drink both," Laine protested. "I just can't abide the thought of wasting good champagne."

"Laine, it's just a cheap bottle. It's justifiable."

"Rachel, dear, I was born during Prohibition and grew up during the Depression. In my world there is no such thing as a *justifiable* waste of champagne."

A few minutes of intense negotiation followed, during which Laine adamantly refused to break the bottle. Several lesbians decided to join the fray, and the point that we were just opening a theater, not actually putting out to sea in one, was actively debated. Finally, it was decided that she would open the bottle, and simply throw a glass of champagne against the ticket booth rather than actually break the bottle.

She handed the bottle to me and I popped the cork. I filled glasses all the way around, and then Laine drew herself up regally, plastic champagne flute held high, stared at the ticket booth and pronounced, "I christen thee the Theater DeLaine. God bless all who are entertained in her." With that, she snapped her hand downward with a flourish reminiscent of Faye Dunaway in *Mommie Dearest*. Champagne splashed against the ticket booth window, and at the same moment, Zach hit the switch. Overhead, there was a momentary pause during which we could hear the buzzing as relays charged and closed. Suddenly, for the first time in about forty years, the ninety-six bulbs in the marquee ceiling began to flicker on and off. A second later, the fluorescent tubes behind the milk glass panels sputtered to life and illuminated the announcement "Duck Soup: A Political Allegory. Opens Friday!" A second after that, the neon tubes on either side of the marquee warmed enough to begin glowing. And lastly, the bulbs behind the brass letters on top switched on, and the name "Theater DeLaine" was backlit against the night sky.

All of us stared at the marquee in silence. I felt tears welling in my eyes for reasons I could not fathom, and my vision blurred. Zach came running out of the theater, turned around, looked up at the marquee and asked softly, "How awesome is *that*?"

How awesome indeed?

We began pouring the *good* champagne for everyone gathered, and were, for the most part, oblivious to Laine dabbing the cheap champagne off the window with her fingers and then licking them.

After that, it was like a spell was broken. Everyone's mood shifted, and we were all in a better place mentally and emotionally. I escorted Rachel back to her apartment, and tucked her back into bed. Then, as I crossed the street to return to work, I had to stop on the sidewalk and just stare. Against all odds, I was about to open a theater. I felt an immense sense of achievement well up in me.

Unbeknownst to me, Archer Bellamy was watching it as well.

Opening night arrived. Well, opening day of opening night arrived. For once, I was up before the Feldmans were. I was a mass of nerves, and I wasn't even the one going on stage that night. Lying in bed, I was also keenly aware of the number of things I felt I *should* have done before opening night that I had not. I had wanted to fix the cracked tiles in the men's room, shampoo the lobby carpet, polish the stair banisters, clean the windows. None of that would get done.

The nervous energy ran through the entire building. Despite the fact it was a Friday, no one in the building went to work except for Zach, and that's only because I made him. Even Laine seemed to be at loose ends, and hardly touched her manhattan at lunch.

I went over to the theater around noon. The building itself seemed to be waiting, expectantly. I had been alone in the theater nearly every day since I had first wandered in, but as I switched on the lights I looked out onto a different room. Each day, prior to this, it had been a project; something I was working towards. Now, despite the cracked tile and tarnish on the banister, I saw it as ready. The newly upholstered seats marched forward to the stage. As I walked down the center aisle, the mustiness that I had come to associate with the place was gone. I mounted the steps and stood beneath the proscenium and turned to look back out into the auditorium. For just a moment I could envision an audience staring back up at me as the lights dimmed. I smiled, walked beneath the proscenium, and pulled the rope for the great curtain. Slowly, it slid downward from the catwalks above. The weights in the hem met the stage with a reassuring brush, and the ghost light teetered slightly. I tied the rope off. She was primed and ready.

I walked upstairs to my office and began to slide the couch out. It was my intent to put it on the balcony, so I could watch the show from there. I had only managed to pull it away from the wall when the buzzer rang.

We had installed a small doorbell button next to the ticket booth, so people could signal whoever was inside when the door was locked. I ran down the stairs, and there was a pretty young woman standing on the other side of the glass. I opened the speaker hole in the ticket window, and she asked whether she could buy two tickets for opening night. We had been selling tickets over the internet via the troupe's website. Excitedly, I ran upstairs, grabbed my laptop, brought it down, and made my very first sale. She paid in cash, and I took the twenty, the *first* twenty the theater had made, and tucked it in my shirt pocket. I would frame it later. It still hangs in the ticket booth.

I managed to get the couch into the outer office when the buzzer rang again. I dashed downstairs and made another sale. Back upstairs, I had it into the hall when the buzzer rang again.

And so it went. I did a brisk business selling tickets and accomplished nothing else, apart from getting my couch into the empty loge. Once it was finally in position, I returned to the office, only to hear the buzzer ring again. I walked back down, beginning to feel a little winded. There was no one down there, but a manila envelope was leaning against the glass.

I walked around the ticket booth, opened the door and retrieved the envelope. It was addressed to Donovan Ford in a handwriting I had come to recognize as Mister Kersey's. I looked either way but there was no one who immediately struck me as an elderly recluse.

I carried the envelope upstairs to my office and opened the window. Even though it was the height of a Georgia summer, I resisted turning on the air conditioning when it was just me in the building. I didn't want to spend the money. I sat down to open the package as outside, our friendly neighborhood saxophonist was playing "Man of La Mancha."

I have a small pewter dagger that I keep in my desk and use as a letter opener. It was a wedding gift from Liv. (Shoulda known, shoulda known.) As I retrieved it and cut open the envelope, I sang along to the saxophone. "…My destiny calls and I go, and the wild winds of fortune will carry me onward, oh whithersoever they blow. Whithersoever they blow, onward to glory I go!"

Inside of the envelope was yet another program. I smiled indulgently for a moment before I realized what it was. On the cover, it announced the grand opening of the Briarcliff. It was a delicate thing, fragile with age, and I laid it gingerly on the desk. There was also a note from Mister Kersey that said, simply, *Break a leg.*

At three, Zach came over to man the ticket booth. He was carrying two garment bags. The previous weekend, on a whim, Chris and I had taken him to a discount men's clothier on the west side of town and bought him his first tuxedo. One bag held his tuxedo, the other held mine. It had been decided that, for all of us at the 'Hurst, tonight would be a black tie affair.

Once Zach was settled into the ticket booth, I returned to my office, pulled a box of stationery out of my desk and dashed off a quick note to Mister Kersey thanking him for all the gifts and consideration. I slipped it into an envelope, and walked back downstairs.

"Zach, pull two tickets for me."

He shrugged. "Sure, for anyone in particular?"

"Don't know," I replied. He gave me a quizzical look, registered the tickets on the computer and handed them over to me. I pulled the note back out of the envelope and added a postscript. "Please feel free to join me as my guest. There will always be a seat in the balcony for you."

"Back in a minute," I told Zach and crossed the street. The saxophone player was still on the street, but talking to one of the locals as I slipped back into the building. I walked quickly past Aunt Laine's door to the one just behind, and gently slid the note underneath. I pictured him as a gaunt, aged, timid little old man. I would be on the lookout for him that evening.

As I crossed back over Highland the saxophone player resumed playing. With my first step off the curb he began "Comedy Tonight," from *A Funny Thing Happened on the Way to the Forum.* I began to sing in the middle of the street. "Something familiar, something peculiar…"

The cast arrived at six and immediately disappeared behind the curtain into the dressing rooms. I saw Miranda only once, looking elegant in a black crepe pantsuit. She informed me that all the typical actor superstitions and good-luck rites were being carried out backstage. I kissed her on the cheek for luck, and told her to join me in the balcony, if she could, once the show started.

She nodded. "Once this turkey is off the ground, we need to get back to work on our script."

"Anytime," I replied.

Charles and Brit helped navigate Aunt Laine across the street. I had perched a stool next to the front door, ostensibly to let Laine hand out programs, but really to give her a spot to feel like she was center of attention, but sufficiently out of the way that she wouldn't bother me.

"Oh, I don't know if he will show," I told her as she stored her thermos of manhattans behind the bar, "But I invited Mister Kersey."

"Really?" she replied, eyebrows raised. "Have you met him?"

"No, I haven't. But since he has been so kind to give me all the memorabilia, I gave him two tickets and a little note telling him he was welcome to come as my guest. I would always keep a seat in the balcony for him."

Her eyes glittered mischievously. "Well, if he comes in, I'll be sure to send him up. In the meantime, hadn't you better change? Doors open soon."

"Yes'm." I headed up the stairs to my office, calling to Zach that he needed to change as well. Once inside the office, I unzipped the garment bag and pulled the tuxedo out, hanging it from the top drawer of the filing cabinet. I pulled the small box of studs and cufflinks out of one of the shoes from the bottom of the bag, and began the ordeal of fastening them to the shirt before I put it on.

Zach knocked and opened the door. "Mine's in here as well."

"No worries," I replied, still stuffing the studs through the shirt. They are sterling-and-pearl, and belonged to my grandfather. I wondered idly if my father knew I had them.

Zach retrieved his tux, and stepped back into the outer office to change. I pulled off my golf shirt, pulled on a tank top and then the tux shirt and began the elaborate process of fastening it. Once I had it on, I kicked off my flip flops and slid out of my shorts. I pulled on the dress pants and sat down to put on my shoes and socks.

"Van?" Zach asked. "I've got four holes and only three studs."

Chris had given him one of his old tuxedo shirts, and the plastic studs that had come with it. "Three is all you need. Top one goes in the first hole below the collar. The fourth is optional."

I finished tying my shoes, stood and retrieved the bow tie and began tying it. Once it was tied, I slipped my white suspenders on and fastened the cummerbund. Zach came around the corner staring at his. "Which way is up?"

"The exact opposite way your instinct tells you."

He stared at it for a moment. "So the folds are up?"

"Yep. Like you *intend* for them to catch crumbs, 'cause that's what they are going to do."

I pulled on my jacket and, out of instinct, felt inside my pockets. Liv always said my jackets were time capsules of memorabilia. Old ticket stubs, valet tickets, the various documentation of where I had last worn that particular garment.

In this particular case I came away with two tickets to a New Year's Eve party at the Algonquin. It had been the last New Year's Liv and I had spent together before the divorce. We knew we were on the rocks at the time, but we were both still giving it a fighting chance to recover.

She had been wearing (uncharacteristically) a red Richard Tyler gown that evening, off the shoulder with a striking white bodice, and the pearls I had bought her with my first profit-sharing check from the magazine. She had been stunning. A strange wistfulness washed over me, and I was totally unaware that Zach had been talking to me.

"Van?" he repeated, rousing me from my reverie.

"I'm sorry, Zach. I went away for a moment. What did you say?"

"I asked if you would help me with my cufflinks. I can't get them together."

"Sure," I replied, standing up and stashing the tickets back in my pocket. I know I should have thrown them away, but I wanted to hold on to that moment for just a while longer.

I clasped his cufflinks and stood him back. Thinking of Liv had somehow made me feel generous. "Y'know, you're a pretty sharp-looking kid. Some guy is going to be lucky to have you."

He blushed and rolled his eyes. Beneath the feigned impatience, though, I could tell he appreciated the compliment. The two of us returned to the first floor.

Jennifer and Rachel had arrived, and were busy setting up the bar. In the ticket booth, Brit and Charles were handing out tickets and ringing up sales at a brisk pace. On the other side of the doors I could see a crowd milling about. Chris stood by the door, chatting idly with Laine. Everyone was bedecked in finery. All the men wore tuxedos. Brit had on a very smart turquoise suit. Laine looked smashing in a black pair of silk pants topped with a paisley jacket and a red Hermes blouse. I complimented myself on how well turned out my theater looked.

My nerves were on edge, so I stepped into the theater looking for a bit of calm. Instead I heard a man's voice coming from the stage. I walked towards it.

"Flee!" called the voice with a slight Long Island accent.

"Flee!" a chorus of women's voices replied.

"Flee fly!" he called again.

"Flee fly!" came the response.

"Flee fly fo!"

"Flee fly fo!"

I slipped behind the curtain to see the entire cast facing a short guy with curly dark hair wearing an Atlanta Braves jersey.

"Bista!"

"Bista!" There was a certain glee in their responses.

"Cumalama cumalama cumalama bista!" I glanced to my right to see Miranda leaning against the set, watching the exchange with a bemused look on her face.

"Cumalama cumalama cumalama bista!"

We made eye contact, and I crossed over to her, mouthing, "What's going on?"

He sang, "Oh, no, no-no capista!"

"It's a combo warm-up, good luck tradition," she replied.

"Oh, no, no-no capista!"

"Who's the guy?"

"Eeney meeny decameeny ooh wanna wanna meany. Decameeny salameeny ooh wanna wah."

"A friend of Cara's. He's in a local improv troupe in town."

"Eeney meeny decameeny ooh wanna wanna meany. Decameeny salameeny ooh wanna wah."

The guy threw his hand out and they all ran forward. All of them chanted together, "Beep bidiobob bebop a bop bop be there!"

There was lots of laughter and clapping. Miranda whispered to me, "We've now exercised every possible good-luck ritual except drinking the blood of an owl and sacrificing a virgin during a full moon."

"Where would you find a virgin in the Highlands anyhow?" I glanced at my watch. "Time to open the doors."

She took a deep breath and nodded. Then she held her right fist forward to me. "Break a leg."

I punched her fist back gently. "Break a leg."

She corralled the cast downstairs to the rehearsal hall, I'm sure for one more last-minute ritual, and I returned to the lobby. The room fairly crackled with energy. I kissed my aunt on the cheek and then announced, "It's time."

A hush fell over the lobby and I crossed to the doors. Under my breath I said, "May good fortune favor the foolish," and unlocked the door to the left of the ticket booth. As I crossed behind the booth, Charles winked at me and pulled the door shut. I unlocked the door on the right side of the booth and pulled it open. The crowd came in, tentatively at first, and then in a great rush.

The lobby filled up almost immediately. I retrieved a small headset that allowed me to communicate with Mac, who was up in the old projection room with the technical staff, and with Miranda, who was backstage. My job was to move everyone from the front of the house into the theater when the show started. I listened to mostly idle chatter over the headset, and stood on the stairs, watching as people milled about the lobby, getting drinks and checking their programs, before deciding to make their way to their seats. We had opened the door ninety minutes before the curtain, so they had time to kill.

I noticed that a fair number of them seemed to know Laine. Talbot came in with some distinguished older gentleman on her arm. She introduced me to him, and over his shoulder I saw Archer Bellamy come through the door. He looked around suspiciously. His overall demeanor fit in with this crowd about as well as an Amish farmer on stage with Cirque du Soleil.

The time sped by, and what felt like minutes later, I got the word from Miranda to flash the lights. I walked up the stairs and flashed the lobby lights, while upstairs in the booth, Mac flashed the auditorium lights. The crowd immediately surged into the theater. I ran up the rest of the steps, down the hidden hallway past the stage left box, and down the steps to the stage. Miranda was waiting at the bottom and I could see the rest of the cast in the shadows. "You ready?" she asked me, and I could her hear her voice both normally and through the headset.

I nodded and pulled off my headset. "Yep."

She nodded and said into the headset, "Cue houselights."

Through a small space between the proscenium and the curtain, I could see the houselights go down. A second later, a spot hit the stage just past the arch. I took a deep breath and, for the first time in my life, stepped onto a stage in front of a live audience.

The audience applauded politely and I walked to the center of the stage. Turning, I smiled, and waited for the applause to die down.

"Ladies and gentlemen, good evening. I'm Donovan Ford, general manager of Theater DeLaine, and I would like to welcome you to both the premiere of *Duck Soup,* and the grand rededication of this theater, after sitting unused for nearly thirty years." More applause.

"Being as most of you probably have never been in here before, please notice the location of the emergency exits." I pointed them out. "And, as a courtesy to our performers, please switch your pagers and cell phones to vibrate." I paused a beat. "But why would you ever wear them any other way?" This received a polite chuckle. "Now, please, sit back and enjoy the show." With that I walked back into the wings, and the spot light went off, plunging us into darkness.

As instructed by Miranda, I found the wall with my left hand and pressed my back against it, while she said into the headset, "Curtain."

The curtain rose, the lights came up on the cast standing there, and Lara spoke the first line.

And, just like that, we were a theater.

I stayed backstage for the first twenty minutes of the first act, and then snuck up to the secret hallway on the second floor. I stopped for a minute in the stage right box so I could watch the audience. They were laughing in all the right places, and seemed attentive enough. We were playing to a packed house, which was definitely a good thing. It occurred to me that, before the show closed in a few weeks, I should sit down and decide what other shows to book until I had mine done.

Other shows to book? I thought to myself as I resumed my walk to the front of the theater. I had dropped even the pretense that I wasn't going to try make a go of this place.

I rounded the corner and let myself through the doors into the balcony. I noticed that someone was already occupying the couch. For a moment I thought it was the elusive Mister Kersey, but closer inspection revealed it was Laine, primly sipping her manhattan.

"I thought you were Mister Kersey," I whispered as I sat down next to her.

"He's taller than me," she replied, giving my knee a little squeeze. "And, he didn't want to come upstairs. He said he'd rather sit in with the audience."

"He's here?"

She nodded. "Downstairs. Came in near the end."

"Can you introduce me to him?"

"If the opportunity presents itself. I expect if it does, though, he'll introduce himself to you."

There was a sudden burst of laughter from the audience. The show was going well. As the laughter died down, I noticed someone sitting on the rail at the left end of the balcony, leaning against the wall. I asked Laine if she knew who it was, and she said he had been up here when she got here, so she assumed he was a friend of mine.

I got up and casually walked to the rail and looked over, glancing to the left. I realized it was the guy who had been backstage leading the troupe through their warm up. We made eye contact and he smiled, so I walked over to meet him.

"Hi," I said. "I didn't get to meet you before. I'm Donovan Ford."

He shook my hand and smiled. "Nathan Kleinmann. My friends call me Klein."

"It's a pleasure, Klein."

"Thanks," he replied. "Great venue you've got here."

I nodded. "We feel lucky to have it."

"Hope you don't mind me being up here. Miranda invited me to stay and told me you wouldn't mind if I watched from up here."

"No worries."

We watched the show for a while. I was amazed to see that we were nearly at the end of the first act. I was sure the show had only been going on for ten minutes.

"That was one weird warm-up you put the troupe through this afternoon," I informed him.

He grinned. "Yeah. Cara asked me to come do that. We used to be in the same improv troupe and that's how we always warmed up."

"What's it mean?"

He shrugged. "No idea. It existed in the troupe long before we got there."

I glanced at my watch. "I need to go downstairs and check on things before intermission," I told him. "Feel free to hang out up here, though. The old gal on the couch is DeLaine Fairchild. She actually owns the place."

"Cool!" he replied. "Thanks."

I descended the stairs to see everyone moving into position for intermission. The ticket office was closed, and Charles and Brit had joined Rachel and Jennifer behind the bar to serve.

Chris and I took up posts at the auditorium doors, and as soon as we heard the huge laugh that Miranda had hoped would signify the end of the first act, we pulled the doors opened. Inside, the stage had just gone dark and the house lights were coming up slowly. The crowd was getting to its feet, and I noted smiles everywhere. Years of shows had taught me that an audience that was smiling at intermission was a good omen for how the show would do. Even audiences attending bleak dramas will smile at intermission if they are enjoying the show. An audience that looks like it is making up its grocery list in its head usually means a quick close.

The crowd came into the lobby and immediately split into lines for the bar and lines for the bathrooms. There was not enough room for me to help behind the bar, and helping out in the restrooms struck me as creepy, so Chris and I retired to the stairs to stand watch.

I noticed Archer Bellamy shoving his way through the crowd. He was not smiling, nor did he look like he was making out his grocery list in his head. He looked pissed. He stormed up to the side of the bar and immediately demanded attention from Charles, who was working the bar.

"You need to open the ticket office back up!" Bellamy demanded. "I want my money back."

Even though Charles had lived in the States since grad school, he had never become accustomed to American indignation. "Sir, I'm handling these customers at the moment," he answered, masking his surprise. "Once intermission is over..."

"I don't care about these customers, I..."

"Apparently," Charles replied icily as he poured a glass of shiraz.

I came to the end of the steps. "I'll handle it, Charles." I remained on the steps so I stood a bit above him, held out my hand and said, "Mister Bellamy, I believe? I'm Donovan Ford, the general manager of the theater."

Bellamy chose not to shake my hand. "Yeah. I want my money back."

When it became obvious that he was not going to shake my hand, I'm sure I flared my nostrils (a trait I had appropriated at some point from Olivia), withdrew it slightly and said, "Why don't you come up to my office and we'll discuss it?"

"Only if it ends in me getting my money back."

I thought of every theater I had ever attended in New York. Money was not returned. You attended the show. If you walked out, it was your problem. Rather than be that blunt, I asked, "What's the problem?"

"This is a piece of trash is what the problem is," he replied. I notice an amused hush fall over the crowd gathered in the lobby. They were pleased to discover that there would be theater during the intermission as well. "It's liberal, anti-American dissent bullshit."

I felt my eyebrows arch in surprise. "Dissent is anti-American?"

"Yes."

"And you learned that *where?*"

I heard a couple of suppressed chuckles from the crowd.

"I'm not paying good money to sit here and watch my president get ridiculed." His puffy face began to grow red. At the back of the crowd, I noticed Raymond the cop leaning against the wall. He was dressed in civvies and sipping a beer, watching everything unfold. Our eyes met for just a second and he winked.

"No one's got a gun to your head," I replied evenly. "However, protest theater *is* perfectly American."

He lost patience with me, clearly not in the mood to discuss the Constitution. "Just give me my money back."

"In a word, no."

The red face began to approach purple. He took a step forward. "Give me my money back," he fairly shrieked.

"You paid to see the show. The show is going on. You can stay or not stay as you like, but we made no warranty that you would like it. Only that we would present it."

He took a deep, snuffly sounding breath. "I'll sue you…"

"Over a ten-dollar theater ticket that had no real or implied warranty? I'm sure you could, but I doubt even the small claims court would be interested in hearing your case."

He took a step towards me, "I should tear you up." I found the concept of it amusing since he was probably forty pounds overweight. However before I could answer, Raymond's hand fell hard on his shoulder. He spun him around and slammed him hard against the stair rail below me.

He fixed Bellamy with a cold, menacing stare and said, "Donovan, did I just hear this gentleman threaten you with bodily harm?"

"Who the f..." Bellamy began, clearly not recognizing him.

I leaned down and whispered in his ear, "This is the same cop you pissed off the day you moved in. I'd keep my mouth shut if I were you." I could see the recognition register in his eyes. He swallowed hard. Turning my attention to Raymond I said, "Thanks officer. Mister Bellamy was just leaving."

Raymond leaned forward so that his nose was a mere inch from Archer's.

"That would be a good thing," he growled. "And I hope *Mister* Bellamy realizes that if anything happens to you or to Miz DeLaine's theater, he will be *the first person I go to to find out what happened.*" He stared at Archer for another moment and then let go of his shirt.

"Good night, Mister Bellamy," I said evenly.

The crowd parted and Archer walked quietly towards the door. When he reached it he opened it, clearly wanting to get the last word in. But he looked back at a crowd of mostly amused liberals, a few lesbians ready for a fight, and one enormous cop, and thought better of it. He turned and walked out into the night. As soon as the door had settled back into the frame, the crowd erupted in laughter and cheering. Raymond turned, looked up at me and said, "What an ass."

I shrugged. "World's full of 'em."

"Yeah, but the Highlands ain't. His type usually sticks to the far outer suburbs where they're sure they only have to deal with other white people and Republicans."

I laughed. Over the headset I heard Miranda say "Curtain in five."

I announced to the crowd, "Ladies and gentlemen, if you would find your way to your seats, act two is about to begin." Then, laying a hand on Raymond's shoulder, I told Charles, "Charles, the cop drinks for free." Turning to Raymond, I added, "Appreciate knowing you've got my back, Officer."

He smiled and we shook hands. "Hey, we appreciate you bringing theater to the neighborhood. Can't wait to see what your next show's gonna be." He accepted a fresh beer from Charles, crossed the lobby and put his arm around a very attractive woman who I guessed was his wife, and escorted her back into the auditorium.

I retrieved two beers from Charles. He leaned in to me and said, confidentially, "Brit told me that Bellamy works at that god-awful church. If there was even a remote chance I would get married in a giant concrete head – and there's not – there's no way I would give money to help pay that asshole's salary. We're very grateful for your offer, and will definitely get married here."

I returned to the balcony. Klein was now sitting on the couch next to Laine. They were laughing conspiratorially like old friends. I came around the couch and offered one of the beers to Klein, who accepted gratefully. As Laine poured herself a fresh manhattan she asked, "What was all the commotion downstairs, dear?"

I shrugged and leaned my back against the rail. "Archer Bellamy didn't enjoy the show and was putting up a ruckus demanding his money back. Fortunately Raymond Franklin was downstairs and put the fear of God in him."

Laine rolled her eyes. "Rube," she pronounced, then abruptly changed the topic. "Donovan, Klein here is an actor and a comedian."

"So I've heard" I said, smiling at him.

"In my spare time. Mostly improv. I'm part of a troupe called Scanlon," he told me. "If you're ever looking for someone to fill the venue, let me know. Or, hell, if you've got a part I could audition for."

I smiled at him. "Never know what's going to happen in this place," I replied. Behind me, the overture for Act Two started, and the house lights came down.

The show ended triumphantly, and the crowd burst out of the theater in a raucous din of laughter, chatter, and praise. Miranda and I stood at the stairway landing, listening. We exchanged smiling glances. "I believe you have a hit," I told her.

She cast her eyes heavenward and wiped imaginary sweat from her brow. "*We* have a hit," she corrected me.

Despite the fact I had never introduced them, Laine had somehow figured out who Talbot was, how to get in touch with her, and how to get her to illegally sell Laine a case of champagne at cost, which she'd had Zach keep on ice someplace where I wouldn't find it. Once the crowd was gone, all of us—cast, crew and sundry residents of the 'Hurst —gathered together on the stage. Bottles were opened, glasses were poured, and Laine stood proudly in the center and made a toast.

"Thank you all for being here tonight at the rebirth of this little theater. Arthur Miller once said 'spirit is like a child, you can never catch it by running after it; you must stand still, and, for love, it will soon itself come back.' This theater has stood here a long time waiting for some spirit to return to it. I'm sure the building thinks it was well worth the wait. I certainly do. So, please raise your glasses in a toast: to *Duck Soup* and the reborn Theater DeLaine."

The assembled crowd cheered the toast and drank their champagne. As soon as it was consumed, the cast meandered out to celebrate opening night, my friends and family dissipated back to their homes, and I found myself alone in the theater to close up. I made a quick tour to ensure no one had remained behind, locked all the doors, and shut off all the lights, save the ghost light on the stage. Then I made my way upstairs to close up my office. I found Miranda on my couch, making pencil edits in my script.

"Shouldn't you be celebrating?" I asked.

She held up her glass of champagne. "I am."

"I meant out there?"

She smiled indulgently at me. "Liz has already gone home to bed. I personally don't like to go out and celebrate the opening night. I prefer the cast party after we wrap. My own superstition, I suppose. Besides, I've got some ideas on the script I want you to consider."

"Funny," I replied, pulling my bow tie so the ends fell loosely away from the knot. "I've got someone I want you to consider casting as the lead."

Crepe Myrtle

For a brief period in their early married life, Laine and Maurice had lived in San Bernardino, California. It was near the end of World War II, and Uncle Mo had been stationed there. Chances that he would be sent overseas were slim, so Laine followed him out. She was recounting this one sultry, humid, early-August Friday afternoon as I drove her home from a day of shopping at Lenox Square Mall with Bitsy Hollander. All through the Highlands, crepe myrtles were blazing into bloom, which is what had prompted the conversation.

"There is a road in San Bernardino called Sierra Way," she informed me, gazing out the window, "And it was lined for miles with crepe myrtles. Simply lovely. Of course, Maurice never noticed. Every summer, after we came back east, I would reminisce about the crepe myrtles on Sierra Way, and he'd always tell me there were no crepe myrtles on Sierra Way."

She paused in a moment of silent reverie and then pronounced, "*Idiot*! He was wrong, of course. But we'd argue about it for the entire month of August." She still missed Maurice, even though he had been dead for years.

I thought idly of Olivia. I wondered how she was doing, more out of curiosity than out of sentimentality.

As we turned past the theater, I noticed a bit of motion in front of it. It was a breeze blowing a corner of the banner I had hung that morning from the marquee announcing the closing of *Duck Soup.*

The show had run successfully for four weeks, and was now winding down to its close that evening. We had received good reviews for the show itself from the various papers in town. Each of them had included a comment or two about what a great venue Theater DeLaine was, and how lucky the city was that this "jewel-box of a theater" had been restored. The local free paper had even done another full-page article on it and its eccentric owner and namesake.

Spurred by how well the show had done, as well as my keen awareness that I had had no income for almost the last year, I had confided my plans to make the theater a going concern to Laine, and had even told her the first show I planned to run would be one of my own. She excitedly encouraged me, and had underwritten my incorporation as Donovan Ford Productions, LLC.

I had made a little money off of *Duck Soup*, but didn't pocket it myself. The manpower to run the theater had been provided by my friends and family. Instead, I put some of it away to throw a fantastic wrap party for all of them to thank them. I put the rest away and, working with Clare, planned to use it to actually pay for a professional cleaning company, as well as a part-time house manager. She also helped me recruit and orchestrate a team of volunteers to be ticket-takers and ushers.

Our timeline was pretty clear. First, the show had to close on Saturday so we could use the theater the following weekend for Brit and Charles's wedding. For convenience, they had elected to get married on the *Duck Soup* set, rather than have us try to *churchify* the theater.

The week after that, we would start work on the new show, tentatively titled *Highlands-A-Go-Go*. Miranda and I had a nearly completed script and score. We were ready to do a staged reading of it, but both of us had been putting it off. I think, subconsciously, we were both scared of it. Neither of us had ever gone this far out on a limb with material we had created before.

Our goal was to have the show cast by Labor Day, and go into rehearsals the following week. As a bit of lyric inspiration, many of the main characters were now named after colleges in the city. My personal favorite was the matriarch, Mercer Oglethorpe.

The real challenge that faced me was what to do with the theater until I could mount my show. This concern must have been apparent on my face because Laine offered, "Penny for your thoughts."

"That's all?" I smirked as I turned down the driveway. "When I was writing for *Gothic* my thoughts earned a lot more than that."

"Only in Manhattan," she confided. "No one read you down here."

"Fair," I pronounced and made the sharp U-turn around Jennifer's Sebring convertible, and pulled into the garage. "In answer to your question, I'm trying to figure out how to get some money out of the theater between now and the time I open Highlands-A-Go-Go. At some point, I have to start making real money again. I can't live in your attic forever."

"You can if you want," she replied.

I shrugged. "I appreciate that, Laine, but I also need to make something of myself."

She said nothing and let the matter drop. I retrieved her bags from the trunk and carted them up the stairs to her apartment. Once she was settled in with her packages and a manhattan, I dropped down the front stoop and walked across the street. It was blisteringly hot outside, and I knew the theater would be beyond stuffy. I briefly considered turning on the air conditioning for a while, thought of the money and thought better of it. Instead I just pulled off my shirt and tucked it into the belt of my shorts.

My office (which was now doing double duty as the headquarters of Donovan Ford Productions) was stifling. I opened the windows and switched on the two fans I kept in there now to try to get air moving. I took a bottle of water out of my small refrigerator and held it against the back of my neck while I played the answering machine messages. They were all ticket requests for that evening and the following. We stood to be sold out both nights.

I spent the next two hours seated at the Casio keyboard Miranda had installed, picking out the melody line of the final production number in the show. I was struggling to find a humorous rhyme for a line ending in the words *Atlanta traffic*. Across the street, I heard a lawnmower fire up. I glanced out the window to see Zach starting to cut the lawn. He had assumed most of the handyman responsibilities around the 'Hurst while

I had focused more and more of my time and attention to the theater. Although he was naturally lean to begin with, a summer of hard work had hardened his body, and he had a nice deep tan across his chest, back and legs. While it had hardened his body, it had also done something to soften his spirit. He was more trusting and the emotional wariness that was the natural outcome of two years living in the basement seemed to be receding as he figured out how his life worked.

At around four, I had to switch on the air conditioning if I wanted the theater to be cool enough for the show. I pulled the windows shut and dropped down to the lobby to fire it up. As I switched it on, I heard a key in the lock and turned to see Miranda letting herself in. I had made a key for her when it became clear we were going to be working together long term. "Thank God you're turning that on," she said without greeting. "It's as hot in here as it is outside. I don't understand how you can work in here like this."

I shrugged. "People worked in hot theaters for thousands of years. Air conditioning is only a recent dramatic device."

"But a welcome one." She followed me up the stairs to the office, settled down at the keyboard and began humming the score I had spent the last two hours working on. "*La la dum dum de dee... the cream of Atlantastocracy are we.*" She turned and smiled at me. "Atlantastocracy?"

I grinned. "Do you like it?"

She nodded. "I do. I think it is time to stage read it. Kind of a backer's pitch. Do you still want that guy, Klein, to play the lead?"

"I think I would. I'd certainly like to have him read for it."

"Do you think he's going to be here tonight?" He showed up every other night or so for the show.

"If not tonight, I'm sure he'll be here for the closing show. When do you want to try to get a group together to read it?"

"Monday night after the close?"

I nodded. We had sketched out a slate of current cast members and a few others who we intended to ask to do the staged reading. The characters of the show itself now only bore a passing resemblance to the residents of the 'Hurst, and I felt that I could skate by on this account. They had all been renamed. The college names we had chosen were good representations of the Atlanta stereotypes the main characters represented. In addition to Mercer Oglethorpe (the character representing Atlanta's white matriarchy), there was Jonetta Morehouse-Spelman (who represented the African-American matriarchy), Diego Kobiashi-Emory (doing triple duty representing Asian, gay and Latin American Atlanta), and Agnes Scott Ponce de Leon (representing the Decatur lesbian power structure). Rounding out the cast was Buzz DeLoitte, a sort of clueless white-boy, Yankee neophyte, a la Leopold Bloom, who finds himself trying to navigate this weird social structure.

There was nothing even remotely politically correct about this lineup. I was envisioning Klein to play Buzz.

Even though I had no problem knocking around the theater in nothing but cargo shorts and flip flops during the day, I had become very sensitive to propriety when we were gearing up for the evening show. Sensitive is probably not the right word. I had become superstitious. I didn't feel I needed to be in a tux every night, but I did feel that, if the business was going to thrive, I needed to at least look professional. I excused myself to Miranda so I could duck across the street and get changed before the volunteers and performers showed up.

Up on the roof, I found Chris sitting in one of the Adirondack chairs, working on his tan. There was no one up on the deck with him. No music was playing; really no noise of any kind. He seemed to be lost in quiet reverie. *Quiet reverie* are not words that are usually, in any way, associated with Chris's life, so I assumed he must be ill and said so. He laughed.

"Not at all. Just having a bit of an existential crisis."

"Existential crisis?"

He rolled his eyes. "Typical flight attendant angst. Bad day, bad trip. The kind of thing that reminds you this really isn't a job for adults."

I nodded understandingly. "Do you need to talk?"

He shook his head. "Far from it. And there's no time. We need to get across the street."

I thought nothing more about it and went to change. When I returned to the theater, most of the volunteers were in place, the ticket office was open and I could hear the cast going through their preshow warm-ups backstage. The presence of a male voice calling "cumalama-cumalama-cumalama-bista" told me Klein had indeed decided to join us that evening. So before opening the doors, I dashed upstairs to my computer and started printing a copy of the script to give him.

Laine arrived as I was coming back down the stairs, resplendent in a pair of black silk pajamas with an ermine collar and a spray of diamonds at her neck. At times, she truly reminded me of Auntie Mame. She had been at every night's performance, and I believe there was greater motivation for doing so than just being a supportive aunt.

When Uncle Maurice had been alive, they had constantly been on the go. They traveled a great deal, and she had had an active role in his business affairs. But after he had died, her world had slowly, inexorably closed in on her in Atlanta. She didn't travel all that much; people came to see her if they came at all. And most of the businesses had been sold, leaving her with nothing but some real estate holdings that largely took care of themselves. In its own way, her life had become as insular as Mister Kersey's.

But the theater was giving her an outlet as much as it was giving me a direction in life. She had been volunteering to do a number of things, and every evening as she took up her perch dispensing programs by the door, I saw her come alive as she reconnected with old friends, made new ones, and generally flirted with the entire crowd. She was more than the namesake of Theater DeLaine; she was becoming its face as well. I made a mental note to get her a nametag.

As soon as the curtain went up, I escorted Laine up to her seat in the balcony. The balcony and boxes still challenged me. I didn't have the money to add seats, and I wasn't sure there was enough demand to fill them anyhow. However, I hated that the space was going to waste. Klein was already seated up there, beer in hand, awaiting us. He and Laine had struck up quite a rapport.

Klein had moved from New York after college to take an accounting job. He, like so many people I had known in New York, hated accounting, but had studied it rather than pursue a career in theater because his parents had pressured him to have a stable job to fall back on. I remembered students just like him from college, who had somnambulated their way through their core curriculum, and only came alive when they attended the theater classes we shared. Now the demands of a daily job kept him from pursuing his passion, apart from weekend gigs performing with the comedy troupe.

I settled Laine onto the couch next to him and then went to retrieve the script from the printer in my office. He and Laine were whispering between themselves when I returned. Having watched the show for a month now, none of us felt any obligation to give it anything more than cursory attention. I dropped down on the couch between them and whispered to him, "Hey, got a proposition for you."

He gave me an inquisitive look that I'm sure was reflected in my aunt's face behind me. I handed him a script. "This is a show Miranda and I have been working on. We want to do a staged reading of it, kind of like a backer's read, week after next. We were wondering if you would be willing to read the main character for us."

His face lit up. "Hell yeah."

"So we are finally going to get to see this mythical show?" Laine asked, reaching for the script. I intercepted her hand and guided it away.

"I want you to see the show cold, meaning no one gets to see the script but the cast."

Laine is not accustomed to being told no, and clearly had no idea what the appropriate response was. Klein flipped open the script. "Which character?"

"Buzz DeLoitte."

He nodded and flipped a page of the script, turning his back slightly so he could read the words by the light from the stage. Laine tried to read the words over his shoulder but there wasn't enough light for that, so she sat back sullenly and held out her empty glass. I retrieved her silver shaker and filled it.

"When do we do the first read?" he asked.

"Monday night."

"You're not wasting any time, are you?"

"Can't afford to let the theater sit empty."

"Yes we can," Laine reminded me.

I started to disagree, thinking of how much energy being involved in something seemed to be giving her, but couldn't find a way to word it that wasn't insulting. So, instead, I conceded the point. "Okay, we could, but I don't think we should. I think we can make something of this place, but we've got to build on the momentum."

"How often are we going to rehearse it?"

"Every night next week."

"Not Friday," Laine cautioned. "That's Charles's bachelor party."

I groaned inwardly. I hated bachelor parties. My own had been a miserable experience, which I guess was an appropriate omen for the marriage that followed. "That reminds me, Klein. Want to come to a bachelor party Friday night?"

The following night, *Duck Soup* closed. We played to a packed house and many neighbors and friends who had been there opening night returned to send us off. (For the record, Archer Bellamy was not one of them.) We rang down the curtain to a standing ovation and three curtain calls. Laine had roses sent for the entire cast, and Cara, who had been playing Groucho's role, took the final bow as the leading lady. The curtain came down with its usual thud, the house lights came up, and the crowd loudly departed.

As per our usual custom, Miranda went backstage to congratulate the troupe, while all the volunteers and I did a five-minute sweep of the auditorium to pick up cups and programs that had been left behind. Then, I thanked all the volunteers, and they adjourned to the 'Hurst , which Laine had offered up for the cast party. I waited behind for the cast to depart. They made their way out of the theater in ones and twos, and soon it was just me, awaiting Miranda to come upstairs and to leave.

As I pulled the ghost light out onto the stage, Miranda appeared from around the corner, putting her things into her backpack.

"I'd say you had a perfect run, Madame Director."

She looked at me and smiled, taking a gracious bow. "Ah thahnk you, suh. And I keep telling you, it's *we* who had a perfect run."

"I'll take credit for the next one." The ghost light flickered a little, and I jiggled the switch.

Miranda sat down on the stage steps and looked out at the auditorium. "You should take credit for a lot more than you are. Look at this place. Three months ago, I never would have believed you could have brought it this far, this fast."

"Most of the problems were cosmetic," I told her absently.

"Oh sure. Cosmetic. Except for no air conditioner, and no carpet and broken seats and no sound system and a homeless kid living in your basement, totally cosmetic." I came down the steps and held out a hand to help her up. "You really don't think you've accomplished anything major, do you?" she asked incredulously.

I looked around the auditorium. "I dunno. I mean, sure, I'm proud of the work I've done here, but it's only been a cleanup. When we are mounting shows consistently, *then* I'll be proud."

She shook her head as we walked up the aisle. I switched off the house lights and we left.

The party was too big for the roof-top deck, so Zach had been assigned to clean out the bottom of the small light well in the middle of the building. I had grown pretty confident in his abilities to handle projects the way I wanted them done around the building, so I had not checked up on him at all during the process. I was, therefore, stunned when I walked through the driveway gate into an elegant Chinese garden with a small, above-ground swimming pool in the corner. Not only had he cleaned out the weeds and dead leaves, he had uncovered the original paving stones laid around the courtyard by Maurice some forty or fifty years ago. Since then, he and Laine had been traveling back and forth to the garden center for a week buying plants and accessories, which Zach had laid out. Then, today, I discovered that he and Laine had purchased the pool on closeout at a home center, and he had spent the afternoon assembling it.

There was a small brass fire pit in the center of the garden, where a fire burned brightly. Citronella torches were bolted to the fence, and strings of Christmas lights and Chinese lanterns ran back and forth from the rooftop high overhead.

There were a few folding tables and some plastic deck chairs scattered about, but the crowd was mostly standing. Along the wall beneath Laine's bedroom windows ran a long folding table covered with appetizers while directly opposite, beneath Mister Kersey's bedroom windows, stood a bar with Jennifer working behind it.

I left Miranda, who had immediately greeted a cast member, and crossed the courtyard to where Zach and Laine were standing next to one of four stone Chinese lions, each facing radially outward from the fire pit.

"There you are," Laine greeted me warmly. "Doesn't the courtyard look grand? Didn't Zach do a marvelous job?"

I looked at him and smiled. "You did indeed. I never would have recognized it. Tells me I should pay more attention to you." He blushed. "Did you assemble the pool yourself?"

"I did," he nodded. "It was easier than I thought. I was thinking that, before I went back to school, we could put a deck around it so it looks more permanent."

I nodded absently. "Definitely, if I can find time from the theater." I turned to Laine and therefore missed the crestfallen expression she would later tell me crossed his face. "There are a lot of people here. Is Mister Kersey going to be okay with this?"

She shrugged. "I'm sure he will be. I asked him to come. Regardless, it's my building so there's really not much he can say, is there?"

I glanced up at his windows, blinds tightly drawn against the outside world. "I suppose not."

"Besides, I think I saw him here."

I scanned the crowd. There were certainly many more people here than just the cast and crew of the show. I saw Bitsy Hollander and most of the rest of the crowd who had been here for Summerfest, and several people I knew from the neighborhood. There also seemed to be a large number of people who I had never seen before, but who had been members of the audience that evening. Laine was not above inviting strangers because she deemed them friendly, or fun, or probably just plain courteous and therefore deserving. In Laine's world, good manners should be rewarded with free cocktails.

I excused myself to get a drink and was joined at the bar by Brit and Charles. Brit assailed me almost immediately. "Darling, have you planned Charles's bachelor party yet?"

I glanced at Charles who looked profoundly uncomfortable. "Uh no, not yet. Got some ideas, but nothing concrete yet."

"Well, you better get with it. Jennifer and Rachel have my bachelorette party planned for the same night, and I don't want y'all hanging about mine."

"What are you doing?" I asked pleasantly.

She gave me a look that indicated how dumb my question was. "We can't tell you that. Don't you know anything about wedding traditions?"

An image of Olivia snapped into my head for a brief second, like a Viewmaster™ slide rolling by. "Apparently not." I looked at Charles and said, "Well, buddy boy, I guess you and I should go talk about what you want to do."

"Buddy boy?" Charles asked as I steered him away from my sister and over towards the pool where a couple of Chris's flight attendant buddies had shucked their clothes and were now floating around with their cocktails.

"American masculine term of endearment," I explained. "Seemed appropriate, given the context of the conversation."

"Ah. Look, Donovan, you really don't have to throw me a bachelor party. I…"

I held up my hand "Hey, it's a best man's duty. I'm proud to be your best man, I'm happy to do it."

"But I…"

"No protests. Just tell me what you would like to do."

He gave me that helpless, exasperated look the British seem to reserve exclusively for Americans before blurting out, "Not have one."

I smiled. "I beg your pardon?"

"I hate bachelor parties. I don't handle liquor at all well, and strip clubs make me profoundly uncomfortable. I find women grinding against brass poles and rubbing their breasts all over me makes me stammer and sweat. Plus all the forced bonhomie among the men at these things strikes me as latent homosexuality."

Oh thank God, I thought.

"Did someone mention a latent homosexual?" Chris asked, walking up to the pool.

"We're talking about Charles's bachelor party."

"Using those terms?" he grinned. "Sounds like my kind of party."

Charles choked on his drink.

"Charles," I began as he recovered his breath. "I couldn't agree with you more. I hate 'em as well. That doesn't mean we still can't celebrate your marriage. Let us take you out for the evening anyhow. I promise no strippers, and however much or little drinking as you would like."

He smiled. "Well, okay then. What do you have in mind?"

"No bloody idea." We all laughed.

"You know what I'd like to try?" he asked.

"What?"

"Something, I don't know, *competitive.* In England, you play soccer or rugby or cricket throughout school, and then are expected to never do anything again once you graduate. You blokes over here play volleyball or bowl or whatever well into your adulthood. In England, once you pass twenty-one, you're not supposed to touch another ball ever again. Even your own."

"You want to go bowling?" Chris asked, horror dripping from his voice. "You do realize that you have to wear other people's shoes."

I smiled at him. "Competition it is. Beginning at noon on Friday. We meet at my place."

"Really?" He grinned like a little kid.

"Here's what I'm thinking. Volleyball that afternoon, bowling that evening, poker that night. A full-fledged boys' day out."

"Smashing!"

"Who do you want there?"

He shrugged. "Well, you two of course. And maybe Zach."

"I hope you don't mind. I invited Klein."

"Not at all. He seems like a nice guy." He puffed out his cheeks, clearly lost in thought. "Other than that, I can't think of anyone. I can't really see Professor Whitaker or Professor Kolby from Emory joining us. Their idea of a rousing good time is to have a hot toddy while watching Bloomberg. And I don't really want any of my grad students there, so I suspect just the five of us."

I nodded. "So it shall be."

Shortly after planning Charles's party, Laine rescued me from an excruciatingly painful conversation with Bitsy. "Dear, I have a favor to ask," she informed me as she tucked her arm in mine and led me off to a the opposite corner of the courtyard from the pool.

"Sure, Laine, anything."

"I know you are busy with the theater, but I also want you to spend a little more time working with Zach."

I immediately felt guilty for shuffling most of my building responsibilities to him over the last month. "I'm sorry, Laine. I thought he was doing an okay job, and so I..."

She held up a hand, silencing me. "His work is fine, what you don't realize is that he needs you."

"Huh?" I asked, not following her.

She took a sip of her manhattan. "Sweetheart, I don't think you realize it, but he looks at you as a mentor. Maybe not a father figure, but someone who definitely took an interest in him and is helping him become a man. An older brother figure, perhaps."

I looked at Laine skeptically. "Laine, I know nothing about being a gay man. He really relies on Chris for that."

She smiled. "I'm not talking about being gay. I'm talking about being a man. He's a boy who is trying to figure out how to be a man. Gay is incidental. There is much more to it than that. He obviously can't talk to his father about the things he's trying to work out, and that oaf doesn't sound like much of a man to begin with. Besides, when it comes to discussing how to be an adult, I'm not sure I would say Chris is the ideal role model, would you?"

I snickered. "No, probably not. But what makes you think I am? I'm sort of leading a slacker's lifestyle these days."

"You made a commitment to adulthood in some form or fashion a long time ago. You also haven't been paying attention to what he's been talking to you about. It doesn't make any difference if you think you are a good life-mentor. He does."

I had not had enough to drink to be as confused as I was and said so. She explained.

"Haven't you noticed that, over the course of the summer, he maintains a nonstop conversation with you? He tells you about his experiences; what he's feeling. He asks you your opinions."

"Yeah, so? He talks a lot."

"He is listening to, and internalizing, everything you say. It may sound like idle chatter to you, but to him those conversations are times for him to test his theories of manhood with you. He sees you as a safe harbor."

I glanced across the yard to the bar where he sat talking to Rachel. It's true that he had discussed a lot of things with me. I had always attributed the conversation to typical young prattle. However, I remembered babbling on like that for hours, first with my father, and then with my dorm advisor at school. I suddenly saw twenty years old from an entirely different perspective. Instinctively, I knew she was right because I had done it myself.

I also realized I had pretty much ignored him for the entire month of July. The theater had been all consuming.

"What do you want me to do?"

"Give him some time. Build the pool deck with him. He desperately wants your attention and has absolutely no idea how to go about getting it."

I nodded, thought, and then nodded again. "Sure, Laine. Sure."

I wandered over to Zach later, leaned my back against the bar, looked at the pool and asked him, "So tell me about this deck you're envisioning."

The party wore on into the early hours of the morning. Zach and I laid out plans for the deck in a discussion where several neighbors participated. Laine and Bitsy got smashed on manhattans. Mister Kersey, if he was in residence, stayed quiet.

Generally, a good time was had by all.

And across the street, at some point during the night and unbeknownst to me, the ghost light burned out.

On Monday evening, the new cast gathered in chairs on the stage for the first reading of *Highlands-A-Go-Go.* The evening was a great deal of fun. Klein was a natural for Buzz DeLoitte, and everyone had great suggestions to help revise the lines so that they were easier to deliver. Miranda and I played through the songs and taught them to the appropriate cast members. We all agreed that we would need some more time to rehearse, so we committed to meet almost every evening for the next ten days to power-learn the script and songs. We wanted to do the staged reading a week from Saturday.

That evening, after everyone adjourned, Klein hung out with me on stage. As I replaced the bulb in the ghost light, he told me, "Y'know, this is a really great script. It could be something fantastic."

"Thanks." I dragged the light to the center of the stage.

"Once we do the staged reading, are you going to produce it?"

"Dunno. Hope so, but I have to figure out where to get the money to do it. The set I envision is complicated, even though there is only one. And, it'll be expensive to get the music recorded."

"You don't think your aunt would underwrite the show?"

"I'm sure she would if she had the cash and I asked her. But this is a bigger production than *Duck Soup* was, and I don't want to ask for that much."

"What's your plan, then?"

I grinned at him. "Wish I knew."

During the days that week, we worked on executing Zach's vision for the deck around the pool. It was an octagonal affair with a circle in the center for the pool. It was not too wide, just wide enough to walk around the edge, but it hid the fact that the pool was a cheap, above ground model. Because the fire escape leading down into the courtyard was accessible from all apartments as well as the roof, I could envision all of the neighbors using it, except Mr. Kersey, of course. I momentarily contemplated raising their rent. Of course, it's not my building, but…

My return gave Zach the opportunity to resume his long litany of questions, discussions, observations, tirades, and opinions. I now understood what Laine had been talking about. He was, indeed, trying to figure out what being a man was about. We covered topics spanning the spectrum from men's dress shoes to second mortgages. During the course of the week, I not only learned how much he needed to know, I learned how much I knew, but took for granted.

By Friday, we had decked the pool, enclosed the front with lattice work, hidden the pump and filter, and stained and sealed the whole thing.

On that day at noon, as planned, Chris, Zach, Klein, Charles, and I assembled on the roof. I had several gifts for my future brother-in-law. We five sat around the deck while he opened the first one I handed him.

"It's a...ball," he said, looking at it.

"It's a volleyball," I corrected.

Next he was handed another that was wrapped much like the first one had been. "Two volleyballs?" he asked, amused.

"Nope," I replied, taking a swig of my beer.

He tore the wrapping paper, "A basketball." He beamed.

We also gave him a baseball, a tennis ball, a super-ball, a cheese ball, and finally, a bowling ball.

"Well, I'm properly amazed. Brit is going to be quite put out with you if you bring me home from this afternoon turned into a redneck."

Once we had finished our beers, I led the crowd downstairs. Charles carried the volleyball and Zach, as punishment for an offhand remark about being the youngest, carried a backpack cooler full of beer. "Where are we headed?" Charles asked.

"Up the street." There was a beach volleyball court in John Howell Park, about three blocks away. Pickup volleyball games were always taking place there. "It's my intent to go challenge a bunch of college-age punks to a game."

"Hey!" Zach protested.

"No offense intended to our own college punk," I amended.

"Each of us has a different competitive outing planned for you today," Chris informed the groom.

The park actually boasted two beach volleyball courts. When we arrived, no one was on the court, so we set about stringing up the net.

"I always assumed you had to reserve these courts," Charles volunteered as he took off his shoes and socks.

"I checked online. They are managed by Volleyball Atlanta, but local residents can use them when they aren't reserved. I checked and no one had them booked until later today."

"So how do you know we will have college punks to challenge?" he asked.

I finished tying off my end of the net. "I have yet to ever see a beach volleyball game not attract college punks. It's like a blonde sitting at a bar with an unlit cigarette."

"Can we lose the term punk?" Zack asked crossly.

"Nope," Charles replied.

We began batting the ball back and forth. It started as two-on-two, with the fifth man rotating off one side and onto the other. It took less than ten minutes for three guys, all in their late teens or early twenties, to find their way to us. Two emerged from a duplex across the street, and the third was riding by on his bike.

We didn't spend much time getting to know each other's names. After all, none of us was looking to begin a relationship; just play some volleyball. In a matter of minutes, we were arrayed four to a side: Charles, Klein, Chris and myself against Zach and the other punks. (Out of courtesy, we discontinued the use of that term while amongst strangers.)

The first game was quite an eye-opening experience. The punks were quite good, *especially* Zach. On our team, Klein and I were passable; I was maybe slightly better. Charles, having only seen the game on television, was not good at all. Chris on the other hand, was amazing. Quickly, a grudge match evolved between him and Zach. They went out of their way to spike each other at every chance. Klein and I exchanged surprised looks at the end of the first game, which we lost.

"Where did you learn to play like that, man?" he asked Chris while retrieving a beer from the cooler.

Chris shrugged as he wiped sand off of his chest. "Flight attendant rite-of-passage. We spend a lot of layovers on beaches. If you don't want to get drug into beach rugby, you go play beach volleyball."

The grudge match continued into the second match. We had agreed to play best two-out-of-three. Despite Chris, we lost the second match as well. Badly. We decided to play the third match as well. First, we shared our beer with the punks, hoping it would slow them down.

It didn't.

Nothing really brings home the metabolism difference between someone in their early twenties and someone in their late thirties like volleyball. Zach beamed at his victory. Chris sulked at the loss. Charles apologized for not being better, so I explained that he was not the issue. Age was. I depressed myself trying to make him feel better, and slammed a beer to get my mind off it.

At four, we returned to the building, hot, sandy and barefoot. Despite the drubbing we had received, Charles was beaming. Actually, everyone had had a great time. As we were coming into the building, Jennifer, Laine, Rachel, and Clare were coming out.

"Where have you five been?" Laine asked, sniffing. "You smell appalling."

"Afternoon volleyball game," Charles replied. "Start of my batch party. Where are you off to?"

The ladies exchanged looks. "Off to collect Britany for, um, *her* evening."

Everyone looked smugly uncomfortable with their various secrets, so we all exchanged farewells. They went on to collect Brit, while we went inside to get cleaned up.

Klein, Charles, and I all went to my apartment, where each of us grabbed a quick shower and changed into jeans and sneakers. Twenty minutes later, we met in the courtyard where Chris provided a tray of tequila shots. Four of us slammed back the shots; Zach deferred since he was not yet legal and would therefore be driving that night. Then we piled into the VeggieRoll and sped off to the bowling alley.

The nearest bowling alley, Midtown Bowl, was located on a loop of road near Buford Highway that had never really found itself. In part, it could have been one of the thousands of similar areas located at off-ramps everywhere: a smattering of diners and fast food, some gas stations, a large motel left over from the sixties. However, this area nuzzled up against the old-money enclave of Ansley Park as well as a strip of eclectic, high-end restaurants. Straddling the uncomfortable boundary between these two worlds was the bowling alley. It is not the kind of place where a Rolls-Royce would typically pull up, but it is strangely not unheard of, either.

The bowling alley itself appears to have been unchanged since 1972. As we waited for shoes, it occurred to me that 1972 might be the last word in bowling alley style. You don't see many new bowling alleys being built these days. Perhaps they are trapped in the faux wood and leatherette miasma of the early seventies for all time, until released from their torpor by the sweet kiss of the wrecking ball.

My colleagues were not interested in such philosophical discussions. Only Klein and I had ever bowled before. Charles was excited, but somewhat unclear on the premise. Zach was interested, but dubious. Chris, appalled by the concept of doing anything in rented shoes, had brought a second pair of socks, with the expressed intention of discarding the outer layer once the game was done.

With two pitchers of beer and the greasiest onion rings on the planet, we selected a lane at the far left end of the alley. The place itself was only moderately full, as we had arrived ahead of the early evening crowd. Having explained the finer points of the game and scoring to Charles, we started the match with Klein rolling first. He scored a strike on the first roll. He turned around, blew on his nails and smugly buffed them on the lapel of his bowling shirt.

"Hate to tell you guys, but you never want to go up against a Long Island Jew when it comes to banking, baking, or bowling."

It was my turn next. I retrieved the ball I had selected, a jaunty little blue-onyx number, and approached the lane. I had not bowled since my sophomore year in college, so I was a little apprehensive. I rolled, and knocked down all the pins on the left side. On the next roll, I was able to pick up the spare.

"Very nice," Klein complimented me.

"Thanks. Zach, you're up."

We had divided into two teams based on family connection; Charles and I versus Klein, Zach, and Chris. The reasoning was that only Klein and I had ever bowled before, and since he was much better than I, he could foot the burden of carrying Chris on his team.

Klein explained the basics of rolling a ball to Zach, who smiled nervously. He approached the lane tenuously, and gently rolled the ball. It dropped into the gutter halfway to the pins.

"Shit," Zach said.

"Don't sweat it," I told him reassuringly. "If you got a strike on your first roll ever, it would have made you a freak or something."

Next it was Charles's turn. Even though I had picked up the bowling ball I had given him earlier at a flea market as a joke, he was determined to bowl with it. We walked him through the basics of how to throw it. He fixed a pensive look on his face, drained the beer I had just poured for him, and picked up the ball. Then, with an expression reminiscent of Montgomery facing battle in Africa, he turned and stalked towards the lane.

Pulling his right arm back firmly, he suddenly launched the ball forward. It met the wood of the lane in smooth arc and sailed straight down the lane, meeting the centermost pin head-on. They split beautifully, each knocking down the two pins behind. It was a textbook perfect strike.

"Rule fucking Britannia!" Charles announced triumphantly.

"A freak or something, huh?" Zach asked sourly, glancing sideways at me.

"I quit," Chris announced flatly. I could tell by his tone that he wasn't joking.

"That was awesome, man," Klein cried, jumping up to hug Charles. Charles was still coming to terms with the concept of men hugging. Nonetheless, he smiled joyously.

Chris did not get up for his turn. I slid over to sit next to him. "C'mon. Give it a shot."

"You do realize that all gay men detest any competition based on putting a ball in a specific location, don't you?"

I smirked at the unintended double entendre, but said nothing. "You're among friends and family. If you suck, we will tease you mercilessly, but it does not mean that we love you any less."

He grimaced and rolled his eyes. Reluctantly, he stood up and walked to the ball return. I followed behind, attempting to explain to him what to do. He turned, held his hand up and said, "Let me just try it once without the helpful straight condescension."

I held my hands up, bowed slightly and took a step backward. As I did so, I noticed his bowling shoe was untied.

"Chris..."

He held up his hand. "Really, just let me try it."

"But..."

He turned, annoyed. "Van, *please*."

I decided to hold my peace. He held the ball up and studied the line of it to the lane in a very professional manner. He began his stride forward, pulling the ball backward in a manner that made it look as if he had done this a thousand times before. Just before he reached the line, his left arm began to descend. Then he stepped on his own shoelace.

He had too much forward momentum to stop. The pulled shoelace turned him around in a nearly full circle, counterclockwise. The four of us, momentarily fearful that the ball would leave his hand towards one of us, dived left and right. The ball did not actually leave his hand until he was approximately 330 degrees though his pirouette.

I could not see the full scene unfold from where I had dived behind the ball return, so it took Klein to describe it later. The ball left his hand and made a majestic arc into the next lane, narrowly missing the elderly gentleman bowling there. It hit the right hand gutter of that lane and bounced out, sailing over the next lane. It landed in the third lane where it made contact with the ball that had just been rolled by the woman bowling in that lane. The collision knocked her ball into the gutter, and sent Chris's ball straight down that lane where it hit the pocket for a perfect strike.

All of us stared, dumbfounded at what had just happened.

"I have no idea if he gets credit for that strike or not," Klein mused.

"Well, that's it for me," Chris announced. It took another pitcher of beer and the arrival of Pinpoint, one of the teams in the gay bowling league, to get him back in the lane.

We bowled three games with Klein, Zach and Chris beating us in all three. However, Charles and I made a respectable showing. He developed the disturbing habit of kissing his ball after every good frame, but I decided to say nothing since I didn't have to kiss him. We departed the alley at eight-thirty and headed back to the Highlands. On the way, Chris ordered a couple of pizzas from the Mellow Mushroom, one of our local pizza joints, via his cell phone. I noticed that he was slurring a little bit as he gave them directions to deliver the pizza to our driveway.

The last part of the evening was given over to poker. However, since it was August in Georgia, the roof would be ungodly hot until well after midnight. So instead, Zach and I had worked up a floating tabletop that we set afloat in the pool. I had found some plastic playing cards at Metropolitan Deluxe, a store around the corner, and poker chips were water resistant.

All of us changed back into the bathing suits we had worn to play volleyball. Chris had a cooler of beers and a set of shots waiting for us as we gathered poolside. I didn't recognize the brand of tequila.

"That's 'cause it's illegal in the States," Chris explained as he poured out five shots. "It is, however, a thousand times better than that straight, gringo swill y'all drink." He placed the shots on a stainless tray with lime and salt. I noticed, out of the corner of my eye, that Zach looked nervous.

"Have you ever done a tequila shot before?" I asked.

"I've never done a shot before," he confided quietly. "Tequila or otherwise."

I explained the ritual of the salt, the shot and the lime as all of us slipped into the water. It was still hot outside (as August in Georgia is wont to be) so the cool water felt good against the muggy night air. Chris dropped in and took up the silver tray, passing out shots to everyone. We each took one of the five cobalt glasses that he offered and waited patiently for him to make the toast.

"Charles," he said gravely, "You are about to embark on a voyage that is denied to ten percent of the population of this country, and executed poorly by fifty percent of those who actually do get to participate. Being barred legally from participating and emotionally incapable of it if I weren't, I have little advice to offer apart from this. Don't screw it up." We all laughed, and then slammed back the tequila. It was the smoothest, mildest tequila I ever remember drinking and I said so.

"That's because you believe Americans are capable of making a decent tequila. No decent tequila has ever been produced north of Juarez. And, the beauty of truly good tequila is that it doesn't give you a hangover."

Chris next produced our floating card table. Since the water was too deep for its legs to touch bottom without becoming entirely submerged, it was strapped to the back of a large yellow inner-tube with an enormous duck head. The table was launched with Charles's proclaiming a jolly "God bless all who sail on her," and the first hand of cards was dealt. I took the hand with a full house, queen high. A round of tequila shots was distributed and consumed.

The deal passed to Klein. "Seven card stud, queens are wild."

"Yes we are," Chris replied.

The hand was dealt and played. Klein won with two pair. A round of tequila shots was distributed.

"Y'know, Chrish," Charles slurred, "I mean no disreshpect to your Latin heritage, but I'm really not mush of a tequila drinker."

"I'm sorry, Charles," Chris replied. "I have other stuff up in my apartment. Do you have a request?"

"Howsabout a shot of rye."

Chris looked at me and silently mouthed, *Rye?* I shrugged. He pulled himself out of the pool and said, "Let me see what I can do."

I began to shuffle while he climbed the fire-escape, still dripping, and entered his apartment through a window. A moment later, he returned, carrying a bottle and descended back towards us. He poured a single shot from a bottle that he kept towards the edge of the pool, jumped back in, and handed the shot to Charles.

"You're in luck. Just happened to have a bottle of rye I picked up on a flight to Manchester."

Charles held the shot up appraisingly, smiled, and downed it. He smiled with satisfaction and said "Ah."

I dealt a hand of five-card stud. Charles won it, sort of, with an ace-high. Chris pulled himself out of the pool to pour another round of shots while Charles shuffled.

Behind the groom's back, Chris smiled at me and held up the "rye." It was actually just a different bottle of tequila. He shrugged elaborately, and then poured another round.

I won the next hand. We then had a delay of game for a few moments because Zach didn't really shuffle all that well, and Klein dropped all of his chips in the pool and had to dive to recover them. Four shots of tequila and one shot of "rye" were consumed.

Two hands later, a ruddy, red, full moon began to pass over the opening of the light well, and we heard a car ease its way down the driveway. As the latest round of shots was consumed, the gate opened and Aunt Laine, Jennifer, Clare, and Rachel entered the patio.

"Are you boys still up?" Laine asked, a smile masking the precaution in her voice.

"We are!" Charles exclaimed. "Come have a shot!"

The four of them advanced towards the pool. "What are you drinking?" Rachel asked bemused.

"Mostly tequila," Chris explained. Then, with air quotes, he added, "And 'rye' for Charles."

"Y'know," Charles told Chris sagely. "I hate to complain, but there'sh sssssomethin' funny tastin' 'bout your rye."

Chris nodded knowingly. "I may not have bought the best brand."

"Ah. Tha's prolly it." He sank back against the side of the pool, smiling and snickering to himself.

Laine surveyed the situation. Zach and Klein were slumped against each other. There were two empty bottles of tequila and several empty beer cans stacked neatly on the side of the pool. Two half-eaten pizzas sat next to the trash. The groom was smashed.

She was suddenly not amused.

"There is a wedding this afternoon. Don't you think maybe you boys should sober up?"

Charles smiled at her. "Has anyone ever tol' you that you look a lot like Helen Mirren?"

Laine fixed me with an icy stare. "Party's over. Get him to bed."

"Yes ma'am," I replied sheepishly. Laine stormed off towards the front door. Although she could have accessed her apartment via the fire escape, she made it clear that no southern woman of character would *ever* come and go via the window.

As we were drying off next to the pool, Chris asked Jennifer, "Where did you guys go tonight?"

"Manicures and pedicures this afternoon. Tapas at Pura Vida. Then a brief trip to Swingin' Richards."

In case you can't infer from the name, Swingin' Richards is a male strip club on the west side of town. Chris and Zach exchanged knowing looks.

"We went to the wrong party," Zach laughed.

"Nah," Chris replied as he poured one last round of shots. "Being gay doesn't mean you aren't one of the guys."

Saturday morning, I arose to a strange sound. Silence. Ordinarily Saturday was the one morning of the week that I was able to sleep in, but the Feldmans always ruined it. Every Saturday morning, I could count on the toilet flushing or the ceiling fan banging or the balcony doors opening themselves up, usually right at 7:30. But nothing happened. I rolled over and glanced at the clock. It was eight forty-five.

Of course, this was one morning I was not supposed to sleep in. I gingerly sat up, trying to ensure my head did not roll off my shoulders. I was hung over, as I expected, but quite a bit worse than I had expected as well. I decided Chris's theory about better tequila not causing hangovers was bullshit.

I stood up and looked down from the balcony. Perhaps the Feldmans were silent out of fear of the macabre scene below. Klein lay on the floor, pretty much where he had fallen last night as we stumbled in, wrapped up in the area rug. Charles lay with his head on the armrest of the couch, his lanky frame splayed wildly across the coffee table and end table and over the backrest. I noticed that he held the last shot of the evening, unconsumed yet unspilled, in his hand where it rested on the table.

Zach, who had helped me get both of them upstairs the previous evening, slept under the desk, only his legs emerging into the room.

All in all, it was like looking down over the scene of a mafia hit. Any self-respecting spirit would have been wise to fear the hangovers brewing in that room. The pain was probably strong enough to be felt in the netherworld.

I descended the stairs to go to the bathroom. While I was in there, I heard a knock at the door. Being in mid-pee, I hoped someone would go answer it. No one did, although I heard a little bit of stirring and groaning. There was another knock.

I finished up, washed my hands and walked out into the living room. I could see a paramedic standing on the other side of the door. Concerned, I opened it quickly and said hello.

"Mister Williams or Mister Ford?"

"Uh, Mister Ford."

"Hi there. I'm Sam Patel. Your aunt asked me to stop by."

"Uh, okay. Why?"

"Hangover relief. She gave me a message for you. Her exact words are…" he consulted a note, "'Donovan, Charles, I am not going to accept a hangover as an excuse for anything going wrong with this wedding. If you do not let this nice young man help you, I swear to God I will kill both of you.' It's signed, 'Love, Auntie Laine.'"

"Nothing like death threats to help make the wedding day a joyous occasion." I stood aside to admit him.

He glanced at the scene. "Whoa. Must have been a great bachelor party. Which one's the groom?"

"That one." I pointed towards the couch, and Charles moaned a soft confirmation and raised his hand. Sam carried a small medical kit and crossed over to him.

"Mister Williams?"

"Uh huh." Charles didn't move or open his eyes.

"Your aunt..."

"I heard. What are you going to do?"

Sam opened the box and began unpacking. "I'm going to give you a saline IV."

Charles opened one eye. "Huh?"

"One of the reasons a hangover hurts so much is because the body is badly dehydrated. The saline will rapidly rehydrate you in time for the wedding."

Charles closed the eye and nodded slightly. I stepped into the kitchen to make coffee.

"I'm going to use your right arm." Sam lifted Charles's limp right arm from the coffee table and sat down on the edge of the couch with the saline bag. He began to swab the arm with an alcohol wipe. By the time I had the coffee maker running, he had my brother-in-law-to-be hooked up to a clear bag, which he rested gently on Charles's chest. Charles flinched slightly from surprise when the cool plastic made contact with his bare skin, but otherwise lay motionless. Sam then turned his attention to me.

"You're up, Mister Ford. You need to be motionless for a while. Where do you want to do it?"

"Donovan," I told him and nodded towards my swivel chair. He followed me over and I dropped into the chair. As he swabbed my arm I observed, "I wasn't aware that paramedics could be called to handle hangovers."

Sam smiled. "Not in an official capacity. I've known your aunt a long time. She called my grandmother at six this morning and specifically asked whether I could do something to help you out. Grandmoms called me."

"Do I know your grandmother?"

"Dunno. Bitsy Hollander?"

I smirked slightly, closed my eyes and nodded. Sam was pretty swarthy, clearly of Middle Eastern descent. I speculated inwardly about what Bitsy's reaction had been when her daughter had *not* brought home the standard-model Buckhead boy, but thought better of saying anything. There was a slight sharp sensation as the needle slid into my skin.

"Okay, neither of you move until those bags are empty." Sam glanced around the room. "Um, I was only expecting two of you, but I brought enough saline for the other guys if any of you want it."

Without moving or saying anything, both Klein and Zach raised their hands. Sam chuckled slightly and moved to Klein.

I had to admit, the saline worked. While I wouldn't say I felt marvelous by the time the bag was finished, I felt human. Sam administered one to Klein and Zach, two to Charles and me. Laine had instructed him to make sure we were fully functioning by ten o'clock.

An hour later, Klein had left for home, and Zach, Charles, and I walked across the street to the theater. During the previous week, while Zach and I had been working on the deck, Laine and the girls had been busy transforming the stage of the theater into an appropriate spot for a wedding. Although the National Palace of Freedonia still stood on the stage, it was bedecked in flowered garland. Metal poles had been affixed to the end of every third seat row, topped with glass hurricane lamps, and many, many more candles graced the stage. A simple kneeler stood in the center, facing a podium where the minister would speak.

As I opened the doors, I was greeted with a blast of cold air. Laine had told me the night before to run the air conditioning on high all night, "budgets-be-damned."

Rachel greeted me immediately, and laid a hand on my chest to stop me while Charles and Zach filed in. "Need to speak to you in my apartment," she whispered.

"What's up?"

"Wait until we are outside," came a hissed reply. Then, loudly, "Charles, your tux is in the dressing room. We're going to use Van's office as the bride's room, so after one o'clock you cannot come forward of the auditorium. Understand?"

"I understand," he replied. "Do me a favor though. When you go back across the street, tell Britany...well, tell her I'm very excited."

Rachel beamed at him. "I will." Then, turning to me, she was immediately businesslike and shoved me backwards out of the auditorium with a terse, "Let's go."

"What's wrong?" I asked as we emerged into the bright afternoon light.

"We don't have a minister."

"What? How can we not? I thought the minister from Church of the Concrete Jesus was doing it."

"He was." She shoved open the doors of the 'Hurst , and we heard Britany scream from Rachel's apartment, "Who the hell is 'Archer Bellamy' anyhow?"

"Uh oh," I said, looking at Rachel.

"Precisely," she replied, and we mounted the stairs to her apartment.

We entered as Brit was slamming down the phone. "Goddamn church people!" she exclaimed, and then turned to see us enter. "Donovan! Who the hell is Archer Bellamy?"

"He lives down the street in the monstrosity. Why?"

"Because he apparently wields enough influence at the Friendship Church of the Light in Christ to convince the minister to bail on my wedding at the last minute," she fairly shrieked.

"Did he give a reason?"

"It would be unseemly to perform a wedding in a facility that has such little respect for patriotism as Theater DeLaine."

I remembered my exchange with Archer, and blanched. Before I could say anything, a clearly hung-over Chris burst into the room.

"What in the hell is all the screaming about? There are people trying to die of hangovers in this building."

Brit explained what was going on, while I racked my brain trying to think of where we were going to get a minister on such short notice. Much to my surprise Chris, who had been listening intently, volunteered, "I'll get you a minister."

"Where? How?" Brit and I asked simultaneously.

"Do you really care?" he asked.

"Not really," Brit replied. "Just as long as he is qualified to marry us in the state of Georgia." Chris exited the apartment silently. Brit looked at me with a mixed expression of worry and optimism. "Do you think he can really do it?"

I had no faith in him at all, but wasn't going to let on to her. I smiled comfortingly and said, "He's a flight attendant. They're trained to think fast on their feet."

At that point, Laine arrived to see what all the commotion was about. In the time it took to explain it to her, Chris was back with a sheet of paper. Silently, he handed it to Britany, who took it with a perplexed look. She read it, and then reread it. Suddenly a smile broke across her face, and she looked at him. "Is this legit?"

"Legit enough. Georgia recognizes ministers ordained by the Grace Seminary of the Internet."

She laughed, handed me the paper, and rushed forward to kiss and hug him. I glanced at the document, which turned out to be the ordination papers of the Reverend Christopher Diaz. The ink was still wet. I laughed as well and handed it to Laine. She read it and then asked gravely, "How much more would it cost to make you a bishop?"

"About fifty," he replied.

"I'll pay it. Go get yourself upgraded." She left to get her purse, and I followed Chris to his apartment.

"That is awfully nice of you," I told him.

"Don't you always say, 'we do for family?'" he asked as he sat down at the computer to pay for his installation as bishop.

"Do you know what you are going to say?" I asked.

"I was hoping you would help me."

An hour later, the newly ordained Right Reverend C. Diaz and I had sketched out his ceremony, his sermon, and his blessing, so I returned to the theater to explain the new scenario to Charles.

Three hours later, Zach and I began ushering guests into the theater. Even though it was midafternoon, the theater had a twilight quality due to the lowered house lights and long line of candles lining the main aisle. The Casio had been set up in the loft and the requisite sappy love songs were played by one of Miranda's friends. In one of the palace windows, a single rose in a crystal vase sat next to another candle to commemorate our mother.

We had opened the bar in the lobby and Jennifer had been pouring mimosas for all the guests to take into the wedding with them. Now, before I go on, I must explain this. There are competing wedding traditions in the South. The "true" southern wedding is a simple affair, maybe fifteen minutes long, followed by a cake-and-punch reception held in the church's basement. Since they are overwhelmingly Southern Baptist or Methodist, they are also typically dry since neither denomination could ever deign to allow alcohol in their sanctuaries. Whatever alcohol *is* there is carefully concealed in brown paper bags and consumed out of car trunks in the parking lot.

However, Yankees have been moving into the South ever since Reconstruction and bringing their dangerous and evil ways with them. Big wedding receptions were far more common in the cities, especially Atlanta, which is sometimes mistaken for a northern city anyhow. (Carpetbagger motto: "We burnt it. We rebuilt it. It's ours.")

It had never been Brit's intention to have a dry wedding. Her original plan called for the "normal" dry wedding at the FCOTLIC, followed by a "real" reception at the Virginia Highlands Inn. However, when FCOTLIC decided to walk her wedding, she became militant about doing things differently. Since we no longer had the expense of renting their church, and since she was quite angry with them to begin with, she had asked that we have a bar in the theater *before* the wedding, so people could toast them during the service.

Obviously, alcohol in the church would have scandalized FCOTLIC, but that was her only method of "tweaking their nose." In retrospect, it was probably a good thing the minister waited until the last minute to bail out on us. If he had done so earlier, her anger might have included getting married in blood-red before an altar to Baal.

I stepped into my office to see Laine fussing with Brit's veil. I had worried that seeing my sister in a wedding dress so soon after my own divorce was going to depress me. Instead, I stood there stunned. She wore a simple sleeveless white satin dress with a v-shaped neckline revealing just enough of her cleavage to be tasteful, but not trashy. She wore our mother's pearls at her neck. Each hand was hidden in white satin gloves that came up to mid-arm. My very non-traditional sister was radiant in a very traditional, understated way.

"Brit," I smiled stepping forward, "you look radiant." I took her left hand, kissed her on the cheek, and then touched the pearls gently. "Mom would be so proud of you."

I saw a tear well up in her eye. She smiled at me a minute, dabbed the tear away with a tissue and said, "Goddammit Van! Don't do that. I've got enough estrogen flowing through me I could make ol' Bitsy ovulate by proximity. Don't say anything that's gonna make me cry."

I looked around her at Laine. "She been like this all day?"

"All day." She replied without looking up from the veil.

"Well alrighty, then. I guess it's about time. You ready?"

Brit took a deep breath and said, "Yeah. I am."

I kissed her on the cheek again and said "See you on the other side."

At precisely three, I stuck my head onto the balcony and gave a high sign to the organist. She finished what she was playing and, in the stage-right box, the soloist stood up and sang "Close to You" by the Carpenters. That was our signal to get into our positions. I repressed a gag and made my way down the side corridor to back stage.

As the soloist was "Sprinkling stardust in your hair" I descended the stairs and met Chris and Charles behind the curtain.

"Ready?" I asked.

Both nodded separately. "Have you seen Brit?" Charles asked.

Chris reached over and straightened the boutonnière on my lapel. "I have."

"How is she?"

"Raging."

He smiled. "I'd be worried if you said anything else."

As "La, lalalala, close to you…" echoed away, we stepped out from behind the curtain and stood by the kneeler, stage left. The organist began Pachelbel's Canon, and Zach slowly escorted Laine down the aisle to her seat. Beside her were seated Jennifer and Clare.

A few moments later, Rachel appeared in the doors. She was wearing a simple black dress, also with pearls, and black gloves to mirror Brit's. She walked halfway down the aisle, and I walked half way up to meet her and escort her back down.

It occurred to me as I walked her back down the aisle that I had not participated in a wedding since my own. I had been in dozens before my wedding, but none since. I wondered if that meant anything, but decided not to think about it.

As we reached the stage, we parted and went to our respective stations. The crowd stood. A moment later, Brit rounded the corner from the lobby on Mac's arm, and passed through the door.

Being the nonconformist that she is, she had elected to wear a white linen riding cape as a veil. It hung about her shoulders concealing her entire body except her hands, in which she held her bouquet. The hood also fell forward so that you could not see her face. It was a very effective sight, but might have been a bit more appropriate if she had been getting married on the Scottish moors in midwinter rather than Georgia in August. Still she looked quite attractive, and I muffled a little laugh out of respect when I realized she couldn't see more than two feet in front of her and was totally reliant on Mac to guide her.

They came to a stop at the bottom of the stage steps, and Charles stepped downward to meet her.

"Who gives this woman in marriage?" Chris asked with surprising authority.

Mac glanced over his left shoulder at Laine, who was beaming at him, and then replied, "We, her family."

With that, he pulled the hood up and off Brit's head, and then stood behind her and helped her out of the cloak. Not knowing what to do with the voluminous garment, he slung it over his left shoulder before reaching forward and to shake Charles's hand. I could see Clare roll her eyes.

Charles and Brit joined hands and ascended to the stage, while Mac went to stand next to Clare. Without taking her eyes off the wedding, Clare took the cape off of his shoulder and laid it in the seat next to him.

Chris smiled at the bride and groom, and then began. "Welcome, Charles and Britany. You stand here today, in a place that many should envy. You are standing in the middle of a tremendous circle of love. Your family and friends who are gathered here today are here because of their love for you and their desire for your happiness."

I registered the shocked expressions on the faces of Mac, Clare, Jennifer, Rachel, Zach, and even Britany that Chris was capable of that kind of warm sincerity. If Laine was surprised, she never betrayed it, looking instead pleasantly confident. I couldn't see Charles's face, but I would later learn he never took his eyes off of my sister. Indeed, at the reception he would admit privately to me he had "no idea what the bloody hell Chris said up there."

Chris went on to discuss the wonderful adventure they were about to begin. As he talked, I became aware of a dripping sound. It was only an occasional, gentle drip, so I decided to ignore it.

A few moments later, it began to increase in frequency. On the other side of the altar, Rachel and I made eye contact, which let me know she heard it as well. We both began to try to subtly look around behind the other to see the source, but could find nothing. I determined that it must be behind the Freedonia set.

It was, in fact, directly above it. As we reached the exchange of vows, when all four of us had to gather close around Chris, I noticed movement out of the corner of my eye. One of the garlands was easing down the set. Glancing at it I realized that was because the set was melting. The cardboard and papier-mâché gargoyle that it was festooned across was dissolving.

Chris, Charles, and Brit all remained focused on what they were doing and didn't notice the water. Glancing to my left, I could see that several members of the audience had noticed it and were beginning to point to it. I racked my mind, trying to figure out what was behind or above that gargoyle that could be the source of the water. Nothing immediately occurred to me.

Suddenly I was aware that the entire attention of the bridal party was on me. I looked back and Chris, apparently repeating himself, said, "Van, the rings?"

I reached into the jacket pocket of my tuxedo and retrieved the rings and laid them on the Bible Chris was holding. It was the first time I had noticed the Bible, and wondered briefly where in the world he had found one.

While Chris talked about the historic significance of the rings (based on information he had gleaned from the internet after his ordination), another garland moved. This time, I noticed that water was now flowing out of the dissolved gargoyle and forming a river down the wall. A massive lump of dissolved papier-mâché slid down the wall and a puddle began to form around it on the stage.

By this time, everyone in the theater was aware of what was going on except Chris, Britany and Charles. The water seemed to be pouring at a fairly substantial rate, convincing me that a pipe had broken in the sprinkler system. A silent dread ran through me that, at any moment, the sprinklers were going to turn on. I considered going back stage to turn them off, but then a greater fear came over me that the building might actually be on fire. I saw Zach stand up and make his way up the side aisle towards the door to see what was going on. I silently applauded him.

The rings were placed on fingers and I silently tried to will Chris to hurry up. Unfortunately, he was basking in the moment of the first selfless act of his life, and was taking his time about things. The puddle was spreading, so that Rachel was forced to take a step sideways so her shoes did not get wet. Another garland gave way, and floated past me on my right to wherever the water was running offstage.

Finally, Chris pronounced them husband and wife and told Charles to kiss his bride. As Charles did so, one of the pillars on the set sagged alarmingly and finally caught Chris's attention. The organist began the recessional march, and Charles and Brit, still oblivious, started up the aisle.

Chris leaned over to me and asked, "What the hell is going on?"

"I guess I've got a broken pipe."

"What are we going to do?"

"We're going to have to get everyone out of here fast."

Charles and Brit reached the back door and made their exit. They were going to go upstairs to my office to await everyone's departure, and then we were going to shoot pictures on the stage.

I took Rachel's arm and we motored up the aisle as fast as we could with any sort of dignity. Chris was right on our heels.

As soon as we entered the lobby, I ran up the stairs two at a time and down the access hallway, nearly knocking over the soloist as I passed the box. Once backstage, I could see that the water was not flowing from the sprinkler system, but rather through the roof. The catwalk swayed and I noticed Zach, completely soaked, trying to reach the water-flow. Since the ceiling was painted black, it was hard to tell where it was coming from.

"Can you tell what it is?" I called to him as I ran down the steps.

"It looks like it's coming out of the air conditioner vents."

Since the old building was not particularly level, the water was running around the set and towards the stage door. I opened it so the water could drain out. Then it occurred to me what he had said. The air conditioning compressors were on the roof directly above the stage. They had never been run all night on high before.

I ran back up the steps to the catwalk and climbed up the access ladder to the roof. Throwing open the hatch, I could see the huge ice block that had formed on the condenser coils. The ice on the outside was forcing the condensation back inside. I opened up the breaker box on the side of the unit and shut it off.

Shutting off the air conditioning not only stopped the water flow, it had the additional desirable effect of accelerating the departure of the guests for the reception. We shot as many pictures as quickly as possible on the stairs and in the doorway of the theater, before the heat became unbearable.

Once Brit realized what was going on, she momentarily lamented the waterfall. However, Laine took her aside, gently sipping a mimosa, and reminded her, "Darling. Everyone knows it's good luck to have rain on your wedding day."

Overall, the damage from the air conditioner was fairly minimal. Moreover, it had resulted from an improperly installed part so it was covered under warranty. Several of my family and friends took me to task that the problem might have been discovered sooner if I wasn't so miserly when it came to running the damn thing.

Each evening, we continued to rehearse for the staged reading, progressively getting better and better. However, each evening I also began to notice a strange series of mishaps. The ghost light began to burn out with alarming frequency. One of my office windows would no longer stay open, sometimes slamming down with such a force that I worried it would crack. The sound system began to pick up music from a local radio station no matter how many filters Mac installed on it.

I passed all of these off as coincidence until the afternoon before the read. I knew I was alone in the building. All the doors were locked. But, as I crossed the lobby, I heard a toilet in the men's room flush.

I crossed over to it, and opened the door. No one was inside but the toilet was silently running. And then it occurred to me.

In my apartment across the street, the Feldmans had not made a single noise, opened a door, or even flushed once, in weeks.

Magnolia

The Feldmans did not like magnolias. We discovered this because Miranda did. On the Monday after Labor Day, she brought a vase with three or four of the massive blooms into the office in the theater. Ostensibly, she brought them because she liked the smell. Zach teased me that it was really to cover up *my* smell from working in the theater with the air conditioning off each day. Regardless of the reason, when we came in Tuesday, the vase had fallen off of the windowsill and was shattered on the floor, the withered blossoms lying in the wreckage.

A few days later, Miranda brought in a fresh vase of the blooms. It took two days, but the Feldmans somehow again managed to knock them off of the top of the filing cabinet.

The third time, she brought in the magnolias and sat them in a metal paint can on the floor in the corner. The Feldmans couldn't knock them over, so instead they blew out about fifteen light bulbs in the marquee, all of them the most difficult ones to reach.

"These are some seriously malevolent spirits," Miranda observed through the window as I stood outside replacing the bulbs. Unlike me, Miranda had no problem believing in ghosts, and accepted the Feldmans' residency as if it was the most natural thing in the world. "I wonder if I just left magnolia blossoms all over the building whether it would drive them out of here and back into your apartment. You know, like garlic."

"More likely just piss them off," I replied. Although they generally seemed to be a benign nuisance in my apartment, they had been taking a much more active role in the theater. Miranda was of the opinion they were just exploring their new digs.

I hauled myself back in through the window. I didn't know what to do about the Feldmans, so I didn't spend a lot of time worrying about them. "Are we rehearsing the whole first act tonight?"

She sighed. "If we can get through it."

Highlands-a-Go-Go was well on its way to becoming a reality. When we had done the first staged reading in August, it had been to just family and close friends. Even though the show's matriarch, Mercer Oglethorpe, was based on Laine, she insisted it was a spot-on interpretation of Bitsy Hollander. My other friends, despite the fact that they acknowledged and could see themselves as the inspiration for the rest of the characters, were more flattered.

Miranda and I had only intended to do one staged reading. However, at Laine's insistence, we did a second for all of her friends. Unbeknownst to me, Laine did it as a backer's audition, and we found ourselves with several thousand dollars pledged to help us stage it. Most impressively Bitsy - who insisted that Laine didn't know what the hell she was talking about because Mercer was obviously based on my aunt – coughed up five grand for us, and offered more if we found we needed something in particular. At Laine's insistence, to thank Bitsy, we named the stage-left box the Hollander Box. It still wasn't reinforced and no one could sit in it yet, but Bitsy was pleased nonetheless.

So, Miranda and I found ourselves staging a new show. We had tentatively slated the premiere for the first weekend in October, and planned for, hopefully, a four-week run.

Although the windfall from Laine's cronies had launched us, it wouldn't be enough to get us all the way through to the premiere. So, in order to raise money I was opening the theater every Friday night for Klein's improv troupe to perform. Thanks to Talbot, we had secured an extended special event liquor license for beer and wine only, and she was busy working on a permanent license for us. I wasn't sure exactly what it entailed, but I knew I was going to have to secure the endorsement of the neighborhood planning unit, an informal government organization or a formal government advisory board, depending on how you interpreted the city's organizational structure.

So, each evening we rehearsed. We had cast a couple of women from *Duck Soup* into the show. Lara (known to Zach as "Earth Mother") was playing Agnes Scott Ponce de Leon, and Rochelle ("Dances with Corgis") playing Jonetta Morehouse-Spelman. Klein was, of course, Buzz DeLoitte, and he had found us our Diego Kobiashi-Emory in the person of one Spencer Han. Jennifer was cast to play Mercer, and so far she was doing a pretty passable job of channeling both Laine and Bitsy into the character.

We had been rehearsing for about two weeks, and the cast had the songs down. They had the script down for the most part, so we had just begun working on putting things together. The work was slow and tedious, and we were continually rewriting lines, but the beginning of the show was apparent. I understood the value of rehearsals.

One thing was abundantly clear, however. The Feldmans may have disliked magnolias, but they hated Spencer. Every time he appeared on stage, lights flickered, microphones stopped working, or speakers buzzed. Once, the theater doors had slammed shut. It didn't take the rest of the cast long to figure out we were haunted, and it was often a topic of conversation when something went wrong.

"I think your ghosts hate Asians," Spencer observed that evening as a breaker tripped, plunging the stage into darkness as he was about to begin his first song. "I suspect Mister Feldman fought in the Pacific theater in World War Two, and assumes all Asians are the enemy."

"Problem is," I explained as a reset the breaker, "Laine remembers World War Two and says the Feldmans were haunting the apartment building long before. Maybe since the twenties."

"They don't hate Asians, Spence," Klein offered. "Just you."

As if in confirmation, the breaker tripped again. "Knock it off, Feldmans," I snarled as I walked back to the breaker box. For the record, if they hated Spence, they loved Klein. He had the opposite experience. Not only did they not disrupt any of his lines or songs, they seemed to interfere with the spotlights so his always was the brightest and most steady.

"You know," Lara offered, "I have a friend who's a spiritualist and a psychic. Maybe she could come figure out what is going on."

I rolled my eyes as I reset the breaker, but Miranda jumped on the idea. "Do you mean Lydia Wells?" she asked excitedly.

"I do! Do you know Lydia?"

"Oh yeah. We go way back. I can't believe I didn't think of her before this. Van, we *must* call her."

Hearing the italics in her voice, I knew better than to fight it, so I simply changed the subject. "Right now, we've got to get through Spencer's song."

The next day, I was outside cutting the lawn at the 'Hurst. Zach was back in school, and I found myself having to pick up more of his duties. Paradoxically, Laine had given him a raise.

Talbot's Mercedes pulled up in front of the building and parked in front of a fire hydrant. She jumped out and walked over to me. I shut off the lawnmower and gave her a perfunctory peck on the cheek. I might have done more, but I was pretty sweaty.

"So who is Archer Bellamy and why does he hate you?" she asked, sitting primly on the front steps.

"He's a neighbor. I don't know that he hates me. He didn't enjoy *Duck Soup* and was a bit bent out of shape when I wouldn't refund his money, but I don't know that he hates me. Why?"

"He's filed an objection against our liquor license application with the licensing board."

"On what grounds?" I asked. Laine came out onto her porch and greeted Talbot.

"On several," she replied after catching my aunt up. She flipped open a portfolio and read. "On the grounds that you are too close to a school…"

Laine scoffed. "The middle school is almost a mile away."

"…and, that the theater is a public nuisance, and something about a pending petition he's planning to submit to have the zoning changed for the neighborhood to refuse the sale of liquor within 500 feet of any form of residential."

"Good luck getting that through," Laine observed.

"Maybe I just need to talk to him," I mused.

"It probably wouldn't hurt to give him a call."

Later that afternoon, as I came out the door heading for the theater, I saw Miranda letting herself in with another woman in tow. I hollered at them and ran across to join them.

"Van," Miranda began, "This is Lydia Wells. Lydia, Donovan Ford."

"Hi Lydia," I said, noting that the psychic looked nothing like I would have expected. No caftan, no turban, no beads. Instead she wore a simple pink sweater set over a pair of jeans and classic strand of pearls.

"Hi Donovan. It's a pleasure." She had a firm handshake, and her overall demeanor made me feel more like she was a good realtor than a psychic.

"I've been telling Lydia about the Feldmans, and we thought we'd just stop by so she could have a look. Well, I guess you don't look, per se. More like a feel." She paused for a beat. "Well, that didn't sound right either. Let's just check them out." She led Lydia into the lobby.

"Now as I understand it," Lydia began, " you think they just recently relocated from your apartment, Donovan, to the theater?"

"I don't know that I even think they exist," I replied. "But yes, whatever odd, annoying coincidences that had been happening in my apartment for years now appear to be happening over here."

"Donovan is a very rational person," Miranda explained patiently. "He can't bring himself to believe in things he can't explain."

Lydia shrugged and patted me gently on the shoulder. "Everyone makes peace with the world in their own way. There's no reason you *have* to believe in the spiritual. Now tell me, is there a place where they seem to be strongest?"

We led her up to our office, then out onto the balcony, down the back hallway and onto the stage, and even to the rehearsal hall beneath. She asked fairly neutral questions and established that they hated magnolias and Spence. She asked if she could come back that night for rehearsal.

"Sure," I replied.

"Do you sense anything so far?" Miranda asked, barely able to contain her excitement.

"I sense something or someone here, but beyond that I can't really make any sense of it. Tell me, though; why did you decide it was the Feld*mans*? Why do you think there are two of them?"

I shrugged. "I don't know. It's just something I started calling them when I began to get annoyed by their high-jinks."

"Did your aunt or sister ever refer to them as plural rather than in the singular?"

I thought. I couldn't remember them really discussing them more than saying the building was "sort of haunted." Calling them Feldmans had been my own device, which I told Lydia.

"Interesting," Lydia observed. "I also sense two presences here. Maybe you're more psychic than you think, Donovan."

Thursday night's rehearsal was entertaining for the cast but hardly productive. When Laine heard we were going to have a psychic try to contact the Feldmans, she came trotting excitedly across the street to join us.

Lydia, in order to get more of a sense of who the Feldmans were and what their issue was returned with a friend, a laptop, and a big bag of magnolia blossoms. She distributed the blossoms around the theater while the cast watched and her friend took random pictures by just aiming a digital camera in different directions from where he was looking.

Miranda and I really just had to play along. At Lydia's request, we started with Klein on stage alone and had him sing his solo. Badly. Always being one for a chance to show off, Klein went over the top. He totally butchered it. No lights flickered, no scenery fell. Everything went just fine.

Then we had Spencer get on stage, and asked him to perform his solo. Lydia also asked him to butcher his as well. He wasn't quite the showman Klein was, but he still made it pretty awful. The lights flickered some, but not as much as we had come to expect. No breakers tripped.

During all of this, Lydia sat motionless in an aisle seat in the middle of the auditorium, her eyes closed. As Spence finished his solo, she opened her eyes and asked him to sing it again.

"Louder if possible," she said calmly, "and directed towards the *back* of the stage."

Spence complied, singing straight into the curtain. Lydia's assistant disappeared behind the curtain. Spence sang louder and worse. Then, at Lydia's request, he sang the solo a third time.

That did it. Candidly, I could sympathize with the Feldmans because the bad singing was starting to get on my nerves. The breakers for the stage lights tripped.

I climbed on stage, slipped behind the curtain and reset the breaker. When I came back out, Spence was staring at me wide-eyed.

"Did you touch me when you went backstage?"

"No. I came up along the right wall."

He turned and looked around at everyone else. They were all seated in the auditorium except the assistant, who came around the curtain on the other side.

"I'd swear someone pushed me in the chest right after the breaker tripped. Hard."

Unwillingly, I felt a cold chill run down my spine and into my legs. A quick look around the cast showed they had all had a similar experience. We all turned to Lydia, who was smiling benevolently.

"I probably really should apologize to the Feldmans since I've done everything possible to piss them off," she said. "Sorry, guys."

"Did you pick something up?" Laine asked, excitedly.

"I did." The cast all came and gathered around her, while the assistant began docking the digital camera with the laptop.

"First of all, congratulations, Van. You're right. There are two spirits here, although I don't think they are a couple. I sense both are male. One of them is fairly benign, docile, almost childlike. But this is the spirit that hates the magnolias. I sensed him first when I came in here today, watching us. But, as soon as I took the magnolias out of my bag, I felt him retreat to the balcony.

"The other spirit has very strong opinions. He's the one throwing breakers. As far as I can tell, you're right. He loves Klein and hates Spence."

"Can you tell why?"

She shook her head. "Typically when a spirit 'hates' something, it's because he associates it with unhappiness. So something about Spence probably reminds him of someone or something he hated when he was alive. Now interestingly, he's not hostile to Spence's presence, just his voice."

"That's not going to make me particularly effective on stage," Spence mused.

"Can you tell how they feel about the rest of us?" Laine asked. "After all, it's *always* about me."

Lydia smiled. "The younger one is pretty much indifferent to everyone and everything except the magnolias. The older one seems to be totally indifferent to everyone else, except maybe you and Van. I'm not basing that on anything I am picking up, just on the fact that both of you have seen or experienced a 'haunting' in the apartment."

Despite my innate skepticism of psychics, ghosts, and the whole bloody process, I felt another involuntary chill.

"Are they still here?" Miranda asked.

"I sense the younger one in the balcony still, and the other one seems to be on stage."

We all turned and looked at the stage. Lydia asked her assistant, "Anything on any of the pictures, Max?"

"Not really," Assistant Max replied. "There's one light spot on the stage that could be something, but nothing definite."

He held up the laptop and all of us looked. The picture was of the fuse box backstage and there was an odd discoloring of the shot in the upper left hand corner.

"For some reason, digital cameras seem to do better at capturing images of spirits," Lydia explained. "Especially if you are looking in a different direction than you are shooting." While she was speaking she looked towards the back of the theater and shot a surreptitious picture of the stage. Nothing showed up on the image.

"What are we going to do?" Miranda asked.

"Well, I guess your only options are to get rid of Spence or get rid of the spirits."

"How do we do that?" Laine asked.

Lydia smiled. "Harvest moon is next week. Perfect time for an exorcism."

During the ensuing week, we continued rehearsals, although Spence got less stage time than he possibly needed. The Feldmans were mostly docile, although Miranda had the distinct sense that they were "watching us and waiting for us to make the next move."

Although I still didn't believe in the whole thing, I begrudgingly went along with an exorcism. Lara knew a woman of Cherokee descent who supposedly practiced the "medicinal arts" and was also an accomplished shaman. ("Of *course* she does," Chris and Zach joked.) The harvest moon would be the following Saturday and that was when the exorcism was scheduled for.

In the meantime, I had my own evil spirit to contend with in the person of Archer Bellamy. He had not taken nor returned several calls to his office over the past week, so on Sunday afternoon I found a reason to wander down to his end of the street just as he was arriving home from church. I happened to be on the sidewalk as he was getting out of his Hummer.

"Mister Bellamy," I called in a friendly tone. Although he was an ass, southern propriety required him to acknowledge me. "Good evening."

"Mister Ford," he replied coolly.

"Hope you are well tonight." I didn't really give a damn if he was or not. "Hey, I've left a couple of messages for you at work this week. I was hoping you could help me better understand your concerns with my liquor license application. If there's a way for me to address them, I'm happy to work with you."

He crossed his arms and leaned against his car with a bit of a pinched expression. "I don't think you can work with me, because I object to drinking. Period."

"Um, okay, but since it's not illegal…"

"No it's not illegal. But that doesn't mean it needs to be expanded in our neighborhood."

"Expanded? You do realize this is a restaurant district. Just about every establishment has a liquor license."

"Oh yes. I realize that. Even the new hair salon has a bar in it. But we don't need more."

I scratched my head, perplexed. "So, if I understand you, you're looking to stamp out the spread of liquor licenses in this neighborhood, starting with me. Do I have that right?"

"Basically, yes."

"Okay, forget about me for a second. This could easily be the next business to open. Can I ask what grounds you are basing stopping the spread of liquor licenses on?"

"Quality of life. Look around you. We've got parking problems every single weekend because all these people come into the Highlands to eat and drink and shop and, now, attend your theater. Every morning there are empty beer bottles on the street and in our lawns. This is a residential neighborhood, not Las Vegas."

"I think drawing a comparison between Vegas and the Highlands might be a bit of a stretch. Yes it's a residential neighborhood, but it is also a business district. In fact, my understanding is that the reason people buy here is precisely for the proximity to the shops and bars and restaurants. Help me understand what I'm missing."

He shrugged. "I really don't have time. Yes, people may have bought here for the bars and easy access to liquor, but they are out of step with the times. Covenants and tight zoning will come to this neighborhood just like they came to the suburbs."

"But how do you..."

He held up his hand to silence me. "Good day, Mister Ford." I watched his back as he walked into the house and shut the door.

"What a sanctimonious twit," Laine opined in her apartment later as I related the exchange. She stirred the manhattans in her shaker rather violently in agitation.

"You can't be serious," Rachel asked. "He wants to improve the Highlands by driving out all the bars and restaurants."

"That's what I heard," I replied. "I guess it's that old 'we had to destroy the village to save it' paradigm."

"Well," Talbot observed, "Now that we understand his game, we know how to fight him."

"What do you have in mind?" I asked.

She smiled deviously. "Lots of my clients are on this street. They buy lots of my wine to sell to all those people he's so unhappy about coming into the Highlands. Let me have a few, well-timed discussions."

The set for the show was taking shape. It was sort of a Highlands street scene, with a house and a shop and a bar. However each one folded open at a different time for the scene that took place inside of it. We were far enough along in building it that we needed to acquire some accessories. I had vaguely hoped I could make off with some of Aunt Laine's bric-a-brac, but she made it clear that none of her treasures were going to start a life in the theater.

"Lakewood is this weekend," she told me. "Why don't you go shopping for props there?"

"What's Lakewood?"

Lakewood, she explained, was a huge flea market on the old Lakewood Fairgrounds, south of the stadium. It occupied seven enormous barns, plus, in nice weather, the lawns in between. I gathered that much of Laine's apartment had been acquired there over the years.

It was Saturday morning, and it had been quite some time since my little "gang" had spent some time together goofing off. It took very little effort to convince Rachel, Jennifer, and Chris to escort me to Lakewood to go on a shopping spree. By instinct, I had started towards the VeggieRoll, but Chris explained that Lakewood Fairgrounds was not necessarily in the best neighborhood, so instead we piled into the Jeep and drove south for flea marketing.

The day was hot and hazy. Late in the summer, rain in Georgia can be sparse, and the air quality declines dramatically. (This is largely a function of the fact that there are approximately 1.5 cars for every man, woman, child, and houseplant in the city.) The result is that the late summer sky is seldom blue, but rather a kind of featureless, dingy taupe. While it's not necessarily depressing, the temperature combined with the diffused light can subdue your mood. As a result, the discussion in the car was less ribald than would normally characterize our group outings, and more a steady stream of mildly surly sarcasm.

"So what are we off to buy?" Rachel asked, settling her Jackie-O sunglasses on her nose. The haze resulted in a glare that was too bright for comfort, but not bright enough for the sunglasses.

"Stuff for the set," I replied, pulling off the Connector on the Langford Parkway exit. "I need some lamps, a percolator, a…"

She laid a hand on my forearm. "Not you, dear. We know what you're looking for. I meant the rest of us."

"Oh, I thought you were just coming to help me."

Jennifer let out her harsh, Cleveland "bwa-ha" laugh that she used when something struck her as absurd. "Oh, doll. Of course not. You're looking for your stuff. We're looking for ours. I, personally, am looking for a velvet painting of a fishing village at night that has the little electric lights in the windows."

"Dear God," I replied, "Why?"

Rachel clutched my forearm, her nails digging nails into my wrist slightly. "Dear, you must never insult someone's Lakewood *fantasy find*. It's like insulting someone's religion."

"Huh?"

"When you go to Lakewood, you are always searching for your fantasy find. Something that you believe will be there, and you'd buy without dickering over the price."

"You're kidding."

"Would I make fun of faith?"

"So Jennifer's a Southern Velvetist?"

Jennifer interjected. "No. *They* only search for velvet Elvises, the heretics. I prefer to think of myself more as a Velveterian. Reformed."

"Chris, what are you looking for?" Rachel asked, taking the sunglasses back off.

"Antique art deco stainless-steel martini shaker."

"Oh, that's not hard to find."

"It is with my initials monogrammed on it. You?"

"Same as always." She put the sunglasses back on and pointed where I needed to turn right. "A nineteen-sixty-four, twenty-six-foot Airstream Overlander Land Yacht."

"You're kidding," I said again.

"I'm not."

"What in the world for?"

Jennifer piped in from behind me. "Van, it's rude to ask about someone's fantasies."

"No, I don't mind," Rachel replied magnanimously. "My grandfather always fantasized about having one. He had a camper and used to take all of us camping, but he didn't have an Airstream. He always said we'd know we had arrived when we could afford an Airstream."

We pulled into the parking lot.

"How in the world would you pull it?" I asked as I got out of the Jeep.

She rested her sunglasses on top of her head. "Quit trying to inject reality into my Lakewood."

We walked up the hill to the gates, paid our three-dollar admission, and walked through. The fair ground was built in 1938 and was the home of the Southeastern Fair until 1975. The fair left four huge turn-of-the-century, barn-like buildings that were stuccoed, and had been decorated in a sort of a faux–Spanish mission/Italianate villa style, complete with bell towers and Roman gods atop pillars. When you came through the front gates, you were on a level plaza between the lower levels of buildings three and four.

Immediately to my right were easily two dozen booths open to the sky. The largest, just to the right of the gate, appeared to be selling doors, windows, pillars and entire porches that had all been salvaged off of Victorian buildings. Next to it was a truck with several tables lined up in front of an old panel van. The tables were covered with an amazing collection of housewares, all in a somewhat disreputable condition. Behind that booth, I could see another booth, filled with nothing but armoires.

"Wow," I said, impressed. "Where in the world do we start?"

"Firehouse," Chris replied.

"Firehouse," Jennifer agreed.

"Firehouse," Rachel declared.

"Firehouse?" I asked as the three of the started off towards a ramp running upward at the far end of the buildings.

The ramp ended at a road that ran in front of Buildings One and Three on the right and Two and Four on the left. On the other side, there was another plaza stretching away into the distance. The plaza was a veritable village of vendors. Some were selling expensive restored Victorian electric light fixtures and some were selling Adirondack chairs. One was selling salvaged stained-glass windows. Many were selling nothing in particular, but some of everything.

A road wrapped around the plaza. Passing in front of Building One on the right, it wound to the back of the fairgrounds, turned left and then returned in front of Building Two. At the back of the plaza, between the buildings was a small fire station. It had been converted into a bar-and-grill. While I tried to look in the booths, Jennifer, Chris, and Rachel made a straight path to the bar without looking left or right. Inside, a particularly cheerful woman with dark hair greeted my friends with a simple "Three Bud Light drafts?"

"Four," Rachel replied. Two minutes and ten dollars later we were back outside, sipping our beers.

"Okay," Jennifer announced. Now we're ready to begin. Which way?"

We decided to tour Building Two first.

"One of the things that is important to note about Lakewood," Rachel said, putting her sunglasses back on as we walked towards the end door of Building Two, "is the search for the *theme ingredient*."

"The theme ingredient?" I asked.

"Yep," Chris replied. "Every Lakewood, every *single* month, has a theme ingredient."

"What does that mean?"

"At every Lakewood," Jennifer informed me, "you will no doubt see something your mother or your grandmother or someone else in your childhood had that you completely took for granted. Suddenly, you come to Lakewood, and you see the object, which you haven't even thought of in twenty years, and there are *thirty* of them in different booths as you walk through the event. That's the theme ingredient."

We walked towards Building Two. I had to admit I was a little put off by the "insiderness" they were bringing to this event. On the other hand, I was mesmerized by both the ritual they were bringing to the event, as well as the sheer amount of *stuff* surrounding us.

We entered Building Two, and I forgot all about the "theme ingredient."

We were greeted by music as we entered, and directly in front of us was an oak player-piano, easily a hundred years old, playing Cole Porter's "Miss Otis Regrets."

Jennifer began singing, "...and found that her dream of love was gone."

Chris and Rachel joined in, "Madam, she ran to the man who had led her so far astray."

And suddenly, much to my amazement, I found myself singing along.

"And from under her velvet gown, she drew a gun and shot her lover down, madam. Miss Otis regrets she's unable to lunch *todaaaaaaaaaay*."

I might have been self-conscious, except no one in the crowded building noticed. It was as if people breaking out into song as they entered the building was the most normal thing in the world. Which, of course, it was.

We started up the first aisle, which stretched away for about five hundred feet, before doubling back. There were four such aisles in the building. About halfway down, I found the first thing my mother had had. On my left was a booth selling all kinds of mid-twentieth-century kitchenware. What caught my attention was a brushed aluminum "honey pot" shaped cookie jar with a black plastic lid. I remember my mother having one. It sat in the corner of her kitchen counter, almost always full of Oreos. I picked it up and studied it, noting that it gave me an odd, comforting sensation.

As I returned it to its shelf, the booth owner told me he could "do better on the price."

I thanked him and noticed a set of glass bowls. They were probably originally envisioned as French onion soup bowls. They were semi-conical with a little handle on the side. They were white on the inside and coppery beige on the outside. I picked one up and examined it.

"Fire King," the booth owner told me appreciatively. "It's Depression-era glass. They were manufactured by Anchor-Hocking. I'll do fifty-five for the set of four."

I smiled at him and put it down. "Maybe not."

"Just looking at them 'cause they've got a story for you?"

I nodded. "I'm sure you hear a lot of stories when people see something from their childhood."

He shrugged, smiling. "Oh sure. That's what we do here. We sell people tangible connections to their past. And, I'm happy to listen to their stories…as long as they buy it."

I laughed and walked away, thinking of my Fire King story. My mother had a set. She never made French onion soup in them though. Rather, they were used to serve Brit and me soft-boiled eggs or oatmeal for breakfast when we were little. Sometimes they were also pressed into service for soup at lunch.

Even though I had not thought of them in years, I knew exactly where my mother's were. Well, the surviving three of the set. They were sitting on the top shelf of the cabinet over the refrigerator in the kitchen of the apartment in New York. I had taken so little with me when I left, it had never occurred to me to go get them. The thought of that depressed me. I took another sip of my beer and walked on.

We finished our tour of Building Two and our beers simultaneously. Nothing had been purchased, although Jennifer briefly considered an aluminum Christmas tree. We returned to the bar to purchase another round and went on to Building Three. It didn't take long to ascertain that the booths at Lakewood fell into three categories.

First there were the specialty booths. These were the booths that focused on a specific theme or item. So, one booth might carry nothing but cast-iron cookware; another might deal exclusively in restored antique telephones; a third might peddle only postcards. These booths were always worth a pause to study, but not much more unless you were specifically interested in its special commodity. They did provoke several unkind comments on exactly what might inspire someone to collect nothing but cracker tins or crocheted doilies. "I never waste time at Doily-Mart," Chris announced out as we cruised past one booth.

The second type of booth was the craft booth. These weren't reselling used stuff, but instead something that the proprietor or their spouse had run up at home. Some of it was edible, like the "Amish" cheese and butter from Ohio. Much of it was apparel, such as the pashmina that cost Rachel twenty bucks. And some was just strange, like the decorative arrangements of flowers made of leather for several hundred dollars.

The third type of booth was my favorite though: the Crap Fest. The Crap Fest was a space that had a little something for everyone. Sad clown paintings might be propped against an exer-cycle, resting next to a table covered with shot glasses, Christmas ornaments, doorknobs, and someone's abandoned super-8 films. There was neither rhyme nor reason to the inventory: just a veritable treasure trove of *stuff.*

Invariably, each booth was presided over by the proprietor, who I began referring to as the Crap-Master. The Crap-Master had too much stuff, and so was desperate to move the inventory rather than having to pack it up and lug it back home at the end of the festival. You just knew that the Crap-Master was dreading the sarcastic comments from their spouse, Mister or Missus Master. They would be there waiting and wanting to know when the Crap-Master was going to give this gig up. The spouse had always envisioned an uncluttered lifestyle in a sleek, ultra-contemporary house, like one of those stark glass-and-metal Mies van der Rohe creations you saw in *Architectural Digest*, where the only thing that could even be classified as bric-a-brac was a bright red apple in the center of an empty black coffee table in the middle of an all-white room. But no, the spouse had to marry for love and was now living in a nineteen-sixties ranch that was stuffed to the gills with the Crap-Master's crap because the Crap-Master was convinced of its hidden value.

"I can do better on the bowls," a Crap-Master near the end of Building Three told me as I examined three Fire Kings that were taped together. "Make me an offer. Don't want to leave with any of this stuff."

"Thanks," I replied, as I put them down and continued to peruse his stuff.

"What would make someone sell their wedding album?" Rachel asked as she flipped through one on the next table that was marked for five dollars. "I mean, even if the divorce was just *horrible*, wouldn't you keep the album?"

Chris looked over her shoulder. "Yellow tuxedoes with ruffles. It was the seventies. They were all stoned."

"I don't have any of my wedding pictures," I told her, examining a large framed oil portrait of a mid-century matron that looked like she had just passed a persimmon. It would work well on the set.

"Of course you don't," Rachel replied. "It's not a guy thing. It's a woman thing. I can't imagine a woman leaving her wedding album."

I offered the Crap-Master five dollars for the portrait, which he accepted. I tucked it under my arm and we walked on.

By the end of Building Three, I had also purchased a big, ancient black fan and an oversized decanter and highball glass, which would all be perfect for Mercer Oglethorpe's house. While the gang went to buy another round of beers, I took my treasures to the Jeep. As I came back into the fairgrounds, I noticed another, single, Fire King sitting on a table on the lower plaza.

"So, what do you think of your first Lakewood?" Jennifer asked when I caught up with them. We started towards Building One.

"Pretty neat," I replied. "The stuff is cool, but what is really wild are the people. You don't expect this kind of diversity outside of New York. Hell, the people are more interesting than the things being sold."

She nodded sagely and belched.

"That said," I continued, "I may have found the theme ingredient."

"Which is?" Rachel asked skeptically.

"The Fire King."

"What is a Fire King?"

I explained the brief history. There were none immediately available to show her.

"Well, if I find my nineteen-sixty-four, twenty-six-foot Airstream Overlander Land Yacht, we shall have to pick up a set for it."

"You're serious about this Airstream?"

She paused to consider. "I am," she replied decidedly.

There were no Airstreams in Building One. There was, however, a pirate.

Well, not so much a pirate as a pirate wannabe. His name was Harry, and he ran the first hybrid booth I had seen: the Specialty/Crap-Fest. Ostensibly, he was selling nautical antiques, but there was more than a fair amount of derelict computer and electronic equipment scattered between the bow lights and Jolly Rogers.

Of course the booth is not what made him the pirate. It was the outfit. Harry was a big guy. (Well, he's not dead; he still is.) Well over six feet, and easily over two hundred pounds. He was wearing a black-and-white horizontally striped shirt under a black vest. What was sad was that he wasn't trying to look like a pirate. He just did.

We saw Harry as we came around the corner into the last aisle of the building. I was about to make a snide comment about him, when he called out a greeting to Rachel.

"Rachel! Hey!"

"Hi, Harry. Haven't seen you in the store lately."

"Yeah, I've been traveling for work a lot. Coming to the end of the project though, so I'll be back into my old routine."

"Great. Hey, let me introduce you to my friends." Chris and I were introduced. Jennifer was somewhere behind us, haggling over a powder-blue pillbox hat with a bit of netting.

Harry was a computer consultant, a Georgia Tech graduate, and just now coming out of the far side of his divorce recovery. I immediately felt guilty for having almost made the pirate comment, and began scouring his booth for Fire Kings.

Jennifer came around the corner, wearing her new hat and carrying a large M&Ms tote bag.

"Hey!" Harry called. "You're the angry bartender at Fontaine's."

When Jennifer wants to, she can command an expression and demeanor that would strike the British royal family as aloof. She uses it to flirt. She took that stance now and replied. "Why, yes. I am. Have we met?"

"Yeah. I was in there about a month ago. You made fun of my drink." He was smiling as he delivered this.

"Well, that certainly sounds like something I would do. Was it 'less than masculine'? Like a crème de menthe frappe?"

"It was a black-and-tan."

"Really? That's not very feminine."

"No one said it was feminine. You said it didn't match my personality."

"Ah. Well, you know I'm a professional. Did I tell you what drink would match your personality?"

"A crème de menthe frappe."

"I thought that sounded familiar." She held her hand out as if there were a ring to be kissed. "Miss Jennifer Mathis."

He took it gallantly and kissed it. "Mister Harry Bornbaum."

Chris leaned over and whispered in my ear. "Courting rituals of the straight just nauseate me. Ready to move on?"

"Yeah."

We moved forward. Rachel excused herself and joined us. The three of us continued to wander and drink, during which time I purchased a couple of silverplate candlesticks for five dollars and a broken mantel clock that looked fine for two. We had also reached agreement that Fire Kings were the theme ingredient. Behind Building Three, there were three more buildings. We had made it to Building Seven before Jennifer finally called Rachel's cell phone to find out where we were.

"She'll be here in a minute," she said, snapping the cell phone shut and re-settling her sunglasses on top of her head. "I told her we would meet her at the Dunky Donuts trailer."

Most of the Lakewood food vendors congregated on the lawn in the plaza between Buildings One and Three, but there were outliers. Dunky was one. It was a small, taupish-orange trailer near the edge of Building One that produced the most delicious smelling donut ever. Whether their name was a rip-off of Dunkin' Donuts or a play on Boston-based Dinky Donuts wasn't quite clear. What was clear was that the aroma emanating from the trailer was one of the only things that could make me crave sugar with beer on a hot afternoon.

Jennifer came around the corner of Building One, still wearing her hat and carrying her bag, but now also lugging an enormous faux anchor that she had bought from Harry. We learned she had also secured a date with him for that evening.

"I wouldn't ordinarily date someone from Lakewood," she told us as she relieved me of my beer to take a swig. "It's kind of like dating carny-folk. But he seems very nice and stable, and I don't typically date that." She took another swig of my beer. "Hell. I don't typically date *anyone*."

"I think that's great, Jen. But aren't you working tonight?"

"Eh, I cover for everyone else when they have dates. They can cover for me for once." She finished my beer, and gazed past Rachel. "Hey. Isn't that your Airstream?"

All of us turned and looked past the donut trailer. The ground sloped downward sharply behind Building One to a parking lot. The lot was reserved for the dealers and was filled with panel trucks, trailers, and miscellaneous recreational vehicles. A few were big, new, lavish and expensive: clearly the domain of the more successful dealers. Most were older models, more appropriate conveyances for the inventory displayed around us.

One was set a little farther away from the rest. It stood near the lower back door of Building One, a bright silver bullet, maybe twenty feet long. In the front window, an orange "For Sale" sign proclaimed its availability.

"Oh my God," Chris gasped dramatically. "It's Rachel's fantasy find."

We all turned and looked at her. She was staring at the trailer, wide-eyed, wary. She settled the sunglasses back on her nose, and started purposefully down the hill towards it. The three of us turned and followed her.

She reached it, and gently touched its chromed front with the tips of her left hand. Slowly, she began to walk around it, counter clockwise, studying it intently.

By the time she had completed her third lap, I wearied of her near-spiritual trance and began to look around. I noticed that there was a door into Building One behind us. I turned and walked over to peer inside.

It was the landing of the stairs. They came down from the main floor of the building and split. The steps to the left led down to the restrooms. To the right, a sign indicated that the steps led down to something called "Down Under One." Rachel was still in her trance, so I wandered down to explore.

It was a semi-finished basement: dirt floors and thick concrete walls. The stairs gave way to a hallway lined with old doors. Front doors, leaded glass doors, even pocket doors with their ancient track wheels still mounted to the top. It was packed, and smelled of dust and mildew. I followed the hallway past the doors. It led to a cross hallway leading back outside. I wandered to the door, and peeked outside. Above on the hill, Rachel was completing another lap. I continued my exploration.

Beyond the cross hall, I entered a huge space that took the concept of Crap Fest to a whole different level. The area, about the size of a small gymnasium, was full of everything from mantels and chandeliers to waffle irons and filing cabinets. There was also a large oil painting in the corner of someone who looked like a Puritan ancestor of Judith Light. The whole place was creepy and yet intriguing. It was like a giant prop closet. It was compelling.

Despite the smell, and the creepy atmosphere, I had to go explore. As I walked in, the old guy sitting next to the door offered the perfunctory "I can do better on the prices," without looking up from his paper.

Twenty minutes later, I had lined up a couple of urns, a mahogany pillar, and a faux-plaster bust that would complete Mercer's house. I was just about to go negotiate the final price when my cell phone rang. I paused next to a long table with a set of Wedgwood china set spread out on it. It was Chris.

"Hey."

"Where are you?"

I glanced around. "In the basement of Building One, in a kind of crypt for Victorian architectural features and housewares. Did Rachel buy the Airstream?"

"Nope. It's not an 'Overlander' Land Yacht. It's a 'Safari,' whatever that means. Are you ready to go?"

On the table next to the china was a lone Fire King. I picked it up and examined it. There was a small chip in it and it was grimy as hell. "Jeez…"

"What?"

"Nothing. I just need to pay for my stuff. Will you tell the girls we'll meet them by the Dunky Donuts trailer and then come down here to help me carry this stuff out? I'm buying a pillar."

"Okay." We hung up and I walked towards the Crap-Master and held up the lone Fire King.

"This one, too."

I paid an additional three dollars for the bowl that I was buying for reasons that totally escaped me. Chris managed to find me just as I was signing the charge card receipt.

"Quite a smell down here," he said, scrunching up his nose. "It reminds me of summer camp."

"I never knew you went to summer camp," I replied absently as I put the receipt in my wallet.

He rolled his eyes. "Camp Voldemort. I don't talk about it a lot. Not my favorite experience."

Thirty minutes later, we had the pillar and Jennifer's anchor tied to the roof of the Jeep, and the rest of the crap in the back, and were driving home. I glanced sideways at Rachel and asked, "So no Airstream?"

She shook her head. "I considered it. It was beautiful on the inside. And it's about the right vintage, but for the money it's not the right model."

Later that evening, after all the new props had been unloaded into the theater, I retired upstairs to the apartment and placed the Fire King on the counter. I took out my cell phone and, with a slight wave of apprehension, pressed the speed-dial for Olivia.

"Well hello, stranger." She sounded friendly and upbeat. "I haven't heard from you in months."

"Hey," I replied. "You sound cheery. Life must be good."

"Eh…what did you used to say? 'It doesn't suck.' How are you doing? Are you still in Atlanta?"

"I am."

"How's Laine?"

I smiled. How unlike her to ask about someone she didn't like. "Just about recovered. Still going in for physical therapy, but it's a minor thing now. As the southerners say, she's 'as full of piss and vinegar' as ever."

"I don't think I've ever heard a more apt description for her. So, why is it I have to hear from Aidan McInnis that my ex-husband has restored a theater entirely on his own?"

I was stunned. There was no mistaking it: behind the mock accusation there was something that sounded like pride.

"Well, I can't tell you how surprised I was to see him. But yes, the theater is kind of restored and our first show had a pretty successful run."

"Yeah. Aidan told me it was something like an all-lesbian version of the Three Stooges."

"Close. The Marx Brothers. *Duck Soup*. Very political piece."

She chuckled. "Is there lesbian theater that *isn't* political?"

I joined the laughter. "Not that I've ever seen. Wow, Liv. It's been a long time since I've heard you this upbeat. Divorce must agree with you."

There was a pause, during which I could imagine her taking a sip of her wine while she contemplated what to say next. "I don't know that I would say *divorce* agrees with me, but I'm having a pretty good year professionally."

I ventured, "Are you dating anyone?"

She laughed. "I'm too old to date, Van. I see some guys occasionally, but no one that I want to really devote a lot of energy to. But that's not really my focus right now. If something happens, it happens."

"You should date. You're too hot to give up punishing men."

I may have gone too far. She didn't change her tone, but she did change the subject. "So to what do I owe the honor of a call from my ex?"

"In the cabinet over the refrigerator, there used to be some bowls of my mother's. Three of them. They were white on the inside and a sort of a brownish-tan on the outside. They've got handles like they were meant for French onion soup, and they say Fire King on the bottom."

"I know the bowls you're talking about. Sort of Depression-era glass?"

I leaned back on the couch and kicked off my flip flops. "Exactly. Do you still have them?"

"Of course. I'd never throw away anything of your mother's. Do you want them?"

"Yeah, I do, actually. Would you mind sending them down?"

"Not at all. I'll take them to work and have Sally pack them up." Sally was Olivia's secretary, assistant, and proto-spouse. During the last years of our marriage, Sally and I had spoken more than Olivia and I had.

In the background I heard her drag a barstool around to the refrigerator. I marveled how the sounds of certain experiences stay with you, even more than a year after hearing them last. I closed my eyes and pictured Liv pulling the glass bowls off the top shelf. I even heard them clink together. I knew she would take them into the foyer and set them on the credenza between her briefcase and the answering machine.

I became cognizant of her talking again and opened my eyes. "So tell me, what's next for this theater of yours?"

"Well, um, we're going to stage a musical about life in Atlanta."

"Really? What's it called?"

"Highlands-A-Go-Go."

"Fun. Who wrote it?"

"Well, it would appear that I did."

"It would *appear?*"

I felt a sudden surge of something that I would later learn is called confidence. "Appear hell. I wrote it."

She became quite animated. "You did?! Van, that's awesome. I'm so proud of you. Tell me everything about it."

We spent the next two hours on the phone together. In retrospect, I realized it was the most we had talked in the last two years. The call ended with her telling me she wanted tickets for the opening. I told her the date of it, but didn't think anything more about it. I had an exorcism to attend.

The nice thing about living in an eclectic, educated, wealthy, liberal neighborhood like the Highlands is that everyone is well connected. If you need to find a plumber, or an attorney, or doctoral candidate working on a dissertation for acoustic modeling of the tonal qualities of choral first-tenor sections, it typically doesn't require more than three phone calls. Laine managed to line up an exorcist in one. The woman Lara had recommended was happy to come exorcise the theater for free.

Now, while I still did not really believe we were haunted, I was in the minority. Sadly, the paranormal is accepted as part of ordinary life in the Highlands. Indeed, for several days Laine, Brit, the cast and the residents of the 'Hurst had been involved in a long, tedious discussion about whether we should exorcise the Feldmans—now known as Daddy Feldman and Junior—or if we should instead contract with a medium and try to reason with them. Consensus had gradually established that the most merciful thing we could do was to help them out of their entrapment and jump-start them on the path to their eternal reward.

The woman retained for this service was a small, middle-aged woman of both Caribbean and Cherokee descent named Martha. "Although she's not technically an Obeah-woman," Laine told me earlier in the week after interviewing her over the phone, "She knows some of their ways. She practices a sort of Native American–Christian spiritualism with some Gullah overtones thrown in for good measure."

"That's all? No Shinto?"

Laine fixed me with an icy stare as she poured vermouth into her martini shaker. She had several shakers. Today she was using the Waterford one. "I'd be careful about ridiculing the spirit world if I were you."

"Why's that?"

"There's lots in the world we don't understand. Sometimes what you don't know can hurt you quite a lot."

"Laine, do you really believe all this?"

She didn't answer immediately. She snapped the top on the shaker and shook it over her right shoulder with one hand, as was her usual manner. Then she popped the top off and poured her manhattan into one of her Baccarat glasses. For Laine, drinking was as much about the accessories as it was about the buzz.

Finally, after taking a sip, she said, "Donovan, there is much I have seen in my life that makes me believe we are more than just flesh and blood. Beyond all the world's Baltimore Catechisms and Talmuds, there is just too much that tells me we transcend this mortal coil."

"Like what? What have you seen?" I sat on her couch, and raised one leg up on her coffee table, resting it so my flip flop hung loosely off to the side.

"Well, not so much what I've seen, but certainly what I've felt. For example, I've always felt like Maurice is nearby, even though he is not here."

"You don't think that maybe that's just you missing him?"

She shook her head and stared into her drink. "No, it's not. I miss him certainly. I can't tell you how much I would give to hear his voice again. But I've never had the sense he was gone. He always feels near me somehow." She straightened up and fixed me with her imperious stare. "The same with your mother. I speak to her often and feel like she's here. In fact, I personally think she guided you here when you broke up with Olivia."

"Oh come on. I don't get any credit for free will?"

"Of course you do. However it doesn't mean you were beyond your mother's influence."

I thought about that. I had always had the sense my mother was nearby after she died. "Maybe. But there's a fine line between a sense of connection to the departed, and a ghost who can't stand Spence's singing voice."

"Do you have another explanation?"

I did not. And so, that Saturday afternoon found me spreading sea salt, per Martha's instructions, in an unbroken circle around the 'Hurst. It was explained to me that, since Daddy Feldman and Junior had departed the building, the circle of sea salt would form a barrier cutting off their return when they left the theater. All of the building residents had been instructed by Laine to leave it undisturbed. (Including, I presumed, Mister Kersey.) Certainly all of them, except him, were planning on being in attendance at the exorcism.

While I had been spreading the salt, the rest of the living residents of the building had congregated over at the theater, along with Miranda, Lydia, and most of the cast. Poor Spencer had been explicitly excluded. Lydia had explained to him that the exorcism would work better if he were not there to agitate Daddy Feldman.

"This is not so much an exorcism," Martha was explaining to the assembled crowd when I joined them in the theater, "as it is a home-going." She was a tiny woman, with a warm gregarious smile that flashed brightly in the middle of an ageless face that was almost a pure mahogany in tone. "Exorcism deals with demons, and in a true exorcism, one doesn't so much expel the demon as place them under an oath."

Everyone was standing in the lobby. While I had been surrounding the 'Hurst with salt, everyone else was apparently getting a lecture on Paranormal 101. Zach quickly and quietly explained to me that she was telling us what to expect so we wouldn't interrupt the ceremony with questions.

"Now, this would be greatly easier if we knew the names of our spirits since then we could better command their attention. It's important for all of us to understand that usually spirits don't mean harm, in fact they can't really *do* harm. Most often, they simply want you to know they are alive. That sounds to me like what they were doing in Donovan's apartment. They are simply looking for recognition."

Martha was barefoot and seated on the stairs. There were tea lights burning throughout the lobby, but no lights were on. Outside, it was early evening, but dusk was still some time off.

"What we will do tonight is help both these spirits move towards the light, unto joy, love and peace.

"Now I must warn you that you must stay calm. We don't know why these spirits didn't go towards the light yet. Could be they were afraid, or they were looking for something or they had a message to deliver. Here's the thing, they only have the power to frighten and hurt you if you let them. Tonight, if you sense a negative spirit or energy, or if something frightens you, first just ask them to stop. Be calm. Be pleasant. Just ask them to stop. If they're enlightened spirits, that should be enough."

"There's a chance that they may be worried about punishment, so we are going to reassure them that nothing waits for them but forgiveness, and others will be waiting for them to help them forgive themselves."

Martha indicated several small terra-cotta strawberry pots that she had with her, and bundles of dried leaves. "During the ceremony tonight, we will smudge the entire theater. Smudging involves burning dried sage in every room of the theater to help drive out the spirits. You could just burn the dried sage, but that only mollifies them. The real secret is to help them understand that it is time for them to move on. If any of you are asthmatic, you may not want to stick around as the smoke is a little acrid."

I glanced to the side and met Chris's eye. We both smirked.

"So, we are ready to begin. Before I start, are there any questions?" There were none. "Okay, then I will ask you to remain silent until the ceremony is complete."

With that she asked me to open all the windows in the building that could be opened. Zach and I bustled through the upstairs and backstage opening windows. The rest were asked to ensure every door in the building was open. Restrooms, fire doors, offices, even fuse boxes were all opened.

While the building was prepared, Martha began distributing the improvised smudge pots about, but she did not light them. Fifteen minutes later, she summoned all of us to the stage, where we stood in a circle.

Martha glanced at Lydia. "I know you said one was a young boy. Do you have any sense of how old the man is?"

Lydia shook her head and replied quietly, "They are in here watching us. But I have no sense of the elder one's age."

Martha nodded and closed her eyes. She quietly directed us to join hands, which we all did. Then she instructed us, "It is important that you summon up as much love and compassion as you can for everyone present, including these two spirits. They must feel the love and goodwill we all wish for them."

I was not surprised that I could easily summon up a warm feeling of affection for everyone present. What surprised me instead was that I had a sense of it emanating from everyone around me. I was standing at the base of the circle, with my back to the center aisle of the auditorium. Martha stood directly across from me at the top of the circle, and Laine stood to her left. Our eyes met, and I could see a kind of warm benevolence shining out of them. Here, after all, were the people she loved.

"Young boy!" Martha announced. "Man! Both of you, who have been watching us. Come. Join us. Join this circle of love."

She stayed silent for a moment, and a chill involuntarily crept up my back, as I wondered if we would see or feel anything. Nothing happened.

"Come!" Martha instructed them again in a voice that was surprisingly powerful, considering the petite frame that it emanated from. "Come into this circle, for this circle is for you.

"We are here praying for you. You see, boy, man, you've been given a great gift. It is time for you to leave on a wonderful journey. Your physical bodies have died, and your immortal souls have been freed. And so it is time to leave this physical realm and move towards the light."

Even though all the doors and windows were open to the outside, there was an eerie silence around us.

"Boy, man, you have nothing to fear. Only great joy and forgiveness lies ahead of you. There are others waiting for you. They will greet you with love, and forgiveness, and joy and help show you your way."

An intense wave of emotion washed over me, and I felt tears well in my eyes. I looked to my left, and a quarter way around the circle, I saw Chris. There were none of the smirking sarcastic looks he and I had exchanged earlier. Instead, I could see a strong, almost nervous apprehension on his face.

"Look!" Martha practically shouted, and all of us jumped with a start. She wasn't talking to us though. "Look for the light! Can you see the light? It is here! The light is the Love of God. Go towards it, boy. Go towards it, man. It leads to peace and fulfillment. You've waited for this moment for so long. So long. Don't deny yourself the joy and fulfillment of moving on any longer. Follow the light. Follow the love."

Martha's voice was not pleading. Instead, it was a calm and forceful, yet hopeful sounding. Perhaps it was her emphasis on joy, perhaps it was my own emotions - hell, perhaps it was the Feldmans – but wave after wave of emotion flowed over me and I actually felt tears running down my face. I glanced around the circle as Martha continued to exhort them towards the light and could see tears on almost everyone's cheeks except Laine's. Instead, Laine looked proud and dignified, almost triumphant. She was wearing a gauzy, off-white linen pantsuit. Perhaps not the most appropriate look for after Labor Day, but I thought, briefly, that to a spirit she might actually appear to be an angel.

Martha had kept her eyes closed throughout the entire process, but suddenly she opened them brightly, and looked up towards the ceiling. It was as if she actually saw the light herself and was smiling into it. Her expression was so rapturous, I looked up involuntarily to see if I could see what she was looking at.

"Yes!" she called, joyfully now. "The gates are open and you are free! Fly towards it! You take our love and our prayers with you! You are free! You are free!" She continued to stare upward for perhaps a minute or two. It could have been longer, I don't really know. Then, bowing her head to look towards all of us, she recited, "Grant eternal rest to their souls, O Lord, and to all the souls of the faithfully departed who, through the mercy of God, may rest in peace."

"Amen," I said reflexively, joining a chorus from around the stage.

No one spoke. No one dared. Martha broke the circle, knelt down, and lit the bundle of dried sage in the pot at her feet. As the tendrils of smoke began to curl upward from the pot, she announced, "This sage cleanses out all negative energies and spirits. All negative energies and spirits must now leave the room by the doors and windows, and must not return." A few moments later, she repeated the same sentence, and then did so a third time. It didn't take the sage long to burn, and as it smoldered she finally announced, "In the name of God, this room is now cleansed."

We followed her to the basement rehearsal hall, where she repeated the cleansing ritual, then up to the balcony, the offices, the stairs, and finally the lobby. Each time, she repeated the instructions to depart and then pronounced the room clean in God's name as the sage burned out.

Finally, she led all of us back to the stage and recited a small prayer for the dead, and I found myself wishing the Feldmans a silent farewell.

Once Martha finished reciting the prayer, she lit a small white candle in the center of the stage. There was a moment for silence, and then she held her hands wide and said, "My friends, this place is cleansed. The service is over."

"Lydia," Laine asked softly, "are they still here?"

"They are not." She smiled. "They left while we were still holding hands."

"Could you, um, *feel* anything when they went?"

She smiled beatifically and said simply, "A profound sense of relief." For reasons I will never understand, I found myself crying. For joy.

"Donovan," Martha told me, "the burning of sage banishes negative spirits and energies. You can leave it like it is, or you can burn some incense now, like maybe some lavender, and invite in positive spirits and energy."

I considered, looking around. I loved the theater, but I had never sensed a positive energy in it. Quite the opposite actually. While I would hardly describe it as sullen, it seemed simply resigned to my presence in it.

But now I sensed something had changed. There were emotions and tears registering on the faces of everyone gathered there. I could also *feel* a different energy in the theater. Perhaps it was the ceremony, or perhaps it was a change inside of me, but I felt a positive, excited, anticipatory energy in the building I had never sensed before. The rooms even looked brighter to me. "You know what, Martha. I think the positive energy may already be flowing in."

She nodded silent agreement and tapped my shoulder.

"Well, everyone," Laine announced. "Back to my place. I've got hors d'ouevres and cocktails for everyone."

Brit laughed loudly. "You *catered* an exorcism?"

Laine fixed her with that imperious stare. "Think of it as the Feldmans' bon voyage party."

The Climbing Aster

"October is the season of shorts and sweaters," Chris informed me over dinner on the patio at Atkins Park. Well dinner might have been a bit of a stretch. We were dining on martinis and a basket of pretzels. As a matter of record, we were indeed both wearing sweaters and shorts.

"You're trying to distract me," I observed, devouring one of the five olives in my martini. We had earlier decided they qualified as our salad course.

"Of course I'm trying to distract you. You're a bit of work to be around when you are like this."

The words *like this* referred to a slight sullenness that was masking (I hoped) my sense of absolute panic over the impending premiere of *Highlands-A-Go-Go.* I swirled the martini and said, "I'm not *like* anything. I'm just quiet tonight."

"Bullshit. What's going on with you? You've been weird all week."

"I've just got a lot on my mind. We're opening in…" I glanced at my watch, "twenty-three hours and seventeen minutes and there's still a lot left to do."

He rolled his eyes and took a sip of his martini. "I can't distract you if you won't cooperate."

The trip to Atkins Park – the oldest continuously licensed tavern in Atlanta which was located a few blocks south of the theater – had been conceived of by Miranda to get me out of her hair as she drilled the cast through the final dress rehearsals. As the show had come closer and closer to fruition and each scene and each song was executed just as I had envisioned, I became slightly frantic. Well, *slightly* is perhaps an understatement. I became psychotic. It was as if the Feldmans had taken my entire sense of sanity with them when they departed the theater.

I had never been prone to paranoid behavior before, but I had also never taken a chance like this before. As we got closer to the show, I became obsessed with polishing. Every inch of wood or chrome in the theater had about thirty layers of wax on it. I had also become convinced that someone was going to fall off the stage on opening night, so I repeatedly hounded Miranda to move the action of the play back twelve or fourteen feet from the edge.

"Theater doesn't work if the audience can't see the actors," she told me dismissively.

When my staging suggestions were rejected, I began to question whether the accents were appropriate, the lighting was right, the sound cues were enough, and the piano was tuned correctly.

I also began to obsessively rewrite songs, which she also would not talk to me about. I was convinced my meters were horribly, horribly wrong.

In other parts of my life, I had stopped eating almost altogether. I just had no appetite. And I couldn't sit still very long. As a result, everyone was either worried about or irritated with me.

"You're freaked out about the show, aren't you?" Chris inquired as he tossed a pretzel into the air and attempted to catch it in his mouth. He missed, and it bounced off his nose, landing on the black-and-gray argyle sweater he was wearing over a gray tee-shirt. It snagged on the fibers near the top of his sternum. He plucked the pretzel off and popped it into his mouth.

"Apprehensive."

"Freaked out." He selected another pretzel from the bowl.

"Nervous, perhaps."

He tossed the pretzel into the air, and caught it in his mouth. He snapped it between his jaws, fixed me with a friendly stare, and repeated, "Freaked out."

"Yeah. Maybe a little freaked out."

"Why?"

"Whaddaya mean, 'why?' We're putting on a show."

"So? What's the worst that can happen?"

"Oh, I dunno," I replied sarcastically. "The set could fall down. The critics could hate it. It could close the night after it opens and we've lost all the backers' money."

He continued to stare at me, saying nothing, until I couldn't stand it. "What?"

"You're afraid of failure, aren't you?"

I was saved from answering by the unexpected arrival of Harry. He and Jennifer had been dating ever since Lakewood. While I would have hardly described it as a classic romance, there was something about them as a couple that made them oddly compelling. We were sitting at my favorite table at Atkins Park. The patio was actually an enclosed alley with a wrought-iron fence at one end. It was through this fence that Harry's face was suddenly thrust with a jaunty "Ahoy, mateys!"

"Hey!" I replied.

"Salud." Chris greeted.

"I'm coming 'round," Harry informed me, "So we can discuss last-minute changes to your script." He disappeared into the bar, which was the only way to access the patio.

"Well, that'll help your stress," Chris observed as he stared deeply into his glass before finishing his drink.

Harry had never seen the show, or even its script, but he had established quite soon after meeting me that the show did not include pirates. He viewed this as a grave mistake. "Pirates are a critical success element to every blockbuster movie," he announced as he came through the door.

"I'm fine, Harry. How are you?"

"He's on a mission," Chris announced as he helped himself to a sip of my drink.

"I see that."

"Truly, Van. Look how many successful movies involve pirates."

"Many do," I replied. "But I'm not filming a movie. I'm staging a musical."

"So here's your chance to cash in on a market."

"I'm staging a musical set in Atlanta."

"So? We can't have pirates?"

"We're a land-locked city located in the foothills of the north Georgia mountains. How would they get here?"

"They'd sail up the Chattahoochee!"

"The Chattahoochee River is only about three feet deep. Do they carry their ship upriver?"

"Look, suppose you had this character. Let's call him Cap'n Davy Flint…"

Sadly, this kind of inane debate is not uncommon in the Highlands. It continued through two more martinis, until Harry was distracted by a phone call from Jennifer who was at rehearsal. She wanted him to bring her some fried chicken.

Harry went off in search of chicken, and Chris and I walked home. All along North Highland, asters were blooming. "People are wondering whether you are going to continue to be insane up through opening night."

"I'm insane?"

"Why, yes. Yes, you are."

I was anxious to change the topic. "Jennifer's new boyfriend is interesting, don't you think?" I mused.

"Do you really think so?"

"Actually, I think his favorite drink in college must have been a Harvey Bong-Water."

He stopped cold in his tracks, turned towards me and favored me with an openly stunned expression. "Why, Donovan. How positively bitchy of you. I'm impressed."

I resumed walking. "It wasn't bitchy. It was sarcastic. Bitchy is more mean-spirited."

He fell back in pace next to me. "Really? Define the difference."

"Oh…I'm not sure I could define it."

"Examples."

"Harvey Bong-Water delivered by Joan Rivers is bitchy. Delivered by Sidney Poitier? Sarcastic."

"So you are putting yourself into the same category as Sidney Poitier?"

"Why, yes. Yes, I am."

"See? You are insane."

"Can we let this die?"

"Okay. Enough about your insanity." We walked in silence for a moment. "Let's talk about your fear of failure."

"I'm not afraid of failure," I lied.

"You're terrified of failure."

"You have a crush on Agnes Moorhead."

"What gay man doesn't? Seriously. What are you so afraid of?"

"What is with all the analysis and probing questions tonight?" We were almost at the theater.

He ignored me. "Let me tell you a story."

"This isn't another one of your stories about the drag queen, is it?"

He nodded.

Before Jennifer had moved into the building, her apartment had been occupied by a drag queen that Chris had known slightly. I can't remember his male name, but her drag name was Plethora O'Toole. Despite only having known her slightly, she appeared in a number of Chris's stories.

"As a matter of fact, it is. When Plethora was living in the building…" He stopped talking when I started around the corner towards the theater, and grabbed my arm, stopping me. "Where do you think you are going?"

"To the theater."

"No you're not."

"Why not?"

"You've been banned for the evening."

I was suddenly indignant. "I cannot be banned from my own theater."

"Van, it's for your own good. You're making everyone crazy. You can't control every part of this production. Sometimes you've got to let things happen."

"I've got a million things to do," I whined.

"Like what?" he asked impatiently.

"Like… well…" I couldn't summon up anything immediately.

"That's what I thought."

"The programs need to be unpacked."

"That can wait until the morning."

"The lobby has to be vacuumed."

"Can't do that while rehearsal is going on."

"Bar stocked?"

"You plan to leave liquor unattended while actors are loose in the theater?"

I felt my shoulders slump. I was defeated. A few feet away, our friendly street musician began playing Billy Joel's "Pressure."

"So, anyway," Chris continued as we started walking across the street, "When Plethora was living in the apartment downstairs…"

I was saved from the tale of Plethora by the ringing of my cell phone. I was surprised to see Olivia's number glowing on the caller i.d. as I pushed the button. "Hey, Liv. What's up?"

"I'm with a cab driver who apparently has never heard of the Four Seasons Atlanta," she growled impatiently. "If I'm coming from the airport, how would I find it?"

I stopped dead in the middle of the crosswalk. "The Atlanta airport?"

"No, Van. LaGuardia. I feel like dropping six grand on a cab ride. Of course Atlanta."

I started to ask her why she was in Atlanta, but then thought better of it. I didn't want to divert her wrath from the unfortunate driver onto me. "You'd take Eighty-Five north to the Tenth-Fourteenth Street exit."

"Eighty-Five north to the Tenth-Fourteenth Street exit," she repeated to the driver. In the background, I could hear a muttered reply. Chris nudged me, and I resumed walking towards the 'Hurst.

"Turn right on Fourteenth."

"Turn right on Fourteenth."

"The hotel will be two blocks on your right, just before Peachtree."

"Got it. Thanks."

"What are you doing in Atlanta?"

"I'm here for your opening night, of course."

"You're…kidding."

"I wouldn't miss it. I was planning on coming in the morning, but the weather in New York is supposed to be foul tomorrow, so I took the last flight out tonight instead."

I felt an immediate sense of dread well up inside of me. "Great!" I replied manically. "Um, do you want to get together for a drink or something?"

"Not tonight, but thanks for asking. It was a long day and I had a talker sitting next to me on the flight. I'm not great company. I just want to get to the hotel, take a bath, and go to bed."

"I understand. Well, I guess I'll see you tomorrow."

"Bye."

We hung up. I stood on the stoop and stared at Chris, wide-eyed. "My ex-wife is in town."

"So?" Chris asked, taking his keys out as he opened the outer door of the building.

"So she's coming to the show tomorrow night."

As he unlocked the inner door of the vestibule, recognition dawned on his face. "Nothing like going out on a limb with the biggest risk of your life and having the ex in the audience, is there?"

"Oh my God!" I said as I followed him inside. "What if this bombs? What if this is a horrible, horrible bomb and she's sitting in the audience?"

He turned around and looked me in the eye. "Van, get hold of yourself. This show is not going to bomb."

"But what if…"

He held up a finger, and said very sternly, "Stop it. It's not going to bomb." Over his shoulder, I could see Rachel coming up the stairs from the garage.

"You don't understand. This woman is an agent. She has a totally different set of standards than normal people. The slightest flaw and I'll…"

"Would you stop it?"

Rachel walked over and asked, "What's going on?"

"My ex flew in for opening night!"

"That's nice of her." I gather the look on my face suggested I didn't agree. "Isn't it?"

"I could do with a little less pressure," I thought I was speaking in a normal voice, but their stunned expressions told me I was shrieking instead.

"I thought you knew she was coming."

"She *said* she was coming, but that didn't mean anything. Olivia's never kept a commitment to come to anything. It was a pattern throughout our whole marriage. She couldn't make it to dinner on our first anniversary because she had to check a client into rehab. But this? *This* she makes!"

Rachel and Chris exchanged looks. "Vodka," Chris prescribed. He took me by the arm and guided me up to the roof. Rachel came behind, stopping at her apartment only long enough to secure a bottle of Skyy and some shot glasses.

I sat down on the deck, and tried very hard to get my breathing under control. "Maybe it's not that bad..." I tried to convince myself. "It could be worse." A sudden chill ran up my spine as a thought occurred to me of how it could, indeed, be worse, and I looked at Rachel. "Rache, why did you say you thought I knew? I didn't tell you that before."

A sudden guilty look passed over her face as she poured the shots, but she said nothing. She handed one to me.

"Rache?"

"Drink," she instructed, handing another to Chris.

"Rache? How did you know Olivia told me she was going to come to this?"

She turned and looked at me. "Aidan McInnis told me. I just dropped him at his hotel."

I have been told that, just before a tsunami comes ashore, the tide suddenly rolls out to sea very quickly as all the water is pulled into the wave. I had a similar sensation at that moment, as all of my emotions seemed to roll out of me. I felt a deadly calm.

"So," I said quietly, holding my shot glass and staring at her. "My ex-wife, who was always much more successful than me, is here to see my first attempt at doing anything of substance."

"Donovan," Chris said, "drink your drink."

"And, the writer whom she has always benchmarked me against..., no, no, let's be fair. The writer whom *I* have always benchmarked myself against and always come up short against is *also* here."

"Um..."

I thought for a minute how else the situation could have been worse. Nothing came to mind. My father was about the only other person whose standards I had never lived up to, and I knew he wouldn't be at the premiere. The reality slowly sank in that the two people who I would most not want to fail in front of would be in the audience in a scant nineteen hours.

And the tsunami hit.

I suddenly began to breathe very, very fast and I felt a strange hollow sensation in my chest and my left arm. I drank the shot of vodka and was only dimly aware of it burning in my throat. The hollow sensation persisted.

"So, anyway, I was telling you about Plethora O'Toole..." Chris began.

"Oh God." I groaned, and leaned my head forward so that it rested against my knees. I held my shot glass out for Rachel to refill it. She did so, and I drank the next shot, leaning back in the Adirondack chair. She refilled it again, and I closed my eyes while Chris droned on with his Plethora story. I didn't actually hear a word he was saying as I contemplated what my options were.

I briefly considered burning down the theater.

Deciding that I did not know enough to successfully conceal arson, I considered just not showing up for opening night. I knew of several playwrights on Broadway who refused to attend their own opening nights, believing it brought bad luck.

The problem with that was that it would prolong the uncertainty over whether the show had bombed or not. I had no desire to wait longer than necessary to validate I had been humiliated.

I considered arson again.

It wasn't bad enough that I was risking failure, I told myself; it was greatly compounded now by the fact that these two people, whose opinions I cared a great deal about, would be in the audience.

That thought caught me off guard. Did I really care about their opinions? I had never particularly liked Aidan, and was no longer in love with Olivia. Why did I care about their opinions?

I became aware that Chris had either said something or reached a point in his story where he was expecting some reaction from me. Unsure of what he had said, I opened my eyes and gave him a sidelong glance and offered a noncommittal "Hmm." It seemed sufficient and so he resumed talking.

I drank another shot of vodka. Despite my best efforts to the contrary, it was indeed calming me down.

I had to admit to myself that it wasn't their opinions that I cared about. It was my own pride. I knew that if I failed they would say all kinds of supportive things. Who needs that kind of patronization?

Patronization? Was I really afraid of being patronized?

I had a great flash of insight that I was more afraid of the embarrassment associated with failure, than I was with the failure itself.

That insight led to another: knowing that a fear of failure was really a fear of embarrassment did not make me any less afraid at all.

I became vaguely aware that Chris was saying something about embarrassment, and I gathered that his story involved Plethora, an audition, and a puppet made from a sweet potato that bore an uncanny resemblance to Chita Rivera.

Wow, I thought. *I'm terrified of embarrassment.* It occurred to me that the worst thing about embarrassment is that you cannot actually die from it. Perhaps it was the calming effect of the vodka, or perhaps it was the droning description of a sweet potato wearing a black pageboy wig that aspires to join the touring company of *Call Me Mad-Yam*, but it suddenly occurred to me to ask myself what was the worse that could happen.

I'd be embarrassed, sure. We'd be out some money. But no one would die. No one would take the theater from us. At the end of the day Olivia and Aidan would fly back to their respective cities, possibly with a lower opinion of me, but nothing else would have changed.

In the end it was, at worst, a zero-sum game.

"So you see," Chris was saying, "If Plethora *hadn't* taken the chance of taking the potato with her to the audition, and if she hadn't failed, she never would have had the idea for an all-vegetable drag-puppet revue."

"And was it successful?" Rachel asked, enthralled.

Chris nodded enthusiastically. "It was. *Kiss of the Spuder Woman* was legendary around Atlanta for years. It would probably still be running if the leading lady hadn't come down with a case of mealy worms. To this day, drag queens still scour the produce aisle at Kroger for celebrity-lookalike vegetables in hopes of staging a revival."

I looked at Chris and smiled, suddenly very calm. "Thanks. That helps put things in perspective."

He patted my arm supportively. "I knew it would."

I would not say I slept restfully that night, but at least I slept. The next morning, before going down to make breakfast for Laine, I called the Four Seasons and left a message for Olivia that two complimentary tickets for her and Aidan would be waiting at Will Call.

It was a clear, cool Friday morning. I decided to wait a bit before going over to the theater and so instead I opened all the doors and windows in the building hallways, and mopped the aging linoleum on each floor. The combination of my realizations from the night before, and the smell of pine-cleaner and fresh air helped me contain my emotions at nervous, instead of panicky.

Once the hallways were mopped, I took a bottle of oil soap and cleaned all of the mahogany banisters. It was an exciting day, I told myself. Yessir, an exciting day.

Cleaning the banisters did not take nearly as long as I hoped it would, so I grabbed some ammonia and gave the elevator a good, strong wipe-down. The chrome deco accents gleamed.

While I had the ammonia out, I decided to clean all the windows in each of the hallways. And since I had the windows open anyhow to vent the ammonia and oil soap fumes, it was a good time to clean the grout between the tiny hexagonal tiles on the vestibule floor with muriatic acid.

At noon, Zach returned from class. He came trotting through the open vestibule doors, stopped for a moment, and gasped. He stepped back to the front door. "Dear God! Did we have a chemical spill?"

I was atop a ladder polishing the silver base plate for one of the lights on the lobby ceiling. "Don't be dramatic. It's just a couple of cleaners."

"It smells like someone put a hospital in an autoclave. Besides, shouldn't you be at the theater?"

"I suppose it's about time I meander over."

"'About time?' That doesn't sound like you. I would have thought you would have gone over at four this morning."

"Needed the time here."

"But with tonight being opening night…"

I looked down at him and held up my hand for him to stop. "Zach, I don't want to think about it right now. I'm nervous, but I'm okay as long as I'm busy. I'd rather go over there and have a lot of work to do, then wander around for eight hours wondering whether I should have rhymed *placid* with *flaccid* instead of *antacid*."

He nodded, rolled his turtleneck up over his nose and mouth, and beat a hasty retreat downstairs. I glanced at him as he went and noticed Laine was standing in her apartment door.

"You're like your mother," she observed.

"How's that?" I resumed polishing the fixture.

"The harsh smell of cleaners soothed her nerves as well. When we were girls and she'd come south to visit in the summer, I'd always fix her up so we'd go out on double dates. Before our beaus would arrive, I'd have a shot of brandy to calm my nerves. She'd take a couple whiffs of Clorox."

I grinned at the truth of the observation but said nothing.

"You didn't tell me Olivia was in town," she said.

"The way news travels around here, I didn't think I had to. I assumed you were notified as soon as you got out of bed this morning."

"It's kind of her to come."

"Yes, it is."

"Almost makes me wonder if she'll come to my funeral to be supportive of you."

I glanced down at her. "You talking about your funeral for any particular reason?"

She shook her head. "Not at all. I just wouldn't have expected it of her. If she showed up at my funeral, I would assume it was to dance on my grave."

I came down off the ladder. "It's a pity the two of you could never put your claws away long enough to give each other a chance. You are both quite similar in many ways. I think if you had tried, you might have learned to like each other."

"Perhaps," she admitted. "Would have made your divorce that much more tragic. You need to get over to the theater."

"I was just telling Zach that I'd rather…"

"I heard you," she interrupted. "But that's not why I'm telling you to go. The caterer just called and is on his way to set up the tables for the intermission and you need to let him in."

I began to fold the ladder. "Besides," she added, "one more hit of ammonia and I'm going to need detox."

Life in the Highlands comes with a few traditions, cocktails and canapés at the forefront. It frequently reminds me of Greenwich Village or Soho in that it is bohemian, intellectual and counterculture, but at a more genteel pace. It is not at all uncommon to see people planning a protest march while sitting on their front porch sipping chardonnay and snacking on pesto crackers. So, of course, something as momentous as opening night requires more than a cash bar. Since most of those in attendance this evening would be complimentary guests - critics, backers, family and the like - Laine had sprung for an open bar and a table of light hors d'oeuvres.

In old Atlanta circles, one maintains relationships with two or three caterers at all times. While one might have a favorite culinary institution that would supply pans of barbecue and potato salad for a summer backyard get-together, or perhaps frequent a shop that puts together fantastic picnic baskets for evenings in the park, one would never think of using those institutions to, say, cater the wedding of one's daughter. (Even if it was—clutch the pearls and gasp—her fourth wedding.) In those circumstances, one would instead opt for a *name.* So, given the familial hoi polloi who would be in attendance that evening, I was not surprised to see a truck from Laine's first string, Affairs to Remember, pulled up in front of the theater.

I opened the door and admitted four young men and one middle-aged woman to the lobby. Under the direction of the woman, tables, chafing dishes, candles, and a large amount of fabric that would be used in "froofing" began to roll in.

I began my pre-show ministrations. Since the theater had been dark for about a month, I had to remind myself a bit of my routine. Unpack the programs. Stock the cash drawers and lock them in the safe. Take down the ticket orders from the answering machine and call back with confirmations. Clean the bathrooms.

I walked into the projection room to switch on the house lights so I could vacuum the theater when I noticed that someone was sitting in the auditorium on the center aisle about ten rows from the stage. I could just make out their silhouette from the harsh glare of the ghost light. I flipped the light switch and watched as they came up slowly. It was Miranda sitting there.

I descended the stairs, pulled the vacuum out of the closet, and rolled it down the center aisle until I came up next to her. She was awake, but staring unmoving at the stage.

"Everything okay?"

She smiled and looked up at me. "Everything's fine. I just like to spend a little time before opening night sitting in the theater and running through everything in my mind."

"How long have you been here?"

"Since about nine-thirty this morning."

"It's almost three. That's 'a little time'?"

She laughed. "Everything is relative."

"Will I interrupt your reverie if I vacuum?"

"Not at all."

I resumed rolling the vacuum towards the stage where the plug was. "I'm surprised you've been here this long. I would have thought opening nights were old hat for you by now."

"Opening nights in general are. This is the first opening night where my name is on the script."

I nodded. "I'm familiar with the feeling."

"Are you nervous?"

I nodded. "Yes. You?"

"No." She paused for a minute. "Which scares the hell out of me."

I chuckled and switched on the vacuum.

Four hours later, at exactly six forty-five, I stood in my office pulling on my tuxedo jacket. Downstairs, I could hear the gentle murmur as the small team of staff, caterers and volunteers readied the bar, the programs, the buffet. I heard Laine laugh loudly, gaily.

I had been sitting at my desk for most of the last hour, trying to steady my nerves. I desperately wanted a cigarette and had twice started out the door for the gas station across the street to buy a pack, but had stopped myself each time. I had also considered having a drink to steady my nerves, but since I had had nothing to eat that day I decided against it.

I turned out the light and crossed the hall to the balcony. The auditorium was ready. The curtains had been dropped but behind them I knew the stage was set beautifully. I could hear the muffled voice of Klein shout "Flee!"

I heard someone behind me and Rachel was standing there, looking stunning in a copper satin gown and a brown sequined jacket. She smiled, pointed to her watch and said, "Ready? Everyone's waiting for you." I knew what she meant. Down below, my own personal entourage awaited, most of whom who did not know me last year. Despite that, they had rigorously demonstrated their faith in me, and were waiting for me to come down and open the doors. I knew they were also waiting for me to say something profound, whereas I was just hoping I could make it all the way down without vomiting on the landing.

I nodded. I no longer felt nervous, simply empty and numb. Whatever would happen would happen. She held out her hands to me. Taking them, she kissed me gently on the lips and said, "Break a leg."

I smiled wanly, and we descended the stairs. As I turned the landing, the conversation and laughter below died suddenly and all eyes turned expectantly upon me. Then, much to my shock and surprise, they began applauding. The clapping lasted for a few minutes, and I started to descend, but Rachel laid her hand on my shoulder so I stopped on the top step.

When they saw I was going to say something, the clapping died down. My voice quivered a bit in the silence as I said, "Um I… actually, um, both Miranda and I want to thank all of you for your support and hard work. We would not have made it all the way here tonight if we did not have all of you helping us out and for that we are both very grateful."

I continued to talk as I resumed descending the steps. "Miranda told me I should say something bold and *articulate* when I came down to open the doors tonight. Something like "may fortune favor the foolish.' Unfortunately, the only quote I've been able to think of is from Douglas Adams's classic, *The Hitchhiker's Guide to the Galaxy.*

"'Don't panic.'"

There was a round of courtesy laughter, and the crowd parted as I crossed the lobby. Outside the glass doors, I could see the smiling, anticipatory faces of the first audience who would ever see a piece of my writing produced. The mental image of the same faces leaving the theater as an angry, torch-wielding mob flitted through my mind.

I took a deep breath and turned to face my friends. "Unfortunately, I don't have anything profound to say. All I have to say is…" a wave of emotion welled up inside me, but I fought it down. "It's show time, folks."

There was a collective nod and an appreciative murmur, and everyone immediately went to their appropriate stations as I turned my back. I checked my watch, smiled, and unlocked the door.

The first person through the door was Talbot, carrying a velvet bottle bag, the gold foil of a nice bottle of champagne poking out of the top. She handed it to me, kissed me on the cheek and said, "This is to celebrate your first opening night."

"Thanks," I replied.

Immediately on her heels was Bitsy Hollander on the arm of her latest boy toy. "Let's hope it's not your last," she added as she came in.

I silently reminded myself she was one of the first backers, and subdued the desire to loosen the wingnuts in her walker.

There were many in the crowd whom I recognized, many more whom I didn't. I don't believe there were any Laine didn't recognize. Perched primly on her stool by the front door, she had pulled out all the stops that evening. She wore an elegant full-length black skirt topped with a white cashmere sweater. The sweater had a white mink stole collar lining a neckline whose cut plunged to a depth that might have been considered racy for a woman her age were it not for the diamond-and-black-onyx necklace that hung dramatically at her throat. Large square matching earrings were clipped to her ears, and she completed the set with the matching ring on her right hand and the bracelet on her left.

"Nice rocks," I told her as I kissed her on the cheek, catching the scent of Worth on her.

She winked at me. "Well, you know what they say. Dazzle 'em with your rocks when you can no longer wow 'em with your rack."

Any feelings of unease I had about the evening were more than trumped by the discomfort of discussing my aunt's breasts, so I moved past and into the theater. No one was seated yet, and I quickly jumped up on stage and slipped behind the curtain.

The stagehands were moving the last few props into place, so I quickly got out of their way. Various members of the cast were doing their warm-ups backstage, and Miranda was going through the a few last minute technical notes with the sound man. I became uncomfortably aware that I had nothing to do. I climbed the spiral staircase and let myself into the upstairs hallway.

I opened the curtain to the stage right box. I had recently begun reinforcing the boxes although I had no idea what I was going to do with them. I glanced out into the auditorium. People were starting down the aisles to their seats.

I crossed back to the front of the building and descended the main staircase again just in time to see Olivia arrive with Aidan. She looked marvelous (as usual) in a tweed jacket and tan slacks; he looked flaky (as usual) in a black velvet sports coat, a striped turquoise shirt, and bright green jeans. From where I stood on the landing, I could watch the scene unfold as she and my aunt made eye contact.

They both stopped, as if surprised to see the other there. Olivia crossed to Laine, who held her hands out. "Hello, dear."

Olivia took them and they kissed primly on the cheek. "Hello, DeLaine. You look marvelous."

"Thank you, dear. You as well."

Olivia turned and motioned to Aidan. "DeLaine, I'm sure you remember my old friend Aidan McInnis."

Aidan held out his hand and Laine shook it. "I do indeed, from the wedding. How are you, Aidan?"

"Well, Miz Fairchild. Thank you. And you?"

"Couldn't be better."

"DeLaine, your onyx is simply gorgeous," Olivia opined.

Laine touched the necklace gently with spread fingertips. "Oh this? Well thank you. It's ancient. My mother received it as a gift in the twenties. I'm surprised you never saw it."

"Your theater is beautiful," Aidan complimented her.

"Donovan's theater," Laine corrected, smiling coolly. "It's really all his work. He's the one who's made it such a success. We're so fortunate to have him down here."

"I had no idea you even *had* a theater," Olivia observed.

"Oh, you know, you never want to let on to your heirs how wealthy you might be. Never know when they might get impatient and knock you off." She gave a sardonic little chuckle.

It suddenly made perfect sense to me why my aunt was dressed so lavishly. She was going to make sure that my ex saw nothing of reproach anywhere around her.

If Olivia saw that, or even cared, she didn't let on. They exchanged a few more pleasantries and then filed past to find their seats.

Later, once the doors were shut and I was escorting Laine up the stairs to our seats in the balcony, I observed, "You were simply charming to Olivia earlier."

"Of course."

"Any particular reason?"

She cast a sidelong glance at me. "Donovan, no proper southern woman of any caliber would *ever* allow her dislike of another woman to be apparent. Dislike is never an excuse for rudeness."

"Really?"

We turned the landing and started up the second flight as the overture started. "Never."

"So then how come you feel free to tell me what you think of her?"

"That's not rudeness, that's gossip. Telling her to her face that I think she's a cold-hearted bitch is rude. Telling someone else I think she's a cold-hearted bitch is idle chit-chat."

"It's not hypocrisy?"

"Not really. You would never say something negative about someone without also saying something positive. That makes it a balanced opinion."

"Such as?"

"Oh…such as, 'bless her heart, she's such a slut.' Or, 'isn't it tragic that such an attractive young man is dumber than a box of hair?' In Olivia's case, I'm sure I've always emphasized her positive traits."

"Oh?" We entered the balcony.

"I'm certain I've never called her a cold-hearted bitch uniformly." She settled herself onto the couch and retrieved her shaker of manhattans. "I'm certain I would have said something like, 'I wonder if being such a powerful and successful businessperson is what has made her such a cold-hearted bitch?'"

I marveled that I had not discovered this earlier, and deeply regretted that I had not. The script would have been that much funnier if I had.

But there was no more time to consider what could or could not have gone into the script. The lights lowered and the curtain began to rise.

Following the opening number, there were seven lines until the first joke in the script. Seventy-six words. Three hundred and forty-two letters, five commas, six periods, and a question mark. I listened nervously as the chorus wound their way through the opening number, awaiting the entrance of ol' Mercer and the gang. They had to deliver those first seven lines. The opening line was delivered by Jonetta Morehouse-Spelman. The next was delivered by Diego Kobiashi-Emory. Then Mercer Oglethorpe. The next was a question asked by Diego, a mildly snide reply by Jonetta. Diego delivers a rejoinder and then Mercer brings it home.

I know it sounds ridiculous, but in my mind everything rode on those first seven lines. I had somehow convinced myself that they set the whole tone of the show and if the first joke fell flat, the whole thing would flop.

The opening number finished and the chorus slowly wandered away singing the last notes. Laine reached over and squeezed my left forearm silently for good luck. Jonetta delivered her first line.

The actress playing Jonetta had the kind of delivery that only a large black woman can have. She could read her grocery list and make it hysterical. Jonetta lived up to the moment. Her line was crisp, well enunciated, and flowed over the audience like a warm, welcoming breeze.

Spencer delivered his line next as Diego. I had a momentary sense of dread that the Feldmans had not actually departed this world and would now vent their full wrath on the poor guy, but the line came off fine.

Jennifer delivered Mercer's line next. Miranda had worked with her for a week on the wealthy clenched-teeth accent of old Atlanta money. It was pure.

"I don't know why everyone says that character is based on me," Laine whispered to me.

Diego asked his question. Jonetta's mildly snide reply came off a little too quick and snarky, but much to my surprise, there were a couple of chuckles in the audience. Diego delivered his rejoinder.

There was a beat, and Mercer turned slowly and rolled her eyes dramatically for the audience. There were a few more chuckles. She drew herself up to her full height and gently brushed something imaginary from her jacket.

"Why, my dear," she said in an exaggerated drawl. "That's because she's so dumb, she'd buy a vibrator and chip a front tooth with it."

There was a long, expectant silence from the audience which lasted, oh, I don't know, maybe eleven million years.

Oh God, I thought, *it's bombing. We're five seconds into the show and it's bombing.*

The expectant pause continued. I felt a sudden tightening in my chest and became light-headed. *I'm having a heart attack. Oh God. We're bombing and I'm going to have a heart attack simultaneously with my ex-wife in the audience.*

At that moment, Mercer added a line that Miranda, unbeknownst to me, had written in the previous night and which the audience was clearly expecting. "Bless her heart."

They erupted in laughter. Laine turned to me and smiled broadly. "See what I mean?"

"I do."

"You're a hit."

"Shhh. Don't jinx it. That's one line. We've got two hours to go."

We were, simply said, a hit.

Miranda had the actors and the crew perfectly timed. Each joke built upon the next beautifully. Klein, with his years of improv training, worked the audience majestically, frequently ad-libbing to keep the laughter going. The first act flew by in a flurry of light cues, set changes, and songs.

During intermission, I ducked down the side hallway to the stage and saw Miranda. We exchanged nervous smiles, but were afraid to say anything. All she said was, "I need you to be sure you are backstage at the curtain." I nodded absently.

I was terrified to go down to the lobby for fear of breaking the spell, so I hung out in the balcony. Chris came up periodically to let me know what the audience was saying. He told me they were wild about the show, but his observations were peppered with so much sarcasm about the audience members, I couldn't take them seriously.

After an intermission that seemed like, oh, I don't know, another eleven million years, the audience began to wander back into the theater. I later learned that the length of the intermission was my own fault because I had forgot to flash the lights. Chris had finally done it.

The start of the second act felt a little low-energy to me, and I had a slap of reality when one of my favorite jokes had fallen flat. Everyone had tried to convince me to take it out, but I thought it was witty and urbane. Instead, it was simply too hip for the crowd. I silently admitted to myself that Miranda had been right when she told me, "George Bernard Shaw would agree with you that it was funny. The rest of the world, not so much."

That dose of reality having been delivered, I watched the second act with a much more critical eye. One of the set changes was a little slow, and someone was a little flat when the chorus sang "The Proper Pronunciation of Ponce." I was alone in noticing these issues. The audience was having a great time.

I would have forgotten Miranda's request if Laine hadn't nudged me at the start of the finale and said, "Aren't you supposed to be backstage?"

"Oh yeah."

I got up to go, but she pulled me down and gave me an affectionate peck on the cheek.

"I'm proud of you."

Chris, who was sitting on the other side of her, added, "Looks like you've got a hit on your hands."

"Shhh. Don't jinx it. The reviews aren't in yet."

"Donovan Sky Ford!" Laine scolded quietly. "Exactly when will you acknowledge this is a success?"

Chris leaned forward with a bemused look on his face. "*Sky?*"

I started to answer, but just smiled and shrugged. Then I made my way back stage. I arrived just as curtain came down. The applause was thunderous, and the cast was nothing but smiles as they quickly ran around to the wings for the curtain call. The curtain rose, and from the right wing I could see the audience rising to their feet.

One by one the cast returned to the stage to take a bow, ending with Klein and then Jennifer. Then, the cast lined up and Klein and Jennifer pointed to our piano player and the spot shone on him brightly.

Then, much to my surprise, the whole cast pointed to their right, and Miranda seized my hand and dragged me onstage. The spot centered on the two of us, and I stood there, dumbfounded. I realized Miranda was bowing so I did the same thing. Then, everyone joined hands and we bowed again. The curtain came down. Then it went up again, and everyone bowed. Then it came down again, and Miranda nodded. One curtain call was good. Three would have been extreme.

"What the hell was that about?" I asked Miranda as I hugged her.

"What?"

"Getting me on stage."

"You're the author. The author gets every bit as much credit as the cast."

The cast quickly ran up the stairs and down the side hallway, so they could greet the audience in the lobby. I high-fived Klein as he went by, and then followed them down the hall. When I reached the balcony, I checked, but Chris had already escorted Laine downstairs. I took a deep breath and followed everyone down.

Chris and Laine stood on the bottom step, watching the mulling as the crowd congratulated the actors. Of course, almost no one knew me, so I could join them on the steps and seem relatively unimportant. Chris turned as I descended the lower flight and asked again, "Sky?"

I nodded. My middle name had been both a source of pride and embarrassment most of my life. At best, people assumed I was just another child of the sixties, and that my sister had some equally bizarre middle name, like Mistletoe. I seldom used it.

"As in Sky Masterson," I told him.

"Truthfully?"

I nodded again. "My mother loved *Guys and Dolls*."

He rolled his eyes. "You were *so* meant to be gay."

Liv and Aidan came out of the theater. I could tell, in an instant, she had not only been laughing, she had been laughing harder than I had ever seen. Her mascara was gone, and her face was flushed. She was smiling. No, smiling was the wrong word. She was beaming.

She stopped as she came out of the doors, looked around and saw me. She made straight for the stairs, Aidan in tow.

"Why the hell didn't you write like that when you were in New York?" she demanded as soon as she was in earshot. The reproach aside, she still hugged me.

"So it was okay?"

"Okay? My God, it was brilliant."

I rolled my eyes. "C'mon. Don't patronize me."

Aidan laid a hand on my forearm. "Dude, she's not. It was incredible theater. Your humor is almost visceral."

"Really Van," she added. "I came down here expecting quaint community theater. You know, Wee Playhouse of Hoboken–type shit. But this was professional caliber. Really amazing."

The *Wee Playhouse of Hoboken* was code language we had always used to be dismissive of anything that was pedestrian or amateurish. Once they had walked beyond, I turned to Laine, smiled, and said, "*Now* I will admit it's a success."

Redbud

A week before Thanksgiving, the redbud that clung to the side wall of the theater announced itself with great flourishes of crimson balls, and I began to think about when and whether I was going to return to New York. It had always been at the back of my mind, but...

Oh, who am I kidding? I had been talking about going back to New York since I had been in Atlanta, but it was always a nebulous, sometime-in-the-future concept. Now, however, Laine was mostly recovered. And, as the suggestion of autumn came to Atlanta, I found myself nostalgic for Manhattan.

Autumn comes late to Atlanta and lasts for weeks and weeks longer than it does in the north. It didn't occur to me during September, when Olivia and I would have ordinarily driven through New Hampshire to look at the leaves. Nor October, when the sweaters came out in New York, and evening walks in the park gave way to late night dinners at Feinstein's at the Regency watching, say, Kitty Carlisle Hart. (God rest her soul.) But now, as the millions of trees that line Atlanta's streets exploded into a myriad of reds and yellows and golds, I found myself longing to walk Union Square Park and skate at Rockefeller Center. (Not that I ever did those things when I actually *lived* there.)

It was a beautiful Sunday afternoon, clear and in the mid-seventies, and Rachel, Zach, Jennifer, Chris, and I were camped out on the roof-top deck playing UNO. We had dragged my stereo out onto the deck, and Zach was sharing everything on his brand new iPod, a recent birthday gift from Aunt Laine.

"This next song has been life changing for me," Zach gushed as it came up in the playlist.

"Uh huh," the rest of us said absently as we arranged the card's in our hands.

"It's called "Ennui" by Mimsy and the Marauders."

Chris, the dealer, flipped over the top card on the stack. "Blue seven. Do you have any idea what the word ennui even means?"

"Yes, I know what ennui means," he replied indignantly as he slapped down a blue skip-card on top of the blue seven, preventing Rachel from playing.

"Aw!" said Rachel.

The song, as best I could tell, dealt with a woman who was dating the perfect guy but couldn't cope with the fact that he wore a mullet.

"This song changed your life?" I asked, playing a reverse card. "Rache, back to you."

"It did. Don't you think it's life-changing?"

"I think it's channel-changing," Rachel replied, playing a yellow skip. "Your play, Chris. Three years from now it's going to be the theme song for Folger's."

"Mimsy would *never* sell out," Zach exclaimed indignantly. The rest of us scoffed loudly.

"Is there anything more tragic than your first sellout?" Jennifer asked as she threw a card. "Mine was when the Talking Heads' 'Wild Wild Life' was used for a car commercial."

I played a card. "Mine was Devo's 'Workin' in a Coal Mine' being used for insurance."

Rachel played a card. "Eartha Kitt. 'Where's My Man' to sell cell phones."

"'Downtown,'" Chris said. "Visa."

"You guys are a real downer," Zach announced sullenly.

The song ended, and over the parapet of the building I heard the saxophone player down in the street start a song. I only heard the few first bars, and recognized them but didn't identify the song immediately. I made eye contact with Rachel, who cleared up the mystery and said "Theme song of *The Munsters.*"

"Huh?" Jennifer said absently. "Whose turn is it?"

"Yours," four of us replied.

"Oh." She played a card. "What about the Munsters?"

"The sax player in the street is playing their theme song."

"You mean 'they're creepy and they're kooky'?'"

"Addams Family," Rachel replied.

Before we could really focus on the music from the street, the next song on the iPod started. Per Zach, it was called "Burdock Root at the Golden Lamb."

"Have you guys ever talked to sax-guy?" he asked.

"No," Rachel replied. "Have you?"

"I have. He's very interesting."

"I've always assumed he was homeless," I replied absently, playing a draw-four on Rachel. "Yellow."

"Doesn't preclude him from being interesting," Rachel replied sullenly as she drew cards.

"You ought to charge him royalties," Chris said, playing a yellow two.

"Huh?" I asked.

"He's added three songs from the show to his repertoire," he replied. "He plays them when the show lets out. I guess he must make about fifty, seventy-five dollars from the patrons coming out and going to the bars."

"I wonder how he learned them..." I mused.

"We're a hit," Chris replied. "That means people will put effort into exploiting us."

Chris's sarcasm aside, we were, indeed, a hit. I had planned to run the show for two weeks, and then start looking for the next one, but we were already sold-out for the entire month, and had bookings through December 15. I had tentatively extended the run until the week of Christmas, although I felt we were taking a chance that people would tire of the show. I didn't mention that, though. Everyone was bored with my cynicism.

We were also a hit with the local critics. Although several of them felt I had written the show from a jaded northern perspective, the general assessment had been that anyone who had lived in Atlanta for at least two years would find someone they knew parodied in the show. There had been at least two features in different papers on the cultural revolution we were perpetrating. I had, in a moment of weakness, sent them to Olivia.

Of course, not everyone loved us. Archer Bellamy, for instance. We were serving beer and wine under a succession of special event licenses that Talbot had helped me secure. I had a liquor license application on file with the city, but Archer had raised a good deal of protest about it. Nothing slows southern bureaucracy like religious controversy.

However, I had not been rejected outright because Talbot had managed to get the local restaurants and bars sufficiently worked up about his plans to turn the Highlands dry. They, in turn, had gone to the local newspapers, especially the community free papers where they advertised heavily, and had exerted a lot of pressure on them to "expose the conspiracy." They succeeded and our little theater found itself to be a *cause célèbre* for the community. One of the papers in particular seemed to see enough meat in the controversy that they had published an in-depth interview with Bellamy just that week. It was not particularly flattering.

I didn't have too much time to think about the controversy though. I had rewritten the show script once to eliminate my favorite-but-failed joke, and to also incorporate a minor reference to a local news anchor who frequently changed her hairstyle. I was also working on a new song for the second act. Its working title was "The Chicos-Wearing, Hybrid-Driving Harpy of Crestridge Avenue."

And, we had Thanksgiving to worry about.

Laine typically hosted Thanksgiving for the entire building every year. All of the tenants came, apart from Mister Kersey. It was a giant potluck affair; she had always taken responsibility for furnishing the turkey. However, this year she had decided that I should be in charge of providing poultry. I was a little sour on the topic because it wasn't like I didn't have enough other things going on. The conversation on the roof turned to it.

"What's everyone bringing?" Jennifer asked.

"Same thing I bring every year," Rachel replied evenly. "Potatoes au gratin. You?"

"I was thinking about brandied fruit, especially since I don't have to perform that night," Jennifer offered.

There was no show scheduled for Thanksgiving evening. The theater was typically dark Monday through Wednesday, and then we did shows on Thursday, Friday, Saturday, and Sunday. I didn't think that l-tryptophan and comedy would work together, but I had been surprised by the number of calls from people trying to get tickets for that evening.

A couple of people were pressuring me to add a Saturday matinee, but I didn't think the cast was up to it. For their part, the cast was completely fine with their current schedule, especially since I was now able to pay them. However, almost all of them were working real jobs during the day, and they were getting no time off. I was sure the time would come when they would want their weekends back.

"Chris? What are you bringing?"

"Paella."

"Paella?" Zach asked incredulously. "To Thanksgiving?"

"Hey, you observe your family's traditions. I'll observe mine."

"What was that?" Rachel asked, cocking her head to one side to listen.

"I told you," Zach replied. "It's called 'Burdock root…' "

Rachel cut him off as she stood up. "No, out in the street. I swore I heard something." She paused the iPod and we could hear it. Someone was speaking from a loudspeaker. We couldn't understand exactly what was being said, so all of us got up and walked into my apartment. I opened the French doors and looked down into the street below.

A white pickup truck was parked in front of the theater and a man in a clerical collar was standing in the bed with a microphone and a loudspeaker. He was carrying on about something. A jogger ran by, and the poor guy found himself singled out.

"All of you runners who run by this corner each day trying to save your bodies are misguided. You need to be running towards the church to try to save your soul. North Highland Avenue is a highway straight to hell and there is only one exit from it."

"Freedom Parkway?" Chris asked, bemused.

"The sanctity that comes from the church," the preacher replied indignantly. So indignantly, I almost thought he had heard Chris.

"No that's wrong," Chris replied. "The church exit from the North Highland highway-to-hell has a very poorly timed stoplight. I'm sure Freedom Parkway is easier."

I watched the scene below me incredulously. The preacher was denouncing the good folk of Virginia Highland for their evil ways. His homily damned them for dining out on Sunday, consuming alcohol on a Sunday, jogging on a Sunday, shopping on a Sunday, and just about everything else that didn't involve sitting in a church.

"Suppose he's going to advocate burquas next?" Rachel wondered aloud.

Then the topic turned to theater. He apparently had a special vehemence reserved for theater in general, and Theater DeLaine in particular.

"This alleged *jewel box* of a theater is a den of iniquity, a nest of vipers peddling filth and smut as art that will lead you and your children astray from the way of the Lord."

"*Oh, we've got trouble my friends...*" Chris sang.

"I don't believe this is happening," I replied. "This is the twenty-first century. Who condemns restaurants and theaters in this day and age?"

"It's the twenty-first century in the Highlands, not everywhere in Georgia. And as to who does this, you should already know the answer." Rachel pointed past the truck at the theater, where Archer Bellamy leaned with his back against it, smiling smugly.

I descended the stairs two at a time, and burst out the front door. DeLaine was standing on her porch, stirring her cocktail with such absent ferocity that I expected the swizzle stick to snap the bowl from the stem. My intent had been to run across the street and tell Bellamy to get his ass off my property before I kicked it off. However DeLaine's eyes met mine as soon as I opened the door. Something in her steel-eyed gaze stopped me instantly. She help up her swizzle stick in warning and added "Don't."

I crossed to her porch rail, and she sat on it. "Shouldn't we do something?" I asked.

"I have. I've called the police."

"I was thinking something more like busting Bellamy's nose."

She rolled her eyes and took a sip of the cocktail before resuming her violent stirring. "First of all, these things are simply *not done* in Atlanta, and in the Highlands in particular. Meeting bad behavior with bad behavior is not only tacky. It's bad business. Especially in this case."

"Why this case?"

"The fanatic card is always powerful in the Bible Belt. If a church victimizes you, as is happening here, and you do nothing but rise above, society will do nothing in the short term and eventually do the right thing in the long term. However, if you fight back against the church, you force the powers that be to take sides, and they very seldom side against the church. The Georgia Statehouse is filled with men and women elected for their ability to pander to the ignorant. The ignorant take preachers seriously and therefore so must we."

While we spoke, a police cruiser pulled up and Raymond Franklin got out. He stood next to the cruiser for a minute, made a long appraisal of the situation, and then went over to talk to Bellamy and the preacher. He fell silent for a minute and the sax player struck up a spontaneous version of the Beer Barrel Polka, which garnered a few laughs from those on the streets and restaurant patios that were watching the street theater.

Raymond talked to the men for a long time. Eventually, the minister started talking again, but the volume was much lower now and couldn't be heard across the street. The police officer left and crossed the street to us.

"Evening Miz Fairchild, Van."

"Good evening, Raymond, DeLaine replied. "Would you care for something to drink?"

He smiled and shook his head no. "Sorry about the disturbance. He's been told to turn the amp down."

"Can't we make him go away?" I asked.

"'Fraid not. He's parked in a public parking space and for all practical purposes he has a right to be here. He's no different than the guy playing the sax on the corner."

"Really?"

"Yep. Think of it as political speech. Annoying, offensive, but perfectly legal."

Much to my chagrin, a news van pulled up and parked in front of the `Hurst.

There were three news vans outside the theater by the time the actors started to arrive that evening. At Laine's insistence, I had told all the reporters "no comment" when they had intercepted me and then called all the actors and asked them to do the same thing when they arrived.

From my office upstairs, I could hear the preacher "shaming" Rachel when she opened the box office, and other damning statements made as the cast began to arrive. Laine sailed across the street like a barkentine putting out to sea. She too, did not favor the reporters with a comment, but even the preacher wasn't man enough to criticize the octogenarian first lady of Virginia Highland.

"Isn't this wonderful?" Miranda clapped as I came down the stairs to the lobby.

"I'm not sure I would describe it as wonderful," I replied sourly. "More like damned inconvenient."

"Van!" She scolded as Laine let herself in through the front door, "it's publicity! Controversy is good for sales."

"You don't think a fanatic denouncing the patrons might put them off a bit from attending?"

"Far from it. It'll make people want to come. The people who would be scared off by this moron don't come into the city to begin with. The city itself is a hotbed of liberal values. They'll *want* to come just to tweak this guy's nose."

"I wonder who he is?" Clare asked.

"I've got Bitsy working on it," Laine replied. While Laine's command of the Atlanta gossip network was masterful, Bitsy could plug into it like she had a USB port in the back of her skull. She would make short work of it.

Much to my surprise, Miranda was right. Not only did all of our reservations show, we had several walk-up requests for tickets.

During intermission, Laine called Bitsy on her cell phone to download the reconnaissance. As the second act started, we adjourned to my office.

"Well," Laine began, "first of all Bitsy said the preacher himself sounds terribly shrill on television. She said his voice records like someone dragging a cat across a chalkboard.

"Apparently he's some itinerant preacher and not actually affiliated with the Friendship Church of Jesus' Head or whatever it's called. Bitsy's hairdresser's husband's niece by his first marriage works at the church and said he's not part of the congregation. Apparently he's someone who Archer Bellamy knows and recruited especially for this."

"This is a hell of a lot of work to put into making a statement," I mused.

She nodded. "Bitsy also said that they showed video of me arriving and this pashmina looks absolutely fabulous on television."

"Bless your heart," I added.

Unfortunately, the preacher was back the next night and the next, as were the news vans. For the next two weeks, it became a form of street theater for the citizens and denizens of the Highlands. The crowds for the show began to gather earlier and earlier each evening for the preacher's pre-performance. We settled into a pattern.

Bellamy and the preacher (whose name we learned was Reverend Reeder) would show up every evening at six, as soon as the parking meters were no longer in effect. (Bellamy learned this lesson the night he showed up at five forty-five and failed to feed the meter. Raymond Franklin ticketed him.) It took about ten minutes to set up the portable generator that powered the amps, and then Reeder would start his nightly harangue.

The sermon always followed a similar pattern. It started with a general condemnation of Highlands and its residents for tolerating the decadent lifestyle in their midst. This usually lasted for about twenty minutes. Then, he would segue into whatever elaborate metaphor for impending damnation he had prepared for that evening. The metaphor took three varieties. He frequently used the transportation metaphor; e.g., "this is a highway to hell," or "you are on a steamship to hell," or even "flying the friendly skies straight to hell."

Other times, he would change it up with the biblically damned who hadn't taken the warnings of the prophets seriously. These were usually the Lot's wife variety of admonitions, and I think the crowd typically found them a little stale or unoriginal.

The third variety of sermons was much more cerebral: the attempt to tie a sequence of events to an impending apocalypse, in which Virginia Highland played a key role.

Now these were always highly entertaining and drew heavily on current events. The connections between the theater and the apocalypse were sometimes convoluted and hard to follow, but the crowd seemed to enjoy trying to decipher them. It was like biblical sudoku.

Once the metaphor was finished, he would move into the impassioned plea, usually just about the time we were opening the doors. This would last until about ten minutes into the first act, and would involve tears, pleading, and a lot of heavy drama. "It's like something from Aeschylus," Miranda observed one evening.

Following the impassioned plea, he would take a break, but would start back up during the curtain calls with a lengthy karmic explanation for the crowd concerning how their attendance at the show would led to all sorts of heartache in their personal life. I felt sorry for the sax player. The drama must have certainly cut into his revenue stream.

Nonetheless, I found inspiration in him.

The incorporation of "The Chicos-Wearing, Hybrid-Driving, Harpy of Crestridge Avenue" in the show had been quite successful. There was also a brief skirmish playing out in the media right then between the governor of Georgia and the school superintendent at that time. So, I had also included a small gag about them being in a fist fight behind the house in the script. It had done well also. I saw some opportunity to leverage current events to keep the show crisp and up-to-date. So, I began to consider what I might do to leverage my own media presence.

At the end of the first act, there was a line in which Mercer explains to Buzz "In the South we don't put our crazy relatives away in some institution. We put 'em in the front parlor where you can enjoy them." It was a mildly successful laugh. On the Saturday before Thanksgiving, I caught Jennifer as soon as she arrived at the show and gave her the new line. "We hand 'em a Bible and put them on the street corner for everyone to enjoy them." She delivered it perfectly and it brought down the house.

I had not told Miranda about the script change and she quickly sought me out after the show to let me know she approved. "You know," she observed as we sat alone in the theater after everyone had left, "If you are going to keep making updates to the script to keep it current, we may never be able to close this thing."

I shrugged. "We may not anyhow." The press coverage had driven so many more bookings that I had extended the show until New Year's Eve. "Why are you smirking?"

"Here's what I'm thinking. Let's keep making changes, but not just an occasional line in the script. Let's *really* make changes. You know, add a song or a number every couple of weeks that's based on what's currently going on, so that people want to come back to the show just to see how it's evolving."

"That's a lot of work," I complained half-heartedly.

"Not really. We still keep the basic storyline and script, but we just swap out songs as they become dated. It's already sort of a musical revue to begin with. Let's build on it."

I told her I needed to mull it over, but by three a.m. the following morning, I not only knew she was right, I had just about completed a new song for the end of the first act. We would take out the current number, "Well, Butter My Butt and Call Me a Biscuit," and replace it with a plaintive ballad sung by a new, yet-to-be-found member of the cast. It was called "The North Highland Highway to Hell."

The Wednesday before Thanksgiving, it poured. Usually massive thunderstorms pop up in mid- to late summer, but November is pretty mild, so this one was a bit of a surprise. There was only one news van parked outside. The story was beginning to wane, but one channel still happened to come by every night and do some live broadcasts from the spot in the hopes that something newsworthy might break.

It had been cloudy all day, but the skies really opened up just as the curtain rose. I was in my office and I noticed that, despite the sudden downpour, Reverend Reeder was still down there, standing in the rain preaching away. The amp had been covered to prevent it from shorting out, and so Reeder was reduced to shouting his message of damnation. Whether I agreed with the man or not, I felt bad for him standing out in a cold November rain.

I'm not really sure what prompted me to do it, but there were a couple of umbrellas in the lost-and-found box down in the box office. I went downstairs, pulled two out, opened one and stepped outside.

I crossed the sidewalk and shouted up to my personal antagonist, "Reverend Reeder?"

He stopped preaching and looked at me. "Yeah?"

I held the umbrella out to him. "Here. If you are going to stand out here, take this. It won't keep you warm but it will at least keep you dry."

He looked at me suspiciously. He was a harsh-looking man; tight unsmiling lips, round dark eyes, and short white hair that I suspected was prematurely gray. Ordinarily he wore steel-rimmed glasses, but I imagine he had taken them off because of the rain. Tentatively, he took the umbrella from me. "Thanks."

"No problem," I replied and returned to the lobby.

Unbeknownst to me, the entire exchange had been caught on camera by the news crew. Within moments of my return to the lobby, a reporter was inside with me. Her name was Cheryl Higgins, and I knew her only from seeing her on television and a week and a half of "no comment"s. She called to me from the door "Mister Ford?"

Her voice was a bit loud, and I turned and held a finger up to my lips. She smiled, embarrassed, and shrugged. I smiled back and walked over to her. "Can I help you?"

"We just saw you give the reverend an umbrella."

I'm sure I had a blank expression on my face. "Yeah?"

"Well, why?"

I still didn't understand her question. "Um…because it's raining out?"

She laughed and wiped the rain off her face. "Well, yeah, okay. But why help him? This guy is trying to put you out of business."

I understood. "Hey, he's got a right to his opinion. He's got a right to protest. I can't fight that. I had a spare umbrella, he was getting wet. Consider it an act of charity." I paused, and then added, ironically, "That's the *real* basis of Christianity, isn't it?"

She grinned and said, "I don't suppose we can get you to say that on camera."

I shook my head no, but then added, "No, but you can quote me on it."

She took me at my word, and at eleven footage of me giving the umbrella to the guy was broadcast on the news with Cheryl quoting me as saying that was the real source of Christianity. I didn't see it because I was still working, but the next morning, a still shot of me handing the umbrella to Reeder and the quote "Charity's the real basis of Christianity, isn't it?" appeared on the front page of the Metro section in the local paper.

"Nicely done!" Laine congratulated me as I came into her apartment to start prepping the turkey. She showed me the paper, and I read over the single paragraph article. "That's the way to damn the bastards with kindness. He ought to be embarrassed as hell now to show his face at the theater."

I shrugged. "It wasn't a political statement. The poor guy was getting drenched."

Regardless of whether it was a political statement or not, it was a hotly discussed topic of conversation all day. No one apartment was big enough to seat everyone, so we set up a couple of big round tables in the lobby. Laine's apartment would serve as the buffet, and we would all eat together in the hall.

As we went through the motions of getting things set up, the opinions and concerns were shared. Rachel thought I was kind, Chris thought I was an idiot and that if I left him out there he would have gone away. Jennifer opined that he would be too embarrassed to return. Mac felt that some people might think that the Reverend actually worked for me and would see this whole thing as a ruse to garner publicity for the show. Harry suggested that the whole thing might never have happened if we had included a pirate in the show.

Regardless, Reeder was back that evening even though the theater was dark. We could see him but, mercifully, not hear him through the big double glass doors of the vestibule. I considered taking him a turkey wing but thought better of it.

The next day, quick discussion with Miranda led to the inclusion of a new character in the show: Uncle Preacher. He would come in and sing the new song at the end of the first act. It didn't work perfectly, but it worked well enough. She knew an actor who was available and cast him, with a tentative start date the following week. The cast took the script changes in good humor and rolled on with it. I briefly considered if it was pushing the envelope too far and then thought, *eh, what the hell.*

That was a mistake.

The Camellia

We premiered the character of Uncle Preacher singing his ballad "The North Highland Highway to Hell" to a very receptive audience on the first Friday in December. He was played by Lamar Fox, an older character actor, who fortunately bore almost no physical resemblance to Reverend Reeder. He did, however, possess such a thorough mastery of the mannerisms and speech patterns of a Southern Baptist fire-and-brimstone preacher, that the audience immediately got the joke. Moreover, and much to my pleasant surprise, Lamar was quite a master of improv as well. He took to sitting in my office with the window open, making notes on what Reeder was hurling at the crowd, and then immediately incorporated some of it into his bit on stage.

I assumed that this would be a small gag of no consequence.

I was wrong.

There were three things I had not counted on. First, this was an unusually slow news cycle, and somehow the story of a protesting preacher being "taught the meaning of charity by the small-time theater owner" made it to the national news. Much later I would learn that the network picked up the story after putting out a call to all local affiliates for stories focusing on random acts of kindness to begin the holidays. Cheryl Higgins's station had submitted the story, along with several others, and it was picked up for a spot on the morning national news.

When I heard they were going to run the piece, I again chose to make no comment. Cheryl Higgins got her first opportunity for exposure at the national level and so put a lot of work into the story. The resulting piece was pretty balanced, and when they interviewed Reeder, he came off like a typical fundy, book-burning nutcase. Bellamy also managed to get himself on the screen.

For the local coverage, he had stayed pretty much in the background. The reason, per Bitsy Hollander's network of informants, was that the church he worked for viewed this as a personal crusade, and did not want their name or their employees publicly associated with it. There were, after all, a large number of congregation members who lived in the Highlands and were perfectly happy to frequent the local establishments. They all politely chose to ignore each other's liquor consumption. Being a smart business, the FCOTLIC recognized the collection plate revenue that was at risk by taking sides in this battle. So, when Bellamy was interviewed, he appeared only with the caption "A. Bellamy: *Concerned Neighbor.*" Another idiot.

While I shrugged off the story, the community didn't. I had to replace the reservations line answering machine with a service because of the need for greater storage capacity. We sold out every performance through the end of December in the four days that followed the network coverage. After consulting with the cast, all remarkably good sports, we extended the show for another two weeks.

The second thing I had not counted on was to think that adding Uncle Preacher would be so transparent to the audience. What I had not realized was that we had begun to build a small cult following of audience members. There were enough people who had been sufficiently enamored with their first experience at the show, that they had come back a second or third time to bring friends. Word quickly spread that the script had been updated and *how.* It was only a matter of time until the story found its way to the media.

The third mistake I made was to discount Archer Bellamy just because he was an idiot. I would come to learn that stupid-but-shrewd is a menacing combination, but more about that later.

Putting up Christmas decorations in shorts was an odd experience for me. The nights had finally started to turn chilly, and each morning when I left to go for my run, there was a light coating of frost on the grass. But, by the time noon arrived and the sun was higher in the sky, the weather was usually in the high sixties and clear. So, on this particular Saturday morning, as I hung from the ladder stringing Christmas lights and garlands across the balconies, I didn't feel particularly Christmassy.

I should mention that I have always loved the holidays. It is the one time of the year when even New Yorkers suspended their belief in the banal and would allow themselves to be cheery. My personal season of good cheer had always begun on Thanksgiving at the parade. It was the one day of the year where I could pretty much count on Olivia not having a client-related crisis. So, we would get up early each year and go to the parade. We'd buy coffee and bagels at the shop the across the street, and hike over to her office. There was a conference room in her building that had a great view of 57th Street, and our favorite part was watching the balloons float by the conference room windows. Afterwards, we would go shopping, and then cook dinner together. That night, we'd do Christmas cards and watch *How the Grinch Stole Christmas*, my favorite Christmas special. It put me into the holiday spirit for the rest of the season.

So, given all the past history, I had been mildly surprised that I hadn't felt more excited about Christmas this year. I couldn't exactly describe what I *was* feeling. It was an odd mix of exhilaration and trepidation. Certainly things seemed to be going well. I had brushed it off to a combination of a different climate and my first Christmas without Olivia. But for the most part, I felt like I was just going through the motions.

Somewhere beneath me, I could hear Laine clipping a couple of blossoms off the camellia that stood at the left corner of her porch. She would clip a few off each morning and put them in small glass bowl on her dining room table. "The news van is here early today," she observed as I descended the ladder.

I glanced over my shoulder and saw the news van was indeed parked in front of the theater and Cheryl Higgins was standing on the sidewalk talking to her producer. It had been a week since the story had appeared on the network, and we had not seen much of her. I had begun to hope that maybe the story had run it's course. Archer and Reeder had had their fifteen minutes in the spotlight, but there really wasn't much more happening that was media worthy. I had even begun to note that Reeder was starting to recycle some of his homilies.

"Maybe," I told Laine hopefully, "maybe she's here to actually report on something else."

"That would be nice, wouldn't it?" she replied, unconvinced. She took the flowers inside, and then returned to the porch with her coffee to stand watch over the street. I took the ladder down and carried it around the side of the house to the garage, and returned with an extension cord and timer to plug in the lights.

I rounded the corner just as Cheryl was coming up the front walk and saying to my aunt, "You're Missus Fairchild, are you not?"

"Yes, I am," replied my aunt in her warmest, most dulcet tones.

"I'm Cheryl Higgins," she told my aunt, crossing the lawn to offer her hand. My aunt leaned down and accepted it graciously. "I'm one of the reporters who has been covering the recent protests against the theater and the shows." Anywhere else the introduction would have probably seemed superfluous and unnecessary. In the South, it was an absolute minimum courtesy.

"Yes dear. I've seen you on television many times. The red blazer and tan sweater you wore to cover the liquor store robbery last night was quite fetching."

"Why, thank you." She noticed I had come around the corner. "Oh, hello, Van."

"Cheryl," I replied coolly. Liked her; didn't trust her.

"I'm sorry to bother you on a Saturday morning like this. I know you prefer not to give comments on video, but I received a call from an informant and I was wondering if I could check some facts with you."

Laine and I exchanged wary glances, and then I asked, "An *informant*?"

She smiled. "Well, a news tip, anyhow. We were told that you have added a song and a character to *Highlands-a-Go-Go* that is based on Reverend Reeder, who has been protesting outside the theater. Is that true?"

"I've added a song and a character, that part is true. The character is not based on anyone though."

"Okay, thanks. Now, we've been told that the character is a southern minister with strong opinions and that the resemblance to Reverend Reeder is uncanny."

"The character is a minister, but any resemblance to persons real or imaginary is purely coincidental."

She smirked. "Shrewd answer. Missus Fairchild, I've been told that you were the inspiration for the main character, Mercer Oglethorpe. Can you confirm that?"

My aunt smiled warmly. "Well dear, I didn't write the show so I can't say who the inspiration was. But I can tell you that I certainly could not be the *character* that Mercer is. I may be a grande dame, but perhaps not quite that grande."

I suppressed a chuckle.

"I'm told that you are and that the character is spot-on, but no matter." Cheryl turned her attention back to me. "So Van, as the author, can you say whether any of the characters are based on real people?"

"The characters are based on stereotypes," I replied. "Yes, my aunt is grande, but Mercer and Diego and Wanda and Buzz and Uncle are all from my imagination."

"Fair enough. The other thing I've been told is that you and the actor who plays the minister can be seen sitting at an open window up there," she turned and pointed to my office, "before the show every night listening to Reverend Reeder, and that the things he says in front of the theater each night immediately show up in the show. Is that true?"

I felt a sudden hollow feeling in the pit of my stomach and the hairs on the back of my neck stood up. Being asked about parody was one thing; being asked about plagiarism was another. I hoped I remained visibly calm because I certainly didn't feel it on the inside. "My office tends to get stuffy, so I open the windows a lot. I'm sure I can be seen in the window. However, we don't use the Reverend's material in the show."

"So how do you explain the reported similarities?"

"I'd have to talk to the people who were reporting them. There're a finite number of topics a minister can discuss, so maybe that's where the overlap comes from."

She smiled. "Okay, great. That's all I needed...unless you are willing to change your mind and go on camera?"

I shook my head no. She turned to my aunt.

"Missus Fairchild, what about you? I have a feeling you would make a great interview."

Laine blushed, "Why, thank you, dear, but no. I'm just an old southern lady. I can't imagine I have anything to add to the story, and I'd be terrified to have people see me on television. There's nothing worse than having people you haven't spoken with in years discover that you have grown turkey skin."

Cheryl laughed, thanked us, and walked back to her news van.

"This can't be good," I told Laine quietly as soon as Cheryl was across the street.

"Let's wait and see how the story turns out," she replied.

It was first aired on the midday news as a developing story. Laine and I sat in her living room and watched. The weekend anchor gave a brief recap of the story thus far, and then cut to Cheryl, standing in front of the theater box office.

"Thanks, Carol. I'm standing here in front of Theater DeLaine in Virginia Highland where we're attempting to verify that the writers and producers of the controversial show *Highlands-a-Go-Go* have struck back at the Reverend Dean Reeder by incorporating a not-particularly-flattering parody of him in the show.

"As you may remember, Reverend Reeder has been protesting several things in the Highlands, namely the availability of liquor in a family neighborhood and the theater's history of airing shows that are somewhat critical of political conservatives."

"History?" I asked to no one in particular. "Two shows makes a history?"

They cut to a clip of Reeder who was saying, "We're not protesting *theater*. We're protesting the moral slide that is going on in Virginia Highland and elsewhere in the city."

Cheryl's voice then overlaid the clip of me handing Reeder the umbrella. "Despite the often hostile sermons, show producer and co-creator Donovan Ford recently demonstrated his belief in Reeder's right to express himself and his belief that Christian values should be more about charity than politics. He gained a great deal of public sympathy from that act. But now, he appears to also have used his show as a bully pulpit to strike back at Reeder."

The picture cut back to a live shot of Cheryl. "We've been told that the show now contains a character named Uncle Preacher, played by actor Lamar Fox, who sings a song called 'The North Highland Highway to Hell.' Sources have told us that Ford and Fox sit in an open window above the marquee," the camera panned to my office, "and incorporate Reeder's sermons into each night's show."

The camera panned back to Cheryl. "Now, I did have an opportunity to talk to Mister Ford this morning. Although he declined to be interviewed on camera, he denies that this character or any character is based on a real person. Others question that, especially since they say that the show's main character Mercer Oglethorpe is very clearly based on Ford's aunt, DeLaine Fairchild, who owns the theater. However Mister Ford says all of his characters are just based on stereotypes.

"Live from Virginia Highland, this is Cheryl Higgins."

I turned the TV off. The ensuing uncomfortable silence was broken by my aunt, who simply said, "Anyone who knows me knows I would *never* wear the rhinestone sling-backs Mercer has on at the start of act two."

I looked at her, and felt an impending sense of dread. "I think I may be in over my head here."

"Perhaps," she conceded.

"I wonder if I should call a lawyer."

"Perhaps," she said again. "But this may also be a blessing in disguise. This may help continue to propel the show's success."

"I don't think I am strategic enough to know how to do that."

She thought for a long minute while inspecting her nails. "Donovan, your lack of self-confidence aside, you probably are. But when in doubt, it never hurts to consult a professional."

"Who did you have in mind?"

I am sure it pained her to say it, which is why she never made eye contact with me over her nails. "I think, maybe, you should call Olivia."

The sun was warm enough on the roof that I briefly considered taking off my shirt to work on my tan while I called her. But the air wasn't quite warm anymore. My nerves were on edge and I really, really wanted a cigarette at that moment. But I didn't go for one and instead dropped into an Adirondack and hit the speed-dial for Olivia's cell.

Saturdays were always workdays for us in Manhattan. Something would have opened or premiered the previous evening, and so I would have to write two reviews late Friday night. One was the summary review, which would immediately be uploaded to my blog on the magazine's website. The other would be the detailed review, which would have to be transmitted to my editor by noon so he could get it in the final proof for the magazine and send it off to the printer. So I typically did not get to bed until around four or five on Saturday morning.

Olivia meanwhile, would get up around eight on Saturday morning and go in to her office. Because the agency was closed on Saturdays, she would take advantage of the quiet to catch up on her email, and do all the industry reading that would stack up on her desk each week. We typically didn't see each other until about six or seven at night, and even then one of us might still have to do something for work that evening.

As the phone rang, I could picture her cell sitting on her desk next to a growing stack of assignments that would be deposited on Sally's desk to await her arrival on Monday morning. I heard the call connect. She didn't bother with a greeting. "Divorced or not, for future reference, if the national news is going to do a story on you I expect a phone call in advance."

I smiled. "Sorry about that, babe. The publicity kind of snuck up on me. Who told you?"

"Who told me? Bloody everybody is who told me. Apparently I'm the only one in our circle of friends who *doesn't* watch ABC in the morning."

"Did you get to see it?"

"Yeah. I was able to download the clip. Great publicity for you. I hope it's paying off."

"Well, it's certainly driving sales, but I'm not sure it's paying off. I need some professional advice."

She immediately put on her professional personality. Olivia's ability to switch modes was amazing. As soon as you mentioned the topic of work, she became a different person. You could almost hear a relay close inside her head. "Tell me what's up."

I explained how we had incorporated the new song and the new character based on Reeder into the show, and how our little trick of incorporating his sermons into the script each night had been discovered and fed to the news. I recapped the discussion with Cheryl Higgins and my responses, and how they had been reported on the news that evening. She said nothing while I talked, but I could hear the methodical click of nails on her laptop keyboard. I knew she wasn't ignoring me; quite the opposite. Her talent for processing data from multiple sources is astronomical. I was sure she was Googling me while we talked to see what news items were out there.

I finished up the story with a plaintive, "So, that's my life in a nutshell. How much trouble am I in?"

"Whether you are in trouble or not is all dependent on how you play your hand. Remember, it's possible to win with an ace high and it's possible to lose with a royal flush."

"The poker analogies are new," I observed.

"Do you like them? I just picked up one of the guys on the national poker tour as a client."

"Very effective. Women using sports clichés has become cliché."

"That's what I thought. Okay, looking on the Web there doesn't seem to be too much traffic out there about this yet, so we can still get ahead of the story."

"Is there a way to kill it?"

She laughed. "Kill it? God, no. Fundies eat this shit up. It's free publicity for them, and they are *all* about publicity. If they can find a way to get it in court, they know they can count on at least a twenty percent increase in media share for the entire time of the trial."

"You think they'll sue?"

"They may try. It won't stick, but you'd still have to defend it."

"Why won't it stick?"

"It won't stick thanks to Larry Flynt."

"The guy who published *Hustler*?"

"Yep. *Falwell versus Hustler Magazine* was based on the earlier standard of *New York Times versus Sullivan*. The Supreme Court ruled that speech that is critical of public figures, including parody, is free speech and therefore constitutionally protected. Parody only loses its First Amendment protection if, um... hold on, I've got it right here. It only loses its protection if it 'contains a false statement of fact, the falsehood is uttered deliberately or with recklessness as to its veracity, and the speech ends up defaming and injuring the figure's reputation or intentionally inflicting emotional distress.'

"So basically, unless you are lying about this fundy minister and doing so with deliberate intent to damage him, your right to parody him is protected."

"But he's not a public figure, is he?"

"That's what they would argue. But he's standing on a pick-up truck outside your theater denouncing you via a loudspeaker. He's going to have a hard time making a case that he's acting in private. The plagiarism charge is going to be harder to beat."

"Say more."

"Well, if he is, say, recording his sermons and can demonstrate that you've copied them into the show, he's got a case. So, you've got to operate with that in mind."

I sat back, impressed. I suppose on some level I always knew that Olivia was brilliant. It was much more impressive to actually see her brilliance working on my own behalf. "Okay, so what should I do?"

"Well, you need to play this game on two levels. First is the defensive front."

"So pull the character out of the show?"

"NO!" she fairly shrieked. I knew that tone; in the back of her mind she was wondering how she could have ever married me. "If you drastically change what you are doing because of media coverage, that's as much as a public admission of wrongdoing. You'd be crucified in the media. You need to tweak what you are doing, but not discontinue it."

"Keep going."

"Okay, so to play this on a defensive front, first you must leave the character in the show. You must continue to open your office windows every evening, even if it's thirty below."

"Thirty below will paralyze Atlanta."

"Open 'em anyhow. By playing on a defensive front you want to show you are doing nothing wrong, but also ensure you give him nothing to prosecute you on. So, also continue to document what he says, but don't incorporate it verbatim in the show. Make it *sound* like what he's saying, but don't incorporate verbatim text."

"Got it. That's kind of what we've been doing anyhow."

"Good. Now, for the offensive. First of all, you unknowingly went on the offensive with the umbrella. You seized the Christian moral high ground from him. So all of a sudden you repositioned yourself from peddler of leftist smut to good Christian. Now, you've opened the door for him to do the same thing to you. You've attacked a poor humble member of the clergy. You'll lose unless you can reposition that fast."

"Thoughts on how?"

"Not yet. If you can add another character and another song that makes fun of another stereotype, that would help a little. Let me think a bit on this. Tell me though, why do you think this preacher targeted you to begin with?"

I explained who Archer Bellamy was and our checkered history.

"So let me get this straight: this guy doesn't have any reason to have anything against you personally. He just generally dislikes you, Brit, Laine, and the Highlands on principle?"

"Best I can tell."

"Okay, let me ponder on this a bit. One thing I think you are going to need to do is talk to the media. Don't commit to anything yet, but start sweet-talking this Cheryl chick. She's obviously trying to stake out her ownership of this story."

I thanked her and we ended the call with me making a sincere commitment to keep her in the loop on all news items as they came up. I subsequently called Lamar and Miranda separately and explained our strategy so they were prepared for that evening.

I hung up and went inside the apartment to change, wondering why I had never had this caliber of conversation with Liv when we had been married.

When I arrived at the theater, Reeder was there, setting up. He looked up, saw me and returned the umbrella with a gracious thanks. I walked inside. A pleasantly terse message on the answering service alerted me that the reservations mailbox was full.

I worked through the ticket requests and allocated out the Will Call envelopes for that night. There was a different energy as the cast, crew, and staff began to arrive. Although almost nothing had been said, there was a distinct sense of defensiveness hanging over the show. Even later, as Lamar sat in the office listening to Reeder and studiously *not* writing anything down, the mood was guarded. I felt like the building itself was girding itself for something unexpected.

When I opened the doors that night, I noticed that Cheryl Higgins and her producer were in line with tickets. *I should have expected that,* I thought to myself. It made perfect sense that she would be here. I greeted her as she entered.

"Hi Donovan. I hope you don't mind, but I need to see the show for myself for this story."

"Hey, as long as you bought a ticket, I'm certainly not going to stop you. I've got nothing to hide."

"Great. Glad you don't mind. The offer to appear in the story is always open."

"You know, the time may come to take you up on that."

She stopped and looked at me. "Seriously?"

"Yes, seriously. Since the story isn't going away, maybe it is best to offer my perspective. You watch the show, let me know what you think, and then we can discuss it."

"Okay, definitely."

"Do you want a glass of wine or something?"

"No, but thank you. I'm back on the air later."

"I understand."

"Hey, if we interview you though, wear the shorts."

"I beg your pardon?"

"Saw you on the ladder hanging Christmas lights. You've got great legs."

I'm sure I blushed.

I thought about telling Miranda and the cast that there was a reporter in the house and then thought better of it. Tensions were already high. Plus, they had been performing in front of critics for a month now. They should have expected it. I did, however let Laine know as soon as I sat down next to her in the balcony.

"Cheryl Higgins is in the audience."

"It's not surprising," she responded, pouring a manhattan from a new Waterford pitcher. To make her life easier, I had stocked a small bar on the balcony so that her drinks could be mixed on site rather than schlepped across the street. "What's surprising is that it's taken this long. Did Olivia have any advice on how to handle it?"

"Some, more to follow." I quickly recounted the highlights of the defensive strategy, and explained that there would be some kind of offensive strategy as well, but in the meantime I was supposed to begin making myself more available to Cheryl. "She also thinks I have nice legs."

"You do, dear." The curtain rose.

Klein had once told me that when performing standup, he never drank or did anything else to help him relax before going on stage. "Edgy is good for comedy. It makes you quicker. Relaxed is bad."

I saw it work firsthand that evening as my very edgy cast put on a phenomenal show. Whereas usually Klein and Lamar were the ones who primarily improvised with the audience, tonight everyone in the cast did. They hit the bulk of my script, certainly, but they added so many more jibes, winks, and asides that it was far-and-away their best performance to date. At the intermission I told Laine, "If it makes them perform at this level, I should freak them out before every performance."

Cheryl and her producer didn't leave the auditorium during intermission. She sat at her seat, scribbling furiously on a legal pad and asking her producer questions. Lamar's song had come and gone, so I thought to myself, *Whatever damage that could be done has been done.*

At the end of the show, I waited anxiously to see her come out. She was flushed from laughter, but when I asked her what she thought, she was professional enough not to let me know her impressions or how it might impact her story. I told her that we might find more opportunities for her to have "access" to the show if she was interested and she told me she'd like to discuss it further.

"Why don't you come by for a drink?" Laine asked her over my shoulder.

"I'd like that," Cheryl replied. "Just tell me when."

"I will, dear. As soon as I see how you treat us on tonight's news." Laine replied with a gleam in her eye.

Cheryl laughed. "Totally understood, Missus Fairchild. May I call you DeLaine?"

"That also depends on how you treat us on tonight's news."

She laughed again and excused herself because she would be on camera in a few minutes for the eleven o'clock news.

Rather than run across the street and watch it on television, I simply followed her out to watch the story myself. Laine joined me directly behind her cameraman to watch, fresh cocktail in one hand, leaning on her cane with the other. I glanced at her. "You're using the cane? Are you okay?"

"Never underestimate the visual power of guilt, dear," she whispered back, and forced a look of pain onto her face when Cheryl glanced at us.

It was not the optimal time to be filming a television piece in the heart of the Highlands. First of all, it was Saturday night and there were a *lot* of people milling about, going to and from different bars and restaurants. Then of course, there was the Reverend Reeder preaching to the crowd, with several audience members gathered nearby discussing how he compared with Uncle Preacher. And on the other side of the street, the sax player was playing "The Proper Pronunciation of Ponce" from the show, and a couple of audience members had gathered around him to sing what they could remember of the lyrics.

Cheryl took up her spot with the theater in the background, and several students from Emory University immediately gathered behind her to mug for the camera. The producer informed her that the studio was ready to cut to her and asked the crowd for quiet, which of course no one complied with. Cheryl had her hand on her earpiece and, when the producer pointed at her, started speaking.

"Thanks, Carol. We're here at Theater DeLaine where this evening's show has just let out.

"As Carol told you at the start of this story, there have been reports that *Highlands-A-Go-Go* has been rewritten to lash back at Reverend

Dean Reeder, the controversial minister who has gone on the attack against the nightlife in Virginia Highland in general, and this theater in particular. In fact, Reverend Reeder is just behind me, still preaching." The camera panned to him briefly, "and I just recently saw Donovan Ford, the producer and co-creator of *Highlands-A-Go-Go* and his aunt, DeLaine Fairchild, who owns the theater, in the crowd." The camera did not pan to us, although Higgins did glance our way. Laine took advantage of the moment and sagged pathetically against my shoulder and the cane. "So, all the players in this conflict are still out and active.

"I had an opportunity to attend the show tonight and see for myself whether the character is indeed based on Reverend Reeder. Now, I have to admit, I did not see the show before the character of Uncle Preacher was added, so I can't exactly say how the show has changed. Mister Ford maintains that none of the characters are explicitly based on any one person, but are rather drawn from Southern stereotypes. It has also been alleged that Uncle Preacher's role is rewritten every night, blatantly plagiarizing what Reverend Reeder is preaching in front of the theater.

"I can tell you that, having listened to Reeder before the show, and then seeing the show, the similarities I saw between the character and the Reverend were not great. The character does indeed seem to be drawn from a stereotype rather than the particular person. And, although the preaching is similar in the show to what Reeder has said outside, my producer and I could not find any examples of anything explicitly plagiarized from Reeder's sermon."

Laine moved her hand holding the cane next to mine and locked her little finger around my own for the briefest second, then returned to her crippled old lady pose.

"I should add, however, that they knew I was in the audience, so I do not know if the show was customized for my benefit.

"In regards to Mister Ford's contention that all the characters are based on stereotypes, I do have to say I question that. I have had the opportunity to meet DeLaine Fairchild, and the main character of the show, Mercer Oglethorpe is definitely not a stereotype. It is the spitting image of her. Let's hope she doesn't choose to sue her nephew.

"Live from Virginia Highland, this is Cheryl Higgins. Back to you Carol."

The producer said, "And, we're clear." The cameraman switched off the spotlight.

Cheryl walked over to us and said, "Donovan, Missus Fairchild. How about that drink?"

Laine held out her hand and took Cheryl's warmly. "My dear, please call me Laine."

The next day, as I recapped the previous evening to Olivia over the phone, she encouraged me to set up a "behind the scenes" tour for Cheryl late the following week. "On Friday," she said over the phone. I recognized the sound of the dishwasher being opened, and I momentarily wondered how long I would continue to remember the sounds of our former life together.

"Why Friday?"

"Because I can be there. I'll take the noon flight from LaGuardia and come directly to the theater. I should be able to be there by three."

"You don't have to take off work and come down here just for this," I told her.

"Who's taking off work? You're still my client." Technically she was right. Olivia became my agent shortly after we got married. Of course, I had never done anything that required her to do any work for me. I was also not the caliber of author that she would have customarily represented, so I was all the more grateful. "Besides, I've downloaded Cheryl Higgins's clips and she's no slouch. A little professional spin might be a good idea. Plus, I may have some other information she might find useful."

"What kind of information?"

"Let's see if it pans out first. I'm going to bring a couple of friends with me. Would you comp two extra tickets?"

That afternoon, I filled everyone in on the plan. Cheryl would be invited for a "behind the scenes" tour of the show, beginning at four on Friday. Cameras would probably be included.

At five that afternoon, when I went across the street to open up the theater, Reeder was there, but he wasn't alone. There were ten people with him, Bellamy among them. I wasn't exactly sure what they were doing, so I went right past them, and set about my normal routine. I didn't know what was going on until an hour later when I carried a case of wine into the lobby for the show and found Talbot waiting for me.

"Hey," I replied, putting down the box. "What are you doing here?"

She kissed me on the cheek. "Hello darling. Need you to sign the event license application for the next two weeks. I'll take them by the liquor board."

I took the papers from her and dug a pen out from behind the bar. "Any idea when they are going to rule on my permanent application?"

She shook her head. "Not until the fiasco out front ends, I'm sure. Speaking of which, have you seen what's going on outside?"

I looked up in mid signature. "No, what?"

"Go see."

I put down the pen and walked to the door. In the fading light, the ten or so folks who had come with Reeder were holding candles and singing. I opened the door to listen.

"...and we will keep this vigil going all night, Lord," Reeder prayed aloud, "and every night until this neighborhood and this theater no longer profane your good name and the holy Sabbath..."

I stepped back inside, shaking my head. "Jesus."

Talbot smiled. "That's what he thinks. Of course, Jesus drank wine. I bet if He were here today, I could sell Him a good meritage to go drink right in front of that asshole."

I resumed signing applications. "Why would Jesus need to buy it? Couldn't he just make it?"

"Good point!" she laughed. "Actually, if He comes back, I could rep him. What a private vintage that would be. We could call it Cabernet of Christ."

I handed the papers back to her and smiled. "You know you are going to hell for that, don't you?"

"Yeah, but the schmuck outside will probably beat me there." She put the papers in her purse. "I'd love to stay for tonight's fireworks but I have a date."

"The lawyer or new talent?"

"New talent. The concierge at the Four Seasons."

I raised my eyebrows, in surprise. Talbot typically only dated older, wealthier, more established men. "Not to be indelicate, but isn't that a bit, um, *off-brand* for you?"

"It is. But every once in a while, I'll shop discount for young and hung."

She kissed me on the cheek and bid me farewell. As her Mercedes pulled away, I saw Cheryl Higgins's news van pull up. I thought to myself, *Well, that saves me from having to call her.* I stepped outside and waited for her to get out. Laine, Chris, and Rachel were coming across the street.

Cheryl got out of her car and took in the prayer vigil. She turned to me and I could see the faintest sign of a smirk as she walked towards me. "Give him credit," she said. "He knows how to escalate in such a way to keep bringing the media back."

"That's what worries me," I replied.

"I don't buy that for one minute. You're getting a ton of free press out of this. One national story already, and possibly a second next week."

"A second?"

She nodded. "The network is mildly interested. Depends on what Uncle Preacher does this week, and how you respond."

I chose to ignore the provocation. "Well, that's got to be great for your career."

"It won't hurt it, that's for sure." The others arrived. Chris and Rachel let themselves into the theater but Laine hovered nearby.

"I was thinking about something anyhow, but I've got an idea that might help you pitch the network. Something more than just an on-camera quote from me."

"Yeah?" she asked, clearly interested.

"Would you want to bring your cameras and film an entire evening backstage? You can stay with me for the entire show if you want, or film from the back. I'll even appear on camera."

"So will I," Laine proffered.

She cocked her head, curious. "Why the change of heart?"

"Well, first of all, because you are pretty balanced in your reporting. Second, yeah, it wouldn't hurt me to have more media. And third, I thought maybe the public should see that there's no pentagrams or chicken blood backstage."

She laughed. "When were you thinking?"

"Next Friday. You can come and shadow me next Thursday to see the whole thing and decide what you want to film."

"Block it out, as it were," Laine added, keen to show she was hip on theater lingo.

I looked at my aunt for a moment and then returned my attention to the reporter. "And then you can film on Friday."

She thought a minute. "I love the idea. I've got to talk it over with my news director. Let me get back to you tomorrow."

"Sure," I replied, as I pulled my business card out of my wallet and scribbled my cell number on the back. "Here's my mobile. Call me anytime."

She looked at me, and I could tell she was trying to decide what was motivating my change of heart. Not seeing an answer in my face, she nodded, and returned to her crew.

Laine took my arm and we walked inside. "Do you think this is going to work?"

I shrugged. "Dunno. At this point, Reeder seems like he is going to be here for the long run, so what harm can it do?"

I didn't see Cheryl's report that night as it was payday. Instead, I cut the checks for the cast and crew during the last act, and then went backstage to distribute them at the end of the show. We were dark on Mondays, so I would close the books for November, pay all the bills and determine if there was any profit for Miranda and me to split. I was excited. This would be the first time I had genuinely earned income in about a year.

Laine's door was open as I let myself into the 'Hurst that evening. As soon as the door opened she called, "Van? Is that you?"

"'Tis," I replied, and stuck my head into her apartment. "Everything okay?"

She was curled up on a fainting couch she kept in one corner. "Oh, fine. Did you see Miss Higgins report tonight?"

"I did not," I confessed. "At some point I'm going to have to put a television in my office. How was it?"

"Again, very balanced, but a little concerning."

"Concerning how?"

"When the camera panned the crowd, Archer Bellamy was there, of course, but so were a couple of people I recognized from the neighborhood."

"Anyone in particular?"

"No. No one I know. Just people I've seen."

"So? This is a big neighborhood. I'm sure there is someone here who agrees with him."

"Well, that's my point. I tend to think of this neighborhood as still very liberal, but I wonder if I'm out of touch."

The uncertainty in her voice was most uncharacteristic and I said so. "Do you think we are doing something wrong?"

"No, of course not. I'm more worried about how it appears."

"Laine! When have you ever worried about keeping up appearances? If you held with what conservatives thought, you would never rent to African Americans or gays. Hell, you wouldn't have half the friends you have."

She thought for a minute, and then smiled. "You're right, of course. I was confusing politics with graciousness. Progressives can still be gracious after all, can't they?"

"Of course."

On Monday, Cheryl's news director approved the story. Miranda and the whole cast loved the idea of the backstage cameras. After all, they were performers and it would be good for their careers. Miranda in particular was enamored with it.

"Your ex advised that we should add a character to the show," she said to me Tuesday evening. I was writing out a check for her share of the November profits, which were not insubstantial. Consequently, we were also sharing a bottle of champagne. "You should add a character based on Higgins. A reporter who is investigating the Highlands about something."

"Wouldn't that mean I find myself in danger of *two* people accusing me of plagiarism?"

"Not necessarily. Higgins is definitely a public figure, so she's fair game."

I tore out the check and handed it across the desk to her. She took it, grinned widely, and then held up her flute. We toasted and drank, and then she slipped the check into the front pocket of her jeans.

"Instead of a character based on her, what about if we gave her a walk-on in the show she was filming?"

She raised her eyebrows in thought. "Hmm…not a bad idea. I wonder if she would think it compromises her journalistic integrity."

"Never hurts to ask."

"Ask Olivia first."

"I'll call her in the morning."

"Call her now."

Despite a certain surliness for being called in the middle of the night by her ex-husband who was drinking – how *cliché!* - Olivia actually loved both ideas. "Get her in the show if you can. That *guarantees* it gets on the air. And pitch a new character idea to her about an investigative reporter, and get her rehearsing it on camera. That documents that the show is an evolving piece of art *and* it pretty much guarantees the network will pick it up."

I hung up with her, looked across the desk at Miranda and said, "Both are a go."

"Both are a-go-go," she replied, amused with herself. "More champagne?"

"Can't. I've got to come up with a new reporter character and work it into the script before Thursday."

I wrote late into the night. There was an exchange between Diego and Mercer in the middle of the second act that never worked for me. It felt contrived, and it only garnered the most modest of laughter from the audience. I reworked it, removing Diego from the scene and added a walk-on for a new character, a budding investigative television journalist that I named Tamara Oncamera. She would have enormous hair, and only be able to talk into a microphone, facing directly at the audience. It amused me. I had no idea if it was particularly funny or not.

I called Cheryl the next morning. Olivia conferenced in with me on the call because… well, let's be honest: she was on the line because she was worried I'd screw it up. But, she was on mute, which left me feeling a little sneaky, if not downright manipulative.

Cheryl answered the phone with a matter-of-fact "Cheryl Higgins."

"Donovan Ford," I replied in an even more reporter-like tone.

"Oh, hey! How are you?"

"I'm good, thanks. You?"

"Never better. What can I do for you? You're not calling to cancel on me, are you?"

"Not at all. Just the opposite, in fact. We've been kicking an idea around that I'd like to try out on you. You're free to say no."

"Okay, shoot."

"Well, we've been working on another new character to add to the show. Let me first go on record as saying that any resemblance of this character to persons real or imaginary is purely coincidental."

She chuckled. "Your disclaimer is duly noted."

"I am adding an investigative television news reporter named Tamara Oncamera in the middle of the second act."

This time, it was a snort of laughter with a bit of commotion in the background. "Oh God. I was drinking coffee when you said that. It's everywhere. I thought you were serious."

"I am serious."

"Um…oh, okay."

"I was thinking about trying this character out on Friday night, and wanted to know if you actually wanted to do it as a walk-on. You still get all the free access to the show to film, but you also get the added news bite of you being in it."

She snickered. "Van, I'm no actor."

"I know you're not. Have you looked around this place? I'm up to my earlobes in actors. But until I get the right one, I thought it would be a lark and help you out."

"And what do you get?"

"Maybe another extension to the run. I'm a media hound, pure and simple."

"How many lines would I have to learn?"

"Three."

There was a long, thoughtful pause. "The station will have to approve it…"

"I'll send the script to you via email. The lines are on page eighty-eight."

"Would I have to wear anything special?"

"A power suit. Something that stresses you're a tough reporter who's also built."

"You think I'm built?"

"I do. But don't wear the red-and-tan. I don't want to be accused of basing this character on anyone."

"Go ahead and send the script over." She gave me her email and promised to get back to me that afternoon. We hung up, and my phone rang again immediately.

"Hey Liv. That go okay?"

"It went fine. I'm proud of you." Her voice was strange. She certainly did not sound proud of me.

"Okay. What time does your flight get in here on Friday? Do you need me to come get you?"

"No, not at the airport. We'll take a cab. But could you get us at the Four Seasons about an hour before the show?"

"I can't but I've got a kid named Zach who works with me. He'll come get you."

"Okay, thanks." There was a prolonged silence.

"Anything else?"

"No. I guess not."

"Okay, then…"

"Van, an observation?"

"Sure."

"You were a little, um, *chummy* with this reporter, weren't you?"

"Eh, it's the South. Everyone here is chummy."

"I see. Well, okay then. Call me back and let me know if she gets the go-ahead from her station."

"Will do. Ciao."

"Bye."

Later that afternoon, Cheryl called me back with a confirmation that she was in.

Ordinarily, Cheryl traveled with one cameraman and, occasionally, a sound guy. On Thursday, though, she had her producer with her, the sound guy, two cameramen, an intern, and some general management–type drone that was obviously there to ensure that the station was not compromised in any way.

It was early afternoon, and so we began with the boring stuff. I took them on a tour of the empty theater, telling its history and showing them the workings of the set. They filmed me taking messages off the reservations line and doling out the Will Calls. "Fascinating stuff, I know," I told the camera. "This is where the *glamour* is, kids."

Miranda showed up around three and all of us camped out in my office. Because my office really is stuffy, the window was cracked open. Nonetheless, I reflected to myself on my positive attention to detail.

We all sat around the office while the camera filmed and did the first dry reading of Tamara Oncamera and her lines. Miranda read for Mercer and coached Cheryl on her delivery. Then we all trooped downstairs to block it out on stage.

At four, it was time to start pre-show preparation, so the cameras split. One, the *winner* of a coin toss, stayed with Cheryl and Miranda as they blocked out the scene and met the other cast members. The other, the *loser* of the coin toss, followed me around the theater, filming all the preshow preparation.

"I'll try not to take being the less desirable assignment personally," I said into the lens as the crew started moving the scenery to the opening marks.

I have to admit, it seemed that my guy did get the bum deal. He got footage of Lamar writing his Uncle Preacher lines in my office, but with the radio on so you couldn't hear the street below. He got footage of me vacuuming the lobby, and of my aunt and cohorts arriving to set up the bar. None of it seemed destined for an Emmy.

Meanwhile, there was more filming of Cheryl rehearsing and learning her lines. It started to appear that the story was going to be about her now, rather than about the controversy with Reeder. That is, until the next day.

The whole crew was there at noon again, and we began by taping an interview with me during which I tried to come across as neutral or indifferent to the Reeder controversy. Cheryl hit me with a lot of tough questions, but I felt like I handled them all okay. I kept bringing the discussion back around to free speech, and that I supported Reeder's right to protest me, even though I disagreed that the Highlands was a cesspool of iniquity.

They also filmed an interview with Laine, perched on her stool in the lobby in front of a piece of Brit's artwork she had insisted we hang there. She certainly had dressed for the part of a successful theater owner. She wore a black turtleneck, offset by three loops of white pearls. Cheryl complimented her on the outfit and she explained, "I'm hoping the pearls and collar will draw attention away from the jowls."

Cheryl laughed. "Laine, I hope I look half as good as you do when I'm your age. The pearls are marvelous though." The cameraman switched on a spotlight and started filming.

"Thank you, dear. They represent a lesson."

"A lesson?"

"I once had a friend, Patti, whose house burned down. It was a great, traumatic loss, but fortunately no one was hurt. The very next day, a FedEx package arrived from her mother with a brand new strand of pearls and a note. It said, 'Remember, a Southern woman can face *anything* as long as she has her pearls.'"

That elicited laughter from everyone. The producer suggested that everyone be quiet, but Cheryl and Laine didn't pay attention and continued to laugh together.

"I once heard that pearls are what distinguishes a southern lady," Cheryl remarked.

"Oh, my dear, it's one of three things. A true southern lady will *only* drink her tea sweet. She will *only* fly Delta. She will *only* wear real pearls."

Cheryl turned and looked at me. "Will that line wind up in the show?"

The camera swung to me. "Well, remember, Mercer is *not* based on a real person. But, yeah. I'll probably sneak that in somewhere."

Having sucked all the material out of pearls that we could, the interview was finally about to start when there was an insistent rap on the front door. I turned to see Talbot standing there, clearly agitated.

I crossed to the doors and unlocked them and she fairly screeched, "Archer Bellamy is an *asshole*!!! He's cost us our event license for the week."

Without even looking, I knew the camera had swung around and was filming us.

"What do you mean?" I asked with exaggerated calmness, trying to indicate with my eyes that there was a camera crew filming behind me. She didn't catch the signal.

"When I went down there to file this week's permit application, he was there with a camera crew and a petition. As soon as I submitted the permit, he cuts in front of me and hands the clerk a petition that he says is from the neighborhood, asking that the city *not* issue a permit."

"You are on camera," I mouthed to her, but she didn't catch it.

"Well, of course this hourly City Hall clerk doesn't know what to do, so she calls her supervisor who sees the cameras, panics, and shuts the office down. We've got no alcohol permit for the next week."

I put my hand on Talbot's arm, who finally made eye contact with me. I motioned over my shoulder and she saw the camera. She rolled her eyes, looked into the camera and said, "Jesus! Why can't you people ever be anyplace I *want* you to be?"

"No matter," Laine announced, taking control of the situation. The camera swung back to her. "We're sold out for the next week. We don't need a cash bar. Until we can get this resolved, the drinks next week will simply be on me."

"Missus Fairchild," Cheryl asked. "Are you suggesting that alcohol is a necessary part of attending theater in the Highlands?"

"Not at all, dear. Good theater doesn't require alcohol. I've attended many fine shows in church basements that only served lemonade. But let's be honest. It *doesn't hurt*, either."

It turned out that Archer Bellamy had been cultivating a local FOX affiliate's reporter about as effectively as I had been cultivating Cheryl. That crew was busy outside filming while Cheryl's crew was busy inside. I found a few minutes to sneak into my office and call Olivia, who had just landed.

She listened impatiently to my rants only long enough to get the gist of the story out of me and then said, "Okay, calm down and shut up. This is not the worst thing in the world. We'll need to get our hands on that petition somehow, but in the meantime, Laine's open bar was a brilliant stroke. It's all very 'the show must go on' and 'the little theater that could.' We can spin this. I need to meet the reporter, though."

"I assumed you would tonight," I replied sullenly.

"We'll need to come early. Have the car meet us at the hotel at six-thirty. You're not sending the Jeep, are you?"

"Of course not. I'm sending a Rolls."

"Yeah, right," she sniffed and hung up.

I stared at the phone for a minute and thought *you bitch*, then called Zach and told him to get my keys and take the VeggieRoll to the Four Seasons.

There was a new energy in the building's atmosphere. Word traveled fast throughout the cast and crew, and the air fairly crackled with tension. Even Cheryl got caught up in it, despite being slightly miffed about FOX muscling in on her story. We had one camera following her around backstage, and the other following me. Eventually, it would be stationed up in the balcony with us, but for now, it was capturing everything I said and did.

I had informed Zach to text me when he turned onto Virginia Avenue so I could go outside and meet the car. I received the message just as the crowd began to arrive. So, camera in tow, I stepped outside as the Rolls-Royce pulled up to the theater.

Liv opened the back door, caught the camera, and a gleam of awareness passed across her eyes. She stepped out, looking stunning in a champagne sequined cocktail dress, a fur stole and ecru Prada pumps. She immediately greeted me with more warmth and affection that she had shown during the entirety of our marriage.

"Van, when you said you were sending a Rolls for me, I thought you were joking. You always did do everything with class."

I made a mental note that I must get a copy of that video.

Two men got out of the car after her. One was shortish, about thirty, with long blonde hair that hung low over his right eye and who had a mousy demeanor. The other, closer to fifty, was much larger in every sense of the word. Taller, broader, greyer, and with a personality that beamed out through his Woody Allen glasses. I recognized them immediately even before she made the introductions.

"Van, I want to introduce you to two of my friends. This is Taylor Hirsch and Jonathan Warsheim."

Hirsch and Warsheim of Warsheim & Hirsch! They were the hottest producers not on Broadway. They specialized in creating edgy, far-reaching shows that would never find a home in Times Square. Shows that were summarized by the mission statement that they put in every program and Playbill: "Enlighten! Amuse! Offend!" They had burst onto the off-Broadway scene when they staged the scathing show about retail called *Abercrombie and Bitch!* It had never made it to a mainstream theater, but had been picked up by HBO as a mini-series instead. They eschewed Broadway, which they viewed as having evolved into a Disneyesque theme park, and preferred instead the lucrative freedom of off-Broadway.

"Gentlemen," I said warmly as I shook each of their hands. "It's a pleasure to meet you. Welcome to Theater DeLaine. I reviewed every one of your shows when I was at *Manhattan Gothic.*"

"We know," Hirsch replied. "We loved every one of your reviews. We used to say your review of *Abercrombie* is what got us noticed."

"The new guy they have at *Gothic* is nowhere near as insightful as you," Warsheim added.

"I would hope not. Please, come inside."

I escorted them into the theater, and directly to the bar. While they ordered their drinks, I pulled Olivia aside, ensuring I was out of range of the camera mic, and said quietly, "You brought Warsheim and Hirsch to my show?"

She shook her head. "Hirsch and Warsheim. When you talk about their shows, Warsheim goes first. In real life, Hirsch does. He's very insecure about that."

"Which one is?"

"Both. Anyway, they are shopping around for something new and I thought, what the heck? This might be it. Make a big deal over them without appearing to make a big deal."

I escorted them to their seats, and, since all three of them were drinking meritage, I went back to the bar, grabbed a full bottle, and subtly took it down to them. They were appreciative of the extra attention and Warsheim tucked it under his seat.

Word of celebrities arriving via Rolls-Royce gets around quick, and there was a heightened murmur running through the crowd. Warsheim and Hirsch were not widely known outside of New York, but they were not unheard of, either. Miranda and I consulted quietly on the matter. Well, I tried to consult quietly. She shrieked when I told her. Anyway, we decided it was for the best not to tell the cast. They were edgy enough. Besides, they would find out soon enough.

I returned to the lobby and stepped behind the bar to flash the lights. Chris leaned over and said, "Tell me that wasn't Warsheim and Hirsch with your ex."

"Hirsch and Warsheim," I corrected. "Apparently it's an issue. And yes, it was."

"Hirsch and Warsheim, as in the producers of *Drive, Fag! Drive!?*"

"Yup."

"Wow. That's pretty impressive."

Because of the open bar, a bit more beer and wine was consumed than usual, so the audience was in a festive mood. I escorted Laine up the stairs as was my practice, but then made a dash backstage.

Most small community theaters usually began their shows with the artistic director or executive director coming out and greeting the audience. Being a for-profit theater, that was not a practice I had ever adopted. It didn't feel appropriate, and I questioned whether it put us in the Wee Playhouse of Hoboken leagues.

However, Miranda had persuaded me that I needed to do so tonight, given that tonight was a special show because of Cheryl's premiere. Plus, we had comped tickets for a couple of local gossip columnists, hoping to garner some free publicity, and it would look good in the papers for me to welcome them. (Of course, had I known Hirsch and Warsheim would be coming, I would have made those columnists pay.)

I do not fear public speaking, but I don't particularly enjoy it either. I always feel like I should be more witty and urbane than I actually am, so it takes me a few minutes to work up to it. I stood behind the curtain, and took several deep breaths before I nodded to the stage manager. The house lights dropped to quarter-power, and she nodded to me. I took a step forward and slipped through the curtains and into a spotlight.

There was polite applause. As soon as it died down, I began. "Ladies and gentlemen, good evening and welcome to Theater DeLaine and tonight's performance of *Highlands-A-Go-Go.* I'm Donovan Ford, producer and co-creator of the show, and we're very happy to have you here tonight.

"Those of you who have been here before know I don't typically come out and open the show. However, we wanted to give you the heads up on a change to tonight's script.

"We have, yet again, introduced a new character to the show this evening." There was a slight murmur in the crowd. "Now, yes, I know all of you who watch the news probably have pretty strong opinions on how smart it was to add a character the last time I did it." The crowd laughed. "And you'd be right. So, trying to be someone who learns from his mistakes, I've solicited professional help. There's nothing in your programs about this because we decided at the last minute to try it, but tonight Cheryl Higgins of WSB News has agreed to help us out and will be appearing in tonight's show."

Appreciative applause rose up from the audience. Cheryl tests well in this market.

"So, anyway, we just wanted you to know what's going on and to give you the heads up that there are some WSB camera operators wandering around the theater. So if you are wanted by, oh, the FBI? You may want to step out when we drop the lights."

There was a little more laughter. "Finally, as always, please turn your pagers and cell phones to vibrate, but why would you wear them any other way?" I held my left hand up as they laughed again and said, "Thanks, and enjoy the show."

With that, we were off and running. On my way back upstairs, I stopped off in the stage right box, and stepped out to see if I could see Hirsch and Warsheim. They were in two seats on the aisle, five rows up. I could tell Warsheim was laughing at the first joke. Hirsch was looking down, and I couldn't tell what he was doing.

I settled onto the couch next to Laine, and she whispered to me, "The cameraman caught me mixing a manhattan."

"I wish that was the most controversial thing he had caught today."

"Who was that with Olivia? They seem to be making quite a stir."

"Jonathan Warsheim and Taylor Hirsch. They're fairly successful off-Broadway producers."

"Ah, how nice. Have they done anything I've heard of?"

"Probably not. They stage pretty controversial stuff. They're sort of considered Satan's answer to Sir Andrew Lloyd Webber."

Ordinarily, I sit with Laine for most of the show, but not all. When I do, I have a notebook with me where I jot down ideas as I watch. It is usually a pretty relaxed time. Tonight, however, I couldn't sit still. Perhaps it was the cameras, or the producers, or the liquor license, or Cheryl's premiere. In retrospect, it was actually probably all of those things. Regardless, I wandered the balcony a good bit during the first act, stopping only to perch on the rail and watch for a while. I know the camera caught at least one shot of me pacing back and forth during one of the numbers.

My restlessness aside, the rest of the audience seemed to be having a grand time. I could tell that Warsheim was laughing a lot, but all I could see of Hirsch was the back of his head.

Intermission was a bit rowdier than normal. The buzz about all our guests, the special appearance, and of course, free booze, made it a loud, boisterous affair. I found myself on the sidewalk with the smokers trying, unsuccessfully, to get them back into the theater. Olivia led her guests outside.

"There you are," she beamed. "The show looks even better than it did opening night. I love Uncle Preacher."

Good agent.

"Thanks. Glad you are enjoying it."

"Van," Warsheim asked, "Could I bum a cigarette off of you? I think I left mine in your car."

"Sorry, Jonathan, I don't have any. I don't smoke."

Olivia spun on me, her positive agent demeanor momentarily shattered. "What do you mean you don't smoke?"

"I gave it up, oh, about six months ago."

"You gave up smoking?" The astonishment was plain on her face.

"Yeah."

"You?"

"Liv, it's not like it was heroin." I bummed a cigarette off a show regular and gave it to Warsheim.

"Well, you sure as hell acted like it was heroin whenever I suggested you give it up."

Anxious not to repeat the uncomfortable exchanges of our marriage, I turned to Warsheim and asked. "What do you think of the show?"

"So far, I like it. It has a highly regional focus, but I'm always amazed that doesn't prevent a show from appealing to a broader audience."

"True," Taylor added. "After all, how many people have adored *Porgy and Bess* for the last century, without ever having set foot in Charleston?"

We chatted a few more minutes while Jonathan finished his cigarette. Afterwards, I slipped him another bottle of meritage, and they returned to their seats.

Intermission went twenty minutes longer than normal, but finally the audience was all back inside. The curtain went up, and we rocketed into the second act.

By now, word of Warsheim and Hirsch's presence had made its way to the cast, who had immediately galvanized from edgy into manic. They were putting on a very good show, and the audience couldn't tell a thing, but I had the sense they were trying awfully hard. And, in a sense, I guess they were. For all practical purposes, this was the audition of their lives.

Finally, Cheryl made her entrance. She had teased her hair up and out into a great-big parody of her normal look. She played her role more than perky; she played it like she had consumed nine espressos. She did a marvelous job of spinning to look into the audience like she was looking into a camera each time she delivered one of her lines, and the audience ate it up. The lines themselves seemed to work better than what I had taken out, but it was hard for me to calibrate whether they were truly better or if the audience was reacting to her (and the free alcohol). Regardless, she was a hit.

I was backstage when Cheryl exited her scene. She came running up and hugged me, squealing. I gestured with my finger for her to be quiet since the audience could hear, and she rolled her eyes and immediately quieted down. "Sorry," she whispered. "I got a laugh! Did you see? I got a laugh?"

"You got *several* laughs. You were awesome."

She noticed the camera over my shoulder, and immediately adopted a more professional demeanor. Looking straight into the lens, she whispered "Giddy Cheryl gets cut from the story. We'll use this instead." She paused, and then continued, "I've just come off the stage and I didn't die. More importantly, I did it in front of Broadway producers. And most importantly, the audience laughed when they were supposed to." She nodded at the camera guy, and he switched it off.

"Technically, they're off-Broadway producers."

"Your average Atlantan won't know that. Hey, I've got some interview questions to run with you after the show."

"Sure. We'll do it on the stage. I've got champagne for you and the cast anyhow."

Thirty minutes later, she was back on stage with the rest of the cast, taking her bows. The audience was on its feet as she came through the curtain, and there were three curtain calls.

The audience came spilling out of the theater happy. I sidelined Liv, Warsheim and Hirsch and invited them to come have drinks with us onstage while I answered some interview questions. Leaving the front of the house to Chris (along with the responsibility to get everyone out and the door locked), I led the three of them backstage and began introducing Warsheim and Hirsch to the cast.

Once the audience was out, we raised the curtain and Cheryl set up her cameras so she could interview several of us. She also asked Hirsch and Warsheim if they would be interviewed. Hirsch said no, but Warsheim was happy to comply. In a very few minutes, we were arranged at different places on the set, and she started asking questions.

Turning to Klein first, she got the basics: his name, his real job, his character's name and description. She then did the same with most of the rest of the cast, as well as Miranda.

Turning to me, she asked, "Okay, Donovan Ford. We've spent a lot of time with you so far, so let me ask you this first. Tonight was the premiere of Tamara Oncamera. How do you think the character works?"

"I actually think she works quite well," I replied. "It may have been the expert casting, but I'm quite happy with it. This role replaces a couple of lines I never liked, and it works much better than what I took out."

"Is it safe to say that the show is still evolving?"

"Definitely. Hopefully the show will always keep evolving."

She then turned to Warsheim. "Jonathan Warsheim, you're one of the hottest producers in New York right now. What brought you all the way to Atlanta to see Highlands-A-Go-Go?"

Warsheim, who was seated on the edge of the stage, took a sip of his champagne and smiled. "My partner, Taylor Hirsch, and I have been looking for a new show to start work on this spring. Donovan's show was suggested as a possibility by a mutual friend so we flew down with her to check it out."

"And how do you think the show fared?'

A gleam reached his eye, "At the risk of undermining any negotiation leverage I have, I think it's safe to say we saw enough tonight to keep us interested."

She went on to get another ten or fifteen minutes of interview questions. Afterwards, Hirsch sat alone in the audience, scribbling furiously into a notebook, and Warsheim went to spend more time in the midst of the adoring attention of the cast. I started to cross the stage to talk to Olivia, but she had connected with Cheryl, and had led her aside. She seamed to be whispering intently to her, so I decided not to interrupt. I thought she also handed over an envelope, but I wasn't sure. At a loss for someone to talk to or something to do, I came down off the stage and crossed to the back of the theater where Laine, Chris, Rachel, and Zach all sat waiting.

It took about ten minutes for everyone to break up and start to move towards the exit. I had hoped to have a few minutes to talk to Cheryl, but as soon as they reached the door, Liv grabbed me by the arm and whispered in my ear, "Drive us back to the Four Seasons, and then come inside and have a drink with us in the bar."

I did as instructed, driving them back to the hotel on Fourteenth Street, all of us chatting amiably about the evening. As I pulled into the driveway, Liv said "Van, won't you come have a drink with us before going home?"

"Sure, I'd love to if you don't mind the company."

"No, please join us," Taylor added showing more enthusiasm than at any other point in the evening. I left the car with the valet, and we four found our way to the bar on the mezzanine of the hotel. We settled into four club chairs just far enough from the piano to be able to engage in conversation. I ordered a glass of wine, and Taylor seconded it. Jonathan ordered a dirty martini, so Liv did as well.

Once we had our drinks, an expectant pause descended on the crowd. Liv broke it. "Well gents, what do you think? Are you interested in the show?"

Taylor flipped open his notebook. As soon as the topic of business came up, and an interesting metamorphosis took place. Whereas in the theater Jonathan was all talk and energy, now Taylor became much more animated, and Jonathan became much more sedate and contemplative.

"Let's cut to the chase first," Taylor said, taking a sip of his wine, his eyes sparkling. "It's a great show and it's got some potential. There's a lot about it that could get backing, but there would also have to be some changes."

"Backing?" I said, confused.

"If we are going to bring a show to Broadway, or even off-Broadway, we have to get backers. Typically Jonathan and I will conduct two or three backers' auditions of different shows, and will produce the one that we can get funding for."

Suddenly it dawned on me how serious having these two men at my show was. Liv wasn't just showing some friends a show that they might enjoy; she was doing what an agent was supposed to. She was actively selling me.

I suddenly felt that old familiar inner-vertigo as the potential of failure stared me in the face again. I made an effort to ensure it did not reach my eyes.

"What kind of changes would you want to see?" Liv asked, stirring her martini with a skewer of impaled olives.

"Well...the whole Yankee in the South concept has a very *Connecticut Yankee in King Arthur's Court* vibe, but Buzz doesn't actually accomplish anything in the show. In Atlanta, Buzz provides a witty counterpoint for the stereotypes to play off of, but in New York he'd need some kind of quest, something to achieve."

Olivia pulled a small notebook out of her pocket and recorded the thought, "Something to achieve. Got it. What else?"

"The songs are all great, but the score as a whole is a little too insular. There needs to be at least one song about the outside perception of the south to offer counterpoint for the audience."

"Counterpoint song. Where would you put it?"

"Early on. Probably right as soon as Buzz comes on stage."

Liv looked at me. "There's not a song right there already, is there?"

I shook my head. "Not immediately. There's about two pages of dialogue that serves as the intro for the song about pronunciations, 'The Proper Pronunciation of Ponce.'"

"That's right. So a song could be crammed in there. What other changes?"

Taylor continued to study the notebook and ran his hand through his hair. "Y'know, most of my notes are about how it would be staged. I guess the biggest change beyond giving Buzz a quest thing would be if you could make the stereotype characters broader."

"Broader?" I asked.

"Yeah." He closed the notebook and looked at me over his wine. "The stereotypes are very powerful in the South, but the rest of the world isn't as versed in them. But, the rest of the world knows southern celebrities who are those stereotypes. The entire world knows Dixie Carter and Ted Turner and…oh, I dunno, Oprah, maybe. They know they are southern, but they don't know the southern stereotypes well enough to pigeonhole them.

"But, if you broaden the characters, say base Mercer Oglethorpe on someone like Rue McClanahan and label her, then the show becomes more timeless."

"The word label makes me a little nervous," I said.

"Don't let it. Once something can be defined, it is no longer threatening. A hundred years ago, no one outside of Jews knew what a yenta or a schmuck was. A few writers starting slipping Yiddish into some shows, they defined the matchmaker character, and by the time the *Fiddler on the Roof* came out in the sixties, half of Middle-America knew Yiddish labels and their corresponding stereotypes even if they had never met a Jew in their lives."

Jonathan piped in. "And, if you label and broaden the characters, you can rotate celebrity parodies into the roles as different celebrities are timely. It makes the entire show timeless because you can always reinvent it by just changing how the character is played, without having to rewrite it."

Liv fixed me in a hard, intense stare that only I would have recognized. She was challenging me. "You can make these changes, can't you?"

I shrugged to indicate that my manhood was not on the line. (At least, I hope that's how it came across. I was feeling a little queasy.) "Sure. The broadening of the characters is the hardest part, but that's more from the need to invent some labels."

Jonathan winked at me. "The labels are probably already there. You just need to ask the locals. I suspect giving Buzz more of a storyline is going to be harder."

Taylor leaned forward. "How quickly could you make the changes and have a new script to us?"

"Uh, three weeks maybe for the basic script, four with the song."

Taylor laid his hand on my knee. "If you can make it two weeks for script and song, we'll definitely consider it for the January backers' audition."

I swallowed hard. "I can have it written that fast, but it won't have been tested with the audience. I'd need…"

"We don't care whether it's been tested for this audience. You're writing for our audience now."

The following Monday night, several of my gang gathered around Laine's small, ancient color television to watch Cheryl Higgins' report.

"When are you going to get a larger TV?" Zach asked as he settled on the floor in front of the couch.

"A larger television would only encourage me to watch it more," Laine retorted from her chaise, stirring her drink idly.

"What's wrong with that?"

"Oh, now you've done it," Brit lamented.

"Television is a drug," Laine began. Brit and I immediately picked up her litany and recited it along with her, word for word. "It exists to provide boring people with the illusion that they lead fascinating lives. I prefer to actually experience a fascinating life, rather than live it by proxy."

On the tube, a deeply botoxed weatherman that I didn't recognize explained that our chances for a white Christmas were practically nil. The door opened and Chris and Rachel arrived, carrying pizza boxes.

"Did we miss it?" Chris asked, handing the pizza boxes to Charles and then pulling off his black leather jacket.

"Not yet," Brit replied. "They've done thirty-five teasers for it though."

The pizza boxes were spread out on the floor and we busied ourselves passing out slices to everyone while the newscaster relayed the story of the latest Hollywood starlet who was melting down in front of the paparazzi.

"Why do they always put the reporters out on the street, even when they're are nowhere near the story?" Chris asked, reaching for a second slice of chicken-bianca-oregonata. "I mean, this story is about a rehab-bound bimbo in Hollywood. Why put the reporter on the corner of Peachtree and twenty-fifth?"

"It shows that they are out, sniffing down the facts for the story," Rachel replied.

"Pffah. Somehow I think this is my tax money at work."

"Shhh," Laine instructed. "Here it is."

On the screen, they cut to a live shot of Cheryl standing in front of the theater. "Thanks, Carol. I'm here in front of Theater DeLaine where, Friday night, I got to be part of the ever-evolving show *Highlands-A-Go-Go*." They cut to some video clips of earlier stories and she quickly recapped the history of the show and all the controversy so far.

"She should not wear argyle onscreen," Laine observed.

The back-story concluded and they cut to a shot of me sitting at my desk talking. "So, after all the publicity," she said through a voiceover, "Donovan Ford agreed to be interviewed."

The shot cut to her. "Mr. Ford, rumors have been swirling that your new character, Uncle Preacher, is based on Reverend Dean Reeder, and that you sit in this office and write down his sermons to incorporate in the show. Care to comment?"

"*Highlands-A-Go-Go* is a story based on life in the South. The absence of a southern preacher was a pretty big miss on my part in the original script. Reverend Reeder is a case in point; the South takes religion seriously. So, we went back and added the character. The timing is coincidental.

"As to whether we sit in here and write down what he says, that's false. Every member of the cast has their own warm-up routine, and the actor who plays Uncle Preacher does his warm-ups in this office."

"And what's your warm-up tradition?" Higgins asked me.

"Sitting at this desk and praying."

They cut back to the Higgins live shot. "Well, I had an opportunity to see first-hand how the cast prepares when Mister Ford invited me to play another character he's added to the show, a news reporter named Tamara Oncamera."

The story followed her through rehearsal, showing several good shots of her working through her lines with Miranda. They showed several seconds of her on stage, and the applause at the end.

"Now, for the record, my appearance seemed to be well received. But then again, there was an open bar that night, thanks to the theater's owner, DeLaine Wagner Fairchild, in response to a protest from a few neighbors which blocked their liquor license application."

They rolled the film of Talbot coming through door. Unfortunately they did not omit her opinion of Archer Bellamy, save for bleeping the word asshole.

"When I went down there to file this week's permit application, he was there with a camera crew and a petition." Talbot screamed from the television. I glanced at the live version of Talbot next to me, and she raised her glass to me and winked. "As soon as I submitted the permit, he cuts in front of me and hands the clerk a petition that he says is from the neighborhood, asking that the city *not* issue a permit. Well, of course this hourly city hall clerk doesn't know what to do, so she calls her supervisor who sees the cameras, panics, and shuts the office down. We've got no alcohol permit for the next week."

There was a cut to Laine announcing, "No matter. We're sold out for the next week. We don't need a cash bar. Until we can get this resolved, the drinks next week will simply be on me."

"Missus Fairchild," Cheryl asked on tape. "Are you suggesting that alcohol is a necessary part of attending theater in the Highlands?"

"Not at all, dear. Good theater doesn't require alcohol. I've attended many fine shows in church basements that only served lemonade. But let's be honest. It *doesn't hurt*, either."

Cheryl Higgins live came back to the screen. "However, the liquor controversy didn't keep away some pretty important guests. New York producers Taylor Hirsch and Jonathan Warsheim showed up tonight to scout out the show for production on Broadway."

They showed Hirsch and Warsheim arriving, and then cut to the interview after the show. "And how do you think the show fared?' Cheryl asked Warsheim.

"At the risk of undermining any negotiation leverage I have, I think it's safe to say we saw enough tonight to keep us interested."

The shot returned to the live shot. "For the record, Warsheim was not interested in me going to Broadway. That aside, the *Highlands-A-Go-Go* controversy doesn't look like it will be going away any time soon.

"Live from Virginia Highland, I'm Cheryl Higgins."

Brit reached over and turned down the volume.

"You know," Talbot observed taking a sip of her wine while picking the green olives off her pizza. "I think you can get away with defaming a fundy idiot on television as long as you wear something with a deep neckline. Next time, I'll show a hint of nipple and all will be well."

I got my wish. The story certainly drove sales. We sold out for another four weeks, and we extended the run again into mid-March. While I worried the cast would get exhausted, they were thrilled. I should have focused more on them, but I was painfully aware that I had two weeks to completely rewrite my show.

Miranda was, of course, wild about the prospect of getting to stage a backer's audition and possibly sell the show. She was a professional; she faced failure every single performance. I, however, was terrified.

Meanwhile, all around me people were focused on Christmas and indifferent to my plight.

We sequestered ourselves in my office, trying desperately to *expand* our story and *label* our characters. We had, through many hours of web surfing and much negotiation, found real-life people who matched our archetypes. Having completed that, we scrubbed the dialogue to ensure the lines and character traits were spot. Unfortunately, Buzz was not that easy.

As a sort of New Yorker everyman, Buzz was hard to model. He wasn't based on me, but he might as well have been. No real-life personality fit him perfectly because he was, essentially, one-dimensional. He didn't really grow during the show, and so we didn't know how to expand him. And so the week wound out in frustration as we tried many different approaches to define and broaden him.

We tried writing his back-story, but we couldn't agree on his educational level, his family, his politics, or even his sexual orientation.

We tried each defining his character separately and then comparing results. Essentially, instead of defining Buzz, we defined Klein.

We even, in a moment of desperation tried drawing him. We don't need to go into the results, save to say that Miranda knows relatively little about male anatomy.

The week ticked on towards our deadline. Loud, defiant ticks that I thought I could actually hear as I lay awake at night looking for inspiration.

As the two of us toiled away in that office, we could not have been more different. She was bright, perky, and upbeat; I was blocked, sullen, and morose. On the twenty-third, as Christmas music drifted in through the open window, I commented that she must feel like Bob Cratchit to my Scrooge.

She chuckled. "Hate to tell you, but it's more like you're the Grinch and I'm Max, the dog."

I laughed, seeing the truth in the observation. "Assuming of course the Grinch, after his redemption, began working in musical theater."

She laughed harder. "Musical theater in the heart of Virginia-Wholand."

"'All the whos down in Virginia-Wholand liked show tunes a lot!'"

She snorted. I continued.

"'But the Grinch, who wrote them, found he was blocked.'"

She groaned. "Bad, bad rhyme. No more."

Unfortunately, I have a horrible malady: once I start talking in rhyming meter, I can't stop. I kept talking in mostly iambic pentameter until she gratefully escaped downstairs to start preparation for the show.

Rhyming all your sentences does nothing to relieve anxiety.

December 24 rolled around the next morning, more or less according to schedule. We were no closer to having the script ready to go to Warsheim and Hirsch. The theater would be dark that night, and until the 26th, and Miranda and I had to take a break. She hadn't done any Christmas shopping and was certain that was responsible for inhibiting her muse. I wasn't sure what was inhibiting mine. So I decided to stay away from the theater and spent my day getting ready for Christmas. After all, I had presents to wrap.

I devoted the early part of the morning to being sullen and wrapping presents. Most of my gifts were fairly mundane, but I had a great gift to give Laine. Brit had designed a tricked-out nametag for her and had connected me to a friend of hers at Worthmore Jewelers who produced it for me.

When I had the gifts finished, I carried them downstairs to Laine's apartment and put them under the tree.

"You're just in time, dear," I heard her call from the kitchen.

"Just in time for what?" I called back. "I didn't think you knew where the kitchen was."

I entered from the dining room to see her unloading a couple dozen bottles from the dishwasher. "Spare me the sarcasm," she replied. "Just because my heart is not centered in the kitchen doesn't mean I've never been in here."

"What are you doing?"

"Making liqueurs."

"Liqueurs?"

"Specifically, Irish crème."

"And, um, why?"

"It's Christmas, dear." She pulled a couple of cans of condensed milk and an enormous bottle of Jameson's from the cabinet over the refrigerator.

"And…"

She looked at me as though I was an idiot. "This is what I give everyone for Christmas."

"Irish crème?"

"Sometimes. Sometimes I make limoncello; sometimes I make peach vodka. This year it's Irish crème." She began to measure instant coffee into a bowl. "So much more original than cookies, don't you think?"

"Can't argue with your thinking," I replied, and came to stand next to her. "What can I do?"

I expected her to tell me to break eggs, or fill bottles, but instead she said, "Go downstairs and talk to Zach."

"How does that help make Irish crème?" I asked dully.

"It gets you out of my way." She began breaking eggs into a bowl. "Besides, he's having a rough time of things, and needs to talk."

I started to ask how she knew, and then thought better of it. She knew all. Obediently, I left the apartment and descended to Zach's basement digs. I rapped on the door.

"Mmm."

"Zach?"

"Yeah." There was not much enthusiasm in his voice.

"Can I come in?"

There was along silence. I tried the knob. The door was unlocked so I pushed it open slightly. "Dude?"

The lights were off, but a few candles were burning on the windowsill and his desk. He lay on his futon, staring at the ceiling. He pulled off his iPod headset, and I could hear Mimsy and the Marauders playing through them. "You okay?"

He shrugged.

"You wanna talk?"

"Nothing really to talk about."

I was a little bit at a loss for something to say. "Laine is making Irish crème."

"What's Irish crème?"

"Bailey's, basically."

He smirked slightly. "She's making liquor?"

I walked inside and shut the door behind me. "It's her form of holiday baking. It's why she's never asked to bring anything to church bake-sales."

He stared at me for a long moment. "Did you want something?"

"To check on you."

"I'm fine, Van. The holidays just get me down."

I crossed over to the futon. "What can we do about it?'

He pulled himself up on one arm. "*Do* about it? Nothing. I'll be fine when the holidays are over."

"Why wait?"

He rolled his eyes. "I swear if you start singing 'We Need a Little Christmas,' I'll go off on your ass."

"I'm not going to sing. I'm going to get you out of here."

"To where?"

I had no idea. Unbidden, the mental image of Rockefeller Center drifted through my head. "Let's go ice skating."

He flopped back. "No."

"Yep." I pulled his sneakers out from under the futon and dropped them on his chest. "Let's go."

"I don't want to." I stuffed his left foot into his sneaker roughly. "Ow."

"Look, I know you want to sit down here and feel sorry for yourself," I told him as I tied the shoe. "I plan to knot your laces."

"Stop. I have every reason to feel sorry for myself."

"Don't disagree," I replied, installing the threatened knot. "You have every reason to. But Zach, honestly?" I glanced around. "Haven't you spent enough holidays sitting alone in a basement feeling sorry for yourself?"

He sat up and glanced around. "It's a much nicer basement this year," he said, dubiously.

"Upgrading the basement is not an improvement to the situation." I stood up and threw his other shoe into his lap. "Let's go."

He looked at the knot I had put in his left shoe. "You ass."

I had no idea where to find an ice rink, so I Googled it quickly from his laptop. "There's a rink in Centennial Park." A few minutes later, we were in the Jeep, driving south. He continued to work the knot in his shoe.

"So," he began, "we've established I'm morbidly depressed. What about you? How are you handling your first Christmas away from Liv?"

I was surprised he asked. "Technically, it's my second. We were separated last year."

"How did you handle it?"

"Being alone at Christmas? Mostly, I drank. Not the most healthy way to deal with it, but there you have it."

He was silent a long time. I pulled up to Centennial Park and parked. We walked across the park towards the rink. I sensed he wanted me to ask. "How did you handle it?"

He shrugged. "I worked as much as I could. Being the holidays, there was always somebody who needed you to work an extra shift for them."

We walked up to the skate rental place and rented skates. As we sat on a bench putting them on, I ventured, "So working a lot would cover everything up until Christmas Eve."

"Uh yup."

We walked carefully to the rink and stepped on. Because I played hockey when I was a kid, it always comes back to me pretty easily. Zach was a little more tenuous. "So then," I asked, gliding around and coming up next to him, "What did you do Christmas Eve and Christmas Day?"

"Sat alone in the theater," he replied flatly.

"That's all?"

"What else was there to do?" he asked sourly.

"I dunno. There's a church about fifty feet away. There are homeless shelters."

"Pfah. Do you really think I was in the mood for God at that point?"

I love the feel of being on skates. I circled him again as we started around the rink. It wasn't Rockefeller Center, but it was just as fun. There were people all around us. Young parents with young kids, teenagers, several figure skater wannabes. The smell of hot dogs was in the air from a lone vendor cart. Christmas carols were playing.

It felt a little like Christmas.

I turned and skated backwards for a few moments, staring at him. He was not at all comfortable on the skates, and his face was furrowed into a frown. "Okay, so that sounds like a couple of pretty crappy Christmases. What about now? Why are you still in a bad mood now?"

He rolled his eyes at me. "Um, still don't have a family…"

"You have all of us."

"Let's see. Rachel's heading home to her parents this afternoon. Chris is flying tonight and will lay over in Miami so he can see his mom. Jen is spending Christmas with Harry…."

"And you are spending it with us."

"Van, I appreciate what you are trying to do, but…"

At that moment, he lost his balance and fell backwards onto the ice. "Dammit! Why are we doing this anyhow?" he asked, with no small amount of derision in his voice.

I was transported back for a moment to a Christmas party Liv and I had attended many years ago, when she was in a particularly foul mood. The playwright Paul Rudnick had been there and they knew each other slightly. He spent a bit of time trying to tease her out of her bad mood, to no avail. All it did was give focus to her bad mood, and I don't believe she ever quite liked him afterwards. I always thought he had her in mind when he was later quoted as saying, "The only real blasphemy is the deliberate refusal to experience joy."

Zach was angry at life, and too absorbed in his anger to see what was going on around him. There was nothing I could say to put him in a better mood. So, I checked him into the boards. He went back down on the ice. "What the hell was that for?!?"

"You are acting like my ex-wife."

He stood back up. "And so you slammed her around? No wonder she divorced you."

I skated behind him, grabbed him by the belt, and swung him around. Once I built up a bit of speed, I let him go and sent him flailing off in another direction. In order to miss colliding with an elderly couple, he slammed back into the boards. "Dammit, Van! Knock it off."

I ignored him, electing instead to skate up and shave ice into his face with my blades. "What I learned about Olivia when she was like this," I explained calmly, "is that if she was going to be mad at the entire universe, her bad mood wouldn't go away for a long, long time." I held out my hand to help him up. He stared at it for a minute, then accepted. As soon as he was standing, I started skating backwards. I wouldn't let go of his hand.

"However," I continued, dragging him along without really looking at where I was going, "If I decided to take one for the team, and did something to piss her off, she would transfer all that anger directly on me, and the mood would change much, much quicker."

"Van, slow down. You're going to hit somebody."

I started skating faster. "Tell me which way to go."

"Just stop."

I spun us around and started skating faster in the other direction, this time against the flow of skaters. I grabbed his other hand as well so he couldn't let go.

"Van, c'mon, stop!" There was genuine irritation in his voice.

"Tell me which way to go."

"You're about to hit a kid!"

"Which way?"

"Left!"

I pivoted left and we did one and a half turns before I had us going back in the flow. I was still skating backwards. "Tell me where to go."

I saw what I was looking for. All the irritation, frustration, and unhappiness in his eyes focused directly on me. "Where to go? Go to hell." Instead of being pulled, he started skating hard. I found myself being pushed backwards with no real control. The boards hit me in the lower back, hard, knocking the wind out of me. I went down, dazed. Meanwhile, he skated off.

Gingerly, I made my way off the rink, sat down and began to take my skates off. Twenty minutes later, he arrived back at my side with two cups of cocoa. It was in the low sixties that day, and so not really cocoa weather, but I accepted it anyhow. I could tell the bad mood had broken when he said idly as he slipped off his left skate, "Y'know, I always really wanted a brother."

Christmas Eve was a quiet affair, due in part to the fact that Laine's Irish crème quality-control process required her to consume about a bottle and a half herself. It was just Laine, Brit, Charles, Zach, and

I. The early part of the evening involved wrapping the Irish crème and adding a Christmas card to it. Then, once the sun had set, we set out with a number of big bags and delivered them. First to every apartment in the building, except Mr. Kersey's, and then to homes in the neighborhood. We dropped off two at the rectory of the Church of Our Savior, and one was even given to the sax player. Then, we returned to the apartment, and sat around eating carry-out Thai.

Laine threw us out at ten, so Charles and Brit returned home. I thought of my laptop across the street, waiting for me to come give my show a new ending, but I still had nothing. And, I could tell Zach didn't want to be alone.

He had been very engaged in the evening, and there was no trace of the bad mood from earlier. His earlier comment about a brother rang true with me. Not that I didn't love Brit, but I had always wanted a brother as well. We were standing in the lobby and he was staring at me with a happy, slightly hopeful expression.

"Go get on some pajamas and come upstairs," I told him.

"Pajamas?"

"Yeah. It's Christmas. Santa doesn't visit if you are dressed in jockey shorts."

He looked confused, but shrugged and went downstairs. I climbed up to my apartment, changed into a pair of pajama bottoms and a t-shirt, and pulled out a pillow and a blanket. I spread them on the couch, and then pulled a small travel-size Scrabble game out and set it up on the floor.

When he arrived, I was opening my bottle of Irish crème so I could add it to the cocoa I had warming in the microwave. He was wearing a pair of sweatpants and a tank top. He glanced at the game on the floor. "Scrabble?"

"Yep," I replied, pouring the crème into the cups. "I plan to kick your ass in Scrabble before we go to bed."

He smirked. "You're pretty damn confident in yourself, aren't you?"

I shrugged, "I'm a writer."

"What's with the couch?"

"You're sleeping there tonight." He raised his eyebrows as I handed him his cup. "You've spent enough Christmas Eves in the basement."

I climbed up to my loft and Zach lay down on the couch at about midnight, but he was in the mood to talk, so I didn't actually go to sleep until two. I didn't sleep particularly well. I thought of the script as I was drifting off, and so images of the show kept sliding through my head all night long, punctuated with images of Olivia.

I was awoken way too early by Brit bounding in the front door. (Somehow, I had never succeeding in getting her key back from her.) "Wake up! Wake up!" she cried out as the door burst open. "It's Christmas!"

I rolled over and looked at my clock. Eight-thirty. I groaned. Over the years I had forgotten exactly how much she loved Christmas morning. She ran up the stairs and sat, bouncing on my bed. "Get up, Van! It's Christmas!"

"Won't it still be Christmas in an hour?" I asked.

"Not as much." She pulled the covers off of me. Reluctantly, I got up. Zach was up and standing with a bright expression on his face by the front door. The three of us descended to Christmas morning at Laine's.

There were a number of presents underneath the tree. I glanced at the gift tags and immediately got choked up. When our mother was still alive, but after the divorce, no Christmas gift was ever signed "Love, Mom." Instead, they were all signed with celebrity names. So, a CD might say "To Van, From Stevie Wonder," or sweater box might proclaim, "For my darling Brit, love Madeleine Albright."

All of Laine's gifts were signed the same way. As per family tradition Zach, being the youngest, had to pass out the gifts. He read the tags as he did so.

"Brit, from Tallulah Bankhead. Who was Tallulah Bankhead?"

Laine rolled her eyes. "The quality of education today. Just pass out the gifts."

"Charles, from Gladstone."

"Brilliant," Charles observed. "Gladstone has been dead for, what, a hundred and twenty years? I'm not impressed with your American postal service."

"Van, from Neil Simon."

"How nice. And I thought Olivia got him in the divorce settlement."

We opened the gifts and cooed or exclaimed as appropriate over each. We then had an immense breakfast. As soon as the dishes were cleared away, we began preparation of a more immense dinner. I tried to bury myself in my cooking and not think of my impending deadline and lack of idea for how to end the show. It didn't work. I was edgy all afternoon.

Chris arrived home from his trip at five, and came directly to the apartment, still in uniform, so as not to miss dinner. Jen was also there. She had just enough time to eat before opening the bar. We dined on roast turkey, brandied fruit cocktail, freshly made bread, whipped potatoes, wilted head lettuce, and many, many other things that I can no longer remember. Dessert was this complex pudding affair that was some sort of Charleston tradition.

After dinner was eaten and the dishes were done, everyone in the building quietly retired to their apartments in an l-triptophan coma. I hadn't eaten much because of my nervousness and anxiety, so I decided to go for a walk. I tried to get Zach to go with me, but the allure of seeing the gifts Chris had received from his mother was greater. So, around nine o'clock I let myself out into the cool night air alone. Around the corner, I could hear a small group of carolers singing "Good King Wenceslas." The local sax player accompanied them quietly from the square.

Across the street, Reeder sat alone in his vigil. He looked cold and, perhaps, a bit defeated.

Some of the bars on the street were open, and there were a few patrons there, recovering from the stresses of the holidays and over-exposure to families. I contemplated walking around to Fontaine's and spending time keeping Jennifer company. Then I remembered that Harry was going to be there, doing just that. I wasn't in the mood to debate pirates.

I glanced at Reeder. Around the corner the choir sang, "Therefore, Christian men, be sure/Wealth or rank possessing/Ye who now will bless the poor/Shall yourselves find blessing."

My mother came, unbidden, to my mind. I knew what she would expect of me.

My mother is still a painful memory. She had been a long-term survivor of breast cancer who had suddenly, unexpectedly died of a heart attack. Having lived for almost fifteen years fighting and winning against cancer, she had developed a generous, profoundly grateful approach to life. She was not a simple woman by any stretch of the imagination, but she lived her life by three simple tenets, which were on a small sign that hung in her kitchen.

Trust God.

Help others.

Clean house.

I guess she believed that as long as God saw you tending to others as well as your waxy yellow buildup, you could rely on Him to do right by you. She tried heroically to install some sense of spirituality in Brit and me, but it never really took with me until after her death. The idea of trusting God seemed metaphorical at best. Helping others in my circles in New York was pretty much confined to getting friends through their divorces or checked into rehab as necessary.

I glanced at Reeder again. I have no use for false piety, but my mother was a stronger influence. I noticed that the coffeehouse behind him was open. I decided I needed coffee. I made my way across the intersection.

Since there was no one to preach to, he was sitting alone on the hood of his truck, candle lit, reading the Bible quietly. I was aiming for the coffeehouse, but somehow found myself standing in front of him instead. He looked up from his book and stared at me, expressionless, over the tops of his steel-frame glasses.

"Merry Christmas, Rev."

The vaguest hint of a smile crossed his face. "Merry Christmas, Mister Ford."

"I was on my way to get a latte. Would you let me buy you a coffee as well?

I saw a flicker of wariness cross his eyes for a second, replaced a moment later by an openness. Perhaps he heard his mother lecturing him someplace as well. "Thank you. That's certainly not necessary, but it is cold out here tonight."

"It is," I confirmed. "How do you like it?"

"Just a little cream. No sweetener."

"Regular?"

"Decaf."

I nodded and stepped past him into the coffeehouse. It was empty apart from a barista who seemed to be in good cheer despite working alone on the holiday. I ordered a latte for myself and a large decaf for Reeder. The latte took a minute, so I added cream to his coffee and then, on a whim, picked up a travel mug from the display next to the coffee condiments. I poured his coffee into the travel mug, took it back to the counter and paid for it all.

I returned to the street and handed him the mug. He looked at it and said, "I know the Highlands is upscale, but this surely is not what they serve coffee in, is it?"

I laughed. "Consider it a Christmas present."

"A Christmas present for me?" He grinned.

"I felt motivated by the season. Besides, it's the least I could do. I may not agree with you, but you've been good for my business."

He shrugged in a manner that indicated to me that he did indeed know that. "Well, I thank you."

We gave each other a little mock toast, and then he sipped the drink. I made no move to leave, although I knew I probably should. He smiled approvingly at the coffee and gave me a little wink.

"Can I ask you what you don't agree with?"

"I feel that you're a pawn of Archer Bellamy. That this whole thing is more about asserting control over the lives of others rather than some real religious fervor."

"I see. But that's not really disagreeing with me, is it? That's disagreeing with Archer Bellamy."

"Fair."

"So why do you disagree with me?"

"Well, you're the active player in this, aren't you? I mean Archer may be the instigator but you're playing along."

"True. I am."

"Well, okay then."

"But, to disagree with me, wouldn't you need to know my motivation?"

That had never occurred to me. "Do I? I've disagreed with people my entire life without knowing or caring why they were wrong; I just thought they were."

"A wise man once said you can never really know another until you've walked in his shoes. So, you may disagree, but you are not doing it from an informed point of view."

I looked into his eyes. There was a worldliness there that I had not suspected. "Fine. Then let me ask you; what motivates you to insert yourself in this battle Archer Bellamy is waging against my poor little theater?"

He laughed heartily. "Your *poor little theater?* You mean the poor little theater that has extended the run of this show through March and received national media attention?"

I smirked, caught up in the humor. "So, I'm winning. So what?"

"Would that all of us could be so poor and little. Seems to me God sent me here just to help guarantee you a profit."

"If He did, I owe Him a nice thank-you note. But you haven't answered my question."

He took another sip of his coffee. "Donovan, I'm here because I need to be here. The battle is between you and Archer. Yes, he's the one who invited me here, but my motivation has nothing to do with your theater. Simply stated, I'm here for the attention."

I was so taken aback by has candor, I did not have a meaningful response. "Well, all right then."

"Let me explain. Yes, I am here, doing Archer's dirty work because he is too wealthy and too politically connected in that God-awful monstrosity he calls a church to actually soil his hands. But be clear on something, Archer was going to fight this war with or without me. If it wasn't me, he would have found some other preacher to do it."

"Hardly a noble motivation."

"Well, I haven't really talked about my motivation yet. If you listen to what I've been saying out here, yes, I am preaching against alcohol on Sunday. But that is an example of a larger message I'm trying to get across. I'm preaching against the secularization of life, of a life without God."

I let that sink in for a minute. "Say more."

"Look, let's be honest, no matter what any church has said, there's always been drinking on Sundays and holy days. The difference being that secular life and religious life could cohabitate. But the world has changed in the last forty years. It's all about the secular, and God has been marginalized, if He's allowed admittance to people's lives at all.

"I have nothing against your show, Donovan, but let's be honest. We've been good for each other. I helped your sales, and in the meantime I've had a forum to get my message across. And that message is: give God equal time."

"But that's not what you are saying. You're advocating an imbalance in the other direction."

He shrugged. "Rhetoric. The way you achieve a middle ground in this country is by pitching the extremes."

"But that doesn't answer me. Why here? Why me?"

"Why you?" He laughed aloud again. "Oh, yes. Why poor you? Why did God inflict His messenger on you and punish you by driving ticket sales?"

He pointed a bony finger towards the center of my chest. "Donovan Ford, be very clear on something. I'm an opportunist in the name of God. All I want is the world to remember Him and keep Him in the forefront.

"Archer Bellamy is a small-minded bigot with deep pockets. He was going to put a preacher on your front step whether you wanted it or not. You should be thanking God that it was me, rather some far more fundamentalist wingnut like Fred Phelps and his *God Hates Fags* message."

I wanted to respond, but didn't have an answer. My head was swimming. I took a sip of the coffee and thought. After a moment, he laid a hand on my shoulder.

"Donovan, there are no chance meetings. The saying that God works in mysterious ways is not a metaphor. It's the truth." I could see a light in his eyes, a genuine conviction he believed with all his heart that God moved with him and through him everyday. "There are no chance meetings. You found your way to this theater and this moment in time because you needed to learn something. I don't know what it is that you needed to learn, but God does and He has set challenges in your path so that you might learn it. I, apparently, am one of those challenges. But please know that no challenge comes without a gift."

For the first moment, the first time, I saw the last year in perspective. Hell, I saw the last ten years in perspective. Everything had led me to this moment, to this place in time. And yes, at that moment, I saw Reverend Reeder as a blessing.

"Oh God," I complained. "How trite."

He took a step back, stunned. "What?"

"I'm a New Yorker. I'm too sophisticated to experience an epiphany on Christmas night."

He laughed, a long, loud, rich laugh. It resonated across the otherwise quiet intersection. "I daresay more sophisticated men than you have had more dramatic epiphanies. Besides, you're a writer. Sometimes the obvious gag is just fine."

He held out his hand and I shook it. "Merry Christmas, Mister Ford."

"Merry Christmas, Reverend Reeder."

With that, I left him to his vigil and I walked towards the 'Hurst. The carolers were gone now, but the sax player still sat on the corner, playing "Amazing Grace." On a whim, I rounded the corner instead and walked up the block.

At the north end of the village is a small, red brick church complex. It's an Episcopal church. I had been raised Lutheran, but hadn't set foot in a church in years. On a whim, I walked into the courtyard between the two buildings where a crèche was set up. I looked down at the small trio of figures and reflected on the sheer amount of crap that had occurred in the last few centuries in God's name. It had never, ever occurred to me that those horrible things could contain blessings. The cynic inside of me would not admit the possibility.

And it was at that moment that I realized I was no longer a cynic. Perhaps it was the divorce, or Laine, or my new friends, or the theater but for the first time in my life I was unabashedly hopeful. I believed great things were in store for me if I just took a chance. And, despite all my best efforts to muster up sarcasm or a cynical point of view, I could not. For the first time in a long time, perhaps ever, I felt blessed.

And, fighting back the tears that were welling up in my eyes, I started walking towards the theater. I suddenly knew what Buzz's quest was.

I knew how his story ended.

The Forsythia

The new story line about the transformation of Buzz Deloitte from cynic to optimist and the new ending worked very well. Miranda and I worked out all the kinks and did a dry read with the cast and the denizens of the 'Hurst in the days after Christmas. Everyone agreed that the show had matured from satire to story.

And so, on December 31st, at precisely noon, I surrendered the package containing three copies of the new script, a CD recording of all the songs - including the new one - and all my hopes and fears to the United Parcel Service. Deep in my heart, I knew it was a good show. In fact, I knew it was the best piece of work I had ever written, bar none. Before now, even though I had always called myself a writer, I had always felt like I was faking it. I knew I was engaged in hack journalism and I relied on the title to lend me credibility. But, now I felt like an author.

We spent New Year's Eve in the heart of the Highlands. No sense driving someplace to drink when you live in the middle of a bar district. The parties in the various bars spilled over and out onto the sidewalk. Music and laughter poured from every door.

Cheryl Higgins had joined me for the evening, but we were undecided whether to call it a date or not. She was a little nonplussed to discover that the show had been modified without her knowledge, and that I wouldn't cooperate with her if she did a story on the backers' audition. If I got one.

We began the evening, just the two of us, having sushi at Mai Li. The Highlands was still quiet at that point. Then, we met up with Chris and Rachel at Fontaine's at around eight. The bar was only moderately full when we arrived. Within thirty minutes it was packed. Jen did her best to keep our glasses full, but the crowds had her in the weeds. She couldn't really complain, though. She'd pocket almost five grand in tips that night. Still, by eleven, we were starting to feel claustrophobic. I slid Jen a hundred, with the understanding that she would let me know later what I had actually owed her.

We slipped out into the cool evening air, and made our way back to the 'Hurst. It was a few minutes before midnight, so we would be with Laine at the appropriate hour. All of the usual gang crowded onto her balcony with several bottles of Dom Perignon and one pitcher of manhattans. The countdown began across the street at Murphy's but quickly spread to the other bars. Everyone at Laine's joined along with the mandatory counting. At midnight, the sax player was just below the balcony and fired up Auld Lang Syne. I gave Laine a chaste little kiss, and one to Cheryl that maybe was a little less chaste than it should have been.

We all toasted each other, and then I noticed that Laine was not among us. A moment later I saw her down on the street, striding gracefully towards the sax player with a champagne flute and her drink. As soon as he finished the song, she handed him the flute and gave him a prim kiss on the cheek. He smiled, toasted her and they shared a drink. They chatted while he finished it. Then she returned to the building.

I studied the sax player for a moment, realizing I had never really looked at him before. He had white hair and a neatly trimmed van dyke. He always wore an oversized khaki Panama hat and a black vest, although tonight there was a chill in the air so the latter was concealed beneath his jacket. He gazed after my aunt as she walked back to the building, and then his eyes flicked upward and met mine. He touched the brim of his hat, and picked up his instrument.

I was about to ask Laine for particulars but my cell rang. It was Olivia. I answered and forgot all about the sax player.

"Happy New Year."

"Yeah, you too," she replied. I heard nothing in the background leading me to believe that, rather than spend New Years at Phil and Adelle Bracken's like we always did, she had elected to stay home. "I promised myself I would not be a shrewish ex-wife. You see, if I called to verify you had sent the script yesterday, that makes me a shrew. However, it's the next day now, which meets the statute of limitations. So now I'm just a good agent. You did send it, right?"

I laughed. "Yes, my shrew. I did."

"Express?"

"Priority Express."

I heard her sigh. "Okay. Good. Sounds like you're at a party."

"Yeah. Laine's. Just the normal building folks."

"And, by chance, a pretty little size four news reporter?"

"Um, yeah."

"Uh huh. Do me a favor and tell her my hunch has been verified."

"Your what?"

"Just tell her."

We exchanged wishes for a happy new year, and hung up. I walked over to Cheryl, who was perched on the railing watching the spectacle in the street. "Are you in some secret society with my ex-wife?"

She looked at me confused. "Not that I know of. Why?"

"She just called me and asked me to let you know her hunch has been verified."

She raised both her eyebrows. "Really?"

"What's going on?"

She patted me. "Nothing to worry your pretty little head about, dear. She was just helping me with a lead on a story."

"What kind of story?"

She became playfully coy. "Never mind, Mister Secret Backers' Audition. If you've got your secrets, I've got mine."

I shrugged and said playfully, "Eh, FOX will probably beat you to the reveal anyhow."

She looked genuinely indignant and punched me in the arm, hard. I could see pursuing the topic would only end badly so I let it drop.

Three days later, as I was sitting at my desk tallying the December totals, my desk phone rang. Accounting does not come naturally to me by any stretch of the imagination, so it requires all my focus. It was from a phone number I didn't recognize. I briefly considered letting it go to voicemail, but I had tallied the same column of numbers three times with three different results and my frustration was palpable. I picked up the phone and said absently, "Donovan Ford."

"Donovan!" enthused the voice on the other end. "Taylor Hirsch. Happy new year."

I turned away from my column of numbers and immediately the frustration vanished. "Taylor! Happy new year to you as well. How are you? Did you have a good holiday?"

I had noticed that, since moving to Atlanta, I had begun inquiring after people's health and well being immediately after greeting them. Not just people I knew and loved, but strangers like servers and random telemarketers. Most people took it in stride. It annoyed Olivia.

"It was a very nice holiday, thank you. And yours?"

"Lovely. Just lovely." Another word that had joined my vocabulary, unbidden, of late. "What can I do for you?"

"Well, for starters you can plan to have your entire cast up here on Monday, January thirtieth."

"Really!"

"Yes really. Jonathan and I have both gone through the new script and love it. The transformation of Buzz from cynical New Yorker to cynical New Yorker with a positive outlook is perhaps a bit overdone, but your treatment of it is pretty damn original. So, we want to see what it reads like on the boards.

"We're going to have ten investors see the read-through, and we're going to have our production designer fly down and visit the show so he can give us some estimates on production costs. Do you mind if he spends an evening backstage?"

"Not at all. Just have him call me and we'll take care of everything."

"Got it." We discussed a few more particulars and then he added, "Now Van, I've got to warn you; you're up against some pretty stiff competition. We're going to make the investors sit through nine shows, and all of them are pretty good stuff."

I waited for the inner-vertigo to start. It didn't. "No problem. I understand. Hell, I'm just happy you thought it was good enough to get this far."

"Hey, it's definitely good enough for Broadway. At this point, it's just a numbers game."

We chatted some more and then hung up. I glanced at the clock. It was twelve o'clock. Miranda was probably already on her way in, possibly even in the building, but I decided I couldn't wait. I called her cell. I heard it ring out in the auditorium.

"Calling me from the upstairs office? How *very* Flo Zigfield."

"Guess what, Miss Bryce," I replied, slightly embarrassed to admit that I got the *Funny Girl* reference.

"What?"

"We got the audition!"

She screamed. Loudly. Continuously. I heard her steps pounding up the stairs over the screaming. She burst into my office and snared me in a bear hug that hurt my ribs. "When?" She asked, jumping up and down excitedly. "When? When? When?"

"Monday the thirtieth. In New York. The entire cast."

"Dear God, that's a lot of airfare. We're awfully close in. How is the cast going to be able to afford it."

I glanced down at the tally sheet. It had been another good month for us. "I'm willing to kick in my half of the December profits." She looked over my shoulder and then nodded.

"Liz is absolutely going to kill me. This is the best paying gig I've had since Sam was born. But yeah, I'm in."

The news traveled fast. I ran across the street to tell Laine in person, and managed to get Clare as well. Then, I called Liv who had already heard from Hirsch. Meanwhile, Laine beat me to the punch and told Brit, Rachel, and Jennifer before I ever managed to dial the first number. I got Zach only because he was in class and wasn't able to take Laine's call.

Rachel got the word to Chris, who was at work. Within hours all of the Delta flight attendants knew that there was a chance that the show was going to Broadway. (As a result, we enjoyed quite a bit of popularity as a layover diversion for the next several weeks.)

Clare of course called Mac and Brit called Charles, both of whom immediately called me with congratulations. (I don't know who told Mister Kersey, but someone did. There was a one-word congratulatory note and a press photo of Douglas Fairbanks and Mary Pickford standing in front of Pickfair pinned to my door when I got home that night.)

I got the pleasure of telling Reeder, who shook my hand politely lest he be seen being social. Then he whispered with a wink, "Make sure you say a prayer thanking God for punishing your heathen ways by sending me."

Despite several calls to Cheryl, I was not able to tell her. Finally I left her a message telling her I had great news and to call me. I found out why she was unavailable that night.

As we were welcoming patrons that evening, Laine's cell phone rang. Her cell phone is a rhinestone-studded monstrosity, and I hate that she carries it with her to the theater. But, after all, it is *her* theater, so who the hell am I to say anything about it?

She took the call, which was from Brit, and then snapped it shut smartly. She leaned in to me and told me "Your sister says we need to go upstairs and watch the news. Apparently your Miss Higgins is doing a story."

"Well, that's her job after all. About what?"

"Archer Bellamy."

We exchanged surprised looks but said nothing. Then, once the show had started, rather than go to the balcony, we went to my office and switched my recently acquired television to Cheryl's station.

It didn't take long to get to the story. Cheryl was standing outside of FCOTLIC, with the blue Christ-eye-skylights glowing serenely behind her. The anchor threw the story to her and she began.

"Thanks Joneeta. I'm standing in front of the Friendship Church of the Light in Christ in Buckhead, the workplace of Archer Bellamy, who has been rumored to be the mastermind behind the recent protests in Virginia Highland over liquor sales on Sunday. Today, WSB secured exclusive documents that show that Archer Bellamy, who is in charge of the church's property management department, was convicted fifteen years ago of a gay bashing in his native Indiana."

Laine and I exchanged looks.

"Luke McKee, who was then a freshman at the University of Indiana, was the victim in that attack."

The television cut to a video showing an interview with a man a few years younger than I. "Several friends and I were at a fraternity rush party. A couple of the brothers knew we were gay but had invited us to come anyhow. Apparently that didn't sit well with Bellamy. He and three other friends jumped us as we were walking home. My friends got away, but I wound up with a broken arm, two cracked ribs, and a concussion."

The shot cut back to Cheryl. "Mister Bellamy and two other students were convicted for assault on the student, and Bellamy served approximately two years before he was paroled.

"Now, we went to the church and asked for them to comment on Mister Bellamy's background and whether they endorse his protest actions in the Highlands. A church spokesman declined to comment on camera but did tell us that the church was in no way involved with the protests, and that they were also unaware of Mister Bellamy's conviction. They did say, however, that they are reviewing whether next steps are warranted and if so, what they will be.

"Live from Buckhead, I'm Cheryl Higgins."

I switched off the television. In the theater, I heard the first song fire up. This was the first time I had ever missed a curtain. My cell phone rang. It was Cheryl.

"Hey. Sorry I've missed so many of your calls. I've been working on a story and I couldn't compromise myself by being linked to you until I had the facts."

"I understand," I replied evenly. "I just saw it. Pretty…um…wow."

"Yeah. This is what Olivia was talking about. She had done some research on Bellamy when he first started the protests, and was eventually able to verify this."

I couldn't find anything to say. After a long pause she asked "So what was your news?"

"Oh. I … uh…We got the backers' audition."

"That's great, Van. When?"

"January thirtieth. In New York."

"Fantastic. Are you excited?"

"Yeah. I am."

"Then why don't you sound it?"

"It's just, well, I guess this story threw me for a loop."

"How so?"

"Well, I mean, this is career-ending stuff for him, isn't it?"

"Probably. Supposedly he lied on a job application so that's usually pretty standard grounds for termination. Do you care though? It'll certainly shut him up."

"Well, sure. Of course I care. But I was really just hoping the story would die on its own, not that we would have to kill it."

Laine went into the theater while I next called Olivia. "Two calls in one day? I'm honored."

"I just saw the story on Archer Bellamy."

"Ah. How did it go?"

"Usual stuff. Man has reputation destroyed, employer has no comment. More at eleven."

"Good enough."

"Liv, why didn't you tell me?"

"I didn't tell you because I didn't know if it was true. When I found out it was, I gave the lead to your lady friend."

I began to feel angry. "You know, the story would have gone away. I didn't need you to protect me."

"Protect you? Hate to bust your bubble, but I'm your *agent,* Van. This wasn't protection. This was business. It's what I do."

"Destroying a man's reputation is business?" I asked incredulously.

I could hear the impatience and irritation slide into her voice. "Van, don't be naïve. It's not like we're talking about George Bailey, here. This guy hides behind religion and false piety to bully others. There's a whole pattern of it."

"A whole pattern? You mean there's more to come?"

"I don't know. Depends what Cheryl Higgins finds out. She's the reporter. I just gave her the lead."

"The story would have gone away," I insisted again.

"Yes, it would have. In about six weeks, followed by a 'where are they now' spot sometime next autumn. And if you were just going to be a small-town, small-time playwright, I'd let that happen. But you're not. You've got an audition on Broadway in four weeks and we needed the media attention. You'll get one more national blitz out of this in the next week, and the hype will be enough to carry you into the auditions. None of the other shows they are auditioning are this controversial."

I sat there for a moment, at a loss for what to say. I felt angry, but more, I felt dirty. I was at a loss which emotion to give in to.

Finally Liv broke the silence by saying, "Now say thank you."

Anger won. Without another word I pushed the End Call button and threw the phone into the drawer.

I went through the rest of the evening's machinations rather robotically. I told no one about the story during the show or the intermission, but did fill Miranda in on it before she left for the night.

I thought back over what Olivia had said that evening as I vacuumed the auditorium. She was right about Bellamy, of course. He was a conniving coward. That said, I was still angry Liv had not consulted me on the story. I would not have agreed to it if she had.

Of course, I thought to myself as I put the vacuum back in the janitor's closet, *Let's be honest. It's not like Liv ever gave a damn about what you thought anyhow. She wouldn't have stopped just because you wanted her to. And then where would you be? If you would have found out in advance, you would have been forced to decide whether to warn him. She did you a favor, really.*

That did little to assuage my guilty conscience. I climbed up to my office to retrieve my cell phone. Three missed calls. One from Brit, one from Cheryl, one from Olivia.

I switched off the lights and descended the stairs. Maybe Olivia had had second thoughts. Maybe she was softening in her old age and my hanging up on her had made her think.

More likely, she was royally pissed I had hung up on her and was calling to tear me a new asshole for it.

I stepped outside, pulled the theater door shut and locked it. When I turned around, there was no one there. Reeder's truck and his little band of followers were gone. Not even the sax player was on the corner. As I crossed the street, I glanced to my left. There was a news van set up on Virginia Avenue, directly across from Bellamy's house. I shook my head sadly and let myself into the 'Hurst.

My guilty conscience over Archer Bellamy aside, we had a show to do. The new script was pretty significantly different from the old one. Although many of the lines were the same, we had changed their order and how they were to be delivered. Moreover, I had completely rewritten the first fifteen pages of the script and added the new song, "Northern Sophistication, Southern Style." Our plan was to completely replace the current show with the new one when we returned on February 1. So, even though we were only going to New York for a backers' audition, we went into full rehearsals. Each night, we did two hours of rehearsal before the show, and two hours afterward. The nights were long and the work was hard on the cast. But for this group of local professionals, the excitement over the chance to audition on Broadway outweighed the demands.

Just down the street, the Bellamy saga unfolded as you would expect. Reporters camped out, dredging up lurid details about a crime that happened fifteen years ago. Because Bellamy had not disclosed the conviction on his application, FCOTLIC was forced to terminate him, although they did so in such a manner as to indicate that it was not an endorsement of homosexuality.

The city's gay community roundly condemned him in the media. I was asked several times to comment on camera, and I declined all of them. Reverend Reeder and the protesters disappeared. There were rumors that he had moved on to the site of some other moral transgression, this time in Savannah.

After a particularly scathing editorial of all parties involved in the protest appeared in the paper, the city liquor board relented and awarded us our liquor license. Talbot arrived on January 15 with it and fifteen cases of Cabernet to stock my new bar. Cheryl and I resumed our tentative courtship, but mostly by phone. Nearly every waking hour I had was spent at the theater.

On January 21, we had a rare and wonderful snowfall. Snowfalls in Atlanta are hilarious things if you are from the North. Everyone leaves work early, and the grocery stores are mobbed with people buying bread and milk. However, when the snow actually does fall, it typically doesn't stick to the streets. Yes, we do have ice—lots of ice, when it happens—but it's all melted the next day and you find yourself wondering what people do with all that milk and bread.

We were planning to run the show that evening, and all the cast dutifully trudged their way to the theater as great white flakes drifted to the ground and covered a bank of bright yellow forsythia that was blooming next door to the 'Hurst. Two inches of snow had fallen throughout the day, closing schools and businesses across the city. As a result, we only had three audience members show up. On the spur of the moment, we decided to conduct a dress rehearsal instead. We offered to refund the audience members' money, but they asked to attend anyhow. We gave them free drinks, and they gave us word of mouth. Four days later, news had spread to the papers that *Highlands-A-Go-Go* had been completely rewritten, was going to be auditioned in New York, and would premiere back in Atlanta on February 1.

Against all the background of work, I kept expecting to feel my sense of inner vertigo, but it never came. I was nervous about ensuring that everything went right, but not terrified that everything would go wrong. I experienced a sense of peace and calm I had never experienced before.

On January 22, Liv finally broke radio silence and called me. Warsheim and Hirsch were hosting a cocktail reception for the media and all the writers, producers, and directors involved in the auditions. It would be in New York the night before the auditions themselves, and she thought it would be a good idea for Miranda and me to attend.

She also informed me that she was emailing me a list of documents to bring to the audition, and a series of questions she thought I should probably be ready to answer. I committed that I would.

The call was cordial enough, but overlaying it was the common knowledge that each thought the other was wrong and an apology was owed. No apology was proffered against the cool, stilted conversation and we hung up having said more by our silences than our words. It was just like being married again.

On Sunday afternoon, Miranda and I boarded a Delta jet to LaGuardia. I experienced a strong sense of trepidation about leaving the theater in the hands of others, but Laine took over competently running the front of the house, and the cast really didn't need Miranda backstage. And, after all as Laine reminded me, it was her damn theater to begin with and if she wanted to run it she was going to run it.

The flight to New York was rough as the MD-88 bounced its way above and around a storm system that extended from Cleveland to Norfolk. Miranda and I were crammed into two coach seats on the left side of the aircraft. We were both jittery, and we told ourselves that it was because of the rough air. Unfortunately, because of the turbulence, the flight attendants didn't conduct a beverage service. Being deprived of alcohol did nothing for our nerves.

The plane touched down in New York under leaden gray skies. We escaped the Delta terminal and caught a cab to take us to our hotel, which was in Hell's Kitchen.

When Olivia and I had met, I had been living in a funky loft in the Village, and she had been in a small apartment on the Upper East Side. We were both wedded to our locations for different reasons. She liked the cachet of a Lexington Avenue address, whereas most of the places I went for work or fun were on the Lower West Side. The issue of where to settle had been a long and contentious one and we almost didn't move in together over it. Finally, a "compromise" was brokered that, in retrospect, was no compromise at all. We moved to an apartment that was still on Lexington, but in the mid-forties, where I had easier access to the subway to get me to the west side.

Olivia had offered to make reservations for Miranda and me at one of the hotels her agency used, but those were all East Side hotels. I declined. I wanted to stay on the west side. After the divorce, I had expected to move back there before I got sidetracked to Atlanta. I had always felt like an outsider on the East Side. I was part of the hip set, not the smart set. I didn't talk about business; I talked about bands. Among the diplomats, movers, and shakers of Lexington Avenue, I was as out of my element as if I had been at lunch with a bunch of wives in Scarsdale or a yacht club christening in Larchmont. Now though, as the cab bounced across Broadway, I felt a sense of home, and told myself that perhaps it was time to come back.

The hotel we were staying at was a small, boutique hotel run by two men and an Albanian woman who shared the business, a bed, and a bad attitude. I had been friends with them in my early days at the paper, and had stayed at their hotel when I first moved out of the apartment. Even though we weren't close and I found their constant bickering a little exhausting, they ran a great hotel at reasonable prices.

After the exchange of hugs and pleasantries, we were shown to our rooms on the fifth floor. We had about three hours before we had to be at a club at Fifty-first and Eighth, time which Miranda insisted she was going to need to get ready. I changed into the clothes Chris had specifically picked out for me for the evening; a pair of pinstriped jeans and a black crushed-velvet jacket over an open-collar maroon shirt. A dab of cologne and I went back downstairs to the small hotel bar.

I enjoy intimate bars, the kind that can be manned effectively by one bartender. I slid onto one of the stools and glanced around at the smattering of people who were gathered there. Even though I recognized none of them, I knew all of them. Two young, would-be actresses from upstate who came into town one week every three months and went to every possible audition whether they were remotely qualified for the role or not; one artist going on and on about the difficulty of getting a show in New York to three friends, all of whom had already had shows of their own; one Midwestern businessman, staying at the hotel because it was close to wherever he would have a meeting the next day who would not set foot outside the building unless it caught fire; and three students, two Asian, listening to the third whine about the difficulty and unfairness of life/school/his parents/his girlfriend/his boyfriend.

Marco, one of the three owners, delivered a round of drinks to the whiner's table and then came back behind the bar. "So what are you drinking these days now that you're living down south?"

"Oh, I have to be on my best political behavior tonight, so let's just make it Guinness." He retrieved a glass and began the laborious task of drawing the beer. "And I'm not sure I'd say I live in Atlanta. I've just been staying there."

"Van, you've been gone for eleven months. Hell, you moved out to Larchmont almost a year before that. Being away from this city that long is like a decade anyplace else."

I acknowledged the truth in the statement with a nod and watched him pull the spoon away and add the appropriate amount of head. I noted mentally that Jennifer could draw the same beer in about the same time.

"So what's Atlanta like?"

I took a sip of the beer he had slid across to me. "Different. Amazingly friendly. Lots of energy. Horrible traffic."

He shrugged. "Sounds like here. Except maybe the friendly part."

"You don't think of New York as friendly?"

"Sure I do, in a keep-your-distance sort of way. What's your life like there?"

I told him about my life, the theater, the show, the audition, my friends. He listened politely, but I recognized the studied demeanor of patience. New Yorkers are always having to listen to how much better life is elsewhere.

When I finished the details of my life he offered, "Wow! It really sounds great. But hey, the truth. Don't you miss all this?" He held his arms in an open bowl shape as if he could encompass everything from the Bronx to the Bowery in his virtual embrace.

I glanced around. "Of course I do, and I'll be back one day soon. But this little southern sojourn has been good for me. It's helped me get my head on straight after the divorce."

"You didn't need to go south for that. You had everything you needed right here. You need to be more like me."

I smirked. "A cranky, pan-sexual innkeeper?"

"You need to draw your strength from the city."

I gazed into my beer. "I always thought I did."

Three hours later, Miranda and I arrived at the club where the reception was being held. It was cold that evening, but because of the close proximity we decided to walk. I arrived red faced because, unfortunately, the only additional protection I had against the cold apart from my jacket was a pair of leather gloves and a scarf. (Chris had insisted that my peacoat would have ruined the effect of my outfit.) As opposed to Miranda, my ever-practical lesbian, who was bundled up in some REI-Northface-synthetic-thermal-polymer hybrid coat-gaucho combination.

The club itself was perfect for the West Side. Exposed brick walls with free-hanging panels of frosted green glass. Square-globed gas lights covered the walls, although their dancing flames were lost in the bright gallery lighting that illuminated the canvases hanging among them.

The crowd itself was pretty much the crowd of near-luminaries I expected. A year's absence had not changed the key players in the arts scene much. I recognized playwrights and production designers, actors and choreographers, and more than a few critics. Ninety percent of the crowd was either partly or fully dressed in black, and all the hair was expensively un-coiffed.

"These," I told Miranda proudly, "are my people."

"These," Miranda replied coolly as she stepped up to the bar, "are too cool to be anyone's people. These people are probably too trendy to even use the word 'people' any more. Beer please." She turned around and leaned her back against the bar. "People is too mundane. They probably use some insider term like *personal embodiment.* There's probably even a manifesto someplace. 'We, the personal embodiments, in order to form a more enlightened manifestation, establish trendiness…' You get the idea."

She turned back around to accept the beer. "You're in a mood tonight." I told her and then stepped up to the bar to order a martini.

"I am. Nerves mostly. Something about auditioning immediately puts me on my period. And, frankly, I'm a little hurt."

I turned around. "Hurt?"

"I thought *we* were your people."

I shrugged and accepted my beer. "You're my new people, but it's not like I really belong in Atlanta. I always belonged here."

"Belonging in Atlanta is accomplished by deciding you belong. Three million carpetbaggers can't be wrong."

We made our way into the crowd and presently found ourselves standing adjacent to Warsheim and Hirsch. They were holding court in the center and we were the next to be received. Miranda leaned close and whispered to me, "How do you remember which one is Warsheim and which one is Hirsch?"

I pivoted momentarily so there was no chance they could hear me and whispered back. "Warsheim is bigger. Bigger name, bigger human."

She nodded knowingly, grateful for the cheat. "I can remember that."

"Donovan!" I turned around and was summarily hugged by Warsheim while Hirsch politely kissed Miranda on the cheek. Then places were traded and Miranda was hugged while I was kissed.

"We're so glad you two were able to fly up early," Taylor told me. "All the other auditioners are local, so we weren't sure you were going to make it."

"Wouldn't miss it," I replied.

"Come, let me introduce you to some of your competition."

They turned towards two severe looking women who had preceded us in the receiving line. "Donovan Ford and Miranda Howard, meet JoEllen Stern and kashi fear."

We all shook hands and exchanged pleasantries. I recognized the receiving line handoff from countless cocktail parties in the past. The hosts receive a couple, introduce them to the previous couple and then turn to meet the next couple. Just as smoothly, Hirsch and Warsheim had moved on to a couple of pasty gentlemen behind us.

"kashi fear," I began. "I reviewed a performance you gave at the Renfro about five years ago."

"I remember," she replied in a perfectly monotone voice. "You called my performance 'a depiction of the fashionable banal.'"

I shrugged. There have been other times when a performer or artist had not appreciated one of my reviews and had committed it to memory. "Such is the life of a critic. Your words always come back to haunt you."

"Not at all," she droned. "That was the exact intent of the piece. You were one of the only reviewers who got it."

"Ah, well. Good for me."

"I heard Taylor say you came from out of town," JoEllen offered. "From where?"

"We're from Atlanta," Miranda replied pleasantly.

kashi's horror was visible. "You live in Atlanta now?"

"For now," I replied.

"Rather unusual move, isn't it? Leaving New York to find your literary pedigree?"

Miranda jovially interjected, "Now you know those pesky pedigrees can just show up in the damnedest of places."

I laughed at her delivery. JoEllen and kashi just looked confused. After a couple more abortive attempts at small talk and a disastrous attempt at humor, we ended the horrifically painful experience. They went towards some art on the wall, Miranda and I towards the buffet.

"So, *your people* include women named after breakfast cereal," Miranda observed as she selected a piece of sushi from a platter.

"Worse, she named herself after that. If I remember right, her bio said something like she chose the name *kashi fear* as a statement against how children are forced to learn certain dietary habits."

"Please tell me you're kidding."

"He's not," Taylor said from over my shoulder, a gleam in his eye. "And, she spells it all lower case, of course."

"Of course," Miranda replied.

I confessed to Taylor, "I'm a little embarrassed to be caught dishing the competition."

He snickered. "Are you under some delusion that they *aren't* dishing you? My dear boy, they are dishing Jonathan and me for even having you in the competition."

"Why?"

"We're *cutting edge* producers. Surely nothing cutting edge could come from the South, could it?"

Although I knew he was joking, it also suddenly dawned on me that, in the New York literary circles, I had done damage to my career. It had never occurred to me before. After all, writers were always disappearing to the Hamptons or Nantucket or some other place to go write, but more often than not that was *after* they had earned their pedigree. And, very few of them went south unless they went all the way to the Caribbean.

I glanced around. My people were not exactly my people any more. And it was my fault. They would point out that I left them; they had always been right here in New York, exactly where they were supposed to be. The shock of that realization hit me like a ton of bricks. I spent the rest of the evening observing myself in contrast to my peers around me. I made eye contact with strangers and smiled, they did not. What's worse, a year ago I would never have dreamt of doing such a thing.

I flirted shamelessly with a couple of older women in the crowd—well, dowagers really—who expected the most minimal form of courtesy. I paused to compliment them on their outfits, and chatted them up shamelessly. Out of the corner of my eye, I saw the shocked look on the face of a couple of guys about my age, most of them writers. I also saw the warm, welcoming expressions of other women who had reconciled themselves to only be acknowledged for certain behavior.

After the party, as we were walking back to the hotel, we stopped into a bar for a nightcap. The bartender was a particularly lovely woman whose dark skin and brilliant smile reminded me of Rachel's. As I paid the check, I told her, "This is not a come on. You have the loveliest smile." She was taken aback as though it was the first time anyone had ever said any of these things to her, especially at work. She thanked me awkwardly, I tipped her and carried the drinks to the table where Miranda was waiting.

I wasn't doing these things deliberately. They came naturally, unconsciously to me.

When the hell did I become gracious?!?!?

I set the drinks down and she looked up smiling, but her expression changed. "What's going on with you? You look troubled."

"I have come to a stunning realization tonight and it has knocked me off balance a bit."

"What's that?"

"I left here."

She looked at me perplexed. "Um, not to be a smartass, but of course you did. Where did you think you had been for the last year?"

"No, I mean, I'm not who I used to be. These may be my people, but I don't think they view me as one of them. Heck, I don't even think I view me as one of them anymore."

She laid her hand on mine. "Van, of course not. You've gone through a pretty tumultuous year or so. Of course you've changed. But it doesn't mean you don't belong here. After all, you came here once upon a time and you didn't belong then."

"But I wanted to, so I made the effort."

"And if you want to belong again, you'll make the effort again. But always remember, people can belong more than one place."

I was too embarrassed to continue the conversation. How could I verbally admit that being the cool, hip, trendy New Yorker had always been core to my identity, and now I was coming face to face with the fact I wasn't that person any more? And, not terribly sure I ever wanted to be again.

There was no time to think about it the next morning. The entire cast, plus a couple of key members of our technical crew and our piano player, had all taken the first flight out of Atlanta. They departed, as Klein put it, at the "butt crack of dawn," and landed at LaGuardia at eight-thirty.

Meanwhile, Olivia arrived at the hotel at seven-thirty with a hired bus. She was coming off of it as Miranda and I came trundling out of the hotel. The tension between the two of us was gone. There was too much riding on the day to be angry. She kissed me on the cheek as always and the three of us climbed aboard. She had coffee waiting.

As we lurched through the traffic towards the bridge, we had a moment of calm before the symphony of nerves and cell phone calls would begin.

"Here's what I know about the competition," she told us. "We're the fourth of the nine stage reads they are going to sit through. Only two are musicals. Ours, and one about pizza delivery drivers in love."

"You're kidding," Miranda replied as she blew on her coffee.

"I'm not. It's called *Pizza Drivers in Love: a Musical.* Three of the shows are political satires, although one is dead on arrival."

"Why's that?"

"It's done in interpretive dance and multimedia. The days of throwing pudding on the audience are over."

Miranda enunciated, "And I say thank God for that." I laughed along with her.

"What are Stern and fear offering?" I asked

"It's a one-woman show about Leona Helmsley. As best I can tell, they are playing pretty free and easy with the facts though."

"And the others?"

"Two commentaries on race relations that sound depressing, a series of vignettes told by different panels on the AIDS Quilt, and something about bestiality and hemophilia, although I couldn't really understand the connection."

"That's quite an odd and varied lot."

She nodded. "It is. Warsheim and Hirsch's past oeuvre has always been pretty varied, but their satires have been the real money-makers. Jonathan just bought a house in the Hamptons, so I'm guessing he needs a cash cow right now." Her cell phone rang.

Miranda leaned across the aisle and whispered to me, "She's the first person I've ever met who could use the word *oeuvre* in a conversation."

"You should hear her when she's mad. She's fired off *dialectic*, *sisiphisian*, and *bifurcated* at me without batting an eye. Wharton, you know."

We pulled up to the Delta terminal. I stepped out of the bus, and actors immediately began pouring out of the terminal. Bags and equipment were stowed, people boarded, and the bus was heading back towards Manhattan in less than fifteen minutes.

Over the last week, we had perfected the backer's audition format for the show. Miranda would narrate the stage direction, and the cast would read their roles, moving only as necessary. We had an hour drive to the rehearsal hall, so the cast did yet another run-through on the bus.

As the rehearsal rolled on, I again noticed that I had no sense of inner-vertigo. I was nervous, sure, but I was also confident we were going to nail the audition. So, wherever this new Donovan Ford belonged in the world, I was pleased to notice that at least he wasn't as terrified as he used to be.

We pulled up to the rehearsal hall. We had been told that we couldn't actually enter the hall until noon, when the previous audition would be ending. Then we would have an hour to get ourselves set up, and the next two hours for the audition, followed by one hour of question and answer. We had to be out by four-thirty.

The reality of what we were about to do hit us collectively as the driver parked the bus. A reverent sort of hush fell over the cast and crew. Miranda and I exchanged glances and realized it was time to say something inspirational. We both stood up in the aisle.

"Van and I realized we should offer some wisdom at this point," Miranda began. Then, after a long pause she added, "But I've got nothing. Van?"

The cast laughed appreciatively, then all eyes turned on me. I cleared my throat.

"Um, y'know it's been strange for me being back here, because I'm not sure New York is a place I belong anymore. All of you have taken me on a long, strange journey this year, and collectively you have made me a different man. I'm not entirely sure who he is yet, but I am definitely different. And I owe much of that to you.

"Now, the reason I intro that way is because I've also learned a hell of a lot about all of you. Miranda and I get a lot of credit, but the truth is we aren't *Highlands-A-Go-Go*. You are. Every one of you has taken ownership of this show. It's part of you. And I'll tell you right now, I may not be sure where I belong, but I am sure of one thing. All of you belong in this show, and this show belongs on Broadway."

The clapping started at that point. I had more that I was going to say, but I knew to leave them on a high note. With that, we all poured out of the bus and made our way to the hall.

The previous cast was leaving and all seemed to be in good spirits. Jonathan welcomed us and immediately showed us into the hall itself. There were about thirty seats arranged at one end, facing the other. He told us we had one hour to get ready and then, with a bellow, he instructed everyone not with me to leave.

It didn't take us long to set up. We put up a movie screen at one end and set our laptop and projector off to the side. I had brought a PowerPoint presentation that would be projected on a screen behind the cast. It would show still shots of everything in the existing production, including sets, lighting, and costumes.

It took us a few minutes to get the lights set up and to orient the piano so that the player could see the cast. We laid programs from our show on every chair.

In what felt like much less time, our hour was suddenly up and Jonathan and Taylor led the various backers and their assorted staff members back in. I was introduced to all twenty of them and because of my nerves immediately forgot all of their names.

Everyone sat down. The audition began.

Miranda took her place at the podium next to the piano. She has a natural projection to begin with, but give her any audience at all and she can be positively booming. "Our show begins at an intersection in Atlanta. This is not a particularly high-profile spot like the famed Peachtree Street, nor is it the legendary Sweet Auburn. In fact, unless you have ever been to Atlanta, you have probably never heard of it. But this is the corner of Virginia Avenue and North Highland, the epicenter of a neighborhood and culture called Virginia-Highland.

This neighborhood is chic, liberal, trendy, religious, conservative, counterculture, elegant, run down, and gaudy all at the same time. It is where all cultures in Atlanta, and most of the cultures of the South, intersect with no other intention besides having a cocktail together." A chuckle rolled through the backers. "The scene opens on a Monday morning with the cast singing..."

And we were off. The cast sang the opening song beautifully. Then we cut to the main characters. They had to deliver the same basic first seven lines as in the old script. I held my breath as they rolled through to the first joke.

Jonetta delivered the opening line.

Diego responded.

Mercer's line.

Diego's question.

Jonetta's snide answer.

Diego's rejoinder.

I held my breath and closed my eyes. Jennifer/Mercer delivered her line.

The backers laughed.

I exhaled. Only three-hundred forty-eight more lines to live through.

I was sitting next to Taylor as the run-through proceeded. When we got to the new song, "Northern Sophistication, Southern Style," it was clearly a hit with the audience. Taylor leaned over and squeezed my knee.

The reading came off without a hitch. We had one minor technical difficulty when a light bulb in one of the overheads exploded, and I wondered briefly whether the Feldmans were still with us after all. But the cast laughed it off by improvising a little reference to it, and I forgot all about it.

It finished with the grand finale song, "The Virginia-Highland Rag," followed by Miranda stating triumphantly, "And...curtain!" The backers all applauded politely, although one actually jumped to his feet. (I would later learn he was originally from Macon, Georgia.)

Taylor and Jonathan led me to the center and pulled two chairs out of the audience for Miranda and me. "Okay," Jonathan began, "You've had a chance to see the show, now's your chance to ask questions. Lets give the cast a minute or two to catch their breath and get a drink of water. So in the beginning, just confine your questions to Miranda and Donovan."

The first question came from a short, balding white gentleman sitting in the second row. "Donovan, what's been your average house since the show opened?'

"Our house seats one hundred forty-eight and we've been pretty consistently sold out every night since the end of the first month. I think an overall average would be about one thirty-five."

The next came from a tall African-American seated in the front row. "Miranda, from the photos and the production manager's report, it seems like the choreography is very subdued. Is that so, and if so why?"

She nodded. "It is subdued. Three reasons. First, it's a bunch of white people in the South who just, generally, are not good dancers." There was a laugh. "Second, the reason they aren't good is because of the Baptist and Methodist cultures. They don't dance so it doesn't naturally lend itself to the show. And third, we have a very tiny stage. Because it's an old movie theater, the stage is extremely shallow and while I would like to do a great production number, in our place people would pirouette right off the stage."

The third question came from a tightly wound Asian woman. "Donovan, are you an Equity theater?"

"We are in the process of becoming one."

"When you overlay the Equity costs against your current cost structure, would this show still be profitable?"

I nodded. "Being a writer, I have an accountant who looks after these things. He's comfortable that, because we've kept so much of the overhead low, the show will still be profitable."

And so it went. We fielded an hour of questions on everything from set design to performer motivation. But the bulk of the questions dealt specifically with the financial aspects of the show. I had to recite margins, ticket grosses, contractor costs all from memory. I was grateful to Liv for prompting me on the questions.

In the end, our overall assessment was that the audition had been a success. Taylor gave me a thumbs-up and Jonathan hugged me as we were leaving. All signs were positive.

On the bus back to the airport, we dissected and analyzed every reaction to every song, and every question of every business decision. No one could come up with anything discouraging. As we pulled up to LaGuardia, Olivia disembarked with the rest of us. The bus would be headed back to Brooklyn and she had arranged for a car to take her home. As the rest of the cast filed into the Delta terminal, I held back and asked her, "Okay, just you and me. How was it?"

She smiled. "Not bad. Really not bad. Very professional, very well executed."

"But?"

She shook her head. "No buts. Van, in this business, its not usually the best show that wins, or the best audition. It's what the backers think they can peddle to the investors. You didn't do anything wrong. We just have no idea if anyone did anything better."

I nodded. "I understand. I, uh, have to go..uh…"

"Go *home*?" she asked brightly.

"Um, maybe."

We parted with a kiss, and I went to catch my flight.

The Daffodil

For the next week, I spoke to Liv almost daily. She kept me abreast on what she had heard from the remaining auditions. All three political satires bombed. *Pizza Drivers* had come in surprisingly strong, but the target demographic was too young for off-Broadway. The AIDS Quilt narrative had been understandably powerful. No one understood *I, Leona!* but lack of understanding didn't mean it was out of the running. (After all, no one understands *Cats* either, and it ran for years. And years. And years.)

I relayed each of Liv's reports to my cast who digested them in turn with only minimal speculation.

Outside, the weather was confusing. It was an alternating mish-mash of cold, ugly, gray days, and bright sunny days that, although not warm, were passable with a jacket. Redbud trees sprang to life one morning all across the city, and the green tops of daffodils started shooting out of the ground.

The call from Taylor Hirsch came as I was getting out of the shower. I heard my cell as I was drying off, so I pulled the towel around me and stepped into the kitchen where it was sitting. I didn't recognize the number, apart from an NYC area code.

"Hello?"

"Donovan, it's Taylor!"

"Hello, Taylor. Good to hear from you. Are you well?"

"I am indeed. Hey, I hope I didn't catch you at a bad time."

A drop of water slid off my bangs and hit the tip of my nose. I flicked it away and said, "No, not at all."

"Great. Great. Listen, I've some news. First of all. We've culled the list down to three shows and…"

He paused for dramatic effect. I closed my eyes and resisted the urge to scream "SPIT IT OUT, YOU MIDGET FAIRY!"

The pause ended. "And you're not one of those eliminated."

I opened my eyes. "We're in the final three?"

"You're in the final three."

A wave of joy rushed over me. "So, here's the deal. We are going to do a pretty elaborate financial modeling of what each show would cost, how long it would take to get up and running, that sort of thing. So I was wondering, can you be here day after tomorrow?"

I closed my eyes. Day after tomorrow was February 8, Laine's birthday. "I'm not sure."

"Here's the deal. We've only got a couple of days to figure out how to make this work, so we need the experts for all three shows here. That's you, right?"

"Yes, I suppose it is."

"So, then, we need you to come."

I nodded my head, scattering small droplets from my hair onto the kitchen counter. "I understand. I'll find a way to make it work."

"Hey, that's great. Appreciate it. See you at our offices on Thursday."

He hung up. I closed my eyes and pressed the 2 key on my phone, which was Chris's speed dial key. I knew he was flying, but I didn't know where. After several rings, he answered. "Hey."

"Hey. Where are you?"

"Paris."

"Oh, how is it?"

"At the moment, miserable. I'm at the airport. I think hell borrows its design from Charles de Gaulle airport."

I chuckled. "When are you coming home?"

"I'll be home tomorrow afternoon. Why?"

"I need help."

"Okay. What?"

"I need a cheap way to get to New York on Thursday. Can I have one of those stand-by guest tickets airline people get?"

"They're called buddy passes. You can't go to New York on Thursday. It's Laine's birthday."

"If I don't go on Thursday, they won't produce the show."

"Laine will understand that. Okay, I've got a couple of buddy passes right now. I'll float you one on Thursday and up you go."

"That's great. Thanks."

"No problem. Good luck telling Laine."

We hung up.

Laine was surprisingly understanding. Brit, Rachel, and Jennifer, who were planning a party for her, a bit less so. But the party was grudgingly moved to Friday evening, so I could attend.

Thursday morning, I boarded the earliest flight to New York to ensure I could get there in time. Once I reached LaGuardia, I caught a cab to Olivia's office.

It had been almost two years since I had set foot in there. As I crossed the office I glanced at the names on the cubes and doors. I didn't recognize many, but that didn't surprise me. There was a lot of turnover at Olivia's office.

The light was on in her office, and Sally wasn't at her desk, so I walked in without knocking. I did it deliberately. Liv hated for anyone to walk into her office unannounced. Few people in her office had the temerity to do it, including her boss. I had begun doing it when we were still married, in part, for attention and in part to show that I wasn't afraid of her.

"Good morning," I said cheerily, flinging my backpack onto her sofa and dropping into a side chair across her desk. She spun around to face me, but masked her irritation.

"Good morning. Are you ready for this?"

"Don't really have a choice, do I?"

"No, you really don't. Not if you ever want to be taken seriously in this town. Did you bring everything I told you to?"

"All my financials, Miranda's staging notes, the Equity agreement, and the media portfolio."

"Very good," she commended without any real warmth. "Too bad you didn't pay this much attention to what I was telling you to do when we were married."

I was not in the mood to be baited. I grinned at her in a way I knew she hated and replied, "Too bad you didn't actually tell me what you wanted when we were married instead of just expecting me to read your mind."

She stared at me. "You know, that *sounds* like something you would have said when we were married, but certainly not in that tone."

I shrugged, still smiling.

She stared at me a moment more, and then turned silently, slipped a couple files into her briefcase and stood. "C'mon, let's go."

We caught a cab and made the cross-town drive mostly in silence. Outside, it was cold. Steel gray skies cast a sullen pall over the streets that made you think it was raining even though it wasn't. Eventually we pulled up to W-and-H's offices, which were located above the rehearsal hall we had used for the audition. A young woman escorted us into a conference room looking out over the street. She offered us coffee, committed to bring it to us, and then stepped out, quite deliberately closing the door behind her. We sat down, with nothing to say to each other.

Liv's surliness didn't surprise me. She was always surly when she was nervous. I was also pleased to discover I was able to ignore it.

The secretary returned with the coffee and then left again. For about fifteen minutes, Liv worked her email on her BlackBerry while I sipped my coffee and jotted notes on a new song in my notebook.

Presently, Hirsch and Warsheim arrived.

"Sorry to keep you waiting," Jonathan said, sweeping into the room and shaking our hands. Taylor followed with several large notebooks in his hands.

"No problem," I replied as I shook Jonathan's hand.

We took our positions around the table. Taylor clasped his hands and leaned forward. "Well, let's talk about how today is going to go. We have three shows that we are pretty excited about. All three offer some upside, so we want to run through business assumptions. This includes the production costs, our estimated residuals, and also what we are going to have to pay you."

I glanced at Olivia, but she was staring intently at Hirsch. We had already discussed our opening offer, but had agreed we would pretty much take anything over minimum wage to get the show produced.

My name on a W-and-H production would make me much more marketable for every subsequent thing I wrote.

Taylor continued. "So here's our plan. From now until lunch you guys will meet with one of our analysts to build the financial model. We have two others working with the other candidates simultaneously, so Jonathan and I will be bopping back and forth between the three rooms.

"After lunch, you guys will meet a director we've chosen to work on this show. We've picked three directors, one for each show. So, those discussions will be going on simultaneously as well. After you finish with her, we'll come back and talk about what the purchase would look like. Does this work for you?"

"Of course," Liv said brightly. "We're sure you are going to find us to be the best deal."

"I have no doubt," Jonathan grinned. He and Taylor exchanged glances, and then they stood. We did as well.

"Okay then," Taylor replied. "We'll send in Tristan, our financial analyst, and we'll get started."

They excused themselves and left. I crossed to a credenza where coffee was set out and poured myself another cup. "This sounds grueling."

"It will be. This is how the business has changed. In order to get backing these days, you need more than a catchy tune and a quick pitch. You need an entire business model you can show the bankers. That's why you see so many movies getting remade into shows. They've already got the proven R.O.I."

There was a knock on the door and the analyst stuck his head in. "Mister Ford? Miz Robideau? Ready for me?"

"Tristan Shaw?" Olivia asked, smiling.

He came into the office, holding out his hand. "Olivia."

She shook it. I asked her, "You know each other?"

"We used to work together," she replied as he turned to shake my hand.

"Together, hell," he said. "I worked *for* her."

"Really?" I had a sudden sinking feeling in my stomach. There are very few people in the world that enjoyed working for Olivia. And by "very few," I mean none.

"Not for very long though," Olivia said as we all moved to our chairs. "As I remember it, you left to go be a photographer. What are you doing here?"

"I still am a photographer. That's my real life. This is just how I pay for it." I felt a small sense of relief. Perhaps he got out before she made him regret his existence. Then again, she may also have been the stimulus for a career change.

He opened his laptop and said, "Let's get started, shall we?"

If he held a grudge against Liv, then he extracted his revenge on me. We spent the next four straight hours reviewing every cent spent on the show and why. We dug into decisions over sets, costumes, casting, and lights. He was relentless. Tax audits aren't as grueling.

At twelve-thirty, he had completed his financial model and excused himself. I looked at Olivia and said, "I can tell he was one of your winged monkeys. He picked up your interrogation skills."

She shrugged, refusing to be baited. "I always did like him. I was sorry to see him go."

"He must be good at his job. He seems to believe that *Phantom* could be produced with the same basic budget as *Equus.*"

"Not that it could be, but probably that it should be," she mused, making quick work of the emails on her BlackBerry.

Lunch was sent in. Olivia never ate more than fruit during her workday. She said it was because food took the edge off. While I snacked on a finger sandwich, she pulled a couple grapes off a bunch and ate them while gazing out the window.

"Do you mind a question?" she asked, not turning to look at me.

"It's not like you to ask permission," I observed, selecting another sandwich.

"What's kept you in Atlanta all this time?"

"Dunno," I said absently. "I mean, I had Laine to care for and the theater to run."

She popped another grape and thought a minute. "Starting a theater, running it, and writing a show is a lot of work. I never knew you to have that much ambition."

"Not sure I ever did," I replied truthfully. "Well, I had dreams. But I never felt like I could…I dunno. I guess I never felt like I could take a chance."

She turned and stared at me. "Did you feel like I wouldn't have supported you if you had wanted to take a chance?"

I thought a minute. "No, I suppose not. I guess if I had asked, you probably would have busted my chops about it, but in the end you would have been supportive. But it would have been so bloody hard here. There are so many people who've had the optimism beaten out of them in this city. It's not like that in Atlanta."

She put her hand on her hip and cocked one eyebrow at me. "C'mon. You're not going to try something as trite as saying your dreams can come true in Atlanta but not New York."

"No. Maybe just that it's easier to find inspiration there. That, and people to believe in you. It seems like everything is possible in Atlanta. Even mutually exclusive things."

She looked like she was about to say something else, but didn't get the chance. There was a knock on the door and we were introduced to Su Jin Han. She was a theater professor at Columbia who had dabbled in some off-off-off-Broadway directing. She was W-and-H's choice to direct our show.

She got down to business and we spent the next three hours dissecting my artistic vision and discussing alternatives to staging, production, and casting. I have to admit that I enjoyed this portion. Miranda and I had shared a common artistic vision from the beginning, so having to explain it to a stranger and work out the details was fun and challenging. I found myself thinking about things that had never occurred to me before.

During the entire three hours, Liv worked her email.

I think that Su Jin and I could have talked all night, but Taylor came to the door and politely but firmly asked her to finish up.

I ran out to the men's room, and when I returned, Taylor was already there, and deeply engaged in a negotiation with Liv. I had been instructed in no uncertain terms that, at this point, I was to keep my mouth shut. Not that I would have much to add. The discussion of residuals, and percentages and ticket grosses left me mesmerized. As best I could tell, we were offering to sell it for relatively little, in exchange for a greater percentage of royalties.

What was supposed to be a two-hour discussion actually lasted about four with no sign of stopping. The time of my flight home came and went. I didn't dare protest, so I just texted Chris to let him know my situation. He sent a message back that there was bad weather moving into New York and if I didn't get to LaGuardia I wouldn't get a flight out until the next morning. I couldn't worry about that.

Finally, at about quarter to nine, as large sloppy snow flakes began to fall outside the window, we finished. We had the terms of a deal inked but not signed. "You understand," Taylor said, "That this is all contingent on yours being the show that makes the best financial sense."

"I understand."

"We better get going," Liv observed. "You've already missed your flight. We're going to have to see what we can get you."

"Looks like nothing," I replied, glancing at the increasingly shrill warnings from Chris on my cell phone. "The weather has reduced operations at the airport. I'm here for tonight."

There was a long, awkward silence as I could tell Liv was weighing whether to invite me to stay at our, her place that night.

I smiled at her. "I'll call Marco and see if he's got a room."

"Marco?" Taylor asked, looking up as he stuffed papers into a folder.

"A friend," I explained. "He and his partners own a small hotel on West Fiftieth."

"I don't live far from there," Taylor offered. "I can give you a lift if you like."

Liv and I exchanged glances again and she subtly nodded.

"You don't have to do that…" I began.

He finished putting papers in his folder. "Nonsense. We got you up here on short notice and then made you miss your flight. Least I could do."

"Well, okay."

He walked towards the door. "I need to go shut down my office. I'll meet you in the lobby. Liv, I'll have Etienne call you a cab."

"Thanks, Taylor."

He left and Liv and I headed towards the lobby. I called Marco from my cell while we waited to ensure that he did indeed have a room. He told me he'd have the key and a cocktail waiting for me in the bar.

As I hung up the phone, Liv asked, "Are you going to be able to get back to Atlanta?"

"I'm sure I will in the morning."

"Work Taylor in the car if you can."

"I'll do my best, Sarge." She rolled her eyes. The cab pulled up outside.

"You're good at your job, Liv."

"Thanks," she said, looking like she wanted to say more. She started out the door, stopped and turned back towards me. "For the record, if you had ever told me you wanted to write a show or open a theater, I would have supported you. We would have found a way to make your dream come true."

"I know you would have, Liv. Here's the problem: I had to get out of New York to discover it's not banal to actually try to make dreams come true."

She looked perplexed, then waved and walked out the door. I watched the cab pull away. Taylor came down the hall and said, "Ready?"

I followed him to a small parking lot a block away where his black Jaguar was parked. We got inside and he started towards Eighth Avenue.

"So," he began. "Did you always want to be a playwright?"

I watched the wipers drag the slushy flakes from the windshield. "I don't know that I wanted to be a playwright. I wanted to write. I'm not sure I ever really believed I could do this."

"Surreal, isn't it? To discover you're capable of actually doing what other people dream of?"

I nodded. "It is. I may write a show about it."

He laughed. "Hey, reach behind my seat and open my briefcase. There's a manila envelope in it. Pull it out for me?" I did as he instructed. "Open it."

I did as instructed and pulled out a script. I read the title. "*The New Rochelle?*"

"It's the script for a TV pilot. CBS would like to produce a sitcom here in New York. Take a quick read of it."

I opened it up and started reading. It was the tale of a small New York hotel. It took me ten minutes to read the first half dozen pages. I skimmed the next twenty or so, chuckling occasionally.

"Tell me what you think."

"Well," I began. "The concept is solid. Mostly a single set show. The characters and the premise are amusing, but… well…"

"Be candid," he instructed.

"Well, the dialog is lame. It's too hip for a television audience. The humor is all inside jokes. The problem is as soon as the audience is let in on the joke, it immediately transitions from hip to passé."

We reached Forty-eighth Street and he turned. "I'm going to park my car at my building and walk you to the hotel," he told me.

"You don't have to do that."

"Yes I do. I'm going to buy you a drink and you are going to tell me what you would do with this script."

His building was one of those excruciatingly new buildings that compensated for limited space with machinery. The parking deck was robotic. We drove into a large metal cage and got out. He entered a code on a small keypad. A moment later, the car was shuttled away into the basement.

We walked up the street through the snow to the hotel in silence. I flipped through the script gathering my thoughts about what I would change. We greeted Marco and settled ourselves into a booth in a corner by the bar. Marco delivered drinks, and I flipped through the script one more time.

"Okay," Taylor said. "You've had enough time to think. What would you do?"

"Well," I said, taking a sip. "Okay. The main character is the innkeeper, his wife, the insane staff…it's kind of derivative of *Fawlty Towers* or *Newhart*. Instead of making it about the staff of the hotel, make it more about the people impacted by the hotel. Relocate the hotel to some resort community, maybe the Hamptons, and make the main characters the long-term hotel residents who resent the guests. You can do more with the eccentricities of the characters if you get them away from the hard-and-fast hotel roles."

He stirred his martini without looking up and said, "Go on."

"The target market of this script reads like it's seventeen to seventeen-and-a-half year olds. I'd expand the appeal to at least the late-twenties set. You also need to overlay some diversity. It needs some multiracial characters, maybe a gay couple with their adopted Russian teenage daughter who *hates* being hip. Make her, oh, I don't know, an aspiring actuary when her fathers really want her to be a dancer."

He laughed at that. "Keep going."

We talked for another two hours. By eleven-thirty, I was exhausted and said so. He nodded, paid the check and stood to go. As we said good-bye, he observed "You really need to be living back here. Atlanta can't know what to do with you." He smiled and shook my hand. "When you get back here, we will."

I made it back to Atlanta by noon Friday. It is almost impossible to know how to dress in Atlanta in the winter because the days can vary so wildly. When I had left Thursday morning it had been cold and rainy, but as I stepped out of the airport and onto the train platform, it was sunny and in the mid-sixties.

As the train wound its way north into the city, I thought back over the previous evening for perhaps the ten-thousandth time. I didn't want to seem overconfident, but I had nothing but good feelings about the discussion. Not only did Taylor not question or challenge anything we had discussed or negotiated, I had noticed that during our entire conversation over the *New Rochelle* script, he had listened to me. Not politely, but genuinely. He didn't argue. He challenged and sought clarity, but he didn't dismiss. For the first time in my career, I felt…

Well, I felt respected.

I stepped off the train at Midtown station and took the escalator up. I had intended to run across the street and catch a cab, but the sun glinting off the marble of the Federal Reserve Bank convinced me otherwise and I started walking east towards the park.

Just outside the train station, there is beautiful old brick Tudor apartment building. It reminds me slightly of Greenwich Village, although I don't remember anything in the village nearly as charming. I began to idly consider what part of Manhattan I would live in when

I returned. Hell's Kitchen, I thought. Close enough to Broadway to check in on the show, but far enough to maintain my literary pedigree. Plus it kept me separated a bit from hopeful actors working as waiters, but not so far I would forget where I came from.

As I walked along Oak Hill, I noticed that green stalks were sticking up everywhere in the grass. On the north-facing side of the hill, they were starting to bud, but on the south-facing side, they were opening up into daffodils.

It took me about forty minutes to walk the three miles from the train station to the 'Hurst. I let myself into the building, went upstairs, changed clothes, and then immediately went to the theater. I had a lot of work to do, and I had to let the caterer in. We were having Laine's birthday party there after the show that night. She had bought out the house for hand-picked guests.

The show that night was a great one. We had found an actress to play Tamara Oncamera full time, and we integrated her into the show as we unveiled the new script. It was a hit. The audience loved it. And, of course, Laine insisted we invite all of them to the party.

The caterers rolled a buffet onto the stage after the curtain call. The bar was opened, and Bitsy was first in line. At about eleven-thirty, it was time for the cake.

Laine stood on stage in front of an enormous pineapple upside-down cake, trying to politely ignore the eighty-five candles burning brightly in front of her while we sang Happy Birthday. I felt my cell phone vibrate in my pocket. Pulling it out, I didn't recognize the number, but the area code was 212. Manhattan.

I pressed the answer key and as soon as the last note of the song was reached, spun around and ducked out the front door onto the street. "This is Donovan."

"Donovan! Taylor!" Taylor always sounded very excited when he announced himself on the phone; it was less a greeting and more the kind of exclamation one might expect after avoiding a near-death experience.

"Hi Taylor. How are you? Thanks again for the drinks last night."

"Hey, my pleasure. Glad you could join me. I enjoyed our chat."

I leaned against the ticket booth as he continued. "Hey, listen. Sorry to bother you on a Friday night. I've got to tell you, we really love your show and you've made a great business case for it."

I looked up at the street lights and smiled. "I'm glad you think so."

"I do. Both Jonathan and I are really impressed. It's amazing that this is your first show. You obviously came to New York to win."

I took a deep breath, smiling inwardly.

"But I'm sorry. We're going to pass."

My elbow slipped off the windowsill. I must have heard that wrong. "You are?"

"Yes, we are."

I was silent, waiting for him to tell me he was joking. He didn't.

"The lack of name recognition is the only thing that is keeping us from it. We think that the AIDS Quilt narrative is going to be more cutting-edge and generate more pre-premiere media. Plus, we think we can bring it to the stage for a little less in production costs, which means we can spend a little more on talent."

I began walking towards the 'Hurst.

"Listen, though, we think there's going to be a lot of other opportunities for you."

Taylor was still talking, but I couldn't focus on what he was saying. All I could focus on was that I had failed. I had given it my best shot, dedicated my heart and soul, blown my whole wad, and I had fucking *failed!* I'm sure Taylor was saying something important, something uplifting, but all I could think of was my fear about being naked in front of the rest of the guys in the high school locker room, my terror while waiting for my SAT scores, my father's rage that I couldn't immediately ride a two-wheeler. All of those potential failures came crashing back. None of them had materialized, and I had lived in fear. And this, the first true risk I had ever taken in my life and I had failed!!!! And I felt…

Nothing.

The universe didn't come to a crashing halt. My family and friends didn't immediately abandon me. Nothing happened. I had just failed.

Nothing.

And the clock ticked over another minute. I waited to feel something, but I only felt a kind of numb shock.

"Van?"

I came back to the call. "Yeah?"

"Are you okay?"

Was I? I had no idea. I expected to feel worse. Hell, I expected to feel something.

"Yeah. I'm fine. I appreciate you calling me in person to tell me. It's very classy."

There was a pause on the other end and he said sincerely, "Thanks. I think it's important. And besides, I don't want to lose touch with you."

I smiled, shrugging off the meaningless optimism. "Taylor, I really appreciate it. But if you don't mind, I'm at a birthday party…" I opened the door to the 'Hurst.

"I understand. Go. Enjoy. I'll call Olivia. She and I need to chat anyhow."

"Thanks. I appreciate it. Have a great weekend and I hope the Quilt is a great success."

"Thanks Van. Talk to you soon."

I switched off the phone and started up the steps. I climbed in silence, still waiting to be emotionally crushed. As I turned the second-floor landing, I felt disappointed, and a little somber, but no sadness. The lack of feeling started to irritate me.

"I cared deeply about this!" I said out loud as I turned and started up the rise to the third floor. "I should feel something."

"I TRIED," I shouted as I turned the third floor and started towards the roof. "I FAILED! WHERE'S THE EMOTIONS? WHERE ARE MY DEMONS?!?"

At the top of the stairs stood the saxophone player. "What demons are you looking for?" he asked, looking startled and a little concerned.

"Um, hi." I was embarrassed. "I was trying to summon up some emotions."

He smirked. "How's it working for you?"

"Not so well. None are coming."

He leaned against the doorframe. "None of my business, but do you mind if I ask why?"

"Because I failed," I confessed.

"At what?"

"I was trying to sell my show."

"Ah."

We stared at each other for a long minute across the span of the staircase. Finally the strangeness of the situation dawned on me. "Um, who are you? Can I help you?"

He smiled benignly and started down the stairs. "Not at all. I just had to make a delivery."

"A delivery?"

"Left you a little gift." He held out his hand to me as he reached the step two up from the one where I stood. "I'm Isa Kersey."

So thirty minutes later, there I was, back across the street, sitting outside the theater, sharing a bottle of wine with my own personal Boo Radley. Mister Kersey thanked me as I refilled his glass. He was telling me the story of the theater's failure. "So, eventually, we were faced with bankruptcy. We had no choice but to start showing adult features."

"Porn," I suggested.

He shrugged. Inside, Laine's party roared along. "Porn's a strong word. DeLaine Wagner would never have allowed the theater to show porn. Besides, by most standards, it was pretty soft-core.

"Anyway, I could read the handwriting on the wall. I had my army pension, so, I decided to step away and decide what to do next with my life."

"How long did the theater last after that?"

"Not long. A couple of months, I think. Not a full year."

I took a deep sigh. "So the theater was a failure then and I'm a failure now."

He smiled benignly again. "You've failed. That's different from being a failure. This theater," he said proudly, patting her marble face, "is no Yoshiwara and you are no 11811."

I stared at him blankly. "That reference is lost on me."

"Did you ever see a silent film called *Metropolis?*"

I thought for a minute. "German? Maybe made in the late twenties?"

He nodded. "Made in 1926. Premiered in Berlin on January 10, 1927."

"Yeah, I saw it. In a film history course in college. I remember it was long. That, and kind of disjointed. I couldn't follow the logic."

"You probably saw the Channing Pollock edit of it. He totally bastardized the film."

"What is 11811?"

"A little history first. When the movie was made by Fritz Lang, it was long, even by modern standards. They estimate that Lang's original version was close to three hours. Conventional wisdom at that time said that a movie couldn't be more than about 90 minutes long; two hours tops. So, after its original release, it was edited down to about two hours in Germany. Then, when it was released in the States, Channing Pollock edited it again. But because the plot was highly socialist, which was controversial in nineteen-thirties America to say the least, he tried to edit out many of the socialist messages. As a result it was considerably shorter and almost totally incoherent.

"Fast forward to the end of the twentieth century. After years of tormenting film history students, the film was cleaned and restored, and all the cut scenes that could be found were edited back in. But the film was only one hundred and twenty-three minutes long. About thirty minutes were lost. Possibly forever."

He paused in reverie for a minute. "11811?" I asked.

He nodded. "One of the missing scenes is the tale of 11811, a worker who trades lives with Freder, the main character. Even though he's given access to the upper world, he doesn't take advantage of the opportunity. Instead, he disappears into Yoshiwara, the red-light district of Metropolis, where he's ruined and broken."

"And the reference means?"

"You are not 11811. He was a failure. 11811 is given an opportunity of a lifetime, the chance to be something more than he was, and he does nothing with it. More importantly, the men who cut and lost his scene from *Metropolis* are worse failures. To create but not reach an audience is not a failure. To dismember art in the name of profit over controversy is."

I thought for a moment while he blew a few notes on his sax. "So, somewhere out in the world, there's a can of thirty minutes of film that the world has been looking for?"

"A negative for most of it was found in Argentina this year. The thirty minutes that some pin-head distributor thought was too controversial is actually the holy grail of film. Some of the very first cut is still missing. Still, something that didn't meet the distributors' vision of art, is now worth millions."

We chatted a while longer as guests left the party. Eventually, it was time for me to take my aunt back home, and she emerged from the theater having said her goodbyes. I said goodnight to Mister Kersey, and thanked him again for all the gifts and kindness he had given me. Laine kissed him on the cheek and we crossed the street.

Later that evening, as I climbed the stairs to my apartment, I noticed the gifts he had left me in front of my door. One was a tube and the other a flat, wide box, very dusty, and held closed by a leather strap. I carried them into my apartment and set them on the counter.

Opening the tube, I slid out yet another movie poster. I had built quite a collection of them, and made a mental note that I had to go get them framed. Pulling the poster open, I was greeted by the gaze of gleaming, metallic woman, staring at me from in front of an art deco cityscape. At the bottom, the poster announced that *Metropolis* would be shown on April thirtieth, nineteen thirty-three.

I opened the box. Inside, a dusty film can awaited me. There was a label, and Mister Kersey's characteristic print spelled out *Metropolis.*

I had begun letting people know that Warsheim and Hirsch had passed on us the previous evening at the party, but put a real effort into making sure I got the word out to everyone the next morning. I registered some sense of disappointment from a couple of the cast members, but no real sense of surprise. (Apparently I was the only one who really had expected us to get picked up.) As Miranda put it, "How can you be disappointed after being taken on the ride of a lifetime?"

I, meanwhile, was still unsure of myself. I didn't feel the horrible sense of failure I expected to feel. Life was going on as normal. Still, when I saw Olivia's number come up on my cell, I didn't want to risk her dampening my spirits, so I let it go to voicemail.

She called again two hours later as I was taking Laine to lunch at the Colonnade, so I let it go to voicemail again.

The Colonnade ostensibly belongs to a southern genre of restaurants called a meat-and-three, meaning an entrée and three side dishes. When Laine suggested we go there, I pictured some quaint old home with a massive veranda that had been converted to a restaurant.

I have no idea where the name Colonnade comes from because there's no colonnade, anywhere. Not even one damn pillar. It looks more like a nineteen-sixties supper club that has been embedded in amber. The clientele was all in their mid-seventies, queer, or both, a fact I would not have commented on had Laine not brought it up as soon as we were seated.

"Welcome, darling, to the Colonnade, known around here as the gay-and-the-gray."

I chuckled a bit. "It does seem to be an interesting demographic."

"You should see it Saturday evenings," she observed as she opened her menu. "You get all this plus the after-temple crowd. Buy the room a round of gin rickeys and you've got a party."

"At least until someone breaks a hip."

My cellphone rang. I looked at the caller i.d., saw Liv's number, and pressed Cancel.

"Who was that?"

"Olivia."

She looked over the top of her reading glasses at me. "You could have taken the call. I wouldn't mind."

I shrugged. "Not in the mood."

I could tell that Laine was quite happy I would not be returning to New York, but she was making a strong effort to hide that happiness from me. The conversation turned to more mundane matters. It was a nice lunch.

Liv called again an hour later when we were driving home, and I briefly considered answering, but still didn't feel like it. Laine observed, "You know you'll have to talk to her sometime. She's relentless."

"I know that better than most men," I replied, pulling into the driveway of the 'Hurst. Ten minutes later she called again, but now

I was more afraid of her reaction when I did answer the phone after having ignored her. I escorted Laine inside and then ran upstairs to my apartment. The phone rang again as I was coming back down. And then again. And then again.

I pushed the talk button. "Hi Liv."

"Thank bloody God!" she heaved at me, sounding more exasperated than angry. "I was starting to get worried."

"Sorry. I've spent most of the day telling everyone that W and H passed on us, and I didn't really feel like talking."

"I understand," she said, which amazed me. She had never understood anything that inconvenienced her before. "I'm sorry they passed, but these things happen. You made it a hell of a lot farther than I would have expected."

"Largely thanks to you," I said.

"No, largely thanks to yourself. Agents open doors. Writers still have to walk through."

"That was unusually metaphorical for you."

I could hear the pride in her voice. "It was, wasn't it? Hey, listen, I had another reason to call other than commiserating about the show."

I sat down on the hallway stairs outside Laine's apartment. "Shoot."

"Well, to start with, apparently you neglected to tell me that you had drinks with Hirsch the other night."

"Oh, yeah. Nothing major. We talked shop mostly. He has a troubled script he asked me to look at. I gave him a couple of thoughts."

"That's all?"

"Yeah, why?"

"You know, for someone who has traded on hipness for so many years, you are surprisingly dense."

I bridled a bit. "Oh?" I said sourly. "And how's that?"

"You were interviewing for a job."

"I was what?"

She chuckled. "Mister Ford, as your agent I am pleased to inform you that Taylor Hirsch has offered you a job."

"What? As what?"

"As principal writer on their new show on CBS, *The New Rochelle.*"

I was silent for a long minute, before saying, "Liv, this would be a terribly cruel joke."

She laughed outright. "No joke, my dear. He's sent over the first draft of the contract and wants you to come back up here."

"I just left there," I replied.

"This is obviously karma trying to bring you back home where you belong."

I sat there in disbelief for a full minute before asking, "How much?"

She told me. It was far more than I had ever made in my life, but she added "It's a good opening deal. We'll counter for more."

"I can't believe this is happening," I replied, excitement creeping into my voice.

"Oh it's happening. And you know who is absolutely going to be green with envy?"

"No," I said honestly. "Who?"

And then, my ex-wife said the nicest thing she had ever said to me. "Aidan McInnis is absolutely going to crap all over himself with jealousy. He's always wanted one of his books to get picked up as a show or a movie."

I laughed with glee. "God, this is fantastic."

Her voice took on its in-all-seriousness tone. "Truthfully, Van. You need to come right back up here. This offer is too good and too unprecedented. Taylor Hirsch sees something in you he likes, and he can be a powerful ally for you. This kind of career jumpstart doesn't come along every day."

"Okay, Liv. I'll come up. I'll try to get a flight tomorrow morning."

"Pay whatever it takes. You'll more than make up for it. Call me when you know what your plans are."

"Will do," I replied. We said our goodbyes and I hung up. I looked up from the phone at my aunt. I had not heard her come out of her apartment. She was standing in her doorway, holding her garbage and looking pale.

"You're going back up to New York? You just left."

I nodded. "I've got to. I've got a job offer."

"What kind of offer?"

"Principal writer on a new show on CBS." I jumped up to my feet.

"What? When did this happen?"

I took the garbage out of her hands. "Just now. They floated an offer to Liv this morning."

"But, would you go back to New York? When? Do you want it?"

"Do I want my big break as a writer? Of course I do. When? I don't know. That depends on when they want to start, but I imagine it would be soon.

"I'll take this out," I said, pointing to the garbage, "and then I've got to go open the theater."

I kissed her on her cheek and ran down the steps to the basement.

My aunt works fast. That afternoon while I was making flight arrangements for the next day, she was manning the phone. Word had spread to the entire cast and all my friends before five o'clock. I was greeted with a mixture of congratulatory messages and nervous musings. Miranda expressed hope that I wouldn't forget her when I got to New York. Rachel was visibly unhappy and only spoke to me in monosyllables. Chris was flying that evening, and so I had no ally to provoke her into good humor.

As the curtain rose, I went to the balcony and settled myself in on the couch next to my aunt. When the first song began she asked me, "So, if you go back to New York, who's going to take over all this?" She was staring straight ahead, swirling her drink slowly in its glass.

I grimaced. "I haven't worked all that out yet. Miranda, I suppose. We can make her the theater's artistic director and she can assume control of the show and figure out what she wants to stage next."

"I see." She swirled the drink some more, finally taking a sip of it. She still continued to stare straight ahead. "And do you think this is the right thing to do?"

"Is what the right thing to do?"

"Just up and leaving like this."

"I hadn't thought about it in terms of *right* or *wrong*. It's just what's next. I've always said I had to go back to New York someday."

"Yes, that's true. You always have." There was no warmth in her voice.

After a very long pause, I asked, "Why? Do you think it's wrong for me to go back?"

Without looking at me she said, "I think it is wrong to just up and leave, yes. There are a lot of people here who are dependent on you. You've woven yourself into lots of lives and to just leave because you have a better offer seems uncharacteristically harsh."

I looked at her incredulously. "What? No one depends on me. For a year I've been the building handyman who's been playing in his aunt's theater."

"If that's all the role you believe you play, than that is probably all you actually are." She stood up. "I'm tired. I think I'll sit out the rest of the show tonight." She placed her untouched drink on the bar-cart, crossed the balcony and left.

It had never really occurred to me that I played any *other* role in people's lives. Atlanta certainly couldn't have adopted me. I'd only been a visitor. For a year. It couldn't have.

Could it?

Regardless of whether it had or not, this was the opportunity of a lifetime.

After the show, the cast and crew all set new speed records getting out of the theater. No one helped me clean up, so I stayed a little later than I expected. That actually worked out okay for me. I was still quite wound up over my new job, so I took advantage of the downtime in the theater. I had brought *Metropolis* over to the theater, and I threaded it into our ancient Bell and Howell projector and started it. I watched it while I finished cleaning up.

The next morning, with precious little sleep under my belt, I drove to the airport to catch the first Delta flight to LaGuardia. I didn't worry too much about the sleep, since I planned to nap on the plane. However, as I descended the jetway, a familiar voice was my first sign that this might not be a restful flight. Chris was standing in the door of the aircraft, greeting customers in his navy uniform.

I smiled at him as our eyes met. He didn't return it. "Hey," I said. "I thought you never flew Sundays."

"Not if I can possibly get out of it," he said. As I came abreast with him he whispered, "I picked up the trip so I could talk to you." Then, resuming his normal voice he said, "Mr. Ford, may I see your boarding pass?"

Confused, I handed him the card.

"Sir, we've had to make a slight adjustment. Would you please take seat forty-two, A?"

I nodded and walked all the way back to my new seat. It was in a small, windowless section at the very back of the aircraft, behind the galley. I settled into forty-two, A, and leaned my head against the wall. Being as it was early Sunday morning, the cabin was mostly empty, and the seats next to me were vacant. I spread out and began to doze.

As soon as the plane was airborne, the flight attendants began the beverage service. I slept through it. Later, I was awakened by a sharp nudge as Chris shoved my legs aside. He squatted down in the aisle, and the look in his eyes indicated that I was expected to sit up.

"Hey," I replied, rubbing the sleep out of my eyes.

"I'll have you know," he replied, taking a sip of his coffee, "I had next to no sleep last night because I had to spend three hours on the phone with Rachel. What's this about you moving back to New York?"

I shrugged. "I'm sure she filled you in on the details. A chance to write for television. My big break. And so on and so forth."

"And is this something you really want to do?"

"Why not? I mean, this is a great opportunity. It's a chance I've got to take."

"A chance you've got to take? You hate taking chances."

I took the coffee from him and helped myself to a sip. "True," I replied as I handed it back. "The same as you."

He fixed me with a skeptical stare. "Don't talk to me about taking chances. I had to come out of the closet to a Cuban mother. That was taking a chance with my life."

It wasn't really. I had heard the story before about how Chris came out, if you could call it coming out. He had never shown any interest in girls, nor ever done much to hide it. Then, one night while in college, he had an accident with his mother's car. He was okay, and the damage was comparatively minor. However, he was cited as being at fault.

When he got home, he walked into the living room where his mother was reading, in order to tell her about the accident. He began with, "Mom, we have to talk."

She immediately jumped to her feet, knocking over a stool and sending her cat flying. She screamed, "I knew it. You're *gay* aren't you?!?"

Startled, all he could say in reply was, "Um…okay. I guess we can start there."

"I'm not sure that's the same kind of chance," I told him.

"Are you sure this is what you want?"

"Why does everybody keep asking me that? Of course it's what I want. Why wouldn't it be?"

He took another sip of his coffee. "Actually, why would it be?"

"Huh?"

"Seriously. What is it about this opportunity that makes you want to go back?"

I had to think about that for a moment. "Well, I mean… well, hell, it's getting paid to do something I love."

"And that is?"

"Write. More than write. To create a whole new show."

"Ah. So this show is going to be your creation?"

"Well, no. It's actually already been created. I'm coming in to save it, I guess."

"Are you? Did they tell you that they needed you to save it?"

"Well no. But it needs saving."

"But did they agree to that?"

"We haven't discussed it yet."

He took another sip of his coffee. "Okay, so right now, you're getting paid a lot of money to possibly save someone else's show, but maybe not. What else is great about it?"

"Well, it's a really big break. I get to show what I'm capable of, and that will lead to other opportunities to get my stuff produced."

"As opposed to Atlanta?"

"Huh?"

"Well, I mean, don't you own a theater? Can't you get your stuff produced anytime you want to?"

"Well yeah, but not in New York."

"Okay, granted. Atlanta is not New York. Nor is New York Atlanta." Outside, the clouds moved as the aircraft banked to the left. "Why else?"

"Well, there's the respect that comes with it. I mean, it's writing in the big time."

"Writing in the big time. Like Michener-type writing?"

"Of course not," I replied irritably. "But it's still the big time."

"Okay, granted. It's the big time. How do writers get respected for that?"

I was silent.

"Really, Van. How? On the Emmys, whenever the writers win, it's always the producer who accepts the award. Do they even get statues? I just ask because you don't usually hear people talk about television writers in the hushed, reverent tones that they use when, oh, say Kitty Kelley releases an unauthorized biography."

I was silent.

"So, what I'm hearing you say is you will get paid a lot of money to write someone else's concept. You'll get a chance to have your work produced sometime later even though you already have a place where you can do that now, and you'll get respect. You're not sure from who, but you're sure it's there. Is that right?"

"Look…" I began.

"No, you look. Here's reality as I see it. You are walking away from people who love you and a pretty fantastic life that fell in your lap. You're not doing this for the money or the opportunity. And as far as respect goes, you're grasping at this as a replacement for self-respect." He stood up.

"Chris..."

"Sir, the captain has turned on the Fasten Seatbelt sign. We're starting our descent into LaGuardia. Please remain seated." He turned and walked towards first class.

There is something particularly galling about being put in your place by a flight attendant.

Olivia had another client meeting that morning, so I was to take a cab directly to a diner on Sixth Avenue to have breakfast with Taylor. I was not, under threat of dismemberment, to discuss or agree to terms in the contract. I was to limit my discussion strictly to the show and establishing our "joint artistic vision."

As the cab crossed the streets of Manhattan, I noticed that the snow was still on the ground and had been plowed into ugly gray heaps. *No daffodils here,* I thought to myself.

Taylor was already at the diner when I arrived. We shook hands and exchanged the normal pleasantries. He ordered a Denver omelet for breakfast, and I ordered a bagel with lox. Coffees were served, and we made small talk until it was finally unavoidable: we had to discuss the reason for my visit.

"I really appreciate your offer," I told Taylor.

"Appreciation is not called for. You're a great writer with a lot of vision. There's a lot you are going to be able to do with *New Rochelle.*"

"So, is it safe to say that we're going to reposition it to someplace like Nantucket?"

"No, not at all. CBS has already bought it, and they like the idea of it being set in the city."

I nodded. "Okay. Fair enough. Um, then, let's talk about how the characters need to change…"

"Oh, the characters aren't going to change, Van."

"They're not?"

"Nope. CBS bought the show as is. That means, at least for the first season, we trot it out with the characters and plot premise they bought."

"I see."

Our breakfasts were served, and we resumed pleasant small talk for a few minutes. As I rearranged the capers on my lox, I asked innocently, "So, tell me. What exactly were you doing with me the other night in the bar?"

"What do you mean?" he asked pleasantly. "I wasn't hitting on you if that's what you're asking."

"No, I mean I guess I'm curious to see why you were asking me how I would change the script if you can't actually use my changes."

"Ah. Here's the thing: I wanted to see what you would do with the concept, how you would change it."

"Okay, but we can't."

"Not overtly. See, Van, I know the show sucks. Lame premise, and horrible, collegiate writing. But, of the five shows I pitched, it's the one CBS bought. All of the changes you proposed are exactly the kind of changes I would make to that show if I could." He began spreading jelly on his toast.

"But, uh, you can't?"

"Not unless the ratings suck. Then, if it's failing, we get to make all kinds of changes. Of course, they may or may not be what we want. The network holds a lot of veto power. But we've got a shot at it."

"Until then, what do we do?"

"Well, fixing the dialogue is a given. No need to keep the teenage mutant idiots who wrote the pilot. As soon as you sign, I fire them. And, we need to write six to ten episodes using the current plotline. That's enough for it to either catch fire or stumble." He took a bite of toast. "And, we get paid until such time that we can save it and look like heroes, or until it dies a slow, agonizing death. But, by that time, we'll be on to the next project. The corporate politics at the network is pretty bloody. Our window to turn it around will be small, if we get it at all."

I couldn't think of what to say. I would like to believe it was because I was tired, but I knew the truth. I was dumfounded by the cynicism of what he was telling me. He wanted me to be midwife to a preordained failure.

He read the expression on my face. "Not pretty, is it? Unfortunately, this is why it's called show business instead of show art. Van, I need you because I need a writer who can deliver the quantity and caliber of work that you're capable of. This is the chance Jonathan and I have been waiting for, the chance to really break into television. Neither he nor I are writers. We're producers. We know what sells. We need someone in the trenches actually creating it. And unfortunately, the only way you get to produce the stuff that is good, that you are proud of, is to first prove yourself by producing the dreck."

I took a deep breath and blew it out forcefully. "Um, not necessarily."

"Oh? You have other ideas?"

"Not other ideas. Other experience, I guess. I get to produce stuff now that is really good, that I am proud of. And I didn't have to serve time in the dreck mills."

He laughed. "See? Dreck mills. That's good stuff. Pure gold." He took another bite of his omelet and then pushed it away. He settled back into the booth, holding his coffee cup and smiled beatifically. "This job is not for you, is it?"

I tried to protest, but I couldn't. Deep in my heart, I knew he was right. "I feel like I should take it," I confessed. "But the experience sounds absolutely miserable. Especially when I compare it to what I have back..." The word caught me by surprise again.

He finished the sentence for me. "Back home."

I nodded. "Back home. It doesn't pay like this but, my God, I get to do what I want with people I love and trust."

He nodded. "I suspected as much."

I leaned back. "If you already knew, then why did you even ask?"

"You're hungry for something. This could have been it. It was worth a shot to ask, anyhow. You don't get to win if you don't take a chance."

He waived down the waiter for the check. "And, to be perfectly honest, I suspect you didn't know how you felt about everything you've got in Atlanta until you had a shot to leave it."

In the back of my head, I heard Reverend Reeder say, "There are no chance meetings. You found your way to this moment in time because you needed to learn something."

I looked at Taylor and said, "Perhaps you're right."

He paid the check and we promised each other we would stay in touch. "And, good luck to you," he said as we stepped out of the diner into the cold winter air. "You're going to need it."

"I am?"

"Of course. I know your agent. I wouldn't want to be the one to tell her you just turned this deal down."

I took a cab across town to her office. I was long past fearing her temper and I'm sure she knew that. I also suspect it pissed her off.

When I arrived at her office, she immediately handed me the contracts without so much as a kiss hello. The offer was highlighted.

I glanced at it as I dropped into a chair. It would be more money than I had ever made from writing in my life. For ten episodes, it would be more than I had made in most of my career.

I smiled at her across the desk. "I turned it down."

She looked shocked. "You did what?"

"I turned it down."

"For the love of God, why? Van, this is all you ever wanted! A great job where you get to truly write!"

"You're right. It is."

She sat down. "Then why turn it down?"

I smiled. "Because I've already got that."

"Oh, don't even pretend to tell me that the theater pays as much as this."

I shook my head. "Of course not. Probably never will. But Liv, here's the deal. I've learned that sometimes people work at the Wee Playhouse of Hoboken because they love it, not because they couldn't do better. I know now, I could do better. I could be a stunning success in New York. But it's not what I want."

Olivia just looked at me for several moments, her face a mixture of shock and wonder. "Who are you?" she asked as I slid the unsigned contracts back across the desk.

"What do you mean?" I asked.

"You aren't the man I was married to. You're… I don't know. I guess you seem stronger now than you used to."

I could feel a wan smile cross my face as I stood up to go. "I guess that's because in Atlanta I had to be. I never needed to be strong like this in New York."

She gave me that quizzical-yet-skeptical look that all New Yorkers favor when someone implicates something unexpected about their city, so I explained.

"New York has an entire infrastructure just to support our emotions. We don't need to fend for ourselves emotionally here. Well, at least *I* didn't need to fend for myself. I had you, I had the magazine, I had my column that was devoted to celebrating the banal. And, what's worse? I was acting like happiness itself was banal.

"You don't get to do that in Atlanta. The only thing that is banal is trying to create banality." I pulled on my coat. "In Atlanta, making your dreams come true is a very acceptable concept. An exciting concept, even."

"I really don't know that I ever understood you," Olivia observed as she stood up and came around the desk.

I held her by the shoulders and said, "On some level, some very deep, very basic emotional level, you have always understood me totally and completely. And, *it scares the living hell* out of you."

We both laughed and I leaned forward and kissed her cheek. As I walked towards the door, I said over my shoulder, "I've got a great idea for a show about people who like each other better after they divorce."

I glanced back over my shoulder and she looked at me warmly. "Sounds banal. Let me know when you're ready to pitch it."

I walked out of the door, and out of New York. It was time to go home. In Atlanta, the Bradford pears were about to bloom, and I really did have an idea for a new show.

I planned on calling it *The Redemption of 11811.*

The end.